Rekin...

# WE~~DDING~~

## *—Vows—*

## I THEE WED

### SHIRLEY JUMP
### LIZ FIELDING
### MYRNA MACKENZIE

# WEDDING
## *Vows*
### COLLECTION

**April 2015**

**May 2015**

**June 2015**

**July 2015**

# WEDDING
## *Vows*
### I THEE WED

**SHIRLEY JUMP**
**LIZ FIELDING**
**MYRNA MACKENZIE**

MILLS & BOON

Published in Great Britain 2015
by Mills & Boon, an imprint of Harlequin (UK) Limited,
Eton House, 18-24 Paradise Road, Richmond, Surrey, TW9 1SR

WEDDING VOWS: I THEE WED © 2015 Harlequin Books S.A.

*Back to Mr & Mrs* © 2007 Shirley Jump
*Reunited: Marriage in a Million* © 2007 Liz Fielding
*Marrying Her Billionaire Boss* © 2007 Myrna Topol

ISBN: 978-0-263-25379-5

011-0715

Harlequin (UK) Limited's policy is to use papers that are natural, renewable and recyclable products and made from wood grown in sustainable forests.The logging and manufacturing processes conform to the legal environmental regulations of the country of origin.

Printed and bound in Spain
by CPI, Barcelona

# BACK TO MR & MRS

## SHIRLEY JUMP

*For the man I married, who fished my manuscript out of the trash and insisted I follow my dream. His support has given me the courage to make writing my full-time job, even though I still whine about deadlines and characters who refuse to cooperate.*

*A special thanks to the coffee shops in Indiana that kept me sufficiently caffeined up, so that I was working instead of napping or perfecting my FreeCell skills. In particular, thanks to the staff at The Grind, who gave me an insider's view of how a great coffee shop operates. All those lattes were research, honest.*

*New York Times* bestselling author **Shirley Jump** didn't have the will-power to diet, nor the talent to master under-eye concealer, so she bowed out of a career in television and opted instead for a career where she could be paid to eat at her desk—writing. At first, seeking revenge on her children for their grocery store tantrums, she sold embarrassing essays about them to anthologies. However, it wasn't enough to feed her growing addiction to writing funny. So she turned to the world of romance novels, where messes are (usually) cleaned up before The End. In the worlds Shirley gets to create and control, the children listen to their parents, the husbands always remember holidays and the housework is magically done by elves. Though she's thrilled to see her books in stores around the world, Shirley mostly writes because it gives her an excuse to avoid cleaning the toilets and helps feed her shoe habit.

To learn more, visit her website at www.shirleyjump.com.

# CHAPTER ONE

IF HER HANDS HADN'T been covered in double chocolate chip cookie dough, Melanie Weaver would have slapped duct tape over her mouth to stop herself from doing it again.

Saying yes when she really meant no.

Even when she had the best intentions of refusing, that slithery yes word slipped out instead. "Do you want a slice of Great-Grandma's fruitcake?" "Can you call Bingo for the Ladies' Auxiliary?" "Don't you just love this orange sweater?"

She hated fruitcake, had grown tired of the "B-4 and After" jokes, and never wore orange. Yet every year, Great Grandma brought a rock-hard fruitcake to Christmas dinner and Melanie choked down a slice, praising the wrinkled dates and dried cherries. On Tuesday nights, she dutifully showed up at the Presbyterian Church and called out letters and numbers in a smoky room filled with frantic reddotters. And in Melanie's closet, there were three orange sweaters, birthday presents from her aunt Cornelia, who took Melanie's compliment of a mango-colored afghan as sure evidence of love for the color.

So it stood to reason, based on her history of always saying the wrong word at the wrong time, that on a bright spring Friday morning she would accept an invitation to her twenty-year class reunion when her life was as jumbled as a ten-thousand-piece puzzle.

"It'll be wonderful to have you!" Jeannie Jenkins, former cheerleader, blasted Melanie out of her reverie with a voice that hit unnatural decibels on the phone. "Everyone is, like, so looking forward to seeing you. I just knew, when I saw your name on the list, that you'd want to go. I mean, you must have just forgotten to RSVP or something."

"Or something," Melanie said. She hadn't returned the card because she hadn't intended to go, nor to answer all those questions about where Cade was.

Or, worse, see Cade there with another woman on his arm. She may be ending her marriage, but she wasn't quite ready to imagine him with someone else.

"The reunion is only, like, a week away. We'll all be together again, in just a few days. Isn't that so exciting?"

"Absolutely." Melanie tried to work some enthusiasm into her voice. She wanted to see her old friends, to catch up on their lives, but the thought of running into Cade, surrounded by memories of happier days, was unbearable. Her resolve would falter, and all those maybes would pop up, the same maybes that had stalled her leaving over and over again because she'd thought things might change. Go back to the way they were.

Either way, there was no return to those days. Melanie had changed, and Cade hadn't accepted those changes. She now had her shop, her new life. A life that no longer included Cade.

It was early afternoon and Cuppa Life was empty, save for Cooter Reynolds, who was sipping his daily mocha latte while reading the *Lawford News* and tapping his foot along with the soft jazz on the sound system. She had an hour until the college student flood poured into her coffee shop on the west side of Lawford, Indiana. And hopefully, only about five seconds until her daughter, Emmie, who worked part-time in the shop, was here for her Thursday shift. Melanie had started the cookies, sure Emmie would be in any second, but twenty minutes had passed since Emmie's shift was due to start and she still wasn't here.

"Did you like, go to college?" Jeannie didn't wait for an answer. "Me, I totally couldn't go. I was *so* done with school when it was over. The last thing I wanted was *more*." She let out a dramatic sigh, as if Westvale High had been the equivalent of a stint in San Quentin.

Jeannie continued chattering on about how hard high school had been, how much she'd hated sophomore grammar, how the guidance counselor had tried to talk her into at least a two-year degree.

The words struck a note of pain in Melanie's chest. Ever since she'd been a kid, Melanie had dreamed of owning her own business. She'd spent her summers here in Indiana, working in this very space, helping her grandparents run what had then been a very successful antiques shop. Her grandfather, who'd seen that spark of entrepreneurial spirit, had encouraged Melanie to go to school and get a degree in business.

Melanie had had a scholarship to Notre Dame— a free ride to the college of her choice—and then been sidetracked by marriage, a child. Always, Cade had said, there would be time for Melanie—until her chance came up and he'd dismissed it faster than a perpetually tardy employee.

But Melanie refused to be put off. When Emmie was grown, Melanie had started taking night classes in business, working part-time at the Indianapolis university's coffee shop.

There, she had found her calling. In the camaraderie and coffee, she'd laughed more, looked forward to her days, and started thinking of that future she'd put on hold.

After leaving Cade, she'd moved to Lawford and

opened her own coffeehouse, to create that community atmosphere in the city's busy business district. She'd gotten her certification as a barista at a conference for coffee shop owners and put those business classes to work.

It may not have been the dorm life and college experience she'd dreamed of during high school, but that didn't matter. She wouldn't have traded those years of raising Emmie for credit hours and a degree.

Emmie had been worth every sacrifice, ten times over. Her giggles, her first day of preschool, her scraped knees and bicycle riding attempts. Even the early years with Cade had been wonderful, filled with laughter and meals eaten while sitting on the floor of their sparse apartment living room, with candlelight providing the mood and pillows serving as furniture.

Melanie shook off the thoughts and concentrated on stirring chocolate chips into the already chocolate dough, while Jeannie chattered on about how cool the reunion would be, how awesome it would be to reconnect with the other Westvale Highers. Jeannie was clearly a woman who didn't need much oxygen.

"So whatcha been doing all these years?" Jeannie asked when she came up for air, her voice interrupted by a blank sound in the phone line. "Oh, damn. Can you hold on a sec? I have another call, probably from ex number-two." Jeannie clicked off to retrieve Call Waiting.

Melanie pictured her personal resume: thirty-seven-year-old woman, almost divorced, running a coffee shop that had finally started showing a profit three months ago. Experience included nineteen years of running a vacuum and a dishwasher. Hey, but she could Calgon with the best of them.

It had been a conscious decision—the only decision she could imagine making—once she saw those two pink lines three weeks after prom night. She remembered being excited and scared, all at the same time. But Cade—and, oh, how she missed that old Cade sometimes—Cade had held her and told her it would all be okay. They'd work through this life twist together.

So she'd married him, had Emmie and then stayed home while Cade worked and went to law school. Later, she'd hosted the dinner parties, sent the thank-you notes and held down the home fort while Cade worked his way up the Fitzsimmons, Matthews and Lloyd ladder.

"Melanie?" Jeannie again, back from her other call. "You still there?"

"Yep." Finished with the cookie batter, Melanie stepped to the right and peeked around the corner of the shop and chuckled. Cooter had fallen asleep on one of the sofas, the paper across his chest, his snores providing an undertow of rhythm to the soft sounds of the stereo system.

"Remember Susan Jagger? She was saludadorian," Jeannie said, mangling the word, "and can you believe she started her own business selling dog sweaters? She's about to hit two million in sales! Oh, and remember Matt Phillips, the kid who always sat in the back and never said a word? He's, like, a famous software nerd now, like that Gates guy. I didn't really listen when he was telling me. I mean, it was *computers*." Jeannie paused to inhale. "And you, why I bet you've, like, invented a cure for cancer or something."

"Not quite." Melanie shouldn't be envious that other people had accomplished more than she had.

But she was. Green as the Jolly Green Giant.

Admitting she'd spent the last two decades helping her husband succeed seemed…embarrassing for someone who had been voted Most Likely to Become President and even more, a woman who had graduated in the top ten of her class.

"Then what *are* you doing?"

Melanie drew in a breath. So what if she wasn't running a huge company. Cuppa Life was something to be proud of. It was hers, all hers, and every inch of its success was due to Melanie, no one else.

She'd done it—opened a business and survived that critical first year. Sure, she was running an espresso machine instead of a multimillion dollar business, but she was happy. And that, she'd found, was all that mattered.

"I own a coffee shop in Lawford," Melanie said. "It's doing really well."

"Well, that's cool," Jeannie said, the words coming out with that exaggerated care that spelled unimpressed. "Like, everyone drinks coffee."

Melanie dropped cookie dough balls onto the sheets, refusing to let Jeannie's tone get her dander up.

"Anyway, I was, like, at the state courthouse the other day. Had a little incident with my neighbor's underwear." Jeannie let out a dramatic sigh. "Long story."

"I bet," Melanie said, biting back a laugh as she slid the first two cookie sheets into the oven. She peeked around the corner again for Emmie, who was now thirty minutes late.

"And while I was there," Jeannie continued, "I ran into Cade. He was doing some kind of lawyer thing. We got to talking and I told him I didn't have your RSVP, and he gave me your number here. So, we owe our little reuniting all to Cade!"

Melanie's breath got caught somewhere between her windpipe and her lungs. When would the mention of Cade's name stop doing that? She no longer loved him, hadn't in a long time, and shouldn't be affected by his voice, the sight of him or a discussion about the man she was about to divorce.

But some part of her, that leftover teenage romantic that had believed in happily ever after, still reacted. Still wanted him and still thought about him when the night closed in and loneliness served as her blanket.

"Anyway, he said you two were still together. Ever since high school. I think that's *so* romantic." Jeannie sighed. "You guys, like, give people hope."

The oven door, released from Melanie's grasp, shut with a slam.

"Still together?" Melanie echoed. How could he? He'd received the divorce papers. Seen her walk out the door a year ago. Except for the occasional conversation about Emmie and seeing him at a distance on the sidelines of Emmie's college soccer games, there had been nothing between them. Melanie had done everything she could to send the message it was over.

Clearly Cade hadn't been listening.

"Here I can't even hold onto a man for five minutes," Jeannie said. "I don't know how you do it." She took in a breath. "You guys got married so fast after graduation, then moved to what, Indianapolis? I don't blame you. When we were kids, we might as well have lived in Mars, what with Westvale so far out in corn cob country. So, did you guys have any kids?"

"Yes, one. But, Jeannie, listen—"

Jeannie barreled on, not even hearing her. "You guys are, like, my idols. I'm divorced, twice now, soon to be three times. But it's not so bad. The alimony is almost like a full-time job." Jeannie laughed. "Anyway, you must have the coolest husband in the world. Especially if you stuck with him and had a rug rat."

At that word, Melanie heard the bell over the entrance to Cuppa Life jingle. She peeked around the corner again, and smiled. Enter one rug rat, or rather, a nineteen-year-old-sweetheart named Emmie.

"Hi, Mom," Emmie said as she headed into the kitchen.

"You deserve it, Melanie," Jeannie was saying. "I mean, like, *someone* should get the fairy tale ending. Besides Snow White. That girl never even changed her dress in the whole movie. I mean, what man wants that? Like, wouldn't she start to smell?"

"Jeannie, Cade and I—"

"Oh, almost time for my manicure! I need to get to the salon."

Melanie looked down at her own hands, glistening with butter. There was dough under her short, no-nonsense nails and in the creases of her knuckles.

She needed to tell Jeannie the truth. That Melanie and Cade, the "it" couple at Westvale High, had fallen prey to the divorce statistics. Melanie had ended up pregnant at eighteen, married and living in a cramped apartment in Indianapolis before her nineteenth birthday. That she was changing diapers and figuring out the best way to potty train before she was old enough to drink.

That *Cade* had been the one to go on to school, thanks to his father funding the tuition and providing a part-time job at the family law firm to cover other expenses. Cade had been the one to rise to the top of his field, with Melanie by his side, providing that home front support.

Since then, her biggest accomplishment had been learning how to make a good latte.

Well, that and Emmie, she thought as her daughter came into the small kitchen area, pressed a quick kiss to her mother's cheek, then slid into place beside her to help with the rest of the cookies. Emmie was tall and lithe, with the same blond hair as her mother, but the wide, deep eyes of her father. She had Cade's athleticism, Melanie's wit, and on most days, a sweet, compassionate way about her that had survived the ugly teen years. She was Cade and Melanie's pride and joy—

The one thing they had done right together.

Yet, since the separation, Emmie had become more distant, more rebellious. Her short cropped hair was now topped with red, her ears tripled in earrings and her attitude less friendly and more filled with annoyance.

Jeannie sighed. "I *so* wish I'd had that kind of happy ending, too."

As Melanie opened her mouth to tell Jeannie the truth, it somehow got lodged in her throat. Maybe it was pride, maybe it was the thought of everyone in her graduating class giving her that pitying look at the reunion, as if she hadn't measured up to their expectations.

Or maybe it was simply that she had yet to take off her wedding ring.

The ring fit tight, considering she'd gained a couple dozen pounds in the years of marriage. That was all. It certainly wasn't because somewhere deep in her heart, she saw taking the ring off as that final, irrevocable step.

"Ohmigod, I almost forgot!" Jeannie said, interrupting before Melanie could stop letting a simple gold band make the decisions. "Me and the committee had, like, this brainstorm last night. I swear, I saw a lightbulb over Susan's head, it was just so cool. Anyway, we were thinking you and Cade could give the welcoming speech together. The sweethearts of Westvale High, still together and happy."

"Sorry I'm late," Emmie whispered in her mother's ear. "My car wouldn't start so I had to find a ride." Melanie put up a finger to signal she'd be done in a minute.

"You guys are, like, the perfect high school love story," Jeannie went on. "Wouldn't it be so neat?"

"I don't think so, Jeannie. In fact, I'm not even sure *I'm* coming." Melanie moved to the sink to rinse her hands. Emmie had already washed hers and was busy dropping balls of dough onto cookie sheets.

Emmie helping with the baking she dreaded—without being asked? And, in a good mood, one that involved an actual smile? Melanie cast a quizzical eye over her daughter. Something was up.

"Oh, come on, Melanie. You have to do it. I mean, you two were prom King and Queen. It'll be like a fairy tale, only in real life." Jeannie sighed.

Melanie remembered that prom night, the magical star-shaped lights twinkling overhead, the way Cade had looked in a tux.

*Especially* the way Cade had looked. The man had yet to meet a suit that didn't make him look more attractive than a ten-pound chocolate bar.

She and Cade had stood on that stage, hands clasped, beaming at each other, thinking nothing and no one would ever separate them.

They'd been wrong.

"Uh, Mom?" Emmie said, her voice now an urgent whisper as she put on a pair of oven mitts and switched out baked cookies for her loaded sheet of dough. "When I needed a ride to work, the only person available was—"

The door to the kitchen swung open and for the second time in five minutes, Melanie drew in a sharp breath that became a block in her windpipe.

Cade.

He entered the small kitchen, seeming to take up half the space without even trying. Melanie swallowed hard, surprised by the instantaneous, explosive gut reaction to her husband.

Correction: almost ex-husband.

Apparently her hormones hadn't received the separation papers, nor read over the draft of the divorce agreement, because they were still screaming attraction.

And why wouldn't they? Cade hadn't changed at all in the year they'd been apart. A few more crinkles around his blue eyes, the perpetual worry line above his dark brows etched a little deeper, but overall he was as handsome as he had been when she'd still loved him. He may be a bit disheveled by the stress of his day, but he was still sexy.

Really sexy. Familiar desire rose inside her, coupled with the longing to touch his face, run a hand down his chest, feel the security of his long, lean body against hers. The temperature in the room seemed to multiply. Melanie pulled at the neck of her T-shirt and checked the air conditioner. Nothing broken there—

Except for her resolve.

Attraction, though, had never been their problem. Marriages weren't based solely on the swirling, tangling pulses of estrogen and testosterone. They needed communication, understanding, give and take.

And a man who wanted more for his wife than perfecting her baked Alaska and diaper changing.

Cade still sported the same athletic physique—trim, broad-shouldered, a chest of hard, tight planes. It had never been solely his body that had attracted Melanie, though she hadn't minded the nice physical package that had wrapped around Cade.

It had been his eyes. And his smile.

Right now, the smile was absent, but those eyes—the same big blue eyes that had drawn her attention that first day in freshman year, standing in the hall outside Mrs. Owen's art class—they now riveted her attention for a brief, taut second, before she remembered the man may have incredible eyes, but horrible husband skills. He'd never listened to her, not really, never heard her when she talked about *her* dreams, *her* goals. He'd been as focused as a horse with blinders, seeing only one road ahead—for both of them.

And when it had really mattered, Cade hadn't been there at all.

The oven timer dinged. Cookies. She needed to tend to the cookies. Melanie grabbed a spatula and a pot holder, but her attention was still all on Cade, not the hot pan she withdrew from the oven.

"Melanie?" Jeannie asked, her voice concerned, seeming to come from a thousand miles away. "I really have to get to the salon, but I wanted to be sure you and Cade can do me this eensy weensy favor. You will do it, right?"

"Hi, Melanie," Cade said, his voice the same deep baritone she'd known for more than half her life. Once upon a time, that sound had made her heart sing. "Is it okay if I stay here for a bit?" he said. "I've got some time to kill before a meeting."

"Yes, yes, of course," Melanie said. And promptly dropped the spatula. It landed on the vinyl floor with a soft clatter.

"Oh, great!" Jeannie cried. "I'll see you a week from Friday then!" She giggled. "You and Cade. It'll be the best speech *ever.* You guys always did have a way with words. And a lot more." She let out another laugh, then hung up.

"No! I meant to say no!" Melanie yelled into the phone, scrambling for the spatula, but Jeannie was already gone, off for some French tips.

The yes had been for Cade, not Jeannie. Somehow, the sight of him after so much time apart had knocked her off-kilter. As it had in the early days, before their "way with words" became more about flinging them around the living room in arguments that went nowhere.

Emmie tossed her mother a grin, then turned away and started sliding the cookies onto the cooling rack. Melanie tossed the spatula into the sink, all thumbs and as consternated as a chicken in a fox den.

She grabbed a warm chocolate chip cookie off

the wire cooling rack and stuffed it in her mouth before she could make the same mistake twice—

Say yes when she really meant to say no.

# CHAPTER TWO

AS HIS DAUGHTER HANDED him a cup of coffee, Cade watched the woman he'd once thought he knew better than himself hurry between the espresso machine and the bakery case, greeting customers by name, laughing at their jokes, dispensing coffee with a happy, friendly cheer—and wondered for the thousandth time when they had slipped off their common track.

Somewhere between "I do" and "I don't," something had gone wrong in his marriage. He was a corporate lawyer. His specialty was fixing tangled legal messes. Why couldn't he fix the one in his own house?

He'd tried, Lord knew he'd tried, but Melanie had thrown up a wall and refused to remove a single chink in the brick.

God, he missed her. Every morning, he woke up to an empty space in his bed and an ache in his chest that no painkiller could soothe. At night, the talking heads on TV kept him company instead of the soft tones of Melanie, telling him about her day, about something Emmie had said or done.

He took a seat at one of the tables, watching his wife's lithe, fluid movements. She was still as beautiful as the day he'd married her. A little heavier, but over the years he'd found he liked the extra weight on her hips and waist, the fullness in her breasts. The womanly curves had always held a magical comfort, soothing him at the end of a stressful day.

Always, Melanie had been there, supporting him in those early days when it seemed he'd never rise above the minion position of law clerk.

He poured sugar into his cup. It dissolved as easily as the bonds of his marriage.

Still, he'd put off signing the papers that would file their divorce. He had hope, damn it, that this could be fixed. That he could broker a mutually satisfactory agreement, a return to business as usual, something he had done a thousand times between warring corporations.

Every time he looked at Melanie, a constant smile curved across her face as she chatted and poured, the ache in his chest quadrupled. Need for her—not just sexual need, but an indefinable, untouchable need that ran bone-deep—stirred in his gut, rushing through his veins. He wanted to take her in his arms, hold her to his chest and kiss her until he made this past year go away.

But deep in his heart he knew they'd gone way

beyond the point where a simple kiss could solve anything.

"Dad," Emmie said, coming over to him. Now a college sophomore, Emmie had the same heart-shaped face and delicate features as her mother, except now her hair was spiked, her lips painted a dark crimson. "Sit at the counter. It's way more comfortable."

Before he could protest, his daughter had taken his cup of Kenyan roast and put it on the laminate surface. Three feet from Melanie. He and Melanie exchanged a quick, knowing glance.

Obviously she knew Emmie was trying to bring them together. Why shouldn't she? Emmie hadn't asked for the divorce and she'd made it clear she didn't like alternating between her two parents' homes for weekly dinners and occasional laundry stops, like a perpetual ping-pong game.

Cade sure as hell wasn't happy watching his marriage whittle away, either.

He rose and crossed to the wooden bar, settling onto one of the cushioned stools. "You've created a nice place here."

He hadn't seen his wife in a year and that was the best he could come up with? This is *nice?*

After this, he was heading to the bookstore to see if there was a *Resurrecting Your Marriage for Dummies*. Because clearly this dummy was failing at Wooing Back a Wife 101.

"Thanks," Melanie said. She wiped off the steamer spout, then tossed the dirty cloth into a bucket of laundry inside the kitchen. She washed her hands and picked up the rack of freshly baked cookies and began loading them into the glass case, arranging them as carefully as she used to arrange the pillows in their living room.

"Is it going well?" Cade asked. "From what I've seen, this place is as popular as an elf at Christmas."

She laughed. "Things are going much better than expected."

He heard the undertones of their last fight in those two sentences. Cade was smart enough to back away from that. "I'm happy for you, Melanie."

Emmie brushed by him, giving him an elbow hint. "Say something, Dad," she whispered.

Cade held up his hands and looked to Emmie for help. She gave him the duh look she'd perfected by her sixteenth birthday. Oh, yeah, he was the dad. He was supposed to have all the answers.

He did—all but this one.

Cade shifted on the stool. "Are you going to tease your hair and unearth that Kiss concert T-shirt for Friday night?"

She chuckled. "Oh gosh, that was a thousand years ago. I don't think I saved the shirt."

"You did. Bottom drawer, on the right." He knew, because he'd been in their dresser after she'd left, looking for something, and come across the worn image of Gene Simmons. For a moment, Cade had been back there, in the thirtieth row, rocking along with Melanie as they held up a lighter during a ballad and sang along until their voices cracked.

"I remember that night," she said softly, then shook her head and got busy with the cookies again. "Anyway, it doesn't matter because I'm not going to the reunion. I'll have to save the Aqua Net for another night."

She'd tried to pass it off as a joke, but Cade wasn't laughing. "Didn't you just tell Jeannie you would go?" He gestured toward the phone. "I couldn't help but overhear. Jeannie's voice is like a bullhorn."

"I only said yes to—"

"Get her off your back?" He chuckled, reaching for that light, easy feeling again. It seemed to flit in and out, as ungraspable as a moth. "I know the feeling. It's why I said yes, too."

Emmie headed into the back of the shop, to get supplies or something, Cade supposed. As soon as their daughter was out of earshot, Melanie stopped working on the cookies, leaned an arm over the glass case and glared at him. "Why did you tell Jeannie we were still together?"

"I think there's still a chance to work this out. You don't throw nineteen years away on a whim."

"You think this was a *whim?*" She shook her head,

then lowered her voice. "It was the hardest decision I have ever made."

Hurt stabbed at his chest, thinking of how quickly she'd been gone, how fast she'd escaped her half of their life. "I doubt that."

She let out a gust of frustration. "Sign the papers, Cade. It's over."

"No." He slipped off the stool and came around to the back of the glass case. "I'm done catwalking around the issue, biding my time. Thinking all you needed was a little space. I want answers, Mel, a solution." He drew within inches of her. "Tell me what went wrong so I can change it."

She threw up her hands. "Our marriage isn't a clock, Cade. You can't replace a couple gears and call it good as new."

"And you can't just throw it out because you wanted a better model."

"That isn't why I left." Melanie circled the counter and began wiping down the case's glass with an ammonia-scented cleaner and a white cotton cloth. An old man snored lightly on the sofa across the room, the paper on his torso fluttering as his chest rose up and down. "We made a mistake," she said under her breath. "Why can't you just let it go?"

"Because I still love you." The words tore from his throat, contained in his chest for so long, fenced in by a hope that grew dimmer with every day Melanie refused his calls, ignored his e-mails, refused his requests to talk.

She shook her head and when she did, he saw the glimmer of tears in her eyes. "You don't even know me."

*I would if you'd give me a chance,* he wanted to scream. *Let me try again. Don't take away the one rock I've always stood on.*

Before he could say anything, the bell rang and a woman in a business suit strode into the small shop and up to the register. Emmie came out of the back, headed to the register and greeted the woman, but her attention, Cade knew, was half on her parents.

Melanie took out some of her frustrations on the glass case, scrubbing it until it gleamed like silver. As her left hand rose up to swipe away a smear, a glint caught Cade's eye.

Her wedding ring.

The same plain gold band he'd slipped on her finger in the county courthouse nearly twenty years ago.

A wave of hope rose within him, but he held it back. Cade was nothing if not a practical man. His wife may still be wearing her ring, but she'd gone back to using her maiden name and hadn't slept in his bed for over a year. A piece of jewelry didn't mean anything.

And yet, he hoped like hell it did.

"Mellie," he said, slipping into the habit of her

nickname. He grabbed her hand, stopping her from cleaning the glass into oblivion. He lowered his voice and turned so that the customer—and Emmie— couldn't see or overhear them. "Go with me to the reunion. Wear that T-shirt and that bright pink lipstick you used to love. Go back in time with me, for one night. We could go out to dinner first, talk—"

"About what, Cade?" A glimmer washed over the deep thunderstorm of green in her eyes. Behind them, Emmie watched out of the corner of her eye, her movements quiet and small as she finished the customer's latte and poured the steamed milk into a paper cup emblazoned with the bright crimson Cuppa Life logo.

Melanie noticed their daughter's interest and led Cade into the small kitchen space, letting the door shut behind them. The close quarters only quadrupled Cade's awareness of Melanie, of the way her chest rose and fell with each breath, the silky blond tendrils drifting about her shoulders, the jeans hugging her hips.

He wanted to kiss her, to close the gap between them. If only a simple meeting of their bodies would be enough to bridge the chasm. But even Cade knew it wasn't that simple.

"Talk about what?" she repeated. "About how I failed you?" she said. "As a wife, a mother? About how you were at work—always at work—even when I needed you most?"

Regret slammed into his gut. He didn't want to think about that day. Ever.

It was the one tape he couldn't rewind. Couldn't delete. Couldn't do over. "Melanie, I've said I was sorry a hundred times."

She sighed. "It's not about being sorry, Cade, it's about changing what got us there in the first place."

"That doesn't work if only one of us is trying," he countered. "And I'm trying damn it. Go with me, Mel. For one night be my wife again."

"I can't put on that show anymore." She held her ground, arms crossed over her chest. "Besides, did Jeannie tell you she wanted us to make a speech?"

"Isn't that supposed to be the class president's thing?"

"She thought it would be…" Her voice trailed off.

"Be what?" Cade asked, leaning closer, inhaling the scent of her skin, the sweetness of fresh-baked cookies, of the woman he'd lived with more than half his life. "Would be what, Melanie?" Cade whispered, his mouth so close to hers, all it would take was a few inches of movement to kiss her. To have her in his arms, against his heart.

"Romantic," she said after a minute, expelling a disgusted sigh on the word. "The whole Prom King and Queen still together thing."

He moved back a step. "But we aren't, are we?"

She shook her head, resolute. "No, we're not."

The need for her smoldered inside him, a wildfire ready to erupt. He still loved her, damn it, and refused to let her quit so easily.

His gaze traveled down, to her lips, her jaw, the delicate arch of her throat. The old attraction that had simmered between them for more than twenty years ignited anew in his chest, the embers never really extinguished.

He wanted her, Lord, did he want her. He wanted to sweep her off her feet, carry her out of this shop and back to their bed. Every fiber in his being ached to feel her familiar, sweet body beneath his, to lose himself inside her, to find that connection he'd never found anywhere else.

A slight flush crept into Melanie's cheeks, warming them to cotton-candy-pink. She opened her mouth, shut it again, then reached for a spoon, succeeding only in knocking it along the counter. It skittered under a display stand of teas. Was she thinking the same thing?

Then it was gone, and she was back to all business. "The idea of going together and pretending we're still together is—"

"Insane," he finished.

Melanie reached for a towel, folding, then unfolding and refolding it, a nervous habit he recognized—and also a sign of hope. Maybe not much, but he'd take whatever he could get.

"Completely insane," she said, watching him, her eyes as unreadable as the Pacific. Her hand stilled, the towel limp in her grip.

A breath hitched between them. Another. Cade's grip curled around the countertop, willpower keeping him from reaching out and pulling her to him.

"If we don't go, or if we go separately, everyone's going to know we're getting…" He left off the word, still unable to believe it was going to happen. It was why he had yet to even look at the divorce paperwork. Seeing the word, speaking it, would make it a reality.

And Cade sure wasn't ready to let go yet.

"Divorced," Melanie finished. The eight letters that were changing Cade's life hung between them, as bright as a neon sign.

"Yeah." His marriage was so far off track—hell, they weren't even on the same cross-country route anymore—that he wondered if there was even a chance of getting it back to where it had been.

"I should probably get back to work," she said, folding the towel one last time before leaving it on the counter.

"I hear you're thinking about expanding this place," Cade said, changing tactics, avoiding the dreaded "D" word.

Someday, he'd have to deal with it. Just not today.

"How did you…?" Surprise flitted across Melanie's delicate features, then disappeared when she realized the daughter outside the kitchen was the source of the information. "Yes, I am planning an expansion."

"As in a mini-mall or world domination of the cappuccino industry?"

She laughed. "Nothing that big." Then her brows knitted together and she studied him. "Do you really want to know?"

He nodded. Was that what it was? He had stopped listening and she had stopped talking? "I do."

"Do you promise not to give me a list of pros and cons?"

He winced at the memory, then put up two fingers. "Scout's honor."

She laughed, the merry sound such sweet music to his ears. "You were never a Boy Scout."

He grinned. "I always had Boy Scout intentions, though."

"I remember," Melanie said quietly.

"I do, too." The memory slipped between them, the shared thought coming easily, as if they shared a brain. Their first date. A car broken down on the side of the road. Two elderly ladies standing outside of the Mazda, looking confused and helpless. Rain pelting down on Cade's head as he filled their radiator with a jug of water he kept in his trunk, then put a temporary duct tape patch on the leaking hose.

Melanie had called him a Boy Scout, then, when the women were gone, drawn him to her, her lips soft and sweet. He'd have rebuilt fifty transmissions that night if he'd known a simple act of kindness would turn Mellie's interest in him from mild to five-alarm hot.

"You wanted to hear my plans," Melanie said, interrupting his thoughts.

Cade recovered his wits. "Yes, I would."

"Okay. It's slow and I could use a break. Let's go in the back." As the customer lingered, asking about the different types of muffins, Melanie poured herself a cup of coffee, then gestured to Cade to follow her to the rear of the shop, where she'd set up a cozy nook with two leather love seats. It was a small area, but the bronze wash on the walls and the deep chocolate sofas made it inviting and warm. Melanie always had had great decorating skills.

She and Cade took seats on opposite sofas, a few feet away from the armchair holding Rip Van Winkle. "My plan is to double the space," she said, laying her cup on the end table. "Add some game tables, a children's play area, build a room for business people to hold meetings. Maybe even add a stage for open mike nights." Excitement brightened her eyes. He got the feeling she wanted to tell someone, to maybe… just maybe, get his take on her idea.

In the old days, before Emmie had come along, Melanie had been filled with ideas, their evenings in that dingy apartment passing quickly with energetic conversations about what could be if they took this path or that path. In the end, there'd only been one road to follow. Cade had always thought it was the right one, but now, seeing his wife's enthusiasm, he wondered if he'd missed a detour.

Beside them, the old man snarfled in his sleep. "Bad deer," he muttered.

Each of them laughed quietly at the non sequiter, providing a moment of détente, connection. Then Melanie cleared her throat and directed her attention to the room. "Anyway, we're really cramped in our four hundred square feet here. I figured if I could get a bit more space, I'd get more of the college crowd. The building next door is up for sale and the owner has already offered it to me. If I could buy it, knock down this wall—" she gestured toward the plaster finish "—I'd double the space."

He let out a low whistle, impressed. The Melanie he knew had been intelligent, witty, cool under pressure—but never had he seen this business savvy part of her. "You've taken this place a lot further than I thought it could go when we looked at it last year, after you inherited it from your grandparents. I guess I didn't see the potential then."

She studied the brass studs on the armrest's seam. "No, you didn't."

A pair of size fifty boots had a smaller heel than Cade. Had he crushed her dream? He'd only been trying to be pragmatic, to steer her away from a potential mistake. Clearly he'd done the opposite. "I'm sorry, Melanie."

She didn't meet his gaze. Instead she smoothed a hand over the leather. "It's in the past. I'm all about moving forward."

The implied word—alone. "You have a lot of plans for this place. For that you need additional funding, right?"

She nodded.

"Something that's hard to get when you're a relatively new business." From Emmie, he knew she'd financed the opening of the shop on her own, with a little from her grandparent's inheritance, the rest from the nice folks at Visa.

"Tell me about it," Melanie said, clearly frustrated. "Banks want me to have years of success under my belt before they'll lend me any money. But I can't get those years of success without investing in my business. It's that old Catch-22."

It was also an area he knew well—and an opportunity to help. And maybe, just maybe, she'd let him in again. At this point, Cade would knock down the damned wall himself if he thought it would help defrost the glacier between them.

"I have a proposition for you," Cade said, deciding he wasn't going to let his marriage go without a fight. He could only pray this was an offer Melanie couldn't refuse.

# CHAPTER THREE

"WHAT DO YOU MEAN—a proposition?" she asked.

Cade rose, slipped over to her love seat and sat down beside her, not too close, but close enough that their conversation couldn't be overheard by the snoring man or the woman still hemming and hawing about blueberry versus peach crumble.

He was also close enough to catch the vanilla scent on her skin, the same fragrance he always associated with Melanie. Like cookies, homemade bread…all the things he'd missed in his childhood and had found in his wife.

*His wife.*

Damn, he missed her. Missed coming home to her smile, missed holding her. Regardless of what that piece of paper on his desk said, he'd never stopped thinking of Melanie as his wife.

"If you stayed married to me…" Cade paused for a second, letting the last word linger in the air as the idea took root in his mind, "just for a while, you could get that funding a lot easier."

She backed up against the arm of the sofa, warding off his idea. "*No.* I want to do this on my own, Cade. *Without* your help or your family money."

He heard the seeds of the familiar argument taking hold in her tone. Eighteen months ago, they'd stood here in this very space, Cade glancing around at the dusty antiques, the cluttered room, seeing only years of books in the red, not potential. He'd offered to help, to give her the business guidance the place clearly needed, to invest some of the inheritance from his grandfather that had done nothing but sit in the bank, but she'd refused.

*I want to do this on my own, Cade,* she'd said then. *I don't need you to tell me what's wrong. I just want you to say go for it and let me do it.*

Instead he'd pulled out a thick stack of research he'd done on the antique industry, statistics proving what worked—and what didn't. She'd shoved the papers back at him, and in doing so, shut the first door on their marriage.

He'd shut the second one himself.

He tossed her a grin. "Just think of it as a little payback for all the years you helped me."

She rose, frustration running through every inch of her face. "Where is this new and improved Cade coming from? Since when did you want me to be all independent?"

He blinked. "I never said you had to be some Stepford wife, Mellie. I've always wanted you to have your own life."

"As long as it wasn't at the expense of yours." Melanie took in a breath, erasing the quick flash of hurt in her eyes. "Cade, you just don't understand how important it is for me to have something of my own. To do this *myself.*"

"I'm trying, Melanie." He paused, waiting until she sank back onto the seat beside him. "I promise not to do anything more than let you have my credit score," Cade continued. "We have a lot of assets together, Melanie, a financial record, a damned nice nest egg of Matthews money. The bank will look more favorably on your loan if—"

"If I pretend I'm still married to you."

"It's not pretending. We *are* married."

"Only because you won't sign the divorce papers."

"I've been busy."

She gave him the eye roll Emmie had inherited. She sighed, considering him for a long moment. "I'm not agreeing to anything. Not until I know what you want in exchange."

"Nothing."

She shook her head. "I know you, Cade. You don't

make a deal without both sides gaining something. You help me get my loan, but what do you get?"

"Nothing, except—" he drew in a breath "—a date to the reunion."

In her green eyes, the thoughts connected. "As your wife, you mean."

Cade had brokered enough deals to know when he'd reached the crux, the point where the agreement could be broken by one party leaning too far or pushing too hard.

Melanie would eventually be awarded the divorce with or without his signature. He glanced at her left hand, at the circle of gold on her ring finger.

He weighed his next words, trying to figure out what wouldn't make Melanie bolt, or worse, encourage her to throw the countertop Capresso machine at his head. "Not as my wife," he lied, "more as a…fellow reunion attendee. Let people assume what they want." He voiced the idea as calmly as he would the terms of a corporate merger. Start with business-only, and pray like hell it turned into something more personal later.

Her gaze narrowed. "Why are you suddenly so interested in going to the class reunion? If I remember right, you skipped the fifth and the tenth. What's so big about the twentieth?"

Cade didn't miss a beat. "Bill Hendrickson."

"The kid who carried a briefcase to school every day?"

He nodded. "He's now the owner of one of the largest law firms in the Midwest and he's looking for a new partner."

That much was true. For a month or so, Bill had been trying to meet with Cade, but their respective schedules had kept them from finding a common time. Bill suggested a quick meeting at the reunion. "Bring your wife," Bill had said, unaware of the rift in the Matthews marriage. "I'd love to introduce her to my Shelley."

Bill had made it clear he liked to employ family men because he thought they were more committed, more honorable. Cade wasn't so sure he agreed with Bill's logic, but he did know one thing for sure—he'd love to work for the massive, national firm that Bill headed. They'd handled clients Cade could only dream of working for; the kind with names that everyone in America knew.

It was what he'd worked for, toiling away under his father's thumb, hoping to prove himself and then break into the big leagues.

"What's wrong with staying at Fitzsimmons, Matthews and Lloyd?" Melanie asked.

Cade's gaze swept over the hourglass shape of his wife, down the dusting of freckles that trailed a pattern from her shoulder to her wrist, a path he'd kissed more than once. The ache that had become his constant companion in the last year tightened its grip. "Because I need a change of pace."

If this divorce happened—and as more time went by with Melanie remaining resolute in her plans, he knew it would—then he knew he'd have to leave. He couldn't stand living twenty minutes from Melanie, knowing she was moving on with her life.

And worst of all—dating other men.

He tore his gaze away from her. A woman as gorgeous and vivacious as Melanie wouldn't be going to bed alone for very long. "Bill's firm is in Chicago and—"

"You're moving to *Chicago?*" she said, her voice soft, surprised.

"I'm considering it, if everything goes well with Bill. Chicago is only a few hours away, which means I can still see Emmie." He grinned. "Half the time she's here or out with friends. I'm more of a laundry dump than a dad."

Melanie echoed his smile. "I know the feeling. She does the same thing to me. If I hadn't hired her, I don't think I'd see her for more than a five-minute conversation a month."

"Our little girl has grown up, hasn't she?" Cade's memory ran through a quick tape of Emmie's first steps, first day of school, first bike. The years had rocketed by too fast. Hindsight berated him for missing far too many of those firsts.

"Yeah," Melanie said, and the bittersweet expression on her face told him she was watching the same mental movie. "If you get the job, are you selling the house?"

Back to the logistics of divvying up a marriage. "I'll keep it for a while," Cade said. If there was a chance Melanie would ever live there again, would ever sit at the oak dining room table they'd bought for their fifth anniversary and share a dinner with him, he wanted to have that familiar three-bedroom in Indianapolis waiting.

He shook off the thought. Cade had to be pragmatic instead of getting caught up in the green of her eyes, the scent of her skin. The sheer magic of being so close to her again, separated only by a few inches of love seat.

This reunion idea was a last-ditch effort, brought about because he'd thought he'd read some meaning in the gold band on her left hand. Assuming, that was, that she'd ever loved him at all. That she hadn't married him just because she'd been pregnant with Emmie. In the still, dark night, *that* was the possibility that haunted Cade. Had he been so clueless, he'd imagined a love that had never existed?

"I had no idea you were considering a move," Melanie said.

"I haven't broken it to Emmie yet, so please don't tell her. I want to have something definite in hand first."

More, Cade needed to know for sure there was zero chance with his wife. All year, he'd kept telling himself that given a little time, Melanie would be back. She hadn't.

With all the signs she'd been sending him, he could have taken out a billboard: Your Marriage Is Over. And yet, the glutton in him continued to hope that the past nineteen years had formed a foundation they could come back to, build a new beginning on, after they moved the last few years of wreckage out of the way.

The realist in him whispered their foundation was made of sand, not stone.

"Oh." Melanie's mouth formed the vowel, held it for a minute, as if it was taking her a moment to get used to the idea of him moving away. "Okay."

"Anyway, you know how I hate to go to those things, especially alone," Cade said, putting on a smile, making his case, treading carefully. "I can never remember anyone's name. I need a wingman."

*I need you.*

It wasn't until Melanie responded with a smile of her own that Cade found himself able to breathe again. "You *are* pretty bad at that. Remember when you kept calling Jim Sacco 'Stan'?"

Cade laughed. "He was a former partner at Fitzsimmons, Matthews and Lloyd, too. We even worked together a couple times. I've never lived that one down."

Melanie joined his laughter. Cade wished he could

reach out, capture that sound in a jar and bring it home with him. The walls in the house had grown as silent as tombs without Melanie.

"Oh, and what about the time you forgot the name of the governor?" She chuckled softly. "So much for any political ambitions you might have had."

"That's when my wingman came in mighty handy," he said, thinking of that nightmare dinner party seven years ago, of Melanie slipping in with her easy touch and smoothing everything over. With them so close together on the love seat, it was almost like before. Cade and Melanie, staying up late, finishing off the appetizers while they rehashed the night. "You told him some story about me getting the flu or something—"

Another smile from her, the kind that could disrupt a man's best intentions. "And I told him the medicine had some kind of mental side effects."

"All that mattered was that he bought it and signed the firm as his personal counsel. *You* made that save, Mellie." He leaned forward, careful not to invade her personal space, to keep it casual, to act as if his heart didn't still trip over itself every time she smiled. "That's why I need you with me at the reunion. You make me look good."

"Oh, I don't know about that." Her glance flitted away. She reached for her coffee, her hand a nervous flutter that nearly toppled the cup. It clattered against the table, then settled into place.

"I'm serious. Your talent is people. Making them feel comfortable, welcome." He glanced around the corner of their little nook, into the main part of Cuppa Life. The cozy coffee shop was beginning to fill with chattering college students, clustering around the tables and doing homework, playing cards, or just talking. It was the polar opposite to the stuffy, serious law offices of Fitzsimmons, Matthews and Lloyd. For a minute, he wondered what it was like to work in a place like this. To escape the daily grind of a job that had never felt quite right, as if all these years he'd been wearing the wrong size suit. "This place is 'Cheers' with caffeine."

She laughed. "Not quite as successful, but, yeah, I guess it does have that kind of atmosphere. Speaking of which, I better get back and help Emmie with the afternoon rush." She rose and turned to go.

Cade reached for her arm. Everything within him begged for more contact, more of her. With reluctance he held back, tempered his touch to border on acquaintance, not spouse. "Melanie, go with me. Please."

She paused, her emerald gaze meeting his for a long, silent second. "Are you really moving to Chicago?"

Once again, the belt tightened around his heart. If this didn't work, there was no way Cade could stay in that house another second. "Yeah."

Emmie shouted to her mother that she needed help making something called a "Frazzle." With an apology, Melanie hurried back to the counter.

In a blur of activity, Melanie dumped a slew of ingredients into a blender and whirred the icy concoction together. She poured the frothy liquid into a cup, handed it to the customer, then set to work on a couple of lattes, filling the orders of the group of twenty-somethings who'd all come in at once. It was a good five minutes before she had a second to return to Cade.

He rehashed their conversation in his head, as if a replay could show him how to fine tune it next time, to get a different result.

"Did you mean what you said about helping me get my loan?" she said when she came back.

He nodded. "As much or as little as you want. I can even give you the money from our account."

She shook her head. "I want to do this alone."

"It's our money, Mel."

"It's *your* inheritance. I want to earn my own. I want this—" she indicated the shop "—to be mine."

"Okay. Whatever you want. You call all the shots, Melanie."

She hesitated so long, worry began to crowd onto Cade's shoulders.

Then she thrust out her hand. He took it, feeling the familiar delicate palm inside his much bigger one, knowing that if he inhaled the fragrance of her skin, he'd be swept back up into what could have been, instead of what really was.

Instead he shook when she did, the businesslike stance feeling so odd, he wanted to laugh.

"Then you have a deal, Cade Matthews."

# CHAPTER FOUR

"WHAT WAS I THINKING?" Melanie slumped into one of the bar stools beside Kelly Webber, a frequent customer turned good friend. The college crowd had begun petering out as night began to fall and discussion of dorm room parties replaced the complaints about professors with homework fetishes. Emmie was sitting at a table in the corner of the room, ostensibly doing her homework, but really chatting with a friend while their dueling laptops accessed Cuppa Life's wireless Internet connection.

Melanie let out a sigh. "Once again, I said yes when I should have said no."

"That's called Momitis. It's how I got roped into doing the PTL dinner and chairing the book drive all in the same week." Kelly took a sip from her decaf iced mocha and gave Melanie a sympathetic smile. She had her dark brown hair back in a ponytail and wore a blue track suit, her usual running-the-kids attire. Her two sons were taking karate lessons at the studio three doors down, giving Kelly a moment for a coffee and friendship break. "Just skip the reunion. Who needs that one-upmanship fest?"

"But Cade needs my help." Melanie sat back and blinked. "What am I saying? I'm not married to Cade anymore, or at least I won't be soon. I shouldn't care if he needs my help or not."

Kelly laid a hand over Melanie's. "But you do."

A sigh slipped from her lips. "Yeah."

"What you have is a conundrum, my friend."

Melanie grinned. "You helping Peter study for his English tests again?" Kelly often used car time with her captive child audience to do test review.

"Hey, it helps dispel my soccer mom image when I throw out a multisyllable word." Kelly winked.

"You'll be ready for *Jeopardy!* before that boy graduates high school." Melanie laughed, then sobered and returned to the subject she'd been avoiding. "I guess the real problem is that I don't want to go to that reunion and tell everyone…" Her voice trailed off. She stirred at her coffee with a spoon, even though it was already fully sugared up. "Well, that I'm not what they expected me to be."

"What? You *didn't* become what you imagined on graduation day?" Kelly clutched at her chest in mock horror. "Who does, Melanie? Heck, most of us have no idea what we want to be when we grow up. And a good chunk of us never do. Take my husband, for instance. He just bought an ATV. *An ATV.* We live in a subdivision, for Pete's sake. Where's he planning on riding it? Around the cul-de-sac?"

Melanie laughed. "I thought he was sold on getting a jet ski."

"Apparently those are a little hard to use on the grass. The man forgets we live on eight acres in *Indiana,* not to mention an hour away from the closest thing to jet ski water." Kelly threw up her hands in a "duh" gesture. "So now he's hell-bent on saving for a lake house. I swear, that man has more toys than our ten-year-old."

Melanie fingered the spoon, then finally let it rest. "At my age, you'd think I'd be well adjusted enough that I wouldn't worry about what people at the class reunion think of me. I mean, I'm a *grown-up.*"

Kelly laughed. "Honey, even Miss America worries about what people will think of her at her reunion. I don't know what it is about those things, but they always bring out our inner seventh-grader."

Melanie nodded in agreement, drew in a breath and held tight to the stoneware mug. "Cade said he'll cosign on my loan if I help him at the reunion."

"A little quid pro quo?" Kelly grinned. "Sorry. That was on last week's test." Her gaze softened. "What does Cade want you to help him with?"

"Networking at the reunion. Cade's a master in the

courtroom, but put him in the middle of a cocktail party and he's totally out of his element. He gives new meaning to the words social faux pax."

Kelly chuckled, twirling the straw in her frozen mocha. "Do you think he asked you for this favor because he secretly wants to try to get the two of you back together?"

Melanie glanced again at her daughter, and wondered about the glances she'd seen Emmie exchange with Cade. The good mood Emmie had been in this morning had lasted all day, clearly a sign something was up.

Ha, like what *Emmie* was trying to cook up was the problem. Today, Melanie had found herself exchanging a few glances of her own with Cade. The year apart had only seemed to intensify her gut reaction to his presence, as if her hormones had been silently building, waiting for the trigger of Cade to set them off.

Hormones could be kept under control. She wasn't going to let a little desire send her running back into a marital mistake.

"Even if he does," Melanie said, "it's not going to happen. I can't go back to being the little wife."

"What if that's not what Cade wants? What if he's changed?"

"If there's one thing I know about Cade, it's how much he likes things to stay exactly the same. He loved knowing I'd be there at the end of the day when he came in from work. He liked wearing his blue suit on Mondays, the gray on Tuesdays. Eating spaghetti every Thursday night, like our lives were a stuck record."

"Surely you don't think he wanted that at the expense of your dreams?"

Melanie considered her friend's comment for a moment, sipping her coffee. "I don't think Cade ever set out to hurt me, to purposely stuff me in this little Stepford box. We stepped into these roles and then it got easier to go on playing them, rather than changing the game halfway through. He wanted a wife who would arrange the dinner parties, pack his suitcases, have his dinner waiting. He's a good man, but a stickler for tradition." Melanie rose and deposited her empty mug in the sink, then returned to Kelly, lowering her voice so Emmie wouldn't overhear. "For Cade, sameness is security and we got into one heck of a secure rut. He needs something different from a marriage than I can give. I don't want a man who loves me for my ability to cook a crown roast for twelve. Whether or not he looks good in a suit on the night of the reunion, I'm not falling back into that same trap and letting my emotions override my brain."

Like that hadn't happened a hundred times already today. When Cade was in the shop, Melanie had been intensely aware of his every move. The scent of his cologne, the blue of his eyes, the very nearness of him.

The bell over the door jingled again, the spring breeze whisking in with Ben Reynolds, the owner of the pawn shop next door. An instant smile lit up his friendly features, putting light into his gray eyes. "Hi, Melanie." He took off his fedora and clasped it between his hands.

"Ben! Hi! Can I get you a cup of coffee?"

"No, thanks. I came by to talk to you." He ran his fingers around the rim of the hat. Clearly he wasn't here for his regular daily chitchat and cappuccino. Dread tightened in Melanie's gut.

She told Kelly she'd be back in a second, then led the way to the love seats, vacated earlier by a couple who had lingered there for a few hours.

"I hate to tell you this because I know you wanted my place," Ben said after they were seated, "but I got an offer today."

An offer already? The place wasn't even listed with a realtor yet, though nearly all of Ben's customers knew he wanted to retire and sell the space. "I'm working on getting the bank loan, Ben, you know that."

"I need to sell as fast as I can. Peggy's mom is getting worse. That heart attack really did a number on her. Peggy wants us to move to Phoenix soon as we can, to help her mom out. Plus, I'm done with

Indiana winters. If I never see another shovelful of snow, I can die happy."

"You've been a great friend, Ben," she said, laying a hand on his arm. "You were the first to welcome me to the neighborhood, and the most vocal advertiser for my shop I've ever met. I understand your position. You do what you need to for your family."

Ben's face took on an apologetic cast. "I still feel bad, knowing how much you want the space. If you could find a way to get the funding faster..." He threw up his hands.

"I understand."

Ben gave her a sympathetic smile. "Think about it for a second. I'm going to take you up on that coffee offer." He headed over to the counter and ordered his usual decaf from Emmie.

Melanie watched him walk away and knew there wasn't another way. Melanie had already talked to two banks this past week and she'd heard the same thing—once she had a couple years under her belt, with the business showing a steady profit, they'd be more inclined to lend her the money. Otherwise, without much for assets behind her, she didn't have a chance of getting the money.

Being a housewife and a room mom apparently hadn't given her the kind of solid financial background bankers liked to see.

Until now, she'd run her company on her own

terms, without needing to use Cade or her marital status. Everything was in her own name. The start-up expenses had been small enough that she was able to cover the majority of them with an inheritance from her grandmother and the sale of the few remaining antiques in the shop. The rest she'd paid for with credit cards, taking a leap of faith that the market for a coffee shop would be much stronger than that of an aging antiques shop.

The gamble had paid off. Melanie had no debt, and was pleased to finally see more pluses on her balance sheet every month.

With the expansion, she could double her sales. Being located across the street from Lawford University provided a steady under-twenty-five clientele that increased by thirty percent each month. Coupled with the businesspeople who worked in the area and stopped in throughout the day for a caffeine boost, Cuppa Life had a pretty continual customer flow.

Melanie glanced at the door. Cade had left an hour ago, for a meeting with a client. His offer still rang in her head.

That offer came with some strings, but they were strings Melanie was willing to accept, if it meant she could finally have the business she'd envisioned. She could handle this—handle being around Cade—all without losing her heart or her head.

"Ben, don't worry," Melanie said, coming up to

the older man just as he was about to put on his hat and head back out the door. "I'll have the funding. Give me two weeks."

The man who had dispensed wonderful business advice in exchange for a free espresso here and there, nodded. "You've got your two weeks, Melanie. But after that...I have to think of my own family. I'm sorry."

"Two weeks," she reiterated. "I'll make it happen."

How hard could it be? She'd attend the reunion next Friday night, help Cade as she always had, just one more time. In the end, it would mean she'd see her dream fulfilled.

All she had to do was pretend she was married to Cade. After nineteen years in the job, she'd perfected the happy wife role.

Too bad her heart was no longer in it.

"You did *what?*"

Cade swung his racket, sending the tennis ball over the net and onto the cushy green court on Carter's side. He was glad for his weekly early Saturday morning tennis match with his twin brother. After all that had happened in Melanie's coffee shop, he needed to expend some energy and frustration. It was either tennis or pounding some walls. Considering his lack of expertise in the handyman arena, this was a better option, particularly for his walls. "I asked Melanie to go to the reunion with me."

Carter lobbed the ball back. "I thought you guys were getting divorced."

"That's the plan." *Maybe*. He smacked the ball over the net.

"Uh-huh. You're thinking you'll get her all dressed up—" Carter let out a grunt as he hit the yellow sphere "—you throw on a tie, take her out on the dance floor a couple of times, waltz around to some Sinatra. Before you know it, you're in love again, just like in high school?"

Cade made an easy return, then shrugged. "Hey, it happens in the movies."

Carter reached high, nicking the ball a moment before it flew past him. "Real life doesn't work like that."

"Why not? Melanie and I were happy for years." Cade waited for the bounce, then returned again.

"Women today expect more."

Cade arched a brow. "Says the man who thinks marriage is a contagious disease."

"At least I know better than to create a business plan to win a woman over. I know you, Cade, you've probably got a ten-point strategic overview all laid out on how to win Melanie's heart. You've analyzed the pros and cons, created a damned spreadsheet for your options and even calculated the odds on flowers versus diamonds."

Cade scowled. "I have not."

Okay, he did have a list. But he didn't have a spreadsheet and certainly hadn't used a calculator to determine the best course of action.

"If you haven't, which I highly doubt, you will." Carter got the serve this time and sent the ball over the net toward his brother. "You're the most uptight man I know. If you weren't my twin brother, I'd think you were an alien."

"Speaking of nonhuman creatures," Cade said, grinning as he slammed the ball back with enough force to tell his brother he was definitely done with the subject of his marriage. "What's new with you?"

"Funny you should ask," Carter said as he waited for the bounce before swinging his racket. "Remember Uncle Neil's will?"

Cade nodded. He'd been at the reading last month. Uncle Neil, a lifelong bachelor, had divvied up his companies and his possessions among his few nephews and nieces. Cade and Melanie had inherited a house in Cape Cod, a nice beach place that he remembered going to as a kid.

Someday, maybe, Melanie would want to go there. More specifically, go there with Cade. Take a weekend, stroll on the sand and rekindle the flame that had seemed to grow smaller since they'd married.

Then again, at the rate his reconciliation efforts were going, he'd be best off selling the place.

"Did you decide what to do with that toy company you inherited?" Cade said.

Carter drew in a breath. "Yep. I quit my job last week and moved into Uncle Neil's office."

"You did?"

"I'm sick of the corporate rat race," Carter said. "I don't know how you've stood it this long."

Cade hadn't. In the last few years, Cade had grown more and more frustrated with his job, with working for his father, and for the first time ever, wondered if he'd made a mistake by following in his father's footsteps. Cade was a good lawyer—but lately not a happy one.

For a second, he envied Carter's ability to chuck it all, take a chance. Pursue a dream that might not work out. Just as Melanie had.

Cade shrugged off the thought. It was probably some early onset midlife crisis. He'd buy a convertible and highlight his hair and be over it.

But as he looked at his twin brother, at the excitement in his eyes as he talked about the toy company between racket swings, Cade had to wonder if he needed more than a few hundred horsepower to erase this feeling.

"Anyway, the company's been struggling for a while," Carter said. "Morale is in the toilet, sea turtles have faster production than I do. I have to do something, but toys aren't quite my strong suit."

"They aren't mine, either," Cade said, sending another serve over the net. "We didn't exactly have a lot of playtime when we were kids."

"Yeah, that being responsible thing kind of kills the opportunity for a little cops and robbers in the backyard."

Cade missed the shot and cursed. He had no desire to revisit his childhood. Once had been enough. It hadn't been happy, it hadn't been fun and no one knew that better than Carter. No need to reopen old wounds.

"Anyway," Carter said, pausing to take a breather, "I was wondering if you knew anyone who specialized in that whole revitalizing a company thing."

"I heard about a firm in Lawford, Creativity Masters. The client I met with, Homesoft Toilet Paper, was singing their praises."

"They found a way to make toilet paper creative?" Carter chuckled, then swung and hit the ball back. "My toy company should be a piece of cake after a few rolls of squeezably soft."

Cade cut off a laugh as he returned the ball with a hard, swift swing. Once again, the feeling that he was missing something returned. Maybe Cade needed a little creativity boost for his own life.

He wondered vaguely what he would have done differently, had he been able to go back to prom night and change the course he and Melanie had taken. Would he have gone into another field? Tried another avenue?

Carter reached to the right, smacked the yellow ball with his racket and let out a curse when it sailed outside of the white lines, bouncing against the fence. He paused, dropping his hands to his knees and inhaling, sweat beading across his brow. "I'm getting my butt beat. Can't you let a man win once in a while? Protect his ego?"

Cade retrieved the ball, then bounced it on the court a couple of times before readying it for serve, giving each of them a breather. "Lay off the dough-nuts in the break room and you'll be able to reach those high shots."

"It's not the doughnuts. It's the receptionist." Carter grinned. "Late night with Deanna. I'm not operating on all cylinders."

"When have you *ever* operated on all your cy-linders?"

"That was always your job," Carter said with a grin.

That was true. Cade had shouldered the paternal expectations, gone into the family firm, fulfilled the next generation of Matthews lawyers. Carter, however, had been the one with charm, who smiled his way through college, with job offers falling at his feet like starry-eyed coeds. He'd had options—some-thing Cade had never even considered.

For a moment, Cade envied his twin, the freedom he had to quit the accounting firm for a spin at toy making. Cade shook it off. It was simply a restlessness, maybe brought about from another birthday that edged him closer to forty. He didn't need an escape from his job, he just needed a way to deal with the fact that his perfect life had disintegrated.

Cade slammed the serve over to Carter's side, making him dash to the right and dive to return. "To win back a woman like Melanie," he said, undeterred by the conversation detour, "you're going to need a hell of a lot more than your navy Brooks Brothers and a spray of roses, you know."

"I know how Melanie's mind works." The ball sailed into Carter's side of the court, an inch past the reach of his racket. Carter cursed again.

"I hate to tell you this, Cade," Carter said, lowering his racket and approaching the net, his breath coming in little gasps. "But you're a detail guy. When it comes to women, detail guys have no chance. You need to be a concept man, so you can see the whole picture and fill in the blanks you've missed with her. It's not about red roses over pink, Cade, it's about seeing what's bugging her."

"I was married to Melanie for nineteen years. I know the whole picture." But clearly, he'd missed something behind the canvas.

"If that's so, why is she divorcing you?" Carter gave him a sympathetic glance. All their lives, Carter had been the only one who knew what made Cade tick, and how to get right to the heart of Cade's problems.

"Sorry to say it, man, but that's the one fly in your ointment. Until you figure out what's behind her leaving, you'll never be able to convince her to stay."

"So now you're the expert on women?"

"Hey, I never said I knew how to keep one." Carter grinned, the same grin that had stolen—and broken—dozens of female hearts. "Just how to get one."

Five minutes later, they called the game a draw. As Cade retrieved the tennis ball and headed toward the locker room with Carter, he knew his twin brother was right. Whatever had caused Melanie to leave was still there, the eight-hundred-pound relationship gorilla in the room.

If his twin could chuck his career and go into toy making, then maybe Cade could untangle the yo-yo string around his heart.

He was, as Carter said, a detail guy. If he could find the one detail he'd overlooked, then maybe he could restore the life he'd had.

And if not, there was always Chicago.

# CHAPTER FIVE

MELANIE STARED AT THE reflection in the mirror. She'd have to be a magician to make this work.

There was no way she could pull off eighteen again. She wasn't sure she could even pull off thirty-seven, not with those crow's feet and hips.

"I'm insane for doing this," she told Kelly, who had volunteered to go dress shopping with her on Saturday morning. Emmie was running the shop, Kelly's kids were at a sleepover party for a cousin, leaving the two free to enjoy a rare couple of hours in the mall. Well, enjoying wasn't exactly the word, considering Melanie was in a dressing room standing in a front of a three-way mirror that made painfully clear the effects of one too many mocha lattes.

"That's a great dress," Kelly said, standing behind Melanie. "It's got a lot of va-va-voom." For emphasis, she gave her hips a little shimmy.

"I don't need va-va-voom for a class reunion."

Melanie pivoted to go back into the dressing room, take the dress off and go for something more in her usual style—meaning something totally *un*-voomed.

Before she could, Kelly caught her by the shoulders and turned her back to the mirror, waiting while Melanie took in the image of the dress. "Look at yourself," she said softly.

Melanie did, shaking off the doubts of a nearly forty-year-old woman, and gave herself a second, less jaded look. The deep maroon fabric hugged along her curves, slipping down her hips before flaring out in a flirty skirt that begged for twirling. The halter top had a deep V neckline and a nice amount of side support, giving Melanie the illusion of far more cleavage than she really had. It was sexy, glamorous, the kind of dress worn by women ten years younger, a hundred times more sophisticated.

Women other than her.

"You look positively gorgeous," Kelly said. "If I had a figure like that after having my two, I'd be celebrating it, not hiding it." She stepped back and indicated Melanie's reflection again. "And whether you do it for Cade or just to make jaws drop, you should buy this dress."

"I'm a jeans and T-shirt kind of girl. I should wear one of the dresses I wore to Cade's lawyer functions." Melanie stepped back, smoothed a hand down the slippery fabric. "Except those are...well, dowdy.

Mom and wife stuff. You don't do va-va-voom at a client dinner."

"Yeah, and that hardworking mom and business owner look is all the rage at reunions this year." Kelly slipped around Melanie to come between her and her reflection. "If you want different results for your life, you have to stop doing—and wearing—the same old thing."

"But—"

"Don't you but me. You know you've done that with everything else—your marriage, your business—everything *but* yourself." Kelly gave her an understanding smile. "We're in the same club, you and I. We sign up for it in that first Lamaze class. It's the Put Yourself Last club, after the guy, after the kid, heck, I'm even after the dog. It's time for you to let Melanie shine. And that dress," Kelly said, "is going to shine so much, you're going to blind everyone." She grinned, then moved away and waved a hand toward the mirror.

This time, Melanie looked with objective eyes, seeing herself as Kelly did, pushing away the thoughts that she was too old, too conservative…too everything for this dress.

A smile curved across her face. "It does look good, doesn't it?" She spun to one side, then the other, watching the skirt twirl against her legs.

"I'd lose the white ankle socks, though."

Melanie laughed at her footwear staple. "I promise."

She stayed there a moment longer, slipping into the habit of envisioning Cade's reaction to her appearance. How he'd smile at the way the dress flattered the parts of her body he most admired.

Like her legs, her breasts. Heck, he'd been happy with about anything, back in those early years, before the sizzle in their marriage had gone from full boil to simmer before finally dissolving.

A memory of him, coming into the bedroom while she was getting ready for a rare evening out—their fifteenth anniversary—sprang to mind. Melanie, in high heels and a little black dress, busy fastening the diamond earrings he'd given her onto her ears, hadn't heard him come in. He'd snuck up from behind, stealing his arms around her waist, pressing a kiss to her neck, then turning her slowly, oh so slowly, in his arms, until her lips were beneath his—

And they ended up twenty minutes late for their dinner reservations.

If she wore this on Friday night, would Cade do that again? Would he kiss her like he used to, erasing the past year, closing the ever-widening gap between them?

Would he once again make her feel like the only woman in the world? She closed her eyes, bittersweet longing washing over her.

"I'll get the dress," Melanie said, still wrapped up

in the luxurious feel of the silky fabric against her legs, the memories of Cade.

"Good. Now let's go pick out my favorite part." Kelly's eyes glistened with excitement. "The shoes."

A few minutes later, Melanie and Kelly left the mall, a little lighter in their wallets. Melanie swung her new dress over her shoulder, matching heels dangling from a bag attached to the hanger.

Kelly held up the bag containing two new pairs of sexy summer sandals. "When it comes to shoes, I might as well just hand over my credit card the second I walk into the department. I never leave empty-handed."

Melanie laughed. "I'm that way with coffee cups. I have a whole collection of them on the back wall of the shop. Some of them are antiques, some just caught my eye in a store."

Her friend shook her head. "You are *so* not normal."

Melanie laughed again. "Thanks for dragging me out of Cuppa Life to go shopping. I needed this."

"As long as you promise to run interference when Roger sees the Visa bill."

"All you have to do is wear a sexy little dress and he'll forget all about it." As the words left Melanie's mouth, however, she realized she'd never really done that with Cade.

Except for those rare special occasions, she'd never donned a sexy dress just to see him smile, or distract him from his day. From the start, their marriage had been wrapped around Emmie, and struggling to survive on the minimal income they'd made while Cade worked his way through law school and then up the firm's ladder. Melanie had worn the uniform of a mom—sweats, no makeup and hair in a ponytail.

Then, as Emmie grew up and Cade grew busier at work, the number of hours in a day seemed to shorten and the distance between her and her husband had seemed to lengthen, regardless of whether she remembered to put on a little mascara and lip gloss. The problems that they had went unresolved, pushed to the side. After too many years of ignoring the issues, those problems had become too big, too complicated to solve with a little black dress.

What had she been thinking? That a dress would somehow magically erase the illusions she'd had about their marriage? That wouldn't happen, no matter how much she might wish it. Melanie had to be realistic, not get wrapped up in a silky fabric and a handful of memories that stubbornly lingered.

In the parking lot, Melanie hugged Kelly and said goodbye, then slipped into her own car and headed back to Cuppa Life, resolved to put Cade from her mind for the rest of the day.

"Hey, Mom! What'd you get?" Emmie handed Cooter his regular blend, stamped his frequent visitor card, then turned to face Melanie as she came around the counter.

"A dress." Melanie slipped on an apron, then whisked her hair up into a ponytail. Back to regular ol' Melanie.

"I know that." Emmie rolled her eyes. "Details, Mom. I need details."

"Well, it's knee-length, a kind of burgundy-pink and…" She paused, avoiding Emmie's inquisitive gaze by busying herself with washing her hands.

Emmie put a fist on her hip. "And what?"

"Well, it's a little sexy."

"Way to go, Mom." Emmie let out a low whistle. "I never would have pegged *you* for a sexy dress."

"Hey, I was sexy once." Put that way, it sounded pretty darn pitiful. When she'd been Emmie's age, she'd worried about her appearance, spending hours in the mall, poring over fashion magazines, and then trying one outfit after another until she had the perfect one. Since she'd gotten married, she hadn't let herself go—exactly—she'd simply had other priorities to take up her days. Priorities that didn't include makeup, curling irons and especially didn't include sexy dresses.

She thought back to the image of herself in the mirror, the way the skirt swirled around her legs, how every inch of the maroon fabric had accentuated curves lost behind her Cuppa Life apron. Maybe it was time to revamp that priority list.

After all, she was thirty-seven, not dead.

"I bet Dad will love what you bought." Emmie threw the words out as casually as bread crumbs.

Melanie started restocking the small under-the-counter refrigerator with milk and cream. "I'm not wearing it for him."

Liar, her mind whispered. She was, too. Because a part of her still craved his sexy smile, that light in his eyes when he looked at her.

"Uh-huh," Emmie said.

Melanie brushed the thoughts away. Thinking about Cade's reactions would only send her back down the very road she'd left last year. A road Emmie seemed to be ignoring lately, as if she saw the separation as a phase her parents were going through.

"Emmie," Melanie said softly, laying a hand on her daughter's. "Dad and I *are* getting divorced. Please don't read anything into a dress."

Emmie scowled. "You guys are always telling me not to give up, to keep going for what I want. Why is it okay for you to do it?"

"I'm not giving up."

"What do you call a divorce? Why don't you two just sit down and talk?"

"We have, sweetheart." But a little voice inside asked if she'd simply taken the easier road.

"Maybe you didn't try hard enough." Emmie's words were sharp with anger.

Melanie sighed. "It's more complicated than trying harder. Than a conversation."

Emmie threw up her hands. "I am so sick of this, of going to your apartment, then Dad's house, and seeing both of you totally miserable. You've always told me relationships take work. Well, why don't you two practice what you preach?" She stalked off to the rest room, ignoring Melanie's calls for her to come back.

Melanie rubbed at the knot of tension in the back of her neck. Emmie didn't know the whole story. And there was no way Melanie was going to fill in the details Emmie was missing. Melanie closed her eyes and those very details came flooding back, ending with that day in the hospital. She'd been scared, crying and alone.

Always alone. Because when it came to priorities, Cade's had always been work.

Emmie's youthful idealization of the situation made her see it in simple black and white terms. Melanie knew there was far too much gray to sort things out. Even if for a little while today, she'd thought maybe—

Maybe they could.

"You got a real firecracker there," Cooter said, raising his coffee in the direction Emmie had gone.

Melanie smiled politely. "Yeah."

"You know, your man trouble reminds me of a story." Cooter rose and crossed to the one of the bar stools. He ran his hand down the length of his white beard, gearing up.

"Cooter, I—"

"There's these two old women, real biddies, the kind who sit in the sun and yak the day away." Cooter looked to Melanie, waiting for her to nod in understanding. "One of 'em, she's got this dog and it's moaning. The other says, 'What's wrong with your dog?' The first lady looks at the idiot of a pooch and says, 'He's been eatin' wood chips. Tears up his belly somethin' fierce.' Second lady shakes her head. 'Why would he do that, if it hurts?' First lady throws up her hands. 'I dunno. Guess he ain't gotten smart enough yet to quit.'" Cooter grinned at her, as if he'd just given her the secret to life.

"That's a…great story," Melanie said. "I think."

"It means," Cooter said, leaning forward, his light blue eyes bright, "you keep doin' stupid things until they hurt you enough and then you get smart enough to quit." He gave her a nod, then returned to his coffee and his paper.

Melanie shook her head. Cooter had a habit of dispensing wisdom wrapped in allegories. She wasn't quite sure if his tidbit today was about her relationship with Emmie—or with Cade. Or heck, the hot plate she'd burned her thumb on earlier today.

The door jingled and Melanie turned, expecting the next influx of college students. Instead Cade stood in the doorway, still dressed in his suit—his fighting clothes, he used to call them—but a little more rumpled than when he'd started his day. His dark blue tie was loosened at the neck of his white button-down shirt, giving him an air of vulnerability. He looked like a little boy trying to escape the confines of his Sunday best.

Then Cade strode forward, with the same comfortable, assured step he'd always had, and any comparisons to preschoolers ended.

Her stomach flipped over, heavy with a desire that she'd thought had long ago disappeared. But no, it was there, just waiting for Cade. His smile. His touch.

"Hi, Melanie."

Two words and everything within her shuddered to a stop. Damn Cade for still having that power over her. A year apart and a simple glance could still awaken the spark that had first drawn her to him.

A spark, however, wasn't enough to rebuild—and maintain—the fire they'd needed as adults. If it had, it would have gotten them through the roughest parts, the days when one needed the other, and that call had gone unanswered.

"Do you want some coffee?" Melanie said, getting to her feet and putting the counter's width between them.

"Sure." He slid onto one of the bar stools. His face was lined with exhaustion. Melanie's hand ached to reach out, to touch him and wipe all that away. Despite everything they'd gone through, she still worried about him. Some feelings, she'd found, couldn't be turned off like a dripping garden hose.

Either way, Cade wouldn't want her to do that. If there was one thing Cade prided himself on, it was his "can do no matter what" attitude. If only he'd relied on her more, talked more.

She slid a cup of black Kenyan roast across the counter, knowing from all their years together that he wouldn't want anything fancier. "Here you go. On the house."

"Thanks."

"So…" she began, after he took a long sip but still didn't speak, "why did you stop in today?" He'd been here twice in the space of two days, after nearly a year of separation that hadn't involved more than a couple of quick run-ins at events for Emmie. There had to be a reason—Cade Matthews was a man who didn't waste time, or make a half-hour journey if he didn't have an agenda.

He cupped his hands around the mug, staring at the coffee for a long second before looking up and meeting Melanie's gaze. "Are you happy here?"

"Yes," she answered, no reservations in her voice. "I love working for myself."

"Good."

He didn't go on and Melanie told herself not to

push. But then she found her mouth opening anyway, out of habit, out of something more, she didn't know. "What's bothering you, Cade?"

He drew in a breath, then slid the coffee to the side. "I don't know. Maybe I've just been putting in too many hours lately. Or had too many frustrating clients."

"You're not enjoying your job anymore?" she asked, surprised. There'd never been a day where she'd seen Cade anything but charged to get to the office. Perhaps that was why he was interviewing with Bill, to find a new challenge. Or maybe he'd finally grown tired of being under his father's demanding rule.

"I have a trial next month," he went on. "Trademark infringement. One of those really big battles. On any other day, I'd be charged up, ready to hit it head-on."

"But not today?"

He shrugged. "It's like I've already been there, done that. I don't know…maybe I'm just looking for something different."

Cade unsure? Questioning his job? Either he was an alien replacement of his former self or—

There was no "or." The Cade she knew hadn't had a day of indecision. Perhaps he felt out of sorts now that the divorce was becoming a reality.

"I stopped by because I had an idea. An idea for you and me," he said, putting up a hand. "Don't say no until you've heard me out."

"Okay…" She leaned back against the small refrigerator and crossed her arms over her chest. The appliance hummed against her back.

"We've been apart for a year and if we go to the reunion as we are now, I'm sure that's going to show."

"Oh, I don't—"

"It will, Melanie. We're not close like we used to be."

"We were never close, Cade." The harsh truth sat there between them, heavy and immovable. She'd thought they were, once, but it had disappeared, lost in Cade's relentless work schedule and her busy days of being room mom and child chauffeur.

In the dark of night, she longed for that closeness again. Longed for Cade, for the days when he'd crawled into bed and wrapped his arms around her, making it seem as if anything in the world was possible. Then work had taken him away more and more—physically, emotionally—and those times had stopped.

"Either way," Cade continued, "I don't want to walk into that room and let the entire senior class know we're having problems."

Those *would* show, without a doubt. The old Cade and Melanie had been glued at the hip, always touching or flirting, and making so many public displays of affection, PDAs, as Emmie called them, that anyone within a five-county radius could tell they were in love. "Since when did you start worrying about what other people think?"

His eyes met hers and in them, she saw much more than exhaustion. Loneliness. Regret. But then he swallowed, and it all disappeared, replaced with Can-Do Cade. Disappointment flickered inside her. "I don't. I just want this to be convincing for Bill."

She slapped a smile on her face. "Of course." The career, always the career. If anything told her Cade hadn't changed, it was that sentence.

"In order to do that, I think we need to spend a little time together."

Time with Cade? That couldn't be good. Judging by the way her hormones were scrambling a counterattack to her common sense, she knew spending more time with him would only give the estrogen a little more ammunition. "Do you mean dating?" she said, nearly knocking over the sugar as she moved away from him and the idea. "Because I don't think that's a good idea."

"Why not?"

She sighed. Why did he have to be so obtuse about this? Wasn't the moving out, the serving of papers, the year apart, all one huge bullhorn announcing that it was over? "We're getting a divorce, Cade. Please don't make it any harder than it already is."

"Is it hard on you, Melanie?" His gaze locked on hers, the deep blue eyes she'd stared into for more than half her life missing nothing, and displaying frustration and hurt. "Because it sure doesn't seem it."

"Of course it is." She turned away, ignoring the sudden burning behind her eyes. Did he think she'd left their marriage impetuously? That any of this had been an easy decision?

She busied herself with wiping an already clean counter, instead of dwelling on the what-ifs and the storm whipped up by Cade's presence.

When she glanced at him again, he seemed to have tamped down the temporary flare of emotion. As always, Cade was back to being cool, calm and collected. Never betray a weakness, he'd always told her, particularly in a courtroom.

And he never had. Especially with her. And especially not when it had mattered.

If he had…

But he hadn't.

"Anyway," Cade said, clearing his throat, "I thought maybe I could work here for a few days. From what Emmie says, this place is busier than a zoo, and you could use the help. She said the student you had working here quit last week." He grinned, and her heart—which had never done a good job of listening to her mind—skipped a beat. "Plus, I'll work for free."

"Work here?" She paused, the sponge dripping onto her toes. Had she heard him right? "Why would you want to do that?"

"I told you. We need to spend some time together. It seems like a win-win to me."

Melanie eyed the man she had lived with for all of her adult years and knew he was hiding something. It wasn't just about putting on a good show for Bill Hendrickson at the reunion.

She had to wonder if Cade's win-win also involved winning her heart again. As much as a part of her—the lonely part that shared a bed with extra pillows instead of a husband—might wish otherwise, Melanie knew that was the one thing not up for grabs.

# CHAPTER SIX

"I'M INSANE," Melanie said to Kelly the next morning. They were alone in the shop, something that wouldn't last long on a Sunday. Soon as church services were over, the shop would pick up again. The college kids wouldn't be here until they rolled out of bed and came in for a little caffeine to counteract the frat party headache, but after that, business would be pretty steady until late afternoon. "Why did I ever agree to let Cade work here? I'm trying to divorce him, not hire him."

Kelly ran a finger along the rim of her coffee mug. "Maybe a tiny part of you doesn't want to divorce him."

Melanie shook her head, resolute. "This is the best thing, trust me. Cade isn't going to change."

Hadn't he proved that yesterday? Just when she thought he might be a little vulnerable, might tell her some of the secrets he kept locked in his heart—

He'd mentioned work. Always the job, never the man, never how he felt.

"Whatever you say." Kelly shrugged, but there was disbelief in her face. "He's your husband."

"Not anymore."

As the words left her, though, they were tinged with sadness. What would her life ahead be like without Cade? She'd been so busy getting the business off the ground that she hadn't paused to dwell on the empty rooms of her apartment, the lack of a second voice at home.

How would it be to wake up in five years, ten, and realize Cade was truly gone from her life? That the man she'd spent half her life loving was with someone else? Melanie shook the thoughts off. A bit of regret was normal with any divorce, no matter how the marriage had ended. After all, she'd been with Cade for twenty years. She'd only dated two other guys before him. He was what she knew, what she'd always known, and giving that up for good was bound to leave her a little melancholy.

Add to that seeing him again after a year apart and Melanie had a Betty Crocker-worthy recipe for regret. That's all it was—the opposite of cold feet. Regardless of what she might think she saw in his eyes or felt in her chest, she wasn't going to change her mind. The decision had been hard enough to make—there would be no rethinking of it.

"So, when's he coming in?" Kelly asked.

Melanie glanced at the clock, watching the hand

sweep upward to nine o'clock. "Any minute now. I thought he could learn the ropes today. The week-days are way too busy for me to have time to show him anything."

"Sure you don't want me to stay?"

Melanie grinned. "You're just looking for an excuse to get out of that baby shower."

"Hey, I am so done with diapers, I don't even want to look at them. Even the smell of rash cream brings back bad memories." Kelly rose, pushing her empty cup to the side. She laughed. "Oh, what am I saying? I miss my boys being little. Every time I turn around, they've grown six inches." She let out a sigh, then swung her purse over her shoulder. "Maybe I'll take a sniff of the Desitin. Just for old times' sake."

Melanie was still laughing after Kelly had left, a second morning brew in a to-go cup. Five seconds later, the bell jingled and Cade walked in, wearing jeans and a blue T-shirt. Emblazoned across his chest was an ad for a wine festival.

*Cade.*

She watched him cross the room, still handsome as any man she'd ever seen in a magazine, with that lazy, tempting grin and a twinkle in his eyes that seemed to always tease at the edges of laughter. She told herself he no longer affected her. That she could get through a day of working with him—

And not lose her mind or worse, her heart.

Yet, as he drew closer and she read the words curving across his chest, her heart stopped with the memory of the fall weekend when they'd driven up to Michigan to attend the wine festival. Two, no, three years ago. She'd planned the time away for a couple of weeks, reminding Cade several times to clear the weekend on his schedule.

She'd rented a room at a bed-and-breakfast, bought a little sexy black nothing, and hoped the two days alone would bring back the magic that seemed to have disappeared sometime between late night bottle feedings and school plays. She'd thought it would be as simple as throwing on a lacy negligee and spending a few extra hours in bed.

It hadn't. The weekend had been a disaster of epic proportions, with Cade talking on his cell phone more than to his wife. There'd been one moment, when they'd spread out a blanket on the grass, shared a bottle of Chardonnay and a block of cheese, and laughed—oh, how they'd laughed. She'd thought maybe…just maybe, they were recapturing the magic.

Then his phone had rung and the spell had shattered as easily as a crystal vase dropped on concrete.

And yet, as Cade approached, Melanie found herself wondering if that spell had really been broken or merely needed to be reworked a bit.

"So," Cade said, "where do you want me? I'm dressed to work."

Cade had taken her "dress casual" advice to heart and was clearly attempting to appear relaxed. Between the Levi's and the way he was leaning on the counter, he was the poster boy for relaxed. Only she knew that underneath that well-pressed T lurked a man who hated any kind of disorder.

Nevertheless, desire stirred within her, picturing them together again. On the counter. Against the wall. In her bed. She ran a hand over hot cheeks and pushed the fantasy away.

"How about we start with the basics?" Melanie said, keeping her focus on work, not the shirt and the memories it resurrected. And certainly not on Cade's face, on eyes that still had the power to set her pulse off-kilter. "I'll show you how to brew the coffee, then we'll work up to cappuccino."

"Before you know it, I'll be a brewmaster." He cocked a grin at her and she found herself returning the smile. He slipped behind the counter to stand next to her. A year ago, when Melanie had opened the shop, the space had seemed so much wider, particularly when it was just her and Emmie. But Cade made the place seem confined, too tight for two.

Or too tight for her and the one man she didn't want to get close to, not again. Too close and she was risking another heartbreak. One was enough.

"Here's our, ah, main coffee station," Melanie said, clearing her throat and indicating a cranberry and black countertop machine with several spouts and dials. "We brew it here, put it in the carafes, then make a fresh pot whenever the coffee's temperature drops below 150 degrees."

"Doesn't that waste a lot of coffee?"

"Not really. On a busy day, we can go through twenty pots or more."

"Can't you use the old coffee to make those iced things?"

"No, not unless you want to risk cross-contamination. For iced coffee, I have a special five-gallon brewing pot." She opened the fridge and indicated a big white plastic container shaped like a coffee urn.

"Do you roast the beans yourself, too?"

She stepped back, surprised. "You've been reading."

He gave her a grin as familiar as her own palm. "You know me. I always do my homework."

Except for with me, she wanted to add, but didn't. Cade, who put thought into every decision from the brand of toothpaste he used to the car he drove, hadn't quite applied those same principles when it came to that night twenty years ago in the back of his car.

Heck, neither had she. In those days, they'd thought of nothing but each other. Nothing but the feel of his mouth on hers, his hands on her body, and the sweet release from the thunderstorm continually brewing between them.

"Uh, no, we don't roast our own beans," Melanie said, returning her mind to the subject at hand. "I'd like to get a roaster, but I don't have the room for it."

"Unless you buy the space next door."

"Right." Melanie turned away from Cade's intent gaze and reached for one of the bags of coffee beans, imported from Columbia. "We grind the beans in—"

"Here?" Cade asked, reaching for the grinder at the same time as she did. Their hands collided, sending a rocket propelled grenade of attraction through Melanie. It was a hundred times more intense, a thousand times hotter, than anything she could remember with Cade, as if the time apart had intensified his appeal.

Sexual appeal, she reminded herself. Not marital appeal.

And yet, she didn't pull her hand back right away. She looked up and their gazes met, held. Want tightened its grip on her, holding her captive to the spot. To Cade.

"Melanie," Cade said in the same soft way he used to, as if they were lying together in the dark, not standing in a brightly lit coffee shop on a Sunday morning.

*Oh, how I miss him,* she thought, the arrow of that lonely, disappointed pain piercing through her. She missed the Cade he used to be, the marriage she had dreamed of having.

Then he leaned down, slow, tentative, his gaze never leaving hers. The heat between them multiplied ten times over with anticipation. With a craving that had never died, despite the year apart.

*Kiss me.* Her mind willed him to read the unspoken words, to hear the message throbbing in her veins.

He reached for her chin, his large hand cupping her jaw. A tender touch, filled with all the things that Cade never said. "Melanie, I—"

Suddenly she couldn't hear him talk about work. Couldn't bear to hear him disappoint her, to shatter her fantasy that someday, Cade would put her—and their marriage—at the top of the list.

Melanie jerked away, then pushed the button on the grinder, pulverizing a lot of innocent coffee beans. "This, ah…" Her mind went blank.

"Grinder?" Cade supplied, withdrawing and giving her a knowing smile.

"Yes, thank you." Melanie shifted to business mode. *Treat him like a customer. Treat him like anyone other than the man you pledged to love forever.* "This grinder will take the beans down to grounds in less than thirty seconds. Grind them too long and the grounds become dust. Too short and they're chunky. Grind size can really affect the finished product, so you want this setting right here," she said, pointing at a number on the grinder's dial, "and then the beans are the perfect size for the filter."

Yet, even as she explained the pros and cons of different grind sizes, she was aware of Cade. A few inches away, close enough to touch, should she have that desire.

Heck, she *had* that desire. Always had it. She simply knew better now than to let her hormones make all the decisions.

Twenty minutes later, Cade was brewing his first latte. He'd picked up the intricacies of coffeemaking quickly, as she'd expected. He was a smart man, one who paid attention to the details.

It was the big picture he so often missed.

"You did great," Melanie said, taking a sip of the small latte breve he'd made. "And you added caramel," she said with a smile, noting the flavors that slipped across her taste buds.

"If I remember right, it's your favorite flavor."

"Cade," Melanie began, intending to tell him to stop trying. Her mind was made up, and there would be no undoing the divorce. Regardless of what might happen in one day, or one night, she had nineteen years of mistakes to look back on. Leopards didn't change their spots and career-driven husbands didn't change into family men.

The bell rang, ushering in the first slew of customers. Before she could finish the sentence, she and

Cade were busy filling orders and dispensing caffeine. For his first day, he kept up surprisingly well, only looking to her for help a couple of times on a complicated order.

She and Cade slipped into a rhythm, maneuvering around each other in the tight space with ease. If she hadn't known better, she'd have thought Cade had been here forever.

"You did great," Melanie said after the last customers had been served and the door stopped opening. The sun was beginning its late afternoon descent, telling her it was nearly closing time.

"Thanks." He leaned back against the counter and took a long drink of ice water. "I'm not used to moving so much, though. Guess all those years behind a desk are catching up to me."

Cade was still trim, a man who worked out three mornings a week, rising at four to fit in a trip to the gym before work. He'd kept the same routine all of their married life, jogging in those early days when they couldn't afford a gym membership. She bit her lip instead of telling him he looked as refreshed as the minute he'd stepped in the shop today, as he had the day she'd met him. As sexy as the day he'd told her he loved her. The day he'd asked her to marry him.

"How long until the next rush?"

Melanie glanced at her watch and for a second

couldn't read the numbers. She redoubled her focus. "Anytime now. It won't be long before the study groups and coffee dates head in."

"I never thought this would be such a busy place," he said.

"Yeah." Melanie didn't add anything more. There was no sense in reopening an old wound.

"I'm sorry," he said. "I should have supported you when you said you wanted to open this place."

Melanie stared at Cade, stunned into silence. The man who rarely admitted fault, had just apologized? And over the last straw, the one that had made Melanie finally realize she was being suffocated by her marriage?

Enough avoiding the subject, Melanie decided. "Are you trying to convince me we should get back together? Is that why you're working here? Why you apologized?"

He gave her a grin she could have drawn in her sleep. "Would that be so bad?"

"Yes, Cade, it would be." She lowered her voice, then waited until the final customer had left the shop before continuing. "It's over between us. Don't read anything into this—" she gestured toward him and the coffeemaking "—or my attending the reunion. We made a deal, plain and simple."

"That's all it is? A deal?" He took a step closer, invading her space, once again making her nerves hypersensitive. "Nothing more, Mellie? If so, then I have a deal for you. A very different kind of deal."

Heat and desire wrapped around his words, awakening senses that had been tamped down for so long. *Kiss him,* her body urged. *Kiss him.*

She wanted to, oh how she wanted to. She wanted to pretend the words had never been said, the hurts never inflicted, and that she and Cade could go back to that fairy tale from high school.

She reached out a hand, craving the feel of his cheek beneath her palm, the hard line of his jaw softened by freshly shaven skin. She inhaled, and with that breath, brought in the scent of Cade, a mixture of woods and mint, the same scents that had filled their shared bathroom for a thousand mornings.

She turned away, and started prattling on about the difference between a cappuccino and a latte. If she talked long enough, maybe her mouth could overrun the pounding drumbeat in her pulse.

Drums pounded in his head, an insistent rhythm of want, beating along with the soft jazz coming from the sound system. For a second, Cade thought he had read the same need in Melanie's eyes.

If he bent down and kissed her, would she respond in kind? Melt into his arms, her lips soft and sweet beneath his?

Before he could find out, she'd turned away and

started a coffee demonstration that Cade didn't hear. Every sense had been attuned to her, and it was a long time until his brain stopped picturing her in his arms and his bed.

Cade had what he wanted—an uninterrupted block of time with Melanie. Now he just had to figure out what the hell to do with it.

He'd already screwed up his marriage once—he wasn't one of those men who planted blame squarely on the wife, there had definitely been moments when he hadn't been the best husband—and he had no intentions of doing it a second time, assuming he could figure out what he'd done wrong.

As he listened to her run down a laundry list of ingredients for a Frazzle, his mind reached back over the past years, but he didn't find one place he could point to as the fault line. Sure, there'd been arguments. Moments when neither of them was especially happy, but no one event that glared back at him, an arrow pointing to the big mistake, saying "fix me and all will be as it was."

His marriage had dissolved gradually, like threads in a blanket that came undone a little more each time you placed it on your lap. At night, he paced the living room of the house where he and Melanie had once lived—happily, he'd thought—and found no clues in the beige wall-to-wall carpet and soft sage walls.

He'd played that mental game a thousand times

since she'd left and never come any closer to finding the solution than wondering if maybe he'd worked too much, been too unavailable to her. He was willing to be available now—and had told her so that night she left—but Melanie had still shut the door and drove away.

Even now, she was shutting him out, except this time she had a cappuccino machine between them, as if holding him at bay with a little steam.

They worked together for a few more hours, the day passing quickly. Before he knew it, Melanie was locking the door and counting the money in the cash register. "We're done already?" he asked.

She nodded. "I close early on Sundays. There's not enough business to justify staying open as late today as I do on the weeknights. During the week, we have the business people and the college students, but on the weekends, the businesses are closed and the students are more often out on dates than here."

Cade glanced at his watch. "It's early." He paused, then figured he needed to bite this bullet someday. "Are the students the only ones with a date?"

"Me?" she looked surprised, then laughed. "No. I wouldn't have the time or the energy even if someone had asked me out."

No man had asked her out. She was spending her nights alone. Cade figured all the men in Lawford had to be either blind or brain dead to not want Melanie.

"Then how about dinner?" he asked, the words leaving his lips before he could think about the wisdom of the question. "With me."

"Oh, Cade, I really don't think—"

"It's dinner, Melanie. Two chairs, a table and a meal. No hidden strings. No innuendo."

Exhaustion had shaded the area below her eyes. No wonder, too, given the hyperspeed she worked at. He wanted to scoop her up, take her home and tuck her into their queen-size bed, letting her sleep until those shadows disappeared and the smile on her face became brighter, more like the Melanie he used to know.

"You need to eat," he said softly.

"No, I need to get home."

"To what?" Cade took a step closer. "To an empty house? An empty fridge?" Two things he was far too familiar with. "Have dinner with me, Melanie, for old times' sake. Not because you're my wife or because it might lead to something else. Hell, just go because you're hungry and I'm offering a free steak."

"Cade, we're getting—"

"You don't need to remind me every five minutes of the divorce," he said, lashing out, unable to hear that word one more time today. "I know where we're heading. I may not like it, but I've accepted the inevitable."

She took a step closer, her chin upturned, her green eyes afire. "Have you?"

Hell no, he hadn't, but he wasn't going to say it. Instead he let his gaze sweep over her, reading in her eyes the same riot of emotions as earlier. He moved closer to her, coming within inches of her lips. Want curled around his heart, humming within him the familiar song of Melanie, of how she would feel, taste. "Have *you?*"

"Of course I have."

"Then prove it," Cade said, lowering his head, his breath whispering across her lips. "And kiss me."

# CHAPTER SEVEN

WHEN CADE KISSED HER, everything within Melanie went from ice-blue to red-hot. It was as if he'd never kissed her before, as if she'd waited for this touch for a lifetime.

With a clarity that astounded her, Melanie remembered every detail of that first, electric touch from twenty years ago, how she'd wanted him all night, fantasizing about the moment when he would finally go beyond holding her hand.

They'd gone to the mall, wandering the tiled space, not buying anything. They'd talked and laughed, all the while aware of the tightening tension between them. When they'd stopped to throw a penny into the fountain, Cade had moved into place behind her, ostensibly to guide her hand, but more, she knew with that instinct every woman possessed, to touch her.

She'd tossed the penny, made the wish that had

simmered inside her all night, then turned to him, hoping. As if he'd heard her thoughts, he'd kissed her, under the pale white cast of the lights above them. It had been everything she'd dreamed about—and more. Cade Matthews hadn't disappointed her with his touch.

Not then, and not now.

Those memories washed over her, whispering against this new kiss. Desire arched within her, rumbling through a body that had been focused on business matters for far too long. His lips were tender against hers, drifting over her mouth, an easy, sweet taste of what was to come. Then, when she didn't pull away, his kiss deepened, taking her down a sensuous path so familiar, it nearly made her cry.

She'd missed him, damn it. Missed his kisses, missed his touch. Before she could stop herself, her arms stole around his neck, feeling the ends of his short hair tickle against her skin, making every inch of her want him with a fierceness that bordered on frenzy.

His tongue slipped between her lips and every resolve she'd had melted in the seductive waltz he played on her mouth. She did the same to him, nerve endings tingling with awareness and memory, one fire stoking the other.

He reached up and cupped her jaw, tenderly, in the way he used to, back when their focus had been on each other and nothing else. Behind her closed eyes, a slideshow of memories flashed through Melanie's mind, teasing at the edges of their kiss, urging her to forget the divorce, forget the hurts.

How she wanted to give in to that kiss, to do nothing more than love this man. To let his touch erase the words, the silences, the nights spent alone.

But she had spent too many regretful mornings knowing no kiss could do that.

Melanie jerked back and broke the connection, ignoring the pull of regret. "Cade, we can't do this."

"Why not?" he asked, his gaze still locked on hers. "We're still married."

She turned away, busying herself with cleaning the counter, trying to tamp down the need still rolling inside her. It had been a long, lonely year but she knew she was doing what was best for her, and in the end, for Cade.

"Don't do this, Cade. I can't..." Her voice trailed off, unable to voice the vulnerability still lingering in her chest. If he touched her again, she'd surely dissolve.

"I need you, Melanie," he said, his voice hoarse. "I've always needed you."

"No, you don't. You never did."

He cupped her jaw, tipping her chin upward, waiting for her to meet his gaze. "Melanie, I'd never be where I was today if it wasn't for you. You were always the better half of my success. Of everything."

She shook her head, causing his touch to drop

away. "Cade, all I did was bake the leg of lamb and set the table for the dinner parties."

"It was much more than that and you know it."

"Was it? Because I never felt that way. I put on the parties, smiled until my lips hurt, served coffee, tea and your best qualities to every guest. At the end of the night, you were toasting another success and I was washing the damned dishes." She put up a finger when he started to protest. "You forgot me, Cade. Left me behind as you hurried ahead in your career. The only time you needed me was when there was a party to host or a client to impress."

"I never meant to do that."

She drew in a breath, cooling her temper. "I know, Cade. I guess I just wanted to feel like something I did, something other than raising Emmie, meant something. I never felt that when I was pulling a roast out of the oven or pouring champagne." She glanced around the coffee shop. "Until now."

"What you did mattered, to me," he said.

"You never said it." She let out a little laugh. "Heck, you were never home long enough to say anything."

He reached for her, but she turned away. Instead of letting her go, Cade moved forward, taking her hand with his. "I'm here now, Melanie."

How she wanted to believe that. To think that it could be different—that she could have the marriage she'd dreamed of, and the dreams she'd just achieved. To trust Cade would be there, physically and emotionally, when she needed him.

But if there was one thing Melanie couldn't take, it was more disappointment.

"Cade, it's too late," Melanie said. "We drifted apart. I became your personal assistant, not your wife. And then, when it looked like I might have my chance, you wanted to put me right back into the same box I was trying to climb out of."

"All I wanted was a family," he said. "How can you hate me for that?"

She reached out, touched his hand, but then retreated. Each of them had been hurt that night, but instead of coming together, they'd ended up on opposite sides of a common fence. "I never hated you, Cade. I just wanted to go down a different road."

"You've never told me why, Melanie," Cade said, coming around her, forcing her to face him. "*Why* did you leave me?"

Melanie sighed. Why couldn't he just let their marriage die? "I told you. A hundred times over the past few years, but you never listened."

"I'm listening now. Tell me what it is, so I can fix it."

She threw up her hands. "That right there, *that's* part of the problem. You can't fix everything, Cade."

"I can fix this, Melanie. Give me a chance."

For a second, she wanted to do just that, but then

she thought back to the dozens of times they'd had conversations that echoed this one. Things would change for a week, maybe two, and then Cade would go back to being Cade, relying on Melanie to do everything but live for herself. When she'd finally had her chance, all he'd wanted to do was return to the status quo.

She shook her head, then crossed the room, her keys in her hand. She held open the door, waiting for him to exit before shutting and locking it. "No, Cade. You can't fix this."

Then, before she did something really stupid, like revisit that kiss, she turned and went home to her empty apartment, her stomach as disappointed as her heart.

An hour later, Cade walked into the offices of Fitzsimmons, Matthews and Lloyd, although Fitzsimmons had died ten years ago and Lloyd last summer, leaving it technically just Matthews. Even though it was late on Sunday night, he found his father exactly where he'd expected him to be— behind his desk.

The imposing office had been a major part of Jonathon Matthews's life for forty-plus years, and it showed in the dark paneling, the heavy furniture, the deep, plush carpeting. Every inch of the room reflected Jonathon's personality, his high expectations.

When Cade entered the room, his father barely

looked up from the brief he was reading. Jonathon had aged well, the only concession to his sixty years a pair of glasses that he wore when no one was looking. His gray hair was cut short, his suit tailor-made. The same attention to detail that marked his office wore well on every inch of the man.

"Cade," his father said, laying the brief aside. "Glad you came in. I wanted to talk to you about the Tewksbury case."

"I'm not here to work, Dad." The look of surprise on his father's face told Cade he'd spent far too many weekends here. "I wanted to talk to you." He slipped into one of the two claw-foot chairs facing his father. "I'm taking next week off."

"Off?" his father echoed, surprise in his tone, his brows arched above the gold frames. "What could possibly be more important than the Tewksbury case?"

"Melanie." Cade swallowed. "I'm going to go work in her coffee shop this week."

The silence in the room was as heavy as a steel beam. "You're *what?*"

"Going to—"

"I heard you the first time." His father scowled. "What the hell are you thinking?"

"I'm trying to save my marriage."

"At the expense of this firm. She's divorcing you, Cade. Let her go, for God's sake."

"She's my wife."

Jonathon waved a hand in dismissal. "You can always get another. A hell of a lot easier than I can find a lead attorney on this Tewksbury mess."

Anger boiled inside of Cade. He knew, since the day he'd told his father Melanie was pregnant, that the marriage had been a disappointment, a detour from the path Jonathon had planned for the son he saw as the heir to the firm. "Is that how you look at wives? Interchangeable?"

"That's how I look at the ones who walk out on their husbands for no good reason." His father dipped his head, attention on his work again.

But just before he dropped his gaze, Cade saw a flash of vulnerability in his father's eyes. A sheen of hurt, that had lingered despite the perfectionist paint job his father had applied to himself.

"Because Mom did it to you?" Cade said quietly, touching on the one nerve that ran through all three Matthews men.

The sore spot made Jonathon scowl and pick up the brief again. "I have work to do. And so do you, if that pile on your desk is any indication." But his voice had lost its punch.

"Answer me, Dad." Cade leaned forward. "Is it because she left you with two five-year-old boys and never came back?"

His father shook his head, dismissing the glistening in his eyes. Because it was too painful? Too hard for Jonathon Matthews to admit failure? "All that's ancient history."

Cade wasn't going to let that history die. After all these years, he and his father had never talked about that October day when Elaine Matthews had packed up her station wagon and headed to California. "Your mother is gone," Jonathon had said to his twin boys, before introducing the new nanny in the next breath, as if the whole thing was nothing more than a shift change in the Matthews household.

"After she was gone, you poured yourself into work, leaving nannies to raise us. Hell, half of them were so bad, we raised ourselves because you weren't there."

"I had to provide for my family."

After marrying and parenting his own child, Cade understood his father better. How would it have been for Cade if he had lost Melanie when Emmie was a little girl? Would he have done the same, retreating into the predictability, the quiet of work?

"Or was it because you had to escape two little boys with a whole lot of questions?" Cade looked at his father and saw himself in twenty years. The thought didn't bring Cade cheer. "And here I followed in your footsteps, right down to the hours at work."

"Law is a consuming business."

"It doesn't have to be. I can have a family and a career."

His father whipped his glasses off and tossed them

to the side. He squeezed at his eyes, erasing the trace of emotion. "What are we living in, fairy tales now? You have a commitment to this firm, to ensuring that our clients are taken care of. If your wife couldn't understand that—"

"She did, Dad. More than any one woman should have had to."

"I didn't make you put those hours in, Cade," Jonathon said. His gaze connected with Cade's. A look of regret flickered in his eyes, then was quickly whisked away. "Before you throw stones at me, you better damned well look at your own garden." His father settled the glasses on his nose again and returned to the brief, to the comfort of work. It had always been Jonathon's escape, and sadly, it was now also his entire life. "Bring me the Tewksbury file, please and we can strategize for court."

Cade bit his tongue before he lashed out. He knew from experience that the only way to deal with his father was calmly and with a good argument. The minute Cade raised his voice, Jonathon would tune him out. "I told you, Dad. I'm working with Melanie this week. Todd can handle my cases."

His father shook his head, negating the idea. "I need *you* here."

"It's only a week, and then I'll be back. Surely the firm can live without me for a few days."

"We probably can," his father conceded. Then he

laid his hands flat against the smooth surface of his desk and leveled his steely gaze on his son. "The point is you've been…distracted lately. I put up with it after Melanie left, because every man is entitled to some time to get over a thing like that."

"A thing like that? We were married nineteen years."

"But then," his father went on, ignoring Cade's words, "you didn't snap out of it. You've been about as useful around here as a puppy."

"I've always given you my best, Dad, you know that." The best years of his life, the best weekends, the best nights. Cade had nearly killed himself, putting in long hours, always trying to please his father, to achieve some impossible standard.

And for what? Cade still didn't measure up and never would. Pleasing Jonathon Matthews was like trying to fill an endless, empty well.

"Have you?" his father asked. "Because there have been rumors. That you're talking to Bill Hendrickson about leaving."

Cade blinked in surprise. "Yes, that's true."

"When were you going to tell me?" A flicker of hurt ran through Jonathon's blue eyes, then disappeared. For a moment, Cade wanted to relent. He knew his father had always thought his son would step into the role of heading the firm, but Cade didn't want this life. Didn't want to sit in this office at sixty because his house was emptier than his heart.

"I just wanted to look at my options," Cade said.

"Options other than working for me."

"Yes."

Jonathon Matthews gave one short, brisk nod. "Fine. Then you might as well leave now. Save me from wondering when you're going to drop the ax."

This was what frustrated Cade the most about his father. His inflexibility. Either you measured up or you didn't, and if you didn't, Jonathon was quick to sever the ties. "Dad—"

"You've disappointed me, Cade," Jonathon said, rising and pushing his chair back into perfect alignment with the desk. "I expected much more from my own flesh and blood."

"You've expected *everything* from me!" Cade shot back. "I've given you nineteen years, Dad. Nineteen years in a job I never really loved."

"You could have told me that before I paid for law school. Saved me the money," Jonathon said. "And now you're leaving me, just like she did."

"I'm not her, Dad. And the sooner you stop taking out her sins on me and Carter, the better off we'll all be. Hell, we might even be happy." When his father buried his head in his work again, refusing to open that door of vulnerability again, Cade turned and strode out of the room, unemployed—and wondering if the mess his life had become was beyond salvageable.

# CHAPTER EIGHT

ON MONDAY MORNING, Melanie opened the shop a few minutes before the usual 6:00 a.m. start. Emmie, never an early riser, rarely worked the morning shift. Usually Melanie was here alone until about ten. Between the busy bursts, she liked the moments of quiet in the shop, the regulars who stopped in before work.

The bell jingled and Melanie turned, expecting to see Max, the owner of the bakery on Fourth Street. He provided the more complicated baked goods—bagels, doughnuts and cheesecakes—that rounded out her food case.

But it wasn't Max. And it sure as heck wasn't a bagel.

It was Cade, looking too handsome for a man who was at work before the sun finished breaking over the horizon. Today, he wore a light blue golf shirt that set off the color of his eyes and a pair of neatly pressed khakis.

Who had ironed them? Cade? The dry cleaner? Or someone else?

The thought of another woman doing what she had done for more than half her life, for the man she had once loved, slammed into her with a power Melanie hadn't expected.

She'd walked out the door of their house a year ago, intent on starting a life that wasn't defined by being Mrs. Cade Matthews.

She just hadn't thought he'd do the same thing.

Melanie shook off the thought. If Cade dated someone else, or married again, it was none of her business. And it shouldn't bother her one bit.

But it did. Oh boy, did it.

She put on a "I'm not affected by you one bit" smile, but suspected it was as see-through as lace. "What are you doing here?"

"Working," he said, grinning. "Wasn't that the plan?"

"I'd say that plan fell by the wayside yesterday." To be honest, after she'd broken off their kiss and turned down his invitation to dinner, she hadn't expected him to come back.

He put his hands up. "That won't happen again. No more kisses."

"Good." A twinge of disappointment ran through her, but Melanie ignored it. "The morning rush will start pretty soon, so put this on," she tossed an apron to him, the white fabric unfurling as it crossed the distance, "and be ready to latte."

Cade gave her a grin. "Sounds kinda kinky."

She laughed, then sobered when she realized that once again, she'd be in close quarters with Cade. Considering how well that had gone yesterday, and how much willpower she'd had, she might as well drop her head into a trough of chocolate. The calories from the sweets would be far easier to deal with than what kissing Cade could lead to.

Before she could tell Cade to stay or go—or even more, kiss her again—Max was there with his baked goods, followed by a trio of customers. The morning flood made both of them too busy for the next two hours to think about anything that didn't involve caffeine. Cooter wandered in, got his cup of coffee, then headed for his favorite armchair with his paper and mug.

When the last customer had been served, she turned to Cade. All morning, she'd been aware of him, brushed against him more than once, igniting the same rush of hormones as before. There was no way she could tolerate a week of this.

She shook off the attraction. It was simply that she had been alone for an entire year. The lack of male company made her more vulnerable. It certainly wasn't the way Cade looked, the sound of his laughter as he joked with the customers, or the

repartee that had flowed between him and Melanie
as easily as milk.

"I know you thought we needed this time together
before the reunion," she said, "but really, Cade, I'm
sure we can pull off being married for a couple of
hours without any additional 'practice.'"

"Oh, yeah?" He quirked a brow at her. "How
about we try it for ten minutes?"

"What do you mean?"

He gestured toward the front door of the shop.
"Because Jeanie Jenkins is just getting out of her car
and coming into the shop."

"This damned place is busier than a garbage truck
full of flies," Cooter muttered, shuffling his paper to
the next section.

"Jeannie?" Melanie wheeled around. An older
version of the Jeannie that Melanie remembered was
indeed, getting out of an illegally parked silver Benz,
striding up the walkway and toward the shop. She
was as thin as she had been in her cheerleading days,
and still sported the same long, curly hair. Even her
clothes were more fitting a twenty-year-old than a
near forty-year-old. If Melanie hadn't seen her face,
she'd have thought Jeannie hadn't aged a minute
since high school.

"Melanie!" Jeannie exclaimed, bursting through
the door with outstretched arms, as if spying Melanie
was like stumbling upon an oasis. She hurried across

the shop and grabbed Melanie from across the counter, gathering her into a tight hug.

"Jeannie," Melanie said, pulling back to inhale after that octopus grab. "What are you doing here?"

"Why seeing your little coffee shop, of course! I just couldn't stay away once you told me about it." A gossip finding mission, more than anything else, Melanie suspected. Jeannie toodled a wave Cade's way. He gave her a hello back.

Melanie had thought she'd have a week to prepare for appearing in public with Cade—not to mention a killer dress to boost her confidence. But standing here in jeans, a T-shirt emblazoned with the shop's logo and an apron that had a chocolate syrup stain on the front did little to boost her self-confidence. Or make her feel like half of Westvale High's equivalent of Romeo and Juliet.

Melanie put a smile on her face, then grabbed a mug from the clean ones on the shelf behind her. "Can I get you something?"

"Sure. Something non-fat, decaf and sugar-free." Jeanie waved a hand vaguely. "Whatever you have that does all that and tastes good."

A tall order, but Melanie did her best, combining skim milk, sugar-free caramel and almond syrups with a couple shots of decaf espresso to make a nicely flavored latte. Jeannie dumped in three packets of artificial sweetener, then took a sip.

"This is great. Who knew you could do all that with a few beans?"

"Lawford's a couple hours from Westvale. I'm surprised you drove that far for a cup of coffee, Jeannie," Melanie said, doing a little fishing of her own.

"Oh, it wasn't just the coffee. I'm also here for a Stickly." She took another petite sip.

"A what?"

"Stickly table," Jeannie explained. "There's this little antique shop in Mercy, which is, like, really near here. Wait…Mel, don't your grandparents own an antique shop?" Jeannie grinned. "Maybe they'd consider beating the Mercy shop's price."

"They used to own one. Right in this space, actually. But when they passed away, I turned the space into Cuppa Life."

"Oh," Jeannie said, clearly disappointed all she was getting out of the visit was some free coffee. "Too bad. I'm *totally,* like, wild about Stickly. I've been looking for ages for a table to finish off my house and then wham, there was one, in this month's issue of *Antiques.* I was up for a road trip, and then I remembered you had this shop here, and then before I knew it, like, here I was!"

"It was nice of you to stop in," Melanie said, wondering how long Jeannie planned to stay, because having Cade standing right next to her had Melanie's pulse skittering. If she inhaled, she knew she'd catch the notes of his cologne—a woodsy scent that had played its music in her heart for years. "Quite the surprise."

"I agree." Cade slipped an arm around Melanie's waist, drawing her inches closer. He pressed a kiss to her hair, soft, gentle. The wall around Melanie began to crumble. She found herself leaning into him, wanting more, wanting to believe this was real—

And not an act for Jeannie.

"Aw, you guys are still so sweet." Jeannie sighed. "I swear, all the good guys are taken."

Melanie didn't answer, just smiled back. Cade clutched her tighter, but as the reality of Jeannie's words hit her, she quit believing this was real. This was, after all, their trial run.

In the end, she'd have her building and Cade would have his job in Chicago. A win-win, he'd called it. Even if right now, it felt like one of them was losing.

"That reminds me." Jeannie grinned at them over the rim of her cup. "I didn't just drive out here for a table and a java. I have *another* ulterior motive. I'm killing three pigeons with one, like, tree."

"An ulterior motive?" Melanie echoed.

"Susan and I were talking the other day and we thought how cool it would be to bring back everything we loved about high school. Like, definitely not the teachers or that awful Algebra torture, but the good stuff." Jeannie grinned, then sipped at her coffee before continuing. "Especially prom night. I mean, everyone's going to be in fancy dresses and suits anyway, so we thought we'd recreate that whole, like, prom thing."

Prom night had been the night Melanie had lost her virginity to Cade. The night they'd made love, and in their youthful rashness of forgotten protection, ended up with Emmie. It was the night that had turned the tide of her life, and though she would never want to give back Emmie, she would have loved to change the way that night had turned out.

"I'm not so sure that's a good idea, Jeannie," Melanie said. "Not everyone had a great experience at prom."

"Well, that's where you guys come in." She leaned forward, eyes glittering with excitement. "You're going to be prom king and queen. Get the crowd all revved up for the whole thing."

"Us? But—"

"Oh, but you *have* to," Jeannie said, laying a hand over Melanie's. "You two are the only ones who are still together, at least of the couples who met in high school."

"What about Jerry Mitchell? Wasn't he with Danielle?" Cade asked.

Jeannie waved a hand. "They broke up ages ago. Something about Danielle having a backup plan."

"Most people have backup plans." Cade sent a glance Melanie's way.

"Yeah, but Danielle's backup plan was to wait for a better offer." Jeannie arched a brow. "From a younger man. A waiter at that. I mean, if you're going to toss a husband aside, at least trade *up*."

Melanie shook her head, thinking of the kid who had sat behind her in sophomore English and complained his way through diagramming sentences. "Poor Jerry."

"It's okay. He's been hitched to someone else for, like, two whole years now. Beat my record already." Jeannie took another tiny sip, so small it would take her an hour to finish the coffee. No wonder Jeannie was so thin. She ate more like a bird than a human. "So anyway," Jeannie went on, "we were thinking you and Cade could be the reunion king and queen. Lead us in the first dance, the toast. All that stuff."

Dance with Cade? This was going way beyond a speech. It meant taking their happily married act to a whole other level. Melanie had intended to go in, help Cade with Bill, make the speech, then leave. Not hang around for a reenactment of The Finest Moments of Cade and Melanie. "Jeannie, I don't—"

"We'd be glad to," Cade said, his arm around her waist feeling so familiar, so warm…

And way too easy to fall into.

"We really can't—" Melanie cut in.

"Oh, please," Jeannie said, hands clasped, eyes as wide as a baby beagle's. "You have to do it. Like, everyone is counting on you."

Guilt—the kind that seemed to come attached to every woman's psyche—forced a reluctant agreement past Melanie's lips. "Okay, but—"

"That is so awesome!" Jeannie blasted, her words riding roughshod over Melanie's. "You two will be, like, the whole reunion." She took one last sip, then rose and sent a two-finger wave at Melanie and Cade. "See you all on Friday night. I need to get my Stickly home!"

Then she was gone, hustling out the door as quickly as she'd come in, her nearly full coffee sending up a final curl of steam.

"Well," Cooter said, rising out of the armchair and plopping his hat on his head, "wasn't that a little bit of vinegar in your honey?"

With that, Cooter left the shop—leaving Melanie and Cade alone. Cade's arm still lingered around her waist, as if he'd forgotten he'd put it there—or fallen into old habits. She wheeled around, causing his touch to drop away. "What were you thinking? We can't play the happy couple all night. We were supposed to meet with Bill, make a speech and get out of there."

He scowled. "It's a dance, Melanie, not a lifetime commitment."

"Is it, Cade? Because it sure seems to me that everything you're doing is designed to get us back together." She shook her head, thinking of how many times she'd come close to doing exactly that this week. How easy it would have been to believe that a few days of making lattes together could solve everything. "It's not going to happen."

"And why is that, Melanie? Don't tell me it's because you don't love me anymore." He took a step closer, his hand going to her jaw.

"I don't." But she couldn't meet his gaze.

"So when you kissed me, you didn't feel anything at all?"

She didn't deny or agree. Melanie might be strong enough to stick to her guns on the divorce, but she wasn't strong enough to deny she hadn't felt a thing in that kiss. "You can't build a marriage on a kiss, Cade."

"No, we can't." His jaw hardened, his frustration clear as he released her. "But we can sure as hell try instead of giving up."

"Is that what you think I did? Give up?"

"You walked out, Melanie. I wouldn't say that was fighting for us."

"I fought for us for nineteen years, Cade. And where were you? At work. On a business trip. Anywhere but with me and your family."

"My job—"

She threw up her hands. "It's always been your job. Your career. What you needed. It was never about me. A marriage takes two. It means *both* people have their needs met."

"But isn't this," he said, indicating the coffee shop, "the need you wanted me to meet? Supporting you in your business?"

"It was part of it, yes."

"And I'm doing that. I'm here, working with you. I'm cosigning on the loan. What more do you want?"

She tore off the apron and tossed it to the side, sliding out from behind the counter. To keep her hands busy, Melanie folded the newspaper Cooter had left behind, fluffed pillows, picked up a couple of stray napkins. "I want a man who knows me. Who knows what I like. What my favorite color is. What I dream of for the future. Who I am, not what he thinks I am."

Cade was there, his hand over hers, stopping her from grabbing a forgotten paper coffee cup, forcing her to face him. "I know all that."

"No, you don't, Cade," she said, yanking away from him. "You stopped paying attention a long time ago. Or you wouldn't have asked what you did that night."

Emmie was striding up the sidewalk and toward the shop. Melanie grabbed her purse and coat, and headed out the door at the same time her daughter headed in. "I'm going to the store to pick up more milk," she said, knowing there were four gallons still in the fridge, but needing to get away from Cade and the conversation more than she needed to replenish her dairy products.

Cade waited a good ten minutes before he started picking Emmie's brain. "Your mom really loves this shop, doesn't she?" he began.

Emmie let out a gust. "Dad, I'm almost twenty years old. If you want to pump me for information, you can get right to the point."

He chuckled. "You've always been too smart for me."

She grinned at him. "No, I just inherited a little of that lawyer gene."

He laughed again, proud as hell of his daughter. She had always been able to hold her own in any argument, often winning over her parents when it came to getting the keys to the car or extending her bedtime. During the teen years, there'd been days when her smarts and argumentative spirit had been a nightmare more than a plus, but that had ended as she aged. "Okay, yes, I wanted to see what you knew about your mom."

Emmie started brewing a fresh pot of decaf. "I don't know why you're asking me. You should be asking Mom."

Cade looked toward the door where Melanie had exited a few minutes before. "I tried that."

"Mom's easy, Dad. Just listen to her."

"I'm trying, Em, but she's not talking."

"Maybe not with words, but she *is* talking."

He poured himself a cup of coffee, then leaned against the counter and looked at his daughter. "What's that supposed to mean?"

"It means," Emmie said, running a hand through her short, red-tipped hair, "that everything that is important to Mom is in this room."

He looked around the space, feeling as clueless as if he'd stepped into a foreign country where he didn't know the language and didn't have a handy travel guide. Had it gotten that bad, as Melanie had said, that he couldn't discern much about his wife from a room? From her own business?

"Looks like I have some work to do," he said.

"I'll say," Emmie muttered. But in her eyes, he saw the glisten of tears. She gave a one-shoulder shrug, as if she didn't care, but he could tell she did. "I hope you guys work it out, Dad."

"Yeah," Cade said on a sigh. "Me, too."

## CHAPTER NINE

THE NEXT FEW DAYS with Cade were business only, which was exactly what Melanie told herself she wanted. Yet even as she watched him move around the shop, interacting with the customers, brewing up their favorite blends, she wanted him. Wondered if their next kiss would be as good as the last one.

When business slowed down on Friday afternoon, she went outside to straighten Cuppa Life's patio furniture. When she was done, Melanie looked at her building for a long minute, then at Ben's shop next door, and its hand-lettered For Sale sign, put up just the other day. As she watched, Ben reached in the window and took the sign down, sending a friendly wave Melanie's way. She'd made her offer yesterday, with tentative bank approval, which Ben had said was good enough for him.

Cade had left to pick up Emmie, whose Toyota was once again putting up a fuss and had broken down two miles from the shop. Once they returned, Melanie and Cade had an appointment with a local bank, to find out if she had received her loan or not.

Given the loan officer's enthusiasm on the phone yesterday, Melanie figured it was probably a done deal—and clearly Ben believed that, too. She'd done it—albeit with Cade's credit score as a boost and their combined savings as well as the house in Indianapolis as collateral—and now she could watch her business become all she'd dreamed. After a year or two, maybe she'd be doing well enough to open a chain of locations. Indiana, Ohio, Pennsylvania— those states were just catching the coffee craze and would make great choices for additional locations.

Melanie had no doubt she could capture a segment of that market, given half a chance. That thought made her excited about the future. She could do this—and do it well. Success with Cuppa Life represented so much to Melanie, and also she knew, to her grandparents, who were undoubtedly watching from above with a smile.

She sighed, missing their calm wisdom, their kind, encouraging words, and most of all, the summers she'd spent here. Not to mention the respite those months gave her from the hectic, messy house in Westvale where she'd spent her childhood. A house where Melanie was often forgotten by her scatter-brained mother and her solitary father.

"We're back," Cade said, striding up the sidewalk with Emmie at his side. Emmie had her book bag over her shoulder, heavy and bulging with homework.

As she watched him stride ahead to hold the door for her and Emmie, Melanie realized how much she'd started looking forward to Cade's arrival. She'd gotten used to him being here, and knew when Monday dawned and he went back to the law firm, there'd be an empty spot in Cuppa Life.

And in her.

"How was school?" Melanie asked as the three of them headed inside, feeling oddly like the family they used to be, or rather could have been, had Cade been home often enough.

Emmie shrugged. "Okay. Though I'd rather watch cockroaches mate than sit through another of Professor Beach's World History lectures."

Cade laughed. "Glad to see our dollars are funding a good education."

"How's Liam?" Melanie asked. Emmie had broken off a year-long relationship at the end of high school and ever since, had been dating casually. It was pretty sad, actually, that her daughter had ten times the dating experience that Melanie had. But she was glad to see it. The last thing Melanie wanted for her daughter was a rush to the altar and a slew of regrets later in life.

"He asked me to go to the movies tomorrow night." Her eyes shone, the excitement clear in her voice, her face.

"He's the one from your Psych class, right?" Cade said.

Emmie nodded, clearly pleased that her father had, indeed, been listening.

Melanie looked from Cade to Emmie, surprised. All the years they'd been married, Cade had been pretty oblivious to Emmie's day-to-day activities. On any given morning, he couldn't have named her favorite cereal, the boy who'd given her that all-important first kiss, or who was taking her to the prom.

She and Cade had joked about being ships that passed in the night, but after a while, Melanie got tired of being another buoy in Cade's busy life.

"You guys have been talking," Melanie said, as Emmie headed to the rest room.

"It's hard not to when we're working together." He watched his daughter's retreating form and smiled. "She's a great kid, isn't she?"

"Yeah." Melanie grinned. "And it's nice to see her attitude improving this week as well."

"I missed a lot with her," Cade said, then sighed. "I should have been here more. Spent more time with her."

Melanie could have jumped on him then, pointed out the mistakes, the weekends he'd spent at work instead of at school events, or the business trips he'd taken, leaving Melanie to help Emmie with a science project on tornadoes. But she didn't.

Regret swam in his dark blue eyes, coated every syllable. Instead of recriminating, Melanie stepped forward and laid a hand on Cade's shoulder. "There's plenty of time ahead," she said softly.

He nodded, mute.

"Working here was one of the best things you could have done to get to know Emmie," she went on. "When she was a little girl, we had some of our best mother/daughter conversations in those odd moments. Like riding in the car or folding laundry."

"You and she always had that closeness," Cade said, turning to his wife. "It made me feel like an outsider sometimes."

Melanie blinked in surprise. "It did?"

"When I came home, I always felt as if I'd walked in after the punch line of the joke," he said, his gaze on some distant point in the past. "You and Emmie are like two peas in a pod."

"She was an only child, Cade. That meant all she had was me." Melanie realized what she'd just said and hurried to make it up. "I meant, you weren't home that much and—"

"I know what you mean." His attention swiveled back toward her, and in that second, a memory slipped between them, written in that unspoken mental language of longtime spouses. "It almost wasn't that way, though, was it?"

"Cade—"

"Are we ever going to talk about it, Melanie? Or just pretend that it never happened?"

She waved toward the back of the shop. "Emmie will be out any second now."

"Fine," Cade said. "But we have to talk about it sometime."

"Sure," Melanie said, intending no such thing. That day had been painful enough. Cade's absence, her guilt. There was enough fodder there for a soap opera.

"Mel, didn't you want the baby, too?" Cade asked, his voice just above a whisper.

She turned away, straightening mugs, aligning the handles until they were like little circular soldiers marching along the shelf. "I can't talk about this."

"Can't or won't? It takes two to kill a marriage, you know. And two to bring it back to life."

"I don't want to bring it back to life," Melanie said, wheeling around. "I don't want to go back to being Suzy Homemaker."

"When did I ever say you had to do that?"

"Last year," Melanie said, "standing in this very space. I said I wanted to run my own shop and you asked me how I could possibly do that if I had another baby. You just assumed I wanted to try again. Assumed I wanted to go back to being a housewife and a mom. Assumed I wanted to put my dreams on hold one more time."

The rest room door squeaked as Emmie opened it and both Cade and Melanie let the subject drop. A couple of students wandered in, followed by two men in suits who took a corner table and flipped out their laptops.

Cooter ambled in next. He tipped his cap Melanie's way and ordered his usual. His light blue gaze flicked between Cade and Melanie. "That old dog, he's still whining from what I can hear," Cooter said, taking his mug. "And there ain't nobody happy when the dog's not happy."

Cade gestured toward Cooter as the old man headed to the back of the shop. "What'd he mean by that?"

"He told me a story about some dog that got sick eating mulch or something." She shrugged. "I don't know, it's supposed to have meaning for my life."

"Mulch? And a dog?" Cade chuckled. "Jeez, if I'd known the secret to life was that easy, I'd have brought home a golden retriever and landscaped the front beds."

Melanie laughed, glad for the break from the tension of their earlier conversation. Emmie joined them, looking from one parent to the other. She smiled. "Good to see you guys getting along so well."

"Oh, we're just—"

"Sharing a joke," Cade intercepted. "Nothing more."

"Uh-huh," Emmie said, clearly not believing them. "Either way, you two better get out of here. Don't you have a meeting?"

"I almost forgot!" Melanie slipped off her apron, grabbed her coat and purse off the hook inside the kitchen. "I'll see you tomorrow, Em."

Emmie smiled, her gaze again split between Melanie and Cade. "Have a good time tonight."

Hidden meaning—work those marital problems out on the dance floor.

"Thanks for taking my shift, honey," Melanie said, ignoring the hint to get back together with Cade and instead laying a quick kiss on her daughter's forehead. Emmie gave her mother another eye-roll, but didn't move away. Despite her being well past the age when kisses were dispensed with the abandon of confetti throwers, Melanie was convinced Emmie still secretly liked the occasional tender touch. Even if it was from her mother.

The shop door jingled and Liam entered, his attention more on Emmie than Cuppa Life's offerings. "Hi, Liam," Emmie said, a soft, private smile curving across her face.

"Hi, Em." He slipped onto a stool and returned her smile.

"I think that's our cue to go," Cade whispered in Melanie's ear.

A thrill charged through her at the feel of his warm

breath along her neck. She closed her eyes for a half a second, giving up to that feeling, before dismissing it. The bank loan, the reunion, it was all part of a business deal. Not a date. There wasn't going to be some miraculous happily ever after created while the band played "Always and Forever."

Even if a tiny part of her was starting to hope otherwise.


Cade stood in his kitchen, wrestling with the black bowtie that went with his tux. Carter leaned against the wall, watching his twin with clear amusement. "Need some help?" he asked.

"No. I can get it."

Carter arched a brow, then glanced around the messy kitchen. "This place is really starting to scream bachelor. You gotta do something."

Why was everyone telling him that? He *was* doing something—it just wasn't working. He'd thought, after the meeting with the bank this afternoon, that things might change. That the minute the loan officer said, "Congratulations," Melanie would have turned to him, and called this whole divorce thing off. But she hadn't. Instead she'd thanked him as politely as she had the bank manager, then told him she'd see him tonight.

It couldn't have been more businesslike if they'd been standing in a boardroom.

"Did you come over just to complain about my decor?" Cade said to his twin.

"Nah. I was hungry, too. You have anything to eat around here?" Carter opened a cabinet, rifled through it for a second, then turned back to his brother. "Are you sure you don't want some help with that tie? It's a mess."

Cade threw his brother a glare.

Carter just laughed. "All right, but don't blame me if you end up looking like a guy who wrapped his own Christmas present." He moved some cans of green beans, found nothing behind them, then shut the cabinet door. "This is sad. Old Mother Hubbard had more than you do, Cade."

Cade hadn't eaten at home in so long, he couldn't remember what he had on hand—if anything. "Check the fridge. There might be some leftover Thai food."

Carter rose, opened the Whirlpool and withdrew one of the paper takeout boxes. He took one whiff, then shoved it back inside the refrigerator and slammed the door. "You need to fix things with Melanie, man, before you die of e-Coli or typhoid or something."

"My vaccinations are up-to-date," Cade said with a grin. "And I'm making progress with Mel."

"How so?"

"I worked with her at the coffee shop all week."

"Five days serving up lattes? Should have been enough time to solve your problems, the world's problems *and* have some time leftover." Carter grinned.

"You don't know my wife."

"Neither, apparently, do you, if you couldn't get her to talk." Carter opened the freezer, but found only several inches of frost and one pizza box that had started to curl at the corners. He shut the door again, fast. "Did you ever try to figure out why she won't talk to you?"

"Because Melanie is more stubborn than a herd of donkeys."

"Or maybe because she *is* talking and you aren't listening."

Cade started in on the tie again. That was the same thing Emmie had said. "What is that supposed to mean?"

"All along, you've been saying it's her that won't talk. Saying she's the one who walked out on the marriage. Did you ever think that it might have been you?"

"That's insane. I've always been there." The final bow tightened against his neck and he turned around. "Well, except when I was at work."

"And how great of a husband do you think Dad would have been if he'd married again?"

"Dad would have been horrible. Heck, he wasn't even good at the father thing. Never home, always talking about the office, leaving us to do our own thing."

"Uh-huh. Do you recognize anyone in that picture?"

Cade shook his head. "I'm not like Dad."

"You are, too. You're just not as crabby as he is." Carter grinned. "And you don't share his opinion that I'm an idiot."

"He just wants you to make something of yourself." Cade had served as the go-between for the two for years, but he might as well have been a brick wall, given how little Carter and their father communicated. Cade wondered sometimes if his Type-A, workaholic father envied Carter's footloose approach to life.

"I did make something of myself," Carter said. "What I made wasn't good enough. He wanted me to be a lawyer. I'd sooner commit hari-kari than spend all day locked up with legal briefs." Carter snorted at the very idea. "Do you even *like* being a lawyer?"

Cade sighed and dropped into one of the kitchen chairs. "No, I don't."

"Then why the hell are you doing it?"

"Because Dad paid for me to go to college. Gave me a job when Melanie and I had nothing. No money, no apartment, nothing but a baby on the way."

"And he's made you pay him back ten times over," Carter said, sliding into the opposite seat. "If you hate your job, quit."

"I don't have a backup plan, Carter. It's not like I can take my law degree and be a really good bartender."

"You took your law degree and made really good

coffee. Mixing a margarita on some beach in Jamaica should be a piece of cake after that."

Cade laughed, then returned to reality. To a mortgage, college tuition and a retirement to fund. "I'm not going to throw away a twenty-year career to serve women in bikinis."

"You have got issues, my brother." Carter chuckled. "I'd do just about anything to serve women in bikinis."

"That's why you're the bachelor and I'm the—" Cade cut himself off. He wasn't the married one, not really. "Okay, bad point. Still, I'm not applying for any jobs in Jamaica."

"There may be an opening as a toy company CEO soon if I keep helping this business run into the ground," Carter said, then glanced at his watch. "Anyway, I have to go. I have a date." He rose. "I may be a bachelor, and a disappointment to my father and a guy whose still trying to figure out who he is, but at least I'm honest about it. One piece of advice. The sooner you get honest with yourself, the sooner you can get honest with Melanie, too."

Then Carter left, leaving Cade with a mental mirror finally large enough for him to see the reflection of himself. He got out a piece of paper and began to write.

# CHAPTER TEN

"LAST TIME I SAW YOU in one of those, it was light blue," Melanie said. "You looked like the Easter Bunny."

Cade chuckled. "If you prefer the blue…"

"Oh, no. the black is nice." Maybe too nice because she had to remember to breathe. She noticed everything about him, especially the way the tux framed the muscles and planes of Cade's body. Every hormone in her body itched to undo the tie, then start on the tiny black buttons, unfastening one after the other until she got him down to his boxers—

And nothing else.

It was a major change from the business casual he'd worn to the bank earlier. True to his word, Cade had stayed quiet throughout the loan process, letting Melanie run the show—and collect the check at the end. Cuppa Life was going to finally fulfill what Melanie had envisioned, which made her excited about the days to come.

But right now, the only thing increasing her pulse was Cade and the sexy cut of the fancy black suit.

"You look amazing." The compliment shone in his eyes as much as it did in his tone. Cade took a step forward, then reached out and ran a finger along the thin strap of her dress. "Absolutely incredible."

Her breath caught in her throat, her gut twisted with a want that had never seemed this strong, this overpowering. Before she could think about what she was doing, Melanie closed the gap between them, lifted her chin and pressed her lips to his.

He groaned, then his arms stole around her waist. He pulled her to him, hard and fast, nearly catching her breath in her throat. She knew all it would take would be one word—no, one glance—and she and Cade could be in her bedroom, undoing all they had so carefully done to get ready for tonight.

"Oh, Melanie," he said against her mouth, his voice heavy with want, need—the same river rushing through her veins, begging for release.

"We should…go," she breathed in the space between their lips, not wanting to go at all, not wanting to do anything but keep on kissing him.

"Yeah."

But neither of them moved.

"I want you," he whispered. "I've always wanted you. From the first time I saw you, there's never been anyone but you, Mellie."

"Cade—"

He put a finger to her lips, shushing her protest. "I've never wanted another woman and I never will."

"We should go," she repeated, but everything within her rebelled against the thought. Of leaving what was happening right now unfinished. "We should go…" and then, the need for him conquered her doubts, and she took his hand. "To my bedroom," she whispered, ignoring the warning bells rung by common sense, heeding only the need that tightened and curled inside her gut, a call that knew exactly how Cade would answer.

"Oh God, Melanie," he said, his voice nearly cracking. He scooped her up, cradling her to his chest, his lips drifting across hers in a soft, sweet caress. Melanie wrapped her arms around his neck, craving more of this, craving him, needing him to fill that empty space inside her.

"I want you, too, Cade," she said.

He pulled back to look at her, his eyes filled with the gentle kindness that was quintessential Cade. "Are you sure?"

She nodded. "First door on the right," she whispered as he headed down the hall, her hands going to his bow tie. She tugged it loose, then worked her way down the tiny black buttons of his shirt, anxious to feel his skin beneath her palms, the sure strength of Cade against her body.

He deposited her gently on the bed, then kicked off his shoes. They landed with a clunk, matched by the twin sound of her heels following. Electricity filled the air, charging the space between them. His mouth on hers was hungry yet still tender, his hands warm and tight on her hips. He lowered himself beside her, their bodies carving together as easily as two puzzle pieces.

She worked his shirt out of his waistband, flicking the last two buttons out of their fasteners, then tugging it down and off his arms. She paused a moment, allowing herself the agonizing pleasure of running her hands along his chest, feeling the planes and muscles she had memorized over the years. He was familiar, and yet new, after all this time apart, and she marveled at the warm hardness beneath her palm.

Their mouths met, a ravenous kiss that tasted lips, tongue, every inch of each other. Cade tugged her dress up and over her body, then paused, his gaze softening as it swept over her body. "I've had this dream many times over the last year."

"Oh, yeah?" She grinned, teasing him. "And how did it end?"

He leaned down, trailing kisses along her neck, between her breasts, skirting the lacy edge of her bra. "Let me show you," he said, his voice nearly a growl.

An instant later, Cade was fulfilling her with the knowledge of a man who had had twenty years of learning his wife's body. He touched all the right places, stroked at just the right pace and sent every one of her nerve endings into another stratosphere.

She ran her hands down his bare back, urging him to quench a thirst that had suddenly become unbearable. He kissed her neck, her breasts, everything he could reach, while her palms explored his firm, amazing body.

It was familiar, yet as new as the first time. Their crescendo built quickly, fueled by the year apart, and before she knew it, she was crying out Cade's name in concert with him. When the sensations finally ebbed, Cade rolled to the side and pulled Melanie into his arms. She couldn't remember feeling warmer, or more secure.

"I love you," he whispered.

Those same three words lingered on the tip of her tongue, but as she came back to reality, Melanie held them inside and pretended she hadn't heard Cade. She couldn't say them back. Because in the morning, all of this would go back to what it had been. Once before, Melanie had lain in Cade's arms, sure that everything would change, then been shattered when it didn't. She couldn't bear to go through that again.

Instead she raised herself onto one arm and glanced at her bedside clock. "We're going to be late."

The magical spell between them dissipated.

"You're right." Cade released his hold on her and rolled away, clearly hurt.

And broke the spell.

He slipped on his clothes while she did the same, neither of them speaking. When she was done, Melanie fixed her hair in her dresser mirror. In the reflection, she saw Cade wrestling with his bow tie, cursing under his breath. "Let me do that," she said, crossing to him.

His dark gaze riveted on hers, making her fingers jumble her first attempt at the tiny silk neckpiece. She dipped her gaze and concentrated on the tie, finally getting it back into proper order. "You're all set."

"Thanks." Cade reached up and brushed a tendril of hair away from her face, weaving that magic around them once again. For a long moment, neither of them said anything.

Melanie tore her gaze away from his. "We have to go."

Cade nodded, disappointment clear in his features. Together, they headed out of the room, the bed linens as tangled as her emotions.

Melanie grabbed her clutch purse from the bench by the door, then walked with Cade out to his car. He opened the passenger's side door—something he had never failed to do in nineteen years of marriage— then waited until she was seated before shutting it and coming around the other side.

"I've missed that," she said when he got in the car.

"What?"

"Someone opening the door for me."

Cade only murmured an agreement before he started his Volvo.

Melanie slid a glance his way. The second the statement left her, she'd expected that he would say something about how she could have him opening her door every day, if only she'd take him back. But he hadn't.

Had that moment in her bedroom been a final fling between them? His "I love you" more of a goodbye than a return to the old days? And if it was, why did that thought send a little shiver of disappointment through her?

During the two-hour ride to the hotel hosting the Westvale High reunion, Cade kept the conversation impersonal, sticking mainly to the subject of buying Ben's building and her plans for the expansion.

He'd clearly been paying attention—to her thoughts, her business ideas. "Thank you," Melanie said.

Cade flicked a glance her way before returning his attention to the road. "For what?"

"For listening."

"I'm making up for lost ground," Cade said. "With Emmie, and with you. And while we're on the topic, I've been meaning to thank you. For letting me work at the shop this week. I really enjoyed it."

She chuckled. "I'm sure those cappuccino skills

will come in handy when you go back to Fitzsimmons, Matthews and Lloyd."

"Yeah, I'll have to get a machine for the break room." He cast his gaze toward the road before them for a moment, then back at her. "I needed that opportunity to do something else. I've worked for my father for nearly twenty years and never had as much fun there as I did in your coffee shop." He reached for her hand, gave it a short, tight squeeze. "You've accomplished so much with your coffee shop. I'm really proud of you, Mellie."

Something softened inside her, giving room for hope to expand its reach. "I appreciate that," she said softly. "I enjoyed having you there, too, this week. Except for Ben, I haven't really had anyone to talk to about the business."

He glanced at her again. "You miss your grandparents, don't you?"

Tears sprung to her eyes, and she nodded, surprised that he had read that in her.

"They'd be proud. Really proud, honey."

Melanie whisked away the tears that dropped from her lashes. "You're going to make me ruin my makeup."

"You'll still be beautiful," Cade said, his words seeming a hundred times more intimate in the darkness. "You do a great job with that shop, Mel. You have just the right mix of location and atmosphere to make it work."

She sat back against her seat and studied him. "I never expected you to say that."

"The truth isn't so hard to say." He grinned.

As Melanie watched the world pass by in a muddled blur of inky night and spots of light, she had to wonder whether that was so.

When they walked into the gaily decorated ballroom at the hotel that was hosting Westvale High's reunion, several people hurried over to Melanie and Cade, calling their names. Even after so many years apart, Cade recognized several of the faces, but was still damned glad the reunion committee had stuck name tags on everyone's chests.

"Paul Klein!" Melanie exclaimed, striding forward, Dave at her side to greet their old friend. At six foot six, he still towered over Melanie, even if his long curly hair had become a buzz-cut. "How have you been?"

"Great, great," he said, giving Melanie a warm hug, before turning to shake Cade's hand. "It's been a long time since those double dates in Cade's Mustang, huh?"

"You guys are *finally* here!" Jeannie enveloped them in a double hug, then pulled back to indicate a trio of class officers behind her. There was a flurry of introductions, of catching up. Somehow, Cade lost track of Melanie, separated by the flood of people.

Then, he caught sight of her, standing to the side, chatting with a brunette whose face rang a familiar bell; Cade didn't remember her name. He wasn't aware of anything really, except for Melanie. In that deep crimson dress, with her hair loose around her shoulders, Melanie managed to pull off both sexy and elegant, the fabric skimming down her curves, making him wish it was his hands running along those feminine lines again.

Their lovemaking had been as intense as it had been in those early days when passion overrode every thought, and yet this time, it had the added depth of years of connection. Cade had thought—hell, prayed—that in the afterglow, Melanie might have been tempted to try again. But her silence when he'd said he loved her spoke more than anything else she'd said in these last few days.

Melanie was right. One kiss, or even a hundred kisses, wasn't enough to rescue their marriage. Making love to his wife had only been a temporary mask for their problems.

On the way over here, he'd intended to play by her rules. To keep it cool and impersonal, but the longer she stayed in his sight, the more impossible it became, especially as his mind replayed the moments in her bedroom, the sweet ecstasy of having his wife in his arms again.

Still, if he rushed her, or he pushed too hard, he knew he could end up driving her away. His fists clenched at his sides, keeping him from reaching for her, drawing her back into his arms. Then she smiled at him, and something within Cade tightened.

Maybe it was the starry lights strung overhead, the way the disco ball above had been adapted to sweep a sparkling of light across the floor. The soft music, the band crooning a ballad from the eighties…

It was as if they had stepped back in time. Cade slipped through the crowd, weaving in and out among the people until he reached his wife. He slipped his hand into hers. Comfort infused him.

"Cade," she said, her voice a warning.

"For just one night," he whispered, not wanting to let go of the veil of intimacy temporarily surrounding them, "let's pretend nothing has gone wrong. Let's just be Cade and Melanie."

She cocked her head. "Wasn't that the plan, so that no one knows what's going on?"

"I don't care what other people think. I want us to forget those papers on my desk, to forget it all, and go back to the beginning."

"But…" Her voice trailed off, as if she were about to reject the idea as easily as she had his whispered confession of love earlier.

"In the morning, we go back to business as usual," Cade said, wishing that wouldn't happen, praying that tonight had turned the tide between him and Melanie. "For tonight, Mellie, just tonight, be my wife. One more time."

She hesitated, then her green gaze met his, and she nodded, her gaze dropping to the ring on her finger. "One night. Like Cinderella."

The band segued from a fast-paced song to a slow and easy ballad. Cade may be surrounded by people whose names he'd long forgotten, but he recognized the familiar notes. The Whitney Houston hit whispered its magical melody, flashing his mind back to late nights in his Mustang, parked wherever they could grab a little privacy, the windows fogged from the steam of young love, while the radio played those same melodic strains. "They're playing our song."

"You remembered," she said, clearly surprised and touched that he recognized it.

He nodded, his gaze locked with hers, searching, still searching, for those lost threads of his marriage. "Dance with me, Mel."

"But I see Bill Hendrickson over there." Melanie pointed to where the punch bowl and appetizers had been laid out. Bill stood beside the cheese platter, chatting with two other men. He sent a wave Cade's way. "Didn't you want to talk to him?"

"Later. Right now, all I want is to dance with you." Cade reached out, waiting until she'd put her other hand in his, then, together, they made their way to the dance floor. As it had in the days before work and nighttime feedings and dirty dishes had taken over their days, the music made the world around them drop away. He swept her against his body, one arm around her waist. Their pulses merged, heartbeats synchronizing with their every step.

She tipped her head up, her eyes dark and unreadable, her lips inches from his. Want brewed inside him, a different and deeper want than what he'd felt earlier tonight. It was as if, at this moment, with Melanie in his arms and the music of their past playing in the background, his life had finally come full circle.

And everything within him was rebelling at the thought of giving that up.

"Kiss me," she whispered. "Kiss me, Cade."

A smile curved across Cade's face, then he dipped his head, and brought his mouth to hers. She tasted of berries, a sweet dessert. She slipped her arms around his neck, bringing them closer, closing in their world even tighter.

"That's *exactly* why you guys are king and queen!" Jeannie exclaimed. "Because you are, like, the ultimate couple."

# CHAPTER ELEVEN

JEANNIE'S LAUGHING VOICE brought the real world crashing back. Melanie stepped back from Cade. "Hi, Jeannie."

Cade didn't offer a greeting. Instead he mentally cursed the former cheerleader's timing.

Jeannie sighed. "You two are *so* Adam and Eve. I wish I had a man like Cade. I mean, not the real Cade," she laughed, "because he's, like, taken, but one who looks at me like that. It'd also help if he had a really high credit limit. Oh, and definitely a Porsche." She grinned, then took both their hands, pulling them from the dance floor. "Anyway, I'm really sorry to interrupt a little marital fun, but it's time to give your speech."

Cade had practiced his speech all afternoon in his head, mentally weighing the combination of a typical welcome with something a little more personal—and that might get Melanie's attention.

Jeannie led Melanie and Cade up to the stage, leaving them in the shadows of the side curtains while she charged over to the microphone, as hyper as a two-year-old. "We're all, like, so excited to see so many Westvale High people! It's totally a rush to see us all together again! But let's get right to it and bring out the couple you've all been wanting to see, our reunion King and Queen, Cade and Melanie Matthews!" Jeannie started clapping, her face bright and eager. She waved at them, gesturing the two forward.

"Are you ready?" Cade asked Melanie.

"As ready as I'll ever be." But her voice shook on the last syllable.

"You'll do fine," he said, then took her hand and strode onto the stage. As soon as they reached the microphone, Jeannie hurried to a nearby stool, grabbed two silver plastic crowns and plopped them on Cade and Melanie's heads. Cade smirked at Melanie, who gave him one of Emmie's eye-rolls back.

"Thank you all for coming," he said into the microphone, withdrawing a sheaf of papers from his inside pocket and smoothing them onto the podium. "On behalf of the class officers, I'd like to welcome you to our twentieth reunion. Jeannie asked Melanie and me to talk about the passage of time—and about how some of us have stayed the same while others have changed, like by putting on a few pounds." At that he patted his stomach, which elicited a burst of laughter. "Don't worry, Dwight," Cade said to the former football captain standing in the front row, "I won't be tackling you tonight. I can't afford the hospital bill."

Another round of laughter.

"But one thing I can tell you that has stayed the same in all those years—" at this he turned briefly to Melanie "—is how we feel about each other, how we feel about those people who were—and still are—closest to us. The years may have aged us, but they have also aged the friendships, the connections, we built up over the years. Those have only grown in depth, even if we now live miles apart."

Melanie felt the words, heard them in her heart. She knew her husband wasn't talking about Bill, Paul or Dwight or any of his high school friends, but of her.

Had those years really intensified their feelings for each other or driven them further apart? She looked at the crowd below them, seeing pairs of best friends who had been separated for years and then picked up as if they'd never been apart. Tonight, she and Cade had done the same in her bedroom—only with a lot more va-va-voom.

Was it possible that the foundation she and Cade had built all those years ago was still there, waiting for them? Or was she imagining it, still caught up in the afterglow of their lovemaking?

"Our job," Cade continued, "tonight and into the

future, is to maintain those connections. To not let the busyness of our lives or the focus of making it through today distance us from those we love and who love us."

Someone in the audience hooted agreement.

"And with that, I'll introduce my lovely wife," Cade said.

The word startled Melanie. How long had it been since she'd heard Cade call her that? Tears threatened at her eyes, as she realized that once the paperwork was filed, she'd never hear those words again.

Cade turned away from the podium, and as he did, the papers in his hand slipped from his grasp, fluttering to the stage floor.

Melanie bent to pick them up. A smaller piece, different in color and shape from the typewritten pages, slid out of the pile.

A list. In Cade's handwriting. With her name at the top, as if she were a task he had to complete. She saw the words "shop, bank loan, baby," before Jeannie scooted in, gathered up all the papers and shoved them at Cade.

"Hey, we got, like, big-time dead air," she hissed at Melanie. "You have to do something. Say your speech."

Before Melanie could react to what she'd just seen, she found herself at the microphone, unfolding the handwritten pages holding her speech.

The spotlights above her gave the ballroom a

sense of being an enormous black hole, an endless sea filled with people expecting a few words of wisdom from the reunion Queen.

Even if she didn't feel like she had any to give.

"I look at the passage of time a little differently from Cade," she said. In her mind, the words on the list flashed in front of her, a trio of warning signals. How could she have been so foolish? To think that things could actually change? "But then again, I'm a woman, which means I rarely agree with him. And of course, when it comes to arguments, I'm always right."

Laughter erupted from the crowd.

"Maybe it's because I'm a mom. When you have a baby, it seems as if the days—and most of the nights—are endless." She paused for another ripple of laughter. Melanie was grateful to have a written speech in hand, which allowed her to keep her mind on speaking, instead of what she'd just seen on that scrap of notebook paper. "But then, you look back and one day realize the years have passed in a blur, and everything around you has changed. I see the years in our wrinkles, our thighs—" at that, she patted her own "—and in our conversations. Where we once talked about who Adam Garvey liked—" she indicated the former hottest guy at Westvale, who'd become a balding veterinarian "—we now talk about our children and how it terrifies us that they're dating. We used to focus on taking tests, now we chat about keeping our jobs. And yet, one thing is still a common topic. The future.

"We look ahead, as we did twenty years ago, and hope that we have made the right decisions. That we will take the paths that lead toward our goals and our dreams. Sometimes, those paths take us in different directions. But in the end, I'm confident that we can all sit around a table, put on the coffee, and in that, find common ground again with those we love." She thanked the crowd and took a step back from the podium.

The crowd erupted in applause. Cade tossed her a grin as easily as a Frisbee. Melanie turned away, unable to look at him without seeing that list.

"That was just totally awesome," Jeannie said, taking over the mike again. "And now, for the couple of the night—and the most happily married people I've ever seen—we have a special prize." She pulled an envelope out from behind her back, then handed it to Melanie, at the same time tugging Cade closer. "A totally romantic weekend away in windy Chicago, provided by Hartstone Travel." Jeannie leaned forward, increasing her vocal volume. "Hartstone, making travel fun for all ages. And a special thank you to Jim Hartstone—" at that, a chubby guy in a suit took a bow, while Jeannie led a round of applause "—for this great gift."

"Uh, Jeannie," Melanie said, trying to interrupt

Jeannie's continued effusive thanks for Jim. The envelope in Melanie's hands weighed heavy with the knowledge that it would never be used, at least not by the Mr. and Mrs. Matthews scrawled across the front.

No matter how romantic it might have been to tango with Cade in bed, to waltz under a faux starry sky, to twirl around the dance floor in his arms, she was fooling herself if she thought Cade would ever change. He'd made that clear tonight, when she'd found that list.

*"Jeannie,"* Melanie said again, louder.

But Jeannie kept on, touting Jim's company as the next best thing to owning your own cruise line, while the band played a soft melody beneath her voice. "I wonder if Cade and Mel are still limber enough to use the champagne glass hot tub. Not that you two need the extra spark," Jeannie said with a grin that seemed tinted a little green with envy. "Everything about you two is just perfect, isn't it?"

"Ye—" Melanie cut off the yes before it could come out. She was done agreeing to keep the peace, to make someone happy, to preserve the status quo. Done with pretending to be something she wasn't. She placed the envelope on the podium. "No, Jeannie, it isn't. And we can't take this gift. I'm sorry."

"What?" Jeannie cupped her hand over the mike. Behind them, the band screeched to a stop. "What did you just say?"

"Mel, it's okay," Cade cut in. "We'll settle this later."

"When, Cade?" She wheeled around. "When are we going to get to the point and quit fooling ourselves that one night in bed, once dance or even a weekend in Chicago—"

"With a destination package valued at six hundred dollars," Jeannie cut in with a hopeful, work-with-me smile.

"—will bring back what we used to have. It's not going to happen, Cade, because we are getting *divorced.*"

A hush rippled through the crowd. Cade's face paled, as if finally speaking the words in public made them irrefutable. Jeannie gripped the mike stand, her face about three shades below death, and swayed a little. *"Divorced?"* she squeaked.

Silence descended its heavy blanket, muting the merry atmosphere of the reunion. The word seemed to echo, carrying through the room, drumming home the reality.

Melanie and Cade—divorced.

And then, it hit her, too. Hard and deep, like a punch to the gut that she'd forgotten to steel herself for. She'd moved out, filed the papers, started over in Lawford, but throughout it all, the actual thought of divorce hadn't seemed as real as it did right this moment.

She and Cade were finished. She would never again feel his hand in hers, his lips against her mouth, hear his voice warm against her ear.

Melanie was giving up her husband. And in doing so, Melanie wondered who the real loser was.

"Got a lawyer yet, Mel? I'm a real shark in the courtroom." She glanced out at the crowd, searching for the voice, but could see only the flash of a white business card against the dark backdrop.

"I'm sorry," Melanie said, then she ripped the crown off her head and escaped the stage.

"Melanie, wait!" Cade called after her, his long legs closing the distance between them quickly and reaching her just as she exited the hotel. "Why are you leaving?"

She spun around. "I don't want what you want, Cade. We're only hurting each other if we keep trying to make this charade work."

"What do you mean? We made love tonight, Melanie. After that, I thought things were going to be different, that maybe a door was opening between us."

"So did I, but I was wrong." She looked away, her gaze going to the wide, white moon, hanging low in the ebony sky. "And I'm sorry about what happened back there. I probably ruined it for you with Bill Hendrickson."

He waved a hand in dismissal. "It doesn't matter. I already turned down the job."

"You did? Why?"

"Because I can't leave you." He grinned, that same

familiar smile that held a special place in so many of Melanie's memories. "I can't go to Chicago and walk away from us. You go ahead and file that divorce, Melanie, if you really want to, but I'm not letting go that easily."

She shook her head. "Cade, I didn't want to bring in lawyers—"

"I didn't mean I would fight you in court. I meant I'd fight you here." He reached forward and pressed a palm to where her heart beat.

She thought of the list. Of the third item Cade had on it. How tempting it would be to give in to the emotions stirred up by those moments beneath the sheets and on the dance floor.

She shoved the feelings aside. It was crystal clear, especially after she'd seen the words in Cade's own handwriting, that his goals were miles apart from hers. "Don't, Cade. We want different things. Just let it go."

"I can't." His gaze locked on hers. "I love you, Melanie. I always have."

"Oh, Cade, please don't make this difficult." Tears burned behind her eyes. She loved this man—she was fooling herself if she ever thought she could stop loving him—but Cade deserved a woman who would give him what he wanted.

And that woman wasn't Melanie, not anymore.

"I'm not making anything difficult," he said, moving closer, taking her hand. "Unless you count kissing as more difficult." He leaned forward, his mouth a whisper from hers.

How easy it would be. But tomorrow, Melanie knew, she'd be back to where she was before and breaking it off a second time would be ten times more painful.

She jerked back. "Don't."

Surprise filled his blue eyes, tinted with hurt at her rejection. "You can't tell me you stopped loving me, Melanie. I saw it in your eyes tonight, felt it when you kissed me. We're meant for each other and whatever problems we have, we can work them out."

The thought tempted her. How easy it would be to believe they could go back to being the Cade and Melanie they had been twenty years ago.

"Tell me you love me, Melanie," he said, "and we'll start all over again, right here."

If she said those words, her life could go back to what it had been before. The problem was, Melanie no longer wanted that life.

"I don't love you anymore, Cade." A single tear fell from her lashes, but she held her gaze steady on his. "I'm sorry."

Cade stood in the hotel parking lot while cars came and went and the world moved on, Melanie's words slamming against his heart like a wrecking ball. He'd hoped, no, prayed, that it wasn't too late. He'd always believed, beneath it all, Melanie still loved him.

He would have given anything to hear her repeat what he'd said. To have her, one more time in his arms, her lips meeting his with desire, her body curved into that same familiar place, against his heart.

He could have fought her, argued back, lashed out and released all the hurt wrapped around his chest like chains. But he couldn't do that to her.

He swallowed hard. He had to let her go, even as every ounce of his soul protested. "Then I guess that's it." He inhaled, then let the breath out again with two words. "Goodbye, Melanie."

Cade turned on his heel, and left behind the only woman he had ever loved.

## CHAPTER TWELVE

MELANIE WATCHED CADE WALK away, her heart shattering. She'd just told the biggest lie of her life.

She sunk against one of the columns supporting the entryway to the hotel, burying her face in her hands. When she did, the memories washed over her, unstoppable. The two of them, welcoming Emmie into the world. Singing lullabies late at night. Cuddling on the sofa. Eating popcorn while a rented movie played on the television and she and Cade got reacquainted after another business trip.

When had she quit believing in that love? In them?

"Mel, you okay?" Jeannie exited the hotel, the hem of her floor-length dress gathered in her hand as she navigated the stone entrance in high heels.

"Yes," Melanie said, then drew in a breath. "No."

Jeannie laid a hand on Melanie's arm. "Do you need a ride home?"

"Are you sure you don't mind?"

"Not at all." Jeannie dug in her jeweled purse for a set of keys, then dangled them in front of the valet, who hurried off to retrieve her car. "If there's one thing I'm good at when it comes to relationships with men, it's making an escape."

Melanie asked Jeannie to drop her off at Cuppa Life. The whole ride back to Lawford was filled with Jeannie's endless chatter about the people at the reunion, a full-out gossip fest that any tabloid columnist would have relished. This time, instead of being annoying, Melanie enjoyed the endless one-sided conversational stream, if only for the distraction.

"Thanks, Jeannie," Melanie said when the car stopped in front of the shop. She paused to look at the woman she'd hardly known in high school but now, ironically, counted among her friends. "You're a great friend and I'm glad you talked me into going to the reunion."

"It was nothing," Jeannie said, then swiped at her eyes. "This whole reunion has me, like, all emotional. It's either that or I'm PMSing."

Melanie laughed, then exited the car, promising Jeannie a free nonfat, noncaf coffee any time she wanted it. As Jeannie drove away, Melanie dug in her clutch purse for the keys to the shop. The entire downtown strip was silent, all the businesses locked up for the night, including Cuppa Life. Melanie let herself in, then turned on one light in the back of the shop. She made some decaf, poured a cup, then sank into Cooter's favorite armchair, kicking her high heels to the side.

The bell over the door jingled and Melanie leaped to her feet, half expecting Cade. Cooter stuck his familiar head inside the door. "You serving coffee?"

She chuckled. "Only decaf. Technically I'm closed. But I'd be glad to get you a cup."

"I could use it. A man my age has trouble sleeping. I decided to take a walk, see if some fresh air might bring on Mr. Sandman but I think he left for the Bahamas." Cooter slipped onto one of the bar stools, thanking Melanie for the mug she slid his way. "You take care of that dog yet?"

It took her a second to figure out what he meant. "Sort of."

"Is it still hurtin'?" He watched her over the rim of the mug.

*Did it still hurt?*

Absolutely. Ten times more than the day she'd walked out on Cade. Now, the end of their relationship was truly final. She almost wished they hadn't had this week together because it had made that last goodbye nearly unbearable. "Yeah," she said. "It hurts."

"Then why the hell are you still eatin' the mulch?" He took another gulp of coffee, then tipped his hat her way as he stood. "You have a good night now, Mrs. Matthews."

When Cooter was gone, Melanie lingered at the counter for a long time, thinking about what he'd said. She busied herself with straightening the shop, wiping tables that didn't need to be wiped. Going home to her empty apartment was too depressing of a thought.

The bell jingled again. Melanie, in the middle of drying Cooter's mug, called out. "We're closed."

"Did you mean what you said back there?"

Melanie wheeled around, nearly dropping the wet, slippery mug. "Cade."

"Did you mean what you said on the stage?" he persisted. His bow tie was undone, along with the top button of his shirt, his jacket probably back in the car. He looked tired and yet, at the same time, determined. And yet, as always, he stopped her heart.

"About what?"

"About us finding a common place, even if our paths have diverged?"

Melanie looked at the man she had loved more than half her life. She wanted to say yes, but couldn't. If there'd been common ground for her and Cade, she had missed it.

"You know speeches," she said, a burning behind her eyes so fierce, she had to blink it away, "you make up stuff that sounds good on paper."

He crossed to the counter, then slipped behind it, once again seeming to consume the space between them. "I don't believe you."

She stepped back, surprised by the strength in his words. "Cade, I told you it was over."

"I heard you. And I'm not giving up that easily. I let you walk out a year ago and I didn't put up a fight. I kept thinking you'd be back. You needed a little time and then you'd change your mind. But you didn't come back. If anything, you got further away from me—from us. And if I let you walk away again, I'd be a fool."

She put the mug on the counter, then wrapped her arms around her waist to keep from wrapping them around him. "I saw the list, Cade. I saw what you expect out of me."

"The list?" It took a moment before the light dawned in his eyes. "That wasn't what you thought. It was—"

"No, Cade." She put up a hand to stop him. "I know you. You talked a good game to me this week about *my* goals and *my* dreams, even complimented me on the shop, but all you really want is for me to go back home and play housewife while you go out and conquer the world."

"You don't really think that, Mel. I don't want to lock you in the house with an apron."

She tossed down the dish towel. "How the hell do you know what I think? You barely know me, Cade."

He scowled. "That's not true. I know you better than you know yourself."

"Then you should have known the last thing I

wanted was to have more children." She exited the kitchen, around the counter and out into the coffee shop, grabbing her shoes and slipping them back onto her feet.

Cade followed, grabbing her arm to make her stop and face him. "That's not what the list was about, Melanie. It wasn't a list of what I wanted for the future, it was a list of things we needed to talk about. And while we're on the subject, what would be so bad about having another child? We always wanted more than one."

"No, Cade. *You* wanted more than one. I wanted a life after I was done raising Emmie. I had her so young, I never got to do anything." Melanie shoved her feet into her shoes, ignoring the pinch at her toes. "I was in that damned apartment all day long, changing diapers, heating bottles and watching my life pass by in a blur of play dates and dirty laundry. And what about you?" She flung out her hand, indicating an imaginary globe, a world that had spun past her, while Cade circled it day after day for his clients. "You were off, traveling the country, enjoying fancy lunch meetings, interacting with *grown-ups,* while the little wife was at home singing along with Big Bird." She drew in a breath, calming the flare of anger in her chest. "I love Emmie, don't get me wrong, and I wouldn't have undone those years with her for a million dollars. But I also—"

She broke off the words and turned away, the tears no longer hiding behind her eyes, but streaming forward, down her cheeks, a burst watershed.

"Also what?" he asked, his voice gentle, concerned.

She shook her head, mute.

"What, Mel?" Cade asked again, tipping her chin up until her gaze met his. "Tell me. *Please.*"

"I resented her," she said finally, the words cracking as the truth exploded from her, coated with guilt that any mother could ever feel that way. "And I resented you. I was *eighteen,* Cade, and my whole life was over. That wasn't the way it was supposed to be."

"You don't think I thought the same thing, honey?" His voice was as ragged as hers, the hurt, the blown chances, all shattering in his words. "I went to work for my father, and stayed there, because a man provides for his family. He doesn't run off on some silly notion that he could be an artist or a musician. He *provides,* Mel. Whether he likes it or not." He drew in a breath, his eyes closing for a second. "I resented the way our lives turned out, too, but I was afraid to say anything."

"Because a man doesn't show weakness, either," Melanie finished, adding another of the lessons Jonathon Matthews had drilled into his sons' heads. No wonder Cade had always been Can-Do, and especially Can-Do Alone. He'd been brought up to shoulder all the weight and never, ever admit a weakness.

"Do you know why I picked apart your coffee shop idea that day?"

She shook her head.

"Because I stood here, in this very space, hearing you talk about your idea for a coffee shop, and all I could think of was how jealous I was of you."

A plane flew overhead, the muted sound of the engine cutting between them for a moment. "Jealous? You? Of what?"

"You knew what you wanted, Melanie, and exactly how you were going to get it. All of a sudden, you had freedom. Choice. I realized I had spent twenty years at my father's law firm and never *ever* felt what I saw in your face that day." He gripped her hands, his touch warm and secure. "After I worked with you this past week, I realized I couldn't go back to law again. So…I quit my job."

The words hit her with surprise. "You quit working for your father? You mean so you can go work for another firm, right?"

"No, I quit law altogether."

If there'd been a game show with the question "what would Cade be most likely to do?" Melanie would have never guessed that. Cade had been more driven and committed to his career than anyone she'd ever known. "But you love what you do."

Cade's gaze met hers, seeing in her green eyes the distance that still existed between them and the price he had paid—they all had paid—for a career he'd never truly enjoyed. "No, I don't. Corporate law was my father's dream. Not mine."

Melanie shook her head, confused. "But you never said anything. You put in all those hours and spent all those weekends at work. Why would you do that if you didn't even like law?"

Cade sank into one of the armchairs, then waited as Melanie took the one opposite. "In my family, you don't complain. You do your job, you do it well and then you come back for more the next day. One day turns into another, and before you know it, years have gone by." He paused and let out a heavy sigh. Finally admitting he was done with practicing law had released a twenty-year-old weight from his chest. For the first time ever, he wondered what was around the corner of his future. "I wish I could have a do-over for those years. I never meant to let the job take over our lives. I never meant to become my father. I looked at him the other day and saw what that life has cost him. He's given up everything, probably because he was afraid of being hurt again, because my mother leaving really did a number on him." Cade shook his head, knowing it might be too late for his father to realize there was a life waiting for him, but it wasn't too late for Cade. For Cade and Melanie. "I won't use work as a wall anymore. And I won't let that become me."

For nineteen years, they had argued about his hours, about her frustration that he'd never been there for the important moments. That his father had gotten more of Cade than Melanie and Emmie ever did.

But now, Melanie understood her husband in ways she hadn't before. She looked around the room and realized she and her husband had more in common than she'd thought. "I get it now, Cade. After a year of running my own business, I've seen how easily work can consume a person. In my case, it's because I'm pretty much everything from bookkeeper to bottle washer. I haven't had time to get a manicure, much less have a relationship. You become so immersed in the job, you forget to live, too."

He nodded, and that thread of understanding between them twisted and thickened into a rope. "And here I went into law because I thought it would *build* the relationship I'd never had with my father. Somehow please the unpleasable Jonathon Matthews. I thought he'd look at me someday and tell me I'd done the right thing. But mostly, I did it because I hoped working in his firm would give us time together. Something we never had when I was a kid."

"And it didn't," Melanie said, already knowing how much Jonathon and Cade had worked, their endless schedules leaving no room for recreation or building a bridge between father and son. She reached out, laid a hand on Cade's arm, knowing from her own childhood how much a person could still crave that parental relationship even when they were long past the age of wanting cookies and conversation after school. "I'm sorry, Cade."

He shrugged. "I guess I pictured us going on these father-son fishing trips or some such idiotic fantasy. But we never did. Dad worked as much as he always had, if not more. And I—" he let out a breath "—I fell into the same trap. What's worse, I *became* the very person I didn't want to be. I worked too much, I saw you and Emmie too little, and in the end, it cost me everything that really mattered." He reached for her hand and squeezed it. "I'm sorry, Melanie."

But the apology wasn't necessary, not anymore. She held onto that rope of understanding, wondering if maybe it was enough to hold them together. "Cade, that's how you are. You're a Type-A. Success at all costs. I can't blame you for that. Besides, part of it was my fault, too."

He blinked. "Your fault? You didn't make me go to work."

"No, but I didn't speak up, either," she said, finally being honest with herself and with him. It had been far too easy all these months—heck, all these years— to just blame Cade, instead of face her own shortcomings. "I realized that tonight, on the stage, when I almost agreed with Jeannie's plan, even when it wasn't what I wanted to do. I'm a yes-man, or woman." She let out a bitter chuckle. "And I was in our marriage, too. I argued about the missed soccer games and the dinners that got cold, but I never told you how much it hurt me that you were gone. I just went with it all, yes-ing it to death."

"Until last year."

She looked away, her gaze filling with tears. "Yeah, until then."

But he moved closer, undaunted, invading her space, forcing her to look at him. "Why can't we fix that, Melanie? If I'm not working myself to death, and you're not saying it's all okay when it's not, then why can't we fix it?"

"Because it wasn't just about the hours, Cade. There was more than that."

He threw up his hands in frustration. "What more? All I want is for you and I to love each other. For you to be there when I wake up in the morning. I'll do whatever it takes, Melanie, to make this marriage work."

"I *can't* go back to that," she said, rising, her voice choked with tears. The idea of being with Cade again was far too enticing, too easy to fall back into. But if she did, if she returned to his bed, his arms, she knew she'd be unhappy. Maybe not tomorrow or next week, but someday, she'd end up in the same place as before. As much as she had dreamed of returning to what they'd had, she realized now the problem was partly that—what they'd had, even in those early years, hadn't been working. "I lost myself in our marriage. When I slipped that ring on my finger, I expected you to complete me, or something like that. And I thought I would do the same for you. Like some big happy Hollywood ending."

His gaze searched hers, regret shining in those familiar blue depths. "But we didn't find that happy ending, did we?"

"No." She smoothed a hand down her dress. "For twenty years, I invested all my energies into making sure you and Emmie were happy, and in the process, I forgot who I was. I lost the things that mattered to me."

"I never wanted that, Melanie. All I wanted was for you to be happy." His shoulders dropped. "I thought you were."

"I know," she said, softer now. "I don't know if it was because we married too young or if I just let myself get swept up in some fairy tale that wasn't real. It was like our marriage was this delicate crystal ball and I was afraid to tip it or add anything to it, in case it broke." She paused, drawing in a breath, feeling her stomach expand against her palms, knowing she had to hit on that nerve someday or it would keep hurting. "Then, we lost the baby—" The word tore out of her throat, raw and painful over a year later.

Tears shimmered in his eyes, and Melanie reached

for him, sharing that loss in a connected touch. Clearly their loss was still an unhealed wound on both sides. Cooter's words of wisdom came back to her.

*Get smart enough and you'll stop doing stupid things that hurt you.*

Like never talking about the night that had formed the final fracture in their marriage. Like never realize her husband had been as stricken by that loss as she had. She saw it in his eyes, in the hunch of his shoulders, the lines in his face. "Cade, I'm sorry," she said, her voice cracking, "so sorry we lost the baby. And I'm sorry we drifted apart after that, when we should have come closer together."

His eyes met hers, clouded by unshed tears. "All I did was work even more than before. I kept thinking that it would help me get over losing the baby, but it didn't. And…"

"What?" Melanie said, soft, easy.

He let out a sigh. "I thought if I avoided you, we wouldn't have to talk about it."

"I did the same thing." She shook her head at the irony of their common thinking, which had done nothing to build commonality. "Avoiding the problem only made it worse."

He took her hands in his, thumbs tracing the lines of her fingers. "And when you started talking about opening your own business, all I saw was that I was losing you, too."

"We should have talked," she said, wondering how it might have been different and whether they could have headed off the twists and turns that had followed. They probably should have talked from day one, about the important things, but they'd been young and their marriage hadn't come with a manual. "I guess I thought we'd been together so long, we should have been able to read each other's minds."

"I can't even remember other people's names," Cade said, that familiar grin on his face. "And you thought I could read your mind?"

She chuckled, glad for the moment of levity. "True."

Then he sobered, his gaze going to their connected hands for a moment before meeting hers. "Do you still think it's too late?"

She turned away, swiping at the tears that began to run down her face as her mind flashed the past year in front of her. "I don't know."

"What happened to you that night, Melanie?" Cade's voice was as gentle as his touch, his eyes dark with empathy and regrets. "We tried for so long to have another child, and then after the miscarriage, you wouldn't even talk about the subject again. You changed."

"No, I realized who I really was." She didn't bother to stem the flow of tears anymore, nor the guilt that had racked her soul for months. "It wasn't just me. Where were you, Cade? Because you weren't there for me. I needed you, but you were gone."

"San Francisco." Cade closed his eyes. "I was in San Francisco."

She leaned against the cushions, her mind rocketing back. Cade, out of town—again—and her hurrying to make it to the dry cleaners before they closed so that she'd have his shirts ready for him when he came home. Emmie in the car, arguing with her mother about something that was unimportant five seconds later. Just enough distraction for Melanie to look left when she should have looked right—to see the SUV running a red light.

She'd woken up in a hospital, the doctor shaking his head, Emmie crying in the chair beside the bed and Cade, unreachable because he'd turned off his cell phone during a meeting with a client.

"I'm sorry, Melanie." Cade drew his wife into his arms, repeating the words over and over, until his voice grew hoarse and the apology finally sank in, a salve for the wounds of the last months. "I'm sorry I wasn't there. I'm sorry I couldn't stop it from happening."

"And then—" She went on, her breath hitching in her throat. She couldn't stop to absorb his touch, his soothing voice. She had to say it and say it now or she never would. "—when the doctor said the accident had done too much damage to my body, you said we could adopt. We'd find a way." She shook her head, thinking of how she had failed, how she couldn't set herself up for that ever again. "I couldn't do that, Cade. I had just inherited this place." She indicated the coffee shop, then faced her husband and the ugly thoughts that had run through her head that night. "And all I could think in that hospital room was how *relieved* I was. That I wasn't going to be tied down. I was free to do what I wanted." Her voice cracked and shattered, and the tears streamed down her cheeks, coupled with a clenching guilt that made her want to run from the room, to hide this other, awful Melanie from him. "What kind of wife feels that way? What kind of mother does that make me?"

"Oh, Melanie, you're entitled to want something for yourself." Cade captured her jaw with his hand.

"Even at the cost of my marriage? No, Cade, I don't agree." She met his gaze, and knew that a lot of things may have changed in the past year—except for one. "I love you, Cade," she said finally, admitting the truth to herself as much as to him, "I always have. But you deserve a woman who wants the same things as you do." She rose, pulling away from him, even as her heart broke with the distance. "Please, just let me go."

"Why? Because you don't want to have more kids? That's not a crime, Mel. And besides—" at that, he grinned "—I'm getting a little old to be chasing after a toddler. I'd much rather chase after you."

The words took a moment to sink in. "You don't want more children?"

"I want *my wife*. My marriage," Cade said. "I meant what I said before. All I've ever wanted is you and Emmie."

"But—"

"Another child would have been a blessing, don't get me wrong. But what would my life be like if I lost you in the process?" His gaze sought hers, holding her there as surely as he'd held her in his arms earlier that night.

"You aren't mad? Disappointed?"

"No, not at all," he said, getting to his feet and pulling her to his chest. She leaned into his touch, feeling as if she'd stepped back in time, to the days when all she'd had to do was love Cade and the rest worked itself out. "I love Emmie and I love you, and if that's all we ever have, that's okay with me."

"But I thought…" Her voice trailed off as this new information filtered in and changed her image of her marriage. Her husband. Suddenly she didn't want to go back to the way it used to be.

She wanted to see what tomorrow would hold. What this new, and older, Cade and Melanie would be like.

"We both thought we knew what the other wanted. Maybe it's because we met when we were so young. Or maybe because everyone called us the perfect couple. Even perfect people screw up, Mel," Cade said. "And neither of us realized what we were missing until what we wanted most was gone."

"Or when it came back," she said, a smile turning her mouth up, filling the empty spaces in her heart. She ran her hands down his back, feeling the strength in his muscles, the solidity of this man. The only man she'd ever loved. "And insisted on manning the cappuccino machine."

He chuckled. "I haven't been all that good about being there for you before, but I'd like to try, if you'll give me the chance."

She considered his words, meeting the same familiar blue eyes she'd known since kindergarten, loved since high school. "That depends."

"On what?"

Her smile widened. "On whether you know how to latte."

"Sounds kinda kinky," he said, grinning.

"Oh, it is, Cade, it is." Then she kissed him, and realized everything she needed for the perfect brew was already in her arms.

# EPILOGUE

CADE AND MELANIE STOOD at the makeshift altar, hands clasped, waiting while the preacher finished his sentence. "I now pronounce you husband and wife. Again." Reverend Martin grinned, then gestured between them. "You may kiss your bride."

"And you may kiss your husband," Cade murmured to Melanie, just before he took her in his arms and revisited another memory.

Behind them, the room erupted in applause and a couple of catcalls. Melanie turned, her face aflame, and laughed. It seemed half the city of Lawford had shown up—and maybe it had, at least the western side. Several of the university students, and even Cooter, stood inside Cuppa Life Deux, the second location in the beginning of what Cade and Melanie hoped would become a franchise. Instead of a ribbon cutting, Cade had suggested a very different ceremony to christen the new location.

"Are you ready, Mrs. Matthews?" he whispered in her ear.

"Ready for what?" Every day with Cade had been an adventure, and she had learned to adapt with this newer, funner man who now shared her business and her life. He'd quit the law firm, opting to spend his days beside Melanie instead. They worked well together, which had given Emmie not only the satisfaction of being right, but enough extra time off to pursue what had become a very intense romance with Liam.

"For a new future."

She nodded, taking her bouquet from her beaming daughter, then strode down the narrow, short aisle, peppered with coffee filters cut out in the shape of flowers.

As they reached the end, Ben gave her a congratulatory hug, his eyes misty. "I'm glad things are going well for you," he said.

"And for you," Melanie replied, smiling at his wife, standing beside him.

"Glad to see you put that dog out of his misery," Cooter said, ambling up to the group.

Cade and Melanie smiled at him, knowing his wisdom—albeit offbeat and often hidden in weird metaphors—had been part of what brought them back together. Cade drew his wife to his side, unable to stop from kissing her again. All this renewal of vows had him feeling as in love as the day he'd first said, "I do."

"If you're done doing what you're doing," Cooter said, indicating the preacher and the altar, "I'd like to try one of those fancy lattes you two keep talking about."

Cade and Melanie exchanged a glance that erupted into laughter. They'd learned how to latte all right, and had plans to keep on doing it.

"Jeez Louise," Cooter muttered as the couple kissed again. "What's a man gotta do to get a cup of coffee around here?"

"Marry the owner," Cade murmured in his wife's ear. "But be sure you win over her heart *and* her espresso machine."

Melanie laughed. The perfect ingredients for her life, her happiness, were all right here. Emmie, the shop, and most of all, Cade.

# REUNITED: MARRIAGE IN A MILLION

## LIZ FIELDING

*For Barb and Jackie, my companions, on the journey—it was a joy working with you. And for Liz and Gil, who did the actual pedalling.*

**Liz Fielding** was born with itchy feet. She made it to Zambia before her twenty-first birthday and, gathering her own special hero and a couple of children on the way, lived in Botswana, Kenya and Bahrain—with pauses for sightseeing pretty much everywhere in between. She finally came to a full stop in a tiny Welsh village cradled by misty hills and these days mostly leaves her pen to do the travelling.

When she's not sorting out the lives and loves of her characters, she potters in the garden, reads her favourite authors and spends a lot of time wondering, 'What if...?'

For news of upcoming books—and to sign up for her occasional newsletter—visit Liz's website: www.lizfielding.com.

'THE car is here. Your paparazzi army are forming their usual guard of honour.'

Ivo was waiting, his face expressionless. Waiting for her to back down, tell him that she wouldn't go, and Belle had to fight back the treacherous sting of tears.

She didn't cry, ever.

Why couldn't he understand? Why couldn't he see that she hadn't chosen to spend twelve days cycling over the Himalayas on some whim?

This was important to her. Something she needed to do.

By demanding she drop out at a moment's notice to play hostess at one of his power-broking weekends at his country house in Norfolk, he was making it plain that nothing—not her career, certainly not some charity stunt—was as important as being his wife.

That he had first call on her.

If only she could have told him, explained. But if she'd done that, he wouldn't want her to stay...

'I have to go,' she said.

For a moment she thought he was going to say something, but instead he nodded, picked up the heavy rucksack that contained everything she would need for the next three weeks and reached for the door handle.

By the time the door was open, Belle was wearing a smile for the cameras. She paused briefly on the step with Ivo at her side, then they made their way to the car.

The chauffeur took the rucksack and, while he was stowing it, Ivo took her hand, looked down at her with grave eyes that never betrayed what he was thinking.

'Look after yourself.'

'Ivo…' She stopped herself from begging him to come to the airport with her. 'I'll be passing through Hong Kong on my way home. If you happened to find you had some business there, maybe we could take a few days…'

He made no comment—he never made promises he could not keep—but simply kissed her cheek, helped her into the car, repeating his directive to 'take care' before closing the door. She turned as the car pulled away, but he was already striding up the steps to the house, wanting to get back to work.

The chauffeur stopped at the airport drop-off point, loaded her bag on to a trolley, wished her good luck, and then she was alone. Not alone, as a woman with a loving husband waiting at home might feel.

Just…alone.

# CHAPTER ONE

'...SO THAT'S it for Day Nine of the Great Cycling Adventure. Tomorrow I'm told it's going to be "a gentle, undulating rise"...' Belle Davenport wiped away a trickle of sweat on her sleeve and smiled into the camera. 'These guys really have a sense of humour. If seeing me sweating and in pain in a good cause is making you feel good, feel bad, feel anything, please remember any donation you make, no matter how small, will make a real difference...'

Belle Davenport wrapped up for the camera, hit send and, as soon as she'd got a reply confirming it had been safely received, unplugged her satellite phone. It was only then that she realised that what she had thought was sweat was, in fact, blood.

'You do know that he brought you down quite deliberately.' Claire Mayfield, an American sharing her tent, as well as her pain, was outraged.

'He helped me up again,' Belle pointed out.

'Only after he'd taken pictures. You should make a complaint to the organisers. You could have been seriously hurt.'

'No whining allowed,' she said, then winced as Simone Gray—the third member of their group—having cleaned up the graze on her forehead, started to work on her grazed thigh.

'Sorry...nearly done.' Then, tossing the wipe away and applying a dressing, said, 'In this world, Claire, it isn't enough for the media that you're putting yourself through seven kinds of torture to raise money for street kids. They want you down in the dirt too.' Simone was executive editor of an Australian women's magazine. She knew what she was talking about.

'Glamour, excitement, sleazebags with cameras waiting to catch you with your face in the mud,' Belle confirmed, with a wry smile.

'In London, okay,' Claire persisted. Then, 'Actually, it's not okay, but I suppose in your business you learn to live with the intrusion. But halfway up the Himalayas?'

'Are we only halfway up? It feels higher.' Then, shaking her head, Belle said, 'Simone's right, Claire. It's all part of the game. No complaints. I've been at the top of my particular tree for a long time. I guess it's my turn to be set up as an Aunt Sally and knocked off.'

'Set up?'

'Put in a position where not to do it would have made me look mean-spirited, all mouth and no trousers, so to speak. The kind of television personality who encourages others to do the hard work while she sits back on the breakfast telly sofa, flashing her teeth and as much cleavage as the network can get away with at that time in the morning.'

'You're not like that.'

'No?'

'No!'

Belle had gone for 'arch', but found herself profoundly touched by Claire's belief in her.

'Well, maybe not this time,' she admitted, smiling to herself as she remembered just how easy it had been to manipulate the people who thought they were pulling the strings. 'It's amazing how far acting dumb will get you.'

'So…what? You really wanted to come?'

'Shh!' She lifted a finger to her lips. 'The walls of tents have ears.' She grinned. 'All it took was, "If we sent someone for this charity cycle ride it would make a great feature. Lots of opportunities to address a real problem. Get the public to join in with sponsorship." An idle, "Who could we send?", accompanied by just the tiniest shiver of horror at the thought, for the director to get ideas about how much the media would enjoy seeing me getting sweaty and dirty on a bike. The publicity it would generate. Got to think of those ratings…'

For Belle the pain was well worth the extra publicity it would generate for a cause dear to her heart, enabling her to support it publicly without raising any questions about why she cared so much.

Knowing that she was the one pulling the strings didn't take the sting out of her thigh, though. And out here, in the rarefied air of the mountains, spending her time with people who'd financed themselves, who were doing it without any of the publicity circus that inevitably surrounded a breakfast show queen putting herself at the sharp end of fund raising, she was beginning to feel like a fraud. The kind of celebrity who'd do anything to stay in the spotlight, the kind of woman who'd put up with anything to stay in a hollow marriage, because without them she'd be nothing.

She pushed away the thought and said, 'If you think this is about the children, rather than ratings, Claire, you are seriously overestimating the moral probity of breakfast television.'

It was the ratings grabbing report-to-camera straight from the day's ride—the never-less-than-immaculate Belle Davenport reduced to a dishevelled, sweaty puddle—that the company wanted and the media were undoubtedly relishing. Why else would they have sponsored one of their own to come along and take pictures? But after a week it seemed that honest sweat had got old; now they wanted blood and tears too.

Today they'd got the blood and no doubt that was the image that would be plastered over tomorrow's front pages and, when she got home, she'd shame them into a very large donation to her cause for that.

No way in hell were they going to get her tears.

She did not cry.

'That's…' Claire grinned. 'That's actually pretty smart.'

'It takes more than blonde hair and a well-developed chest to stay at the top in television,' Simone pointed out. Then, regarding her thoughtfully, she went on, 'So the street kids get the money, the spotlight on their plight, the television company get the ratings. What are you getting out of it, Belle?'

'Me?'

'You could have stayed at home, squeezing your viewers heartstrings, but you wanted to come yourself. You must have had a reason.'

'Apart from getting myself all over the newspapers looking like this?'

'You don't need publicity.'

'Everyone needs publicity,' she said, but her laughter had a hollow ring and neither of her two companions joined in. 'No, well, maybe I just wanted to feel good about myself. Isn't that why everyone does this kind of stunt?'

'If that's the plan,' Claire said, lying back on her bedroll with a groan, 'it isn't working. All I feel is sore.'

'Maybe the feeling good part kicks in later,' Belle replied sympathetically.

She knew she hadn't been the only one who'd gone through a three-ring circus to get here. No matter how much she hated it, she understood that even when the redtops had people digging in your dustbin for dirt they could use, it wasn't personal.

For Claire, though, a pampered princess with a token job working in her father's empire, the sniggering criticism had been just that. Deeply personal.

What the hell; they'd shown them. With a determined attempt at brightness, Belle continued, 'In the meantime I've lost weight, improved my muscle tone, gained some blisters…'

'No.'

She gave up on the distraction of her newly-defined calf muscles and caught something—a bleakness to Simone's expression that was new.

'What *have* you got out of this?' she demanded. 'Seriously.'

'Seriously?' She looked from Simone to Claire and realised they were both regarding her with a sudden intensity, that the atmosphere in the tent had shifted. Darkened.

'Seriously.' Belle took a deep breath. 'Seriously' meant confronting the truth. 'Seriously' meant having to do something about it. But, forget the publicity, forget the cameras—that was what this trip had been all about. Stepping out of her comfort zone. Putting herself out there. Doing something real. Except she wasn't, not really. She was still hiding. From the world. From her husband. Most of all from herself.

'You can see so far up here,' Belle began uncertainly. Not quite sure what she was going to say. Where this was going. 'When we stopped for that drinks break this afternoon, I looked back and you could see the road we'd travelled winding all the way back down to the valley.'

She faced the rangy Australian, the petite American, who shared her tent. They'd tended each other's grazes, rubbed liniment into each other's aching muscles, they'd eaten together, battling with chopsticks while vowing never to travel again without a fork in their rucksack. They'd laughed, ridden alongside each other since they'd found themselves sharing a cab from the airport to the hotel when they'd first arrived, each of them scared in a what-the-hell-am-I-doing-here? way, yet excited by the challenge they were facing. Outwardly, they were women who had everything and yet they'd seemed to recognise something in each other, some hidden need.

Instant soul mates, they had become true friends.

It was a new experience for Belle. She'd never had girl-friends. Not as a kid, struggling to survive, not in the care home, certainly not in the stab-in-the-back atmosphere of daytime television.

The media bosses, the tabloid hacks, the gossip mags, all used her to lift circulation in a way that made her sister-in-law curl her lips in disdain. And her husband, money-machine tycoon Ivo Grenville, whose eyes burned with lust—the only thing he was unable to control—despised himself for wanting her so much that he'd committed the ultimate sacrifice and married her.

None of them bothered to look deeper than the 'blonde bomb-shell' image that she'd fallen into by accident, to find out who she really was. Not that she blamed them. She wore her image like a sugar-coated veneer; only she knew how thin it was.

These two women, total strangers when they'd met a couple of weeks earlier, knew her better than most, had seen her at her most vulnerable, had shared their lives with her. All of them, on the surface, had everything; Claire was the daughter of one of the world's wealthiest men and Simone had risen to the top in a very tough business. But outward appearances could be deceptive. She'd been trusted with glimpses into their lives that few people had seen, which was why she knew that Claire and Simone would understand what she'd felt when she'd looked back down the road.

It was steep, hard going, and all the twists and turns were laid out before her—a metaphor for her life. Then, before the threatening crack became unstoppable, she let it go and said, 'How many more days is this torture going to last?'

'Three,' Simone said quickly, apparently as anxious as she was to step back from a yawning chasm that had opened up in front of them.

'Three? Can I survive three more days without a decent bed, clean sheets?' Claire asked.

'Without a hot bath.'

'Without a manicure,' Belle added, apparently intent on examining her nails, but she was more interested in Simone's obvious relief that the moment of introspection that she herself had provoked had been safely navigated. Then, because actually her nails did look terrible, 'I'm going to have to have extensions,' she sighed.

Normally long, painted, perfect, she'd trimmed them short for the ride, but now they were cracked, dry, ingrained with dirt that no amount of cold water would shift. As she looked at them, dark memories stirred and she curled her fingers into her palm, out of sight.

'What's the first thing you'll do when we hit that hotel in Hong Kong?' she asked.

'After I've run a hot bath?' Claire grinned. 'Call room service and order smoked salmon, half a ton of watercress served with dark rye bread cut wafer-thin and spread with fresh butter.' Then, as an afterthought, 'And chocolate fudge cake.'

'I'll go along with that and raise you ice-cold champagne,' Belle added, grinning.

'The champagne sounds good,' Simone said, 'but I vote we pass on the healthy stuff and go straight for the chocolate fudge cake.'

'White chocolate fudge cake,' Belle said. 'And a hot tub to sit in while we eat it.'

'Er…that's a great idea,' Claire said, 'but won't your husband have ideas of his own in the hot tub department?'

'Ivo?' Belle found herself struggling to keep the smile going.

'He *is* coming to meet you?'

For a moment she allowed herself that fantasy; that she'd reach the end of the journey and he'd be there, scooping her up into his arms. Carrying her off to a luxury suite to make hot sweet love to her.

With the slightest shake of her head, she said, 'No.' About to make some excuse for him—pressure of business was always a safe one—she found she couldn't do it. 'To tell you the truth,' she said, 'I'm in the marital doghouse.' With the smallest gesture she took in their cramped surroundings. 'He didn't want me to do this.'

'You're kidding?' Claire frowned. 'I thought he was so supportive. I've seen pictures of you guys in those lifestyle magazines. The way he looks at you. The way it reads, you have the perfect marriage.'

'You mean captions like… "Breakfast television's bombshell, Belle Davenport, ravishing in Valentino, arriving at a royal gala last night with her millionaire businessman husband, Ivo Grenville."?'

They always printed one of her arriving—that moment when she leaned forward as Ivo helped her from the car. The one that never failed to catch the look of a man who couldn't wait to get her home again, feeding the fantasy that had grown around them after their 'couldn't wait' runaway marriage on a tropical island.

At least the looks were real enough. His desire was the one thing she'd never doubted. As for the rest…

'I'm sorry to disappoint you, but I'm the original one hundred per cent genuine trophy wife.' The bitter words spilled out of her before she could stop them. The only difference was that he hadn't dumped a long-serving first wife for her; on the contrary, she was the one who'd be dumped when he wanted a proper wife. The kind you had kids and grew old with. 'He was throwing a shooting party last weekend on his estate in Norfolk. A business thing. He wanted me on show. The hostess with the mostest.' She pulled a face. 'I don't have to explain what I've got the most of, do I?' she said as, hand behind her head, she leaned forward, giving the girls a mock cupcake cleavage pose.

'You've got a lot more than that,' Simone chipped in. 'Holding down a job in television takes a lot more than a perfect pair of D cups. And the kind of party you're talking about takes a serious amount of organising.'

'Not by me.'

Her sister-in-law, Ivo's live-in social secretary and a woman with more breeding than a pedigree chum, handled all that. But then she had been born to it. Benendon, finishing school in Switzerland, the statutory Cordon Bleu, Constance Spry courses for the girls-in-pearls debutantes. Another world…

'I'm just there for display purposes to show his business competitors that there isn't a thing they can do that he can't do better.'

'Oh, Belle…' Claire seemed lost for words.

Simone was more direct. 'If that's all there is to your marriage, Belle, why do you stay with him?'

'Honestly?' They were high in the Himalayas, the air was stingingly cold, clear, cleaner than anything she'd ever known. Anything but the truth would pollute it. 'For the security. The safety. The knowledge that, married to him, I'll never be hungry or cold or frightened ever again…'

The truth, but not the whole truth. Passion, security, she would admit to. Falling in love with him had been the mistake…

'But you're bright, successful in your own right—'

'Am I?' She shrugged. 'From the outside I suppose it looks like that, but every day of my life I expect someone to find me out, expose me as a fraud…' Simone made a tiny sound, almost of distress, but shook her head quickly as Belle frowned. 'Let's face it, there's no one as unemployable as a past-her-sell-by-date breakfast television host.' Even as she said it, she knew that she was just making excuses. She was not extravagant and with Ivo's skilful investment of her money, the only thing she truly needed from him was the one commodity he was unable to give. Himself.

There was an emotional vacuum at the heart of her life that had started long before she'd met him. He was not the only one incapable of making a wholehearted commitment to their part-nership. She was equally to blame and now it was time to call it a day. Make the break. Let him go.

She'd known it for a long time, just hadn't had the courage to admit it, face up to what that would mean.

'If you want the unadorned truth,' she said, 'I hate my career, I hate my marriage—'

Not that she blamed Ivo for that. He was trapped by his hormones in exactly the same way that she was trapped by her own pitiful fears. They were, it occurred to her, very bad for each other.

'In fact, when it comes right down to it, I hate my life.' She thought about it. 'No, scrub that. I guess I just hate myself—'

'Belle, honey…'

As they reached out to offer some kind of comfort, she shook her head, not wanting it. Not deserving it from these special women. 'I've got a sister somewhere, back there. Lost on the road.' She didn't have to explain. She knew they'd understand that she wasn't talking about the road they were travelling together, but the one leading back to the past. 'I haven't seen her since she was four years old.'

'Four?' Claire frowned. 'What happened to her? Did your family split up?'

'Family?' She gave a short laugh. 'I'm not like you…' She sucked in her breath, trying to hold back the words. Then, slowly she finished the sentence. 'I'm not like you, Claire.' She glanced at Simone, who was unusually quiet, and on an impulse she reached out, laid a hand over hers. 'Or Simone.' Then, lifting her chin a little. 'We're here to raise money for street kids, right? Well, that was me. It's why I made such a big thing of this fund raiser. Why I'm here.' Feeling exposed in the way an alcoholic must feel the first time he admitted he had a problem, she said, 'My real name is Belinda Porter and I was once a street kid.'

She'd never told anyone where she'd come from. Anything about herself. On the contrary, she'd done everything she could to scrub it out of her mind. Not even Ivo knew. He'd had the tidied-up fairy story version of her life: the one with kindly foster parents—who she'd conveniently killed off in a tragic car accident— a business course at the local college—not the straight from school dead-end job in a call centre. Only the lucky break of being drafted in to work the phones on the biggest national fund raising telethon had been true, but then she'd been 'discovered' live on air; everyone knew that story.

How could she blame him for a lack of emotional commitment to her when she had kept most of her life hidden from him? A husband deserved more than that.

She swallowed. 'My mother, my sister, the three of us begged just to live,' she said. 'Exactly like the children we're here to help.'

For a moment no one spoke.

Then Claire said, 'What happened to her, Belle? Your sister.'

That was it? No shrinking away in horror? Just compassion? Concern…?

She shook her head. 'Nothing. Nothing bad. Our mother died.' She shook her head. That was a nightmare she'd spent years trying to erase. 'Social Services did their best, but looking back it's obvious that I was the kind of teenage girl who gives decent women nightmares. Our mother was protective, would have fought off a tiger to keep us from harm, from the danger out there, but I'd seen too much, knew too much. I was trouble just waiting to happen. Daisy was still young enough to adapt. And she was so pretty. White-blonde curls, blue eyes. Doll-like, you know? A social worker laid it out for me. It was too late for me but, given a chance, she could have a real family life.'

'That must have hurt so much.'

She looked up, grateful for Claire's intuitive understanding of just how painful it had been to be unwanted.

'It's odd,' she said, 'because I was the one named after a doll. Belinda. Maybe it was some need in her to reach back to a time of innocence, hope.' She shook her head. 'It never suited me. I was never that kind of little girl.'

'You have the blonde hair.'

'Bless you, Claire,' she said with a grin, 'but this particular shade of blonde is courtesy of a Knightsbridge crimper who charges telephone numbers. She pulled on a strand, made a face. He's going to have a fit when he sees the state of it.'

She reached for the sewing kit. There was no hairdresser here and no wardrobe department to produce a clean, fresh pair of trousers for the morning. If she didn't stitch up the tear, her thigh would be flapping in the wind.

'Daisy was different,' she said, concentrating on threading a needle. 'I hated her so much for being able to smile at the drop of a hat. Smile so that people would want to mother her, love her.' Her hands were shaking too much and she gave up on the needle. 'I hated her so much that I let someone walk away with her, adopt her, turned my back on her. Lost her.'

'I lost someone, too.'

Claire, suddenly the focus of their attention, gave an awkward little shrug. 'It must be this place, or maybe it's just that here life is pared down to the basics. The next marker, the next drink of water, the next meal. Meeting with the people who exist here on the bare essentials.' She took Belle's needle, threaded it, began to work on the torn trousers. 'There are no distractions, none of the day-to-day white noise of life to block out stuff you'd rather not think about and with nothing else to keep it occupied, the mind throws up stuff you've put in your memory's deep storage facility. Not wanted in this life.'

'Who did you lose, Claire?' Simone, pale beneath the tan that no amount of sun screen could entirely block in the thin air, almost whispered the words.

'My husband. Ethan. A decent, hard-working man…'

'I had no idea you'd been married,' Belle said.

Claire looked at her ringless hand, flexed her fingers, then with a little shiver said, 'As far as the world is concerned, it never happened. One messy little marriage discreetly dissolved with a stroke of a lawyer's pen.'

'It can't have been that simple.'

'Oh, you'd be surprised just how simple money can make things.' Then, 'In my defence, I was twenty-one years old and desperate to get away from my father. He isn't that easy to escape. He paid my husband to disappear and I was weak, I let him.'

'Twenty-one? You were practically a kid.'

Claire lifted her head, straightened her back. 'Old enough to have known better. To have been stronger.' Then, 'He's been on my mind a lot lately. Ethan. I guess it's all part of this.' Her gesture took in the tent, their surroundings. 'I work for my father, but as far as the rest of his staff are concerned I'm a joke, a pampered princess with a make-work job whose only concern is the next manicure, the latest pair of designer shoes. I came on this charity ride to shake up that image, to prove, to myself at least, that I'm better than that.'

'And finding Ethan would help?' Belle asked. 'He did take the money and run,' she pointed out.

'Why wouldn't he? I didn't do anything, say anything to stop him.' She shook her head. 'It would undermine a man's confidence, something like that, don't you think? I need to find him, make sure that he's all right.' She swallowed. 'More than that. I need him to forgive me. If he can find it in his heart to do that, then maybe I'll be able to forgive myself.'

Simone, who'd been increasingly quiet, covered her mouth with her hand to stifle a moan. 'Forgive yourself? Who will forgive me?' As Claire, all concern, reached out to her, took her hand, a sob escaped her and then it all came pouring out of her, like a breached dam. A story so terrible that it made Belle's own loss seem almost bearable.

For a heartbeat, after she'd finished her story, there was total silence as Simone waited, her eyes anticipating horrified rejection. As one, Belle and Claire put their arms around her, held her.

'I can't believe I told you that,' she said finally, when she could speak. 'I can't believe you still want to know me.'

'I can't believe you've kept it bottled up for so long,' Claire said tenderly.

'Some secrets are so bad that it takes something special for us to be able to find the words,' Belle said quietly. 'It seems that each of us needs to walk back a way, make our peace with the past.'

'This journey we're on isn't going to be over when we fall into a hot bath, crawl between clean sheets, is it?' Claire whispered. 'This has just been the beginning.'

'The easy bit.' Belle swallowed, feeling a little as if she'd just stepped off the edge of a precipice.

'But at least we won't be alone. We'll have each other.'

'Will we? You'll be home in America, Simone will be back in Australia and I'll be in England, looking for Daisy. She could be anywhere.' Then, 'I could be anywhere.'

Belle closed her eyes and for a moment the fear was so great that all she wanted to do was turn the clock back to the second before she stopped on the road and looked back. If she just kept facing forward, moving forward, she wouldn't see the demons snapping at her heels. Then, as if sensing her fear, Claire took one of her hands, Simone the other.

'It's not just Daisy I have to find,' she said, turning her hands to grasp them. 'I've been living behind this image for so long that I'm not sure who I am any more. I need to be on my own. To get away from all the pretence.'

'Belle…' Simone regarded her with concern. 'Don't do anything rash. Ivo could help you.'

She shook her head.

'I've used him as a prop for long enough. Some journeys you have to take alone.'

'Not alone,' Claire quickly assured her. 'You'll have us.'

'If you have to do this, Belle, we'll be there for you.' Simone straightened. 'For each other. Support, encouragement, a cyber-shoulder to cry on and with three time-zones we'll have 24/7 coverage!'

They both looked to Belle and the three of them clasped hands, too choked to speak.

Belle hadn't told anyone when to expect her. If she'd phoned ahead, the television company would have sent a car or Ivo's sister would have despatched the chauffeur to pick her up. But having made the decision to cut her ties with both marriage and job, it seemed hypocritical to use either of them.

Or maybe just stupid, she thought as she abandoned the endless queue for taxis and headed down into the underground to catch a train into London.

She'd have to turn up for work until her contract expired at the end of the month.

She pulled a face at this reminder that her agent—right now pulling out all the stops as he negotiated a new contract for her—was someone else she was going to have to face…who was never going to understand.

She wasn't sure she understood herself. It had all seemed so clear up in the mountains, so simple when she'd made that life-changing pact with Claire and Simone and they'd sealed it with their last bar of chocolate.

Back in London, faced with reality, she felt very alone and she shivered as, with a rush of air, the train pulled in to the station.

She climbed aboard, settled into a corner and automatically took out a book to avoid direct eye contact with the passengers opposite. Scarcely necessary. Who would recognise her, bundled up against the raw November chill, no make-up, her hair covered in a scarf twisted around like a turban to disguise the damage wrought by six weeks without the attention of her stylist?

How easily one slid from instantly recognisable celebrity to some woman no one would glance at twice on the underground.

Without the constant attention of those people whose job it was to polish her appearance, the lifestyle magazines, the safety net of her marriage, her career, who would she be?

What would it take for her to fall right off the face of civilisation, the way her mother had? One bad decision, one wrong turning and she, too, could be spiralling downward…

Fear crawled over her, prickling her skin, bringing her out in a cold sweat, and an urge to abandon all her grand ideals, crawl back into the comfort zone of the life she had and be grateful for it, overwhelmed her.

Daisy didn't need her.

In all likelihood she'd forgotten she even existed. What would be the point of selfishly blundering in, disturbing her doubtless perfect life with memories they'd all rather bury, just to ease her own conscience?

Wouldn't the selfless thing be to trace her, find out what she needed and help her anonymously, from a distance, the way she had always supported charities that helped street kids?

Daisy was nineteen, at university in all likelihood. She'd probably die of embarrassment to be confronted by a sister whose success was due solely to the size of her bosom, the huskiness in her voice.

Worse, once the press found out about her sister—and it was inevitable that they would—they'd keep digging until they had it all.

No teenager needed that and there were other ways to redeem herself. Daisy would need somewhere to live. She could fix that for her somehow. Ivo would know…

She caught herself.

Not Ivo. Her. She'd find out.

She exited from the underground station to the relative peace of Saturday morning in the capital before the shops had opened and was immediately confronted by a man selling *The Big Issue*—the badge of the homeless. She fought, as she always had to, the desperate urge to run away and instead forced herself to stand, take out the money to buy a copy of the magazine, shake her head when he offered her change. Wish him good luck before hailing a passing black cab and making her escape. Pushing away the thought that she could have done more.

The driver nodded as she leaned in to give her address. 'Welcome back, Miss Davenport.'

The immediate recognition was a balm, warming her, making her feel safe. 'The disguise isn't working, then?' she said, relaxing into a smile.

'You'd have to wear a paper bag over your head, miss.' Then, when she'd given him her address, climbed in the back, 'The missus'll be chuffed when I tell her I had you in the back. She's been following your bike ride. Sponsored you herself.'

'How kind. What's her name?'

She made a mental note so that she could mention her donation when she went back on air on Monday, chatted for a few minutes, then fished the cellphone out of her pocket and turned it on.

It hunted for a local network, then beeped, warning her that she had seventeen new messages.

'Please call…' from her agent.

'Please call…' from the director of her show. 'Please call… Please call…' The reassuring template messages of her life. And, just like that, the fear, never far below the surface, dissipated.

Smiling, she flicked the button to next and found herself reading, 'I wish you were my sister, Belle. Good luck. Hugs.' Not a template message, not business, but a 'care' message from Claire, sent before she'd boarded her own plane back to the States.

The next, from Simone, said, 'Are you as scared as me?' Scared? Simone? Brilliant, successful, practically perfect Simone who, like her, like Claire, had a dark secret that haunted her.

She'd left them in the departure lounge at the airport in Hong Kong and it had felt as if she was tearing off an arm to leave them. And now they'd reached out and touched her just at the point at which her resolve was on the point of crumbling. For a moment she was too shaken to move.

'We're here, Miss Davenport,' the driver said and she looked up, realised that the cab had stopped.

'One moment.' She quickly thumbed in her reply to Claire. 'I wish you were, too!'. True. If Claire were her sister she wouldn't be faced with this.

To Simone she began, 'We don't have to do this…' Except that wasn't what Simone wanted from her. What they'd all signed up to. She wanted, deserved, encouragement, the mutual support they'd promised each other. Not permission to bottle out at the first faint-heart moment from someone who was looking for an excuse to do the same.

A week ago in the clear, clean air of the Himalayas, in the company of two women who, for the first time in her adult life she'd been able to open up to, confide in, be totally honest with, she'd felt as if she'd seen a glimpse of something rare, something special that could be hers if only she had the courage to reach for it.

The minute she'd set foot in London, all the horrors of her childhood seemed to reach out from the pavement to grab at her, haul her back where she belonged and, terrified, she couldn't wait to scuttle back into the safety of her gilded cage, pulling the door shut behind her.

She looked at the phone and realised that whatever message she sent now, fight or flee, would set the course of the rest of her life.

She closed her eyes, put herself back in the place she'd been a few days ago, then wrote a new message.

*'Scared witless, but we can do this.' And hit send.*

A fine sentiment, she thought as she climbed from the cab and stood, clutching her rucksack, outside the Belgravia town house that had been her husband's family home for generations.

Now all she had to do was prove it.

# CHAPTER TWO

BELLE walked through the open front door and, if her heart could have sunk any lower, the view through the dining room doors to the chaos of caterers and florists in full cry would have sent it to her boots. She'd arrived in the middle of preparations for one of Ivo's power-broking dinners that her sister-in-law would be directing with the same concentration and attention to detail as a five-star general planning a campaign.

About to toss in the proverbial hand grenade, she kept her head down and headed straight for the library, where she knew she'd find her husband.

The fact that it was barely past nine o'clock on a Saturday morning made no difference to Ivo Grenville, only that he'd be working at home rather than at his office.

He didn't look up as she opened the door, giving her a precious few seconds to look at him, imprint the memory.

One elbow was propped on the desk, his forehead resting on long fingers, his world reduced to the document in front of him.

He had this ability to focus totally on one thing to the exclusion of everything else, whether it was acquiring a new company, a conversation in the lift with his lowliest employee, making love to his wife. He did everything with the same attention to detail, intensity, perfectionism. If, just once, he'd cracked, had an off-day like the rest of the human race, seemed *fallible*…

The ache in her throat intensified as, with a pang of tenderness she saw the dark hollows at his temple, a touch of silver that she hadn't noticed before threaded through the thick cowlick of dark hair that slid across his hand. He was tired, she thought. He drove himself too hard, working hours that would be considered inhuman if he'd expected his staff to emulate him, and she longed to be able to just go to him, put her arms around him, silently soothe away the stress...

Just be a wife.

He dragged his hand down over his face, long fingers pinching the bridge of his nose as, eyes closed, he gathered himself to continue.

Then, maybe remembering the sound of the door opening, he looked up and caught her flat-footed, without her defences in place.

'Belle?' He rose slowly to his feet, saying her name as if he couldn't believe it was her. Not that surprising. He'd never seen her looking like this before. The advantage of not sharing a bedroom with her husband was that he never saw her with morning hair, skin crumpled from a night with her face in a pillow. Definitely not in clothes she'd been travelling in for the better part of twenty-four hours, with nothing on her face to hide behind but a thin film of moisturiser. It was little wonder that for a moment he appeared uncharacteristically lost. 'I didn't expect you until tomorrow.'

Not exactly an accusation of thoughtlessness, but a very long way from expressing delight that she was home a day early.

'I switched to an earlier flight.'

'How did you get from the airport?' That was all the time it took him to gather himself, concentrate on the practicalities. 'If you'd called, Miranda would have sent the car.'

Not him, but his ever present, ever helpful little sister. Always there. As focused and perfect as Ivo himself. Too rich to have to bother with building a career, she was simply marking time until some man—heaven help him—who met her requirements in breeding, who was her equal in wealth, realised that she would make the perfect wife.

It was Miranda, not her, who was the chatelaine here, running her brother's social diary and his house with pinpoint precision. The person the staff looked to for their orders.

Who'd had a separate suite ready for her when they'd returned from their honeymoon so that her 4:00 a.m. starts wouldn't disturb Ivo.

That was the inviolable rule of the house. Nothing must be allowed to disturb Ivo.

Not even his wife.

Little wonder, Belle thought, that she'd always felt more like a guest here. Tolerated for the one thing she could give him that not even the most brilliant sister could deliver.

Even now she had to fight the programmed need to apologise for her lapse of good manners in arriving before she was expected. The truth was that she hadn't rung to tell Ivo the change to her schedule because to call would be to hope that just this once he'd drive down to Heathrow himself, join the crowd of eager husbands and wives waiting for that first glimpse of a loved one as they spilled out into the arrivals hall. Just as she'd hoped that he would, despite what she'd told Claire and Simone, fly to Hong Kong to meet her.

Her heart just wouldn't quit hoping.

But his momentary lapse from absolute certainty had given her the necessary few seconds to gather herself, restore the protective shell she wore to disguise her true feelings, and she was able to shrug and say, 'It seemed less bother to get the train. No,' she said quickly, as he finally abandoned his papers, stopping him before he could touch her, kiss her. 'I've been travelling for twenty-four hours. I'm not fit to be touched.'

For a moment he looked as if he might dispute that. For the second time she glimpsed a suggestion of hesitation, uncertainty. She was usually the one hovering on the edge of the unspoken word, afraid that the slightest hint of emotional need would bring the whole edifice of her marriage crashing down about her ears.

Outside, in the real world, wearing her Belle Davenport persona, she wasn't like that. She could play that part without thinking.

And at night, in the privacy of her room where, with one touch, the brittle politeness melted away, his distance dissolving in the heat of a passion that reduced their world to a population of two, it seemed anything was possible.

But afterwards there was no tenderness, no small talk about their day. He was not interested in her world, had no desire to discuss his own concerns with her. Felt no need to sleep with his arms around her, holding her close for comfort, but left her to her early morning alarm call while he, undisturbed, got on with his real life.

It was the role of wife—beyond the basics of the bedroom—that she'd never been able to fully master. But then, with Miranda immovably entrenched in every other aspect of the role, there had never truly been a vacancy for a wife. Only a concubine.

Hard as this was going to be, she knew it could not be as difficult as staying. 'Can we talk, Ivo?'

'Talk?' His frown was barely perceptible, but it was there. 'Now?'

'Yes, now.'

'Don't you want to sort yourself out? Take a shower?' He glanced back at his desk. He didn't have to say the words; it was plain that he had more important things to do.

'For heaven's sake, Ivo, it's Saturday,' she snapped, losing patience, needing to be done with this. Get it over. 'The stock markets are closed.'

'This isn't…' he began. Then, 'It'll take ten minutes, fifteen at the most.'

She'd been away for weeks. Any other man would have dropped whatever he was doing, eager to see her, talk to her, ask how she was, how it had been. Tell her that he was glad to have her home. If he'd done that, she thought, the words sitting like a lump in her throat would have dissolved, evaporated. She could not have said them. But for Ivo business always came first, while she was an inconvenience, a constant reminder of his one weakness…

'Why don't you go up? I'll be there just as soon as I've

finished this,' he suggested and, without waiting, he turned back to his desk. 'We can talk then.'

No. That wasn't how it worked. Not that he wouldn't come. Fifteen minutes from now she'd be in the shower and he'd join her there, demonstrating with his body, as he never could with words, exactly how much he'd missed her.

The only thing they wouldn't do was talk.

Afterwards, after the drugging pleasures of his body that would drive everything from her mind, she'd wake, as always alone—he'd have gone back to work—and there would be some trinket left at the bedside: something rare and beautiful, befitting her status as his wife, an acknowledgement that he'd been selfish, unreasonable about the Himalayan trip. She would wear whatever it was at dinner, a wordless acceptance of his unspoken apology.

Not today, she promised herself, her hand tightening around the tiny cellphone in her pocket—a direct connection to Simone, Claire. Women who knew more about her than her own husband. They'd spent every free minute of the last few days talking about their lives, the past, the future; they had listened, understood, cared about her in ways he never could. With them to support her she would find the strength to break out of the compartment he'd made for her. He might be satisfied with this relationship—and why wouldn't he be?—but she needed more, much more…

'No, Ivo.' Already, in his head, back with whatever project she'd interrupted, he didn't seem to hear her. 'I'm afraid it won't.' He stopped, turned slowly. 'Wait.'

His skin was taut across his face, emphasising the high cheekbones, the aristocratic nose, a mouth that could reduce her to mindless, whimpering jelly and, looking at him, Belle found it achingly hard to say the words that would put an end to her marriage.

He did nothing to help her but, keeping his distance, the tips of his fingers resting on the corner of his desk, a barrier between them, he waited, still and silent, for her to speak. It was almost, she thought, as if he knew what she was going to say. If so, he knew more than she did.

'This is difficult,' she began.

'Then…then my advice is to keep it simple.' His voice, usually crisp and incisive, was slightly blurred. Or maybe it was him that was blurred behind a veil of something she was very afraid might be tears.

'Yes,' she said, and blinked to clear her vision. No tears. She'd learned a long time ago not to show that kind of weakness. 'Yes,' she said again. This was not something that could be wrapped up in soft words. Somehow made less painful with padding. Simple, direct, to the point, with no possibility of misunderstanding. That was the way to do it. 'I'm sorry but I can't live with you any more, Ivo. I'm setting you free of our deal.'

'Free?'

'We said, didn't we, that it wasn't a till-death-us-do-part deal. That either of us could walk away at any time.' Then, when he did not respond, 'I'm walking away, Ivo.'

Predicting his reaction to such a bald announcement had been beyond her, but if she'd hoped that his cool façade would finally crack, she'd have been disappointed. There was no visible reaction. He looked neither shocked nor surprised, but then he'd made a life's work of being unreadable, keeping the world guessing. The fact that he could do it to her confirmed everything she had known about her marriage, but until last week had been too weak to confront.

His response, when it finally came, was practical rather than emotional. 'Where will you go?'

That was it?

Not, 'Why?' Or did he believe he already knew the answer to that? Assumed that the only reason she would leave him was because she'd found someone else? The thought sickened her…

'Does it matter?' she asked abruptly.

'Yes, it matters…' He bit off the words, shook his head. 'Manda will need to know where to forward your mail.'

On the point of saying something very rude about his sister, she stopped herself. This was not Miranda's fault. And she was not hiding from him, running away. Just distancing herself. For both their sakes. 'The tenants moved out of my flat last month,' she explained. 'I'll stay there.'

'That won't do—'

'It's what I want,' she cut in before he could take over and set about organising accommodation that he considered more acceptable for someone who bore his name.

He didn't look happy about it, but he let it go and said, 'Very well.' Then, 'Is that it?'

*No!*

Her heart cried out the word, but she kept her mouth closed and, getting no answer, he nodded and returned to his desk to resume the work she had interrupted.

Numb, frozen out, cut off by a wall of ice, she was left with nothing to do but pack her immediate needs and leave.

Miranda emerged from the dining room as she headed for the stairs.

'Belle? What are you doing here? I didn't expect you back until tomorrow.'

'It's lovely to see you too,' she said, without stopping, without looking back.

Ivo Grenville was staring blindly at the document in front of him when his sister, taking advantage of the door that Belle hadn't bothered to close on her way out, walked into the library.

'What's the matter with Belle?' she asked. Then, without waiting for an answer, 'Honestly, she might have had the good manners to let me know she was coming back today.'

'Why should she? This is her…' He faltered on the word 'home', but his sister was too busy waving his objection away with an impatient gesture to notice.

'That's not the point. Even if I can drum up another man for tonight, I'll have to totally rearrange the seating. And the caterers are going to—'

'No.'

'No? You mean she won't be joining us for dinner?' She relaxed. 'Well, thank goodness for that. To be honest, she did look a mess, but I've no doubt people would run around, pull out all the stops for her. One smile and people just fall over themselves—'

'No!' He so rarely raised his voice, and never to her, that she was shocked into silence. 'You won't have to rearrange the seating because tonight's dinner is cancelled.'

'Cancelled?' Her laugh, uncertain, died as she saw his face. 'Ivo…?' Then, 'Don't be ridiculous. I can't cancel this late. The Ambassador, the Foreign Secretary… What possible reason can I give?'

'I neither know nor care, but if you're stuck for an excuse why don't you tell our guests that my wife has just announced that she's leaving me and I'm not in the mood to make small talk. I'm sure they'll understand.'

'Leaving you? But she can't!' Then, flushing, 'Oh, I see. Who—'

'Manda, please,' he said, cutting her off before she could put into words the thoughts that had flashed through his mind. Thoughts that shamed him. Belle had never been less than forthright, honest with him. She'd wanted security; he'd wanted her…'Not another word.'

He heard the door close very quietly and finally he sat back, abandoning the documents that moments before he'd insisted were too important to wait. Nothing was that important but, in the instant when he'd looked up and seen Belle, he'd known what was coming. It was in her eyes, the look he'd been waiting for, dreading, had always known would one day come. Security, for a woman of such warmth, such passion, was never going to be enough.

His first thought had been to postpone it, delay it, do anything to give himself time.

Another hour. Another day…

Each and every day of his working life he took a few precious minutes out of his morning to watch her as she lit up the television screen in his office. Each day, while she'd been away, he'd seen the change in her, had felt her moving away from him, had recognised the danger. Maybe it had begun even before she'd left; he just hadn't wanted to see it. Maybe that was why he had tried so hard to stop her going on the trip.

He opened the desk drawer, pushing aside the ticket to Hong Kong, bought on the day he'd watched, agonised, as she'd talked into the camera, smiling even though there was blood trickling down her face. Plans he'd been forced to abandon when a crisis had blown up over a project he'd embarked upon.

He'd told himself that it didn't matter. That he would drive down to the airport and meet her flight. Give her the necklace he'd had made for her with the diamonds his mother had worn on her wedding day.

Wrong on both counts.

Belle didn't bother with the shower; she didn't want to spend one minute more than necessary in this house. What she did need were clothes, and since she was due back at work first thing on Monday morning that involved rather more than a change of underwear and a pair of jeans.

She stared helplessly at the dozens of outfits that had been carefully chosen to provoke the desire in the red-blooded male to wake up each morning to her presence on the television screen, the wish in every female breast to be her best friend.

It was a difficult trick to pull off. Between them, however, the designers and the image consultants had managed it. Everything about her that the public recognised as 'Belle Davenport', her life, her marriage, had been airbrushed so thoroughly that she'd forgotten what was real and what was little more than a media fabrication.

Maybe that was why, for so long, she had felt she was running on empty. That if she stopped concentrating for a second the floor would open up beneath her feet and she'd disappear.

Suddenly losing it, unable to keep up the pretence for another minute, she turned her back on them and tossed the bare essentials in a holdall—underwear, shoes, a few basics, the first things that came to hand.

What else? She looked around. Make-up...

She grabbed for a gold-topped glass pot but her hands were shaking and it slipped through her fingers, shattered, splashing pale beige cream in a wide arc over the centuries-old polished oak floor, an antique rug. With a cry of dismay, she bent to pick up the pieces of glass.

'Leave it!'

Ivo....

'Leave it,' he said, taking her hand, pulling it away from the glass. 'You'll cut yourself.'

Her skin shivered at his touch; his hand was cool and yet heat radiated from his fingers, warming her—as he never failed to warm her—so that the siren call of everything in her that was female urged her to let him lift her up into his arms, to hold him, tell him that she didn't mean it. That she would never leave him. That nothing else mattered but to be here with him.

He touched her cheek, then pushed back her hair to look at the graze on her forehead, regarding her with eyes the colour of the ocean, a shifting mix of blue, green, grey that, as with the sea, betrayed his mood. Today they were a bleak grey, her doing she knew, and she forced herself to turn away from his touch as if to gather up the rest of her make-up. It was easier to cope with his reflection in the mirror than face to face.

'Is this because I didn't want you to go away, Belle?' he asked, his hands on her shoulders, his thumbs working softly against the muscles, easing the tension as they had done times without number in a prelude to an intimacy that needed no words.

His touch shivered through her, undermining her will. She'd lingered too long. He'd taken it as a sign that she was just having a bit of a strop, throwing her teddy out of the pram, was waiting for him to come up and make a performance of appeasing her.

'No,' she said. That he didn't want her to go away was understandable, but she couldn't allow him to use her weakness to stop her from leaving. 'It's because we don't have a marriage, Ivo. We don't share anything. Because I want something you're incapable of giving.'

In the mirror she saw him blench.

'You're my wife, Belle. Everything I have is yours—'

'I'm your weakness, Ivo,' she said, cutting him short. This wasn't about property, security. 'You desire me. You have a need that I satisfy.'

'And you? Don't I satisfy you?'

'Physically? You know the answer to that.' When he held her, the flames of that desire were enough to warm her, body and soul. But when he turned away she was left with ice. 'You have given me everything that I asked of you. But what we have is not a marriage.'

'You're tired,' he said, his voice cobweb-soft against her ear. The truth was it didn't matter what he said, her response to his undivided attention had always been the same; she was a rabbit fixed in the headlights of an oncoming car, unable to move, save herself and her body responded as it always did, softening to him. He felt the change and, sure of his power, he turned her to face him. Instinct drew her to him and she leaned into the haven of his body, waiting for him to tell her that he'd missed her, to ask her what was wrong, to do what she'd asked and talk to her.

Instead he took something from his pocket. A strand of fire that blazed in the light as he moved to fasten it about her neck.

'I had this made for you for our anniversary next month.'

'It's not our anniversary…'

'The anniversary of the day we first met.'

Belle felt as if she were being split in two. The physical half was standing safe, protected, within the circle of Ivo's arms. But all of her that was emotion, heart, the woman who'd dug deep and, with the help of her friends, found the strength to confront her past, stood outside, looking on with horror as she was drawn in by this glittering proof that he had thought of her, cherished the memory of the moment when their lives had first connected.

'No…'

She barely whispered the word as the gems touched her throat. A single thread of diamonds to circle her neck. Beautiful.

Cold.

If his heart was a diamond, maybe he could have given her that. But the warm, beating flesh required more, something that was beyond him. That she had once thought was beyond her…

'Please, Ivo. Don't do this…'

It took a supreme act of will to force up her chin, look him directly in the face, find the strength to break free, for both of them.

'No,' she repeated, this time with more certainty. And, taking a step back, she brushed the necklace away, taking him by surprise so that it flew from his hand, skidded across the floor.

This wasn't about desire. Not for him. It wasn't even as basic as lust. This was all about control.

'No more.'

She took another step away, then turned and, abandoning her make-up, she picked up her bag, holding him at arm's length when, instinctively, he made a move to take it from her.

Only then, when she was sure he would keep his distance, did she turn, walk away on legs that felt as if they were treading on an underfilled airbed. On feet that didn't seem to be one hundred per cent in contact with the ground.

Every part of her hurt. It was worse than that first day on the mountains when she'd thought she'd die if she had to force her feet to push the pedal one more time.

That had been purely physical pain. Muscle, sinew, bone.

This cut to the heart. If she'd ever doubted how much she loved him, every step taking her away from him hammered the message home. But love, true love, involved sacrifice. Ivo had taken her on trust, had accepted without question everything she'd told him about her life before they'd met. Before she became 'Belle Davenport'. She'd done two utterly selfish things in her life—abandoned her sister and married Ivo Grenville. It was time to confront the past, find the courage to put both of those things right.

Her rucksack was where she'd left it, battered, grubby, out of place in the perfection of the Regency hall. They were a match, she thought, as she picked it up, slung it over her shoulder. She'd always been out of place here. A stranger in her own life.

The door had been propped open by the florists who were ferrying in boxes of flowers. Grateful that she wouldn't have to find the strength to open it, she walked down the steps and out into the street.

On her own again and very much 'scared witless...' but certain, as she hadn't been for a very long time, of the rightness of what she was doing.

Belle's flat—small, slightly shabby—welcomed her as the great house in Belgravia never had. Unable to believe her good fortune, she'd bought it the moment she'd signed her first contract following one of those chance-in-a-million breaks. Her fairy-god-mother had come in the unlikely guise of a breakfast show host who, when her brief appearance manning the phones on the telethon he was presenting had lit up the switchboard, had run with it and, playing up to the public's response, had offered her a guest appearance on his show. Not quite knowing what to do with her, he'd suggested she do a weather spot.

For some reason her flustered embarrassment at her very shaky grasp of geography had touched the viewers' hearts.

One of the gossip magazines had run a feature on her and within weeks she'd had an agent and a serious contract to go out and talk to people in the street, in their offices, in their homes, asking their opinions on anything from the price of bread to the latest health fad.

Even now she didn't understand how it had happened but, from a situation where she and her bank did their best to ignore each other, suddenly she was being invited into the manager's office for a chat over a cup of coffee. They hadn't been able to do enough for her, especially once she'd demonstrated that investing in bricks and mortar—securing herself a home against the time when the sympathy wore thin—had been her first priority.

Against all the odds, she'd gradually moved from her spot as light relief to the centre of the breakfast television sofa, picking up the long-term security of a multi-millionaire husband on the way.

But she'd kept her flat.

She hadn't needed Ivo—financial genius that he was—to advise her to let it rather than sell it when they'd married. She would never part with it. It wasn't just that it was a good investment, that it had been her first, her only proper home; it represented, at some fundamental level, a different, truthful kind of security.

After her last tenant had left she'd made the excuse that it needed refurbishing and taken it off the agency books. Almost as if she'd been preparing for this moment.

Shivering, she dumped her bags in the hall, switched on the heating. Looked around. Touched one of the walls for reassurance. The stones in her wedding ring caught the light, flashed back at her, and she stood there for a moment, lost in the memory of the moment when Ivo had placed it on her finger. Then it had been the sun that had caught the stones in the antique ring as he'd pledged to keep her safe, protect her.

He had. He'd done everything he'd promised. But it wasn't enough. And she slipped the ring from her finger.

Then, in a frenzy of activity, she made the bed, unpacked her things. Stuffed everything into the washing machine.

Ivo was wrong. She wasn't tired. Her body clock was all over the place and she was buzzing. Once she'd showered, she sorted herself out a pair of trousers, a shirt, a sweater from the jumbled mess in her bag, made a cup of tea and switched on her computer.

Her first priority was to send emails to Claire and Simone to let them know that she was home safely. Update them.

...I've moved into my old flat. It needs redecorating, but that's okay. It'll be something to keep me busy in the long winter evenings.

She added a little wry smiley.

I hope you both had uneventful trips home since I suspect life is about to get a little bumpy for all of us. Take care. Love, Belle.

She hit 'send'. Sat back. Remembered Simone's face as she'd warned her against doing anything hasty. Telling her that Ivo could help...

No. This was something she had to do herself. And, brushing aside the ache, she began to search the 'net for information on how she could find her sister.

The good news was that new legislation meant that not only mothers could register to contact children given up for adoption, but family too.

The bad news was that Daisy had to make the first move.

Unless she'd signed up to find her birth family—and, for the life of her, Belle couldn't imagine why she would want to—there would be no connection.

*Ivo could help...*

The tempting little voice whispered in her ear. He would have contacts...

She shut it out, filled in the online form with all the details she had. If that produced no results, there were agencies that specialised in helping to trace adopted family members.

She'd give it a week before she went down that route. Right now, she had a more pressing concern. She had to call her hairdresser and grovel.

'Eeuw...' George, her stylist, a man who understood a hair emergency when he saw it, picked up a dry blonde strand to examine its split ends and shuddered. 'I knew it was going to be bad but really, Belle, this is shocking. What have you being doing to it?'

'Nothing.'

'I suppose that would explain it. I hope you haven't got any plans for the rest of the day. It's going to need a conditioning treatment, colour—'

'I want you to cut it,' Belle said, before he could get into his stride.

'Well, obviously. These ends will have to go.'

'No. Cut it. Short. And let's lose the platinum blonde, um? Go for something nearer my real colour.'

'Oh, right. And can you remember what that is?' he asked, arching a brow at her in the mirror.

Vaguely. She'd started off white blonde, like her sister, but her own hair had darkened as she'd got older. She'd reversed the process as soon as she'd discovered the hair colouring aisle in the supermarket, but if she was going for 'real', her hair was as good a place as any to start.

'Cheerful mouse?' she offered.

'An interesting concept, darling. Somehow I don't think it will catch on.' Then, having examined her roots, presumably to check for himself, he said, 'Have you cleared this with your image consultant? Your agent?' When she didn't respond, 'Your husband?'

The mention of Ivo brought a lump to her throat.

She fought it down.

It was her hair, her image, her life and, by way of answer, she leaned forward, picked up a pair of scissors lying on the ledge in front of her, extended a lock of hair and, before George could stop her, she cut through it, just below her ear. Then, still holding the scissors, she said, 'Do you want to finish it or shall I?'

# CHAPTER THREE

SHOPPING was not Belle's usual method of displacement activity, but when she'd finally woken on Sunday the reality of what she'd done, of being alone—not just alone in her bed but alone for ever—had suddenly hit home and the day seemed to stretch like a desert ahead of her.

Finding herself sitting at her computer, waiting for an email with news of Daisy, leaping on an incoming message, only to discover it was some unspeakably vile spam, she forced herself to move.

She didn't know how the Adoption Register worked, but it was the weekend and it seemed unlikely she'd hear from anyone before the middle of the week at the earliest. More likely the middle of next month.

For the moment there was nothing more she could do and, besides, she had a much more immediate problem. She had nothing to wear for work on Monday.

Clearly, she rationalized, the sensible thing would be to call Ivo and arrange to go and pick up at least part of her wardrobe. She had a new pale pink suit that would show off her tan, look great with her new hair colouring. And she had to have shoes. There were a hundred things…

Or maybe just one.

Last night she'd felt so utterly alone. She had yearned for that brief flare of passion in Ivo's eyes. To know that there was one person in the world who needed her, if only for a moment.

Pathetic.

But if she went back today, if he launched another attack on her senses when she was at her lowest, she suspected she would not be strong enough to resist. And what then?

If, by some miracle, she found Daisy, she would be torn in two. She would have to deny Daisy a second time or tell him everything. Tell him that, far from being up front and honest with him, she had lied and lied and lied. That he didn't know the woman he'd married.

And she'd lose him all over again.

At least this way she retained some dignity, the possibility that if, when, the truth came out, he would—maybe—understand. Be grateful for the distance. Even be happy for her.

Which was all very well and noble, but it still left her with the problem of what she was going to wear tomorrow.

Since she needed to get out of the flat before she succumbed to temptation, she dealt with both problems in one stroke and called a taxi—no more chauffeur on tap—and took herself off to one of the vast shopping outlets that had sprung up around London and lost herself among the crowds.

She had been told often enough that the golden rule was to change your hair or change your clothes but not both at the same time. As she flipped through the racks of clothes, she ignored it. She was done with living by other people's rules.

She fell in love with an eau-de-nil semi-tailored jacket. Exactly the kind of thing her style 'guru' had warned her not to wear. She wasn't tall enough or thin enough to carry it off, apparently. On the contrary, she barely made five and a half feet and her figure was of the old-fashioned hourglass shape. But all that cycling had at least had one good outcome—she was trimmer all over. And with her hair cut short she felt taller.

She lifted the collar, pushed up the sleeves and was rewarded with a smile from the saleswoman.

'That looks great on you.' Then, 'Did anyone ever tell you that you look a lot like Belle Davenport?'

'No,' she said truthfully. Then, 'She wouldn't wear something like this, would she?'

'No, but you're thinner than her. And taller.'

Belle grinned. 'You think so? They do say that television adds ten pounds.'

'Trust me, you look fabulous.'

She felt fabulous, but she was so accustomed to listening to advice that she had little confidence in her own judgement. But the other jackets—neat, waist-hugging 'Belle Davenport' style jackets in pastel colours—that she'd tried were more expensive, so the woman had no incentive to lie.

'Thank you,' she said. And bought its twin in a fine brown tweedy mixture that looked perfect with her new hair and matched her eyes. Then she set about teaming them with soft cowl necks, classic silk shirts, trousers—she always wore skirts on air—and neat ankle boots.

More than once, as she browsed through the racks, she saw someone take a second glance, but her new haircut and George's brilliant streaky blend of light brown through to sun-kissed blonde—his very inventive interpretation of cheerful mouse—fooled them. She couldn't possibly be who they thought she was.

There was an exhilarating freedom in this moment of anonymity and when she spotted a photo booth she piled in with her packages, grinning into the camera as she posed for a picture so that she could share the joke with Claire and Simone.

Then she passed an interior design shop.

She wasn't the only one that needed a make-over and if time was going to be hanging heavy on her hands she might as well make a start on the flat.

When she was done there, she was so laden with the in-house designer's print outs, swatches, carpet squares and colour charts that she had to call it a day and take another taxi. At which point she wondered about buying herself a car.

One of her very early 'make a fool of Belle' projects for the television had been a driving course. Not that much of a fool, actually, since she'd taken to it like a duck to water and ended up doing an off-road course, a circuit in a grand prix car and driving a double-decker bus through a skid test. And earned herself another contract.

She'd bought a little car then, but once she'd married Ivo there had always been a chauffeur in town and there had been no point in keeping it.

The taxi driver was a mine of information on the subject and by the time he delivered her to her door he'd made a call arranging for her to test drive a zippy little BMW convertible the following afternoon.

'You did what?'

She hadn't long been home from the studio on Monday afternoon when the doorbell rang.

Her first thought was that it was the press who, following up her appearance on the television that morning, would be clamouring for the story behind her 'new look'. Since neither her agent nor her PR consultant could answer their questions—she hadn't talked to either of them yet—the gossip columnists would have called the house, which meant they would now have a much bigger story.

That she was no longer living with Ivo. That the 'perfect' marriage was over.

Of course it could be her agent—he kept a television on in his office so that he could keep an eye on his clients—demanding to know what on earth she thought she was doing, messing with success. Ruining the image he'd gone to so much trouble and expense—he always took expenditure personally, even when it was her money he was spending—to build. Anxious to arrange interviews, a photo session so that he could 'sell' her new look. Wanting to know what spin the PR guys should put on the fact that she'd moved out of the family home, since, like the press, he'd go there first.

A new romance for her? *Positive, upbeat, radiant...*

A cheating husband? *Sympathetic, brave...*

A marriage that had collapsed under the strain of the pressure of their careers? *Very sad. Still good friends...*

She'd seen it all a hundred times.

The light on the answering machine had been flashing when she'd got home. She had ignored it, just as she now ignored the doorbell.

Instead, she was glued to her laptop, anxiously checking through the messages to see if there was anything from the Adoption Register.

Nothing. Instead she clicked on the site she'd bookmarked, the one with personal adoption stories.

A second longer peal on the bell warned her that whoever was at the front door wasn't about to go away and, knowing that she would have to face the music sooner rather than later, she picked up the entry phone.

'Yes?' she said, her voice neutral.

'Belle...'

She caught her breath, almost doubling up with shock at the sound of Ivo's voice...

No...

It was the middle of the afternoon. He should be in his office, all of London at his feet, both figuratively and metaphorically. He didn't do 'personal', not in office hours. Not ever...

She didn't answer, couldn't answer, just buzzed him up, taking the time it took for him to walk up to her flat—an old converted town house, there were no lifts—to recover. Taking those few moments to put herself back together before she opened the door.

For a moment he just looked at her.

Then he reached out, as if he needed to touch the short flicked up layers of her hair before he could bring himself to believe what she'd done. Curled his long fingers back into his palm before he made contact.

'You look...'

Words apparently failed him. That was twice in three days. If she wasn't struggling for words herself, she might have derived a certain amount of satisfaction from that.

'Different?' she managed, when it seemed that nothing would break the silence.

He shook his head, but offered no alternative, just lifted the thick wad of envelopes he was holding as if that was enough to explain his presence.

For a minute there her heart, not quite keeping up with her head, had hoped for something more. What, quite, she didn't know, but something. Doing her best to ignore its dizzy spin—she'd had a lifetime of hiding her thoughts, her feelings; three years of marriage to practise hiding them from Ivo: it shouldn't be this hard—she said, 'I thought Miranda was going to forward my post.'

'It's piled up while you were away. Some of it might be important.'

So important that he'd left his office early to bring it to her, rather than send a messenger? *Was* there anything that important?

She held out her hand to take the bundle of envelopes, but he didn't surrender it.

'I called earlier.'

*Twice? He'd come twice...*

'I have a letterbox,' she said. 'You could have left it.'

'It wasn't just the mail.' No. As she'd suspected, his presence on her doorstep had nothing to do with her post. 'You're usually home long before this.'

'Today wasn't usual. I've been away and there was a lot to catch up with. And I had a couple of meetings that ran on.' A bit of an understatement. Having done the hard one—telling Ivo that she was leaving him—her calm announcement that she wouldn't be renewing her contract to anchor the breakfast television show had been a piece of cake.

And yet here she was making excuses like some kid justifying herself for being late home from school. Not that she ever had been. School had been a dangerous luxury, something she'd had to steal...

It was time to remind Ivo, as well as herself, that she had to make excuses to no one.

'And then I bought a car,' she added, as casually as if she was telling him she'd bought a new pair of shoes.

Which was when her very cool and detached husband became distinctly heated.

'You did what?'

Not so much a question as a man displaying outrage that a woman—his wife, no less—had the audacity to believe herself capable of making that kind of decision for herself.

It had, actually, been quite a week for decisions:

*Left her husband.*

*Had her hair cut.*

*Bought a car.*

So far, it was the car that had got the biggest reaction so she stayed with that.

'It's a BMW convertible,' she told him. 'Silver. Only twenty-two thousand miles on the clock. It's being delivered tomorrow.'

'It's not new?' First outrage, now concern. 'Has it been checked? Please tell me it's not a private sale.'

Extraordinary. If she'd realised it would get this kind of response she'd have bought a car before. Several of them. Maybe gone into the used car business…

'Would that be bad?'

'I'll need the registration number so that I can run a check. It could be stolen. Or a couple of stitched together wrecks. And the mileage is undoubtedly fake. Have you any idea—'

'Oh, no,' she assured him. If he was going to treat her like a dumb blonde, then—hair colour notwithstanding—she'd had plenty of practice playing the role. 'I'm sure it's fine. I bought it from the brother-in-law of a taxi driver I met yesterday.'

He didn't actually groan, but he didn't look impressed. He wasn't meant to.

'Give me his name and address.'

'The taxi driver?'

'His brother-in-law,' Ivo said, not quite through gritted teeth, but she could see that it was a close call.

It served him right for acting as if she was too stupid to live, she thought. If he'd watched her show once in a while he would have known that they had, on more than one occasion, run features on all aspects of buying used cars.

'Oh, Mike!' she said, determined to rub it in. 'Such a sweet man. Hold on, I've got his card somewhere.' Her bag was lying on the hall table and she opened it, produced a business card, offered it to him.

Ivo took it, looked at it, then at her. 'Mike Wade is the taxi driver's brother-in-law?'

'Yes.' Then, 'Is there something wrong?' Beyond the fact that, too late, he'd realised she'd been winding him up since Mike Wade was a senior representative at one of London's premier BMW dealerships rather than some dodgy character selling used cars off the street.

'He asked to be remembered to you,' she added. 'Said you'd been in to talk about exchanging your car for one of the smaller models. Very green…'

Then, exhilarating as it should have been to discover that Ivo was not made of stone, that it was possible to wind him up, she found herself regretting it. He was just looking out for her. Making sure that she was okay.

Actually, she was doing fine and he had to understand that so, dropping the teasing, refusing to hope that the thought that she might be with someone else had been gnawing away at him all weekend, until he'd been driven to come and find out for himself, she said, 'Why are you here, Ivo?'

'I wondered what you wanted to do about your clothes,' he said, returning the card, then running his fingers distractedly through a lick of hair that had the temerity to slide across his forehead. 'There must be things you'll need.'

'Yes.'

The word came out on a sigh that she was unable to quite stifle.

Not uncontrollable jealousy, then, just the practicalities. And of course, infuriatingly, he was right. It took more than a day of self-indulgence to replace an entire wardrobe. A few jackets and shirts wouldn't take her far. Apart from anything else, she had a television awards dinner coming up.

She'd already bought an antique Balenciaga gown for the occasion. It would be her first public appearance without Ivo and if the clothes were eye-catching enough, maybe people wouldn't remark on his absence. Maybe she wouldn't notice it too much.

'And we need to talk,' he added. 'About what happens next.'

'You'd better come through,' she said, turning away, leaving him to follow. Then, because facing him in her small sitting room while he coldly deconstructed their lives was unbearable, she veered off into the kitchen and once there needed to do something with her hands. 'Are you hungry?' she asked. 'It seems forever since lunch.' A sandwich at a hastily convened meeting in the boardroom. Not that she'd eaten any of it. One mouthful had warned her that it would stick like a lump of glue in her throat. Then, when he didn't immediately answer, she turned and realised he hadn't followed. She retraced her steps and found him staring at her laptop. The adoption site.

'You're busy,' he said. 'I've disturbed you.'

He'd disturbed her the moment she'd turned and seen him looking at her at some charity function. When she'd felt the heat reach out and touch her from the far side of the room.

It had been new then, but the effect did not diminish with familiarity; even now it seemed to burn through her silk shirt, warming her skin.

'I'm researching a new project,' she said, her fingers itching to close the lid, but her brain warning her that hiding what she was doing would only arouse his interest. Then, 'I haven't got much in. Food,' she added. Just the basics she'd picked up at the eight-'til-late on the corner.

The computer beeped to warn her of an incoming email and the sound seemed to vibrate through her. *Daisy…*

It took every bit of will-power she possessed to turn away and walk into the kitchen.

'It'll have to be something on toast,' she said. 'Cheese? Sardines?' The kind of comfort food that had no place in his Belgravia kitchen, but which she craved right now. 'Scrambled eggs—'

'We could go somewhere.' Clearly he felt as out of place in her kitchen as—all Savile Row tailoring and handmade shirts—he looked.

'I don't think so.'

'Somewhere quiet,' he persisted, unused to his suggestions meeting with resistance.

She didn't argue, just took a box of eggs from the fridge. 'You'll find some bread in the crock,' she said, as she set about cracking them, one by one into a bowl.

For a moment he didn't move, then, dropping the envelopes on the counter, he reached for the loaf.

'You didn't know I could cook, did you?' she said, reaching up to unhook a whisk, doing her best to keep it light.

'You've never needed to,' he said as he put the loaf down beside her.

Not since she'd married him.

She'd watched the television chefs who'd been on her show. Had bought books, taught herself. It had been such a luxury to have her own kitchen. Such a pleasure to be able to go to the supermarket and buy what she wanted. But in Ivo's house there had always been someone on hand to produce anything from a sandwich to a banquet at the drop of a hat and her early visits to the kitchen had been firmly discouraged by Miranda on the grounds that it would upset the staff.

'Maybe I did,' she said.

When he didn't answer, she looked up, realised just how close he was. How foolish she'd been to invite him in. She needed to keep her distance…

'Why don't you make the toast?' she suggested, moving away to pour egg into a pan. Scrambling eggs was not rocket science, but it did require total concentration, which was why she'd made that the comfort food of choice. 'You *do* know how to make toast?'

'I went to a spartan, character-building public school in the wilds of Scotland,' he reminded her. 'Followed by four years at university, Belle. Without a toaster I'd have starved.'

His words, about twice as much as he'd ever said before about his school days, were unexpectedly heartfelt. He didn't talk much about his childhood. All she knew she'd learned from Miranda. Their summers in France and Italy, the ponies, the pets…

Now she wondered. Had he been as happy as Manda had implied?

'There's a difference between being hungry and starving,' she said, refusing to weaken, look at him. Besides, she wasn't talking about food.

She'd only ever envied Ivo one thing. Not his wealth, a house filled with treasures gathered over generations, the half a dozen places around the world he could call home if ever he had the time to visit them. Only his education. The fact that he and Miranda had conversations about art, music, literature that passed right over her head. That, courtesy of summers spent in France and Italy all through their apparently idyllic childhood, they spoke both languages fluently.

She'd missed out on so much, had spent all her adult life reading voraciously in an attempt to fill the gaps, but mostly learned just how much she didn't know.

He'd had every advantage. Had no business complaining.

'My staff sponsored you,' he said, assuming that she was referring to the kids they'd been raising money to help. 'Supported what you were doing.'

'Am I supposed to be grateful?' she asked, unimpressed, as she continued to stir the egg. 'They were just sucking up to the boss, Ivo.'

'You underestimate yourself.' Then, when she was surprised into looking at him, 'They were genuinely touched by your empathy with those children.'

'Oh.' Throat suddenly dry, she said, 'And you?'

'I supported you too. A cheque was sent into your appeal this morning from all of us.'

'Thank you,' she said, knowing that it would be generous, wishing she hadn't been quite so sharp. 'But I was asking if you were "genuinely touched".'

'Belle…'

Stupid question…

The bread popped up and, glad of the interruption, she took the eggs from the heat, reached for plates from the overhead rack. 'Will you pass me the butter from the fridge?'

He didn't move. 'What is this all about? Why now?' When she didn't answer, he added, 'If there's no one else?'

The painful edge of uncertainty in his voice was so rare, so unexpected, that she had to put down the wooden spoon she'd been using to stir the eggs. The one thing about Ivo that was unchanging was his sureness of purpose and she longed to go to him, to reassure him that this was not his fault.

Unfortunately there was only one way that would end, so instead she fetched the butter herself, spread it on the toast, piled on the egg and hitched herself up on a stool with the breakfast bar between them. Only then could she trust herself to say, 'There's no one else, Ivo.'

She picked up a fork, going through the motions of normality for both of them.

'As for why now—well, maybe distance lends perspective.' She toyed with the egg, searching for words that would explain how she felt without unnecessarily hurting him. 'We never pretended that this was a fairy tale marriage, Ivo, and we've had three years.' She managed a wry smile. 'That's at least two years longer than most people gave us at the start. Almost a record for someone in my business. At least we knew what the score was. Didn't make the mistake of having children…' Her voice faltered and she gripped the fork more tightly, as if it were a lifeline. 'There's no one to be hurt.'

Grateful…

Now that really was a fairy tale.

She'd longed for Ivo's baby, a part of him who would love her unreservedly, accept her as she was, but she had married him for security, he'd married her for lust. Children needed more than that.

Maybe 'grateful' was the right word.

Babies would have been no more than a sticking plaster to cover over the hollow place in her life. The Daisy-shaped emptiness that, until now, she'd refused to acknowledge.

Until she'd confronted the past, found her sister, she had no right to children of her own.

'Just accept that I'm doing us both a favour,' she said, a little desperately. 'Let it go. Find someone who'll fit your world…'

*Grateful.*

The small kitchen seemed to darken and Ivo felt something inside him contract.

Belle had always been too big to squeeze into the narrow confines of his cold world. She had always been brighter, warmer, more alive. A place where he could lose himself, forget who he was for a while. When he was with her, he was the best he could be but she deserved more and had, apparently, finally realised that.

It was as if, out there in the high mountains, she had reached into herself, had found the confidence to abandon a perfectly honed image that the public adored, replacing it with a new, more powerful, maturer look to take her into a new decade. As if she'd somehow tapped into an inner strength that made her at once more desirable, less attainable.

She no longer needed a prop. No longer needed him.

Once, all he would have had to do was reach out, touch her and she would have been his but his attempt to stop her from leaving had, in its desperation, been so clumsy that she'd rejected him out of hand.

To bring her back now, to hold on to her, would be selfish beyond belief. And yet he could not let her go. And did not know how to keep her.

If she were a company he'd know what to do. He could interpret the balance sheets, analyse performance, formulate a plan...

'Someone who will give you what I never could,' she finished.

'You give me—'

The words began to spill out before Ivo could stop them.

'I know what I give you,' Belle said, cutting him off before he made a total fool of himself.

The world might think them lost in love, but the world knew nothing.

'I'm sorry,' he said abruptly, indicating the food she'd made him, an ache as familiar as breathing in his throat. To stay and eat with her in such intimacy, such closeness, was a sweetness, an indulgence he would not, could not permit himself. 'I'll have to leave this. I have a meeting.'

Meetings. Mergers. Takeovers. More money. More power. Anything to fill the aching void within him.

Then, unable to just walk away, 'Is there anything you need? Anything I can do for you?'

That was almost a plea, he realised with a jolt and for a moment he thought he might have got to her, but she shook her head.

Finding it harder to leave than he would have believed possible, he looked around the small, hard-used apartment. 'You can't stay here. Give me a day or two and I'll arrange for somewhere more comfortable for you to live.'

'Is that what's worrying you?' she demanded, taking him by surprise as she flared up at him. 'That it won't look good if the world discovers that I'm holed up in a tiny flat near Camden Lock rather than expensively housed in a penthouse in Chelsea Harbour?'

'This isn't about me.' Except that it was. He needed to rid himself of this feeling of helplessness. If he could do something, regain some measure of control...'I just want you to be comfortable. To be safe.' *To come home.* 'This is a very mixed neighbourhood.'

'I know you mean well, Ivo—'

Was a man ever damned with fainter praise?

'—but I need to be in my own place right now.' Then, before

he could argue, 'I'll call Miranda and make arrangements to have my things moved from your house.'

Your house...

Not *our* house. Not even the more neutral *the* house, but a place that had been furnished over the centuries, decorated to match its historic importance. More like a museum than somewhere offering the comfort of home.

Somehow they got through the awkwardness of goodbye without touching, using the meaningless words that people say when they don't know what to say.

'If you need anything...'

'I'll call.'

He nodded. 'I'll see myself out,' he said as she made to follow him to the door, not able to face that moment at the door when to kiss her would be unacceptable, not to kiss her would be impossible.

And while he was still strong enough to resist the tug of some force that seemed to draw him inexorably towards her, just as a current drew a drifting ship on to rocks, he walked away, out of her flat, down the steps and out into the busy streets.

His chauffeur opened the door of the Rolls, ready to whisk him back to his ivory tower, but, on the point of stepping in, he changed his mind. Stood back.

'Call the office, let my secretary know that I won't be back today, Paul.'

The man cleared his throat. 'She rang a few minutes ago, Mr Grenville. Threadneedle Street called to ask where you were.'

He had a meeting at the Bank of England and he'd forgotten. Something that had never happened to him before.

'Ask her to call and make my apologies, will you?' Then, 'I won't need you until the morning.' And, without waiting for a reply, he began to walk.

If Belle were a company that he wanted to acquire he'd know what to do.

*Look at the balance sheets. Analyse performance. Formulate a plan...*

# CHAPTER FOUR

BELLE forced herself to eat. She had not been hungry. Cooking had been no more than a distraction, a focus for her eyes, something safe to do with her hands, but the horror of wasting food was too deeply ingrained to simply tip it into the bin and so she chewed food she could not taste, swallowing down a throat choked with pain.

Just because she knew what she was doing was right—right for her and right for Ivo—didn't mean it was easy.

Even now his presence filled the small kitchen, marking her space, owning it with a faint trace of something that lingered in the air. The warmth of his skin, the clean scent of perfectly laundered clothes, something that she couldn't name, but which left her weak with longing, hanging on to the edge of the worktop as if it were a lifeline.

In desperation she grabbed an air freshener from the cupboard beneath the sink and sprayed it around. What had been proved to eradicate the odour of sweaty socks, however, had no discernible effect on the subtler, pervasive essence of Ivo Grenville.

The scent, she realised, was in her head; she would have to live with it until it wore away under the attrition of everyday life. Fading like a bittersweet memory. Or a photograph left in the light.

On autopilot, she forced herself through the motions, rinsing the dishes, putting them in the dishwasher. She wiped down the work surfaces, counting to a hundred before she allowed herself to go to the computer and check the email. Appeasing the Fates with patience, so that the news was more likely to be good. Or maybe just afraid that it wasn't the one she was waiting for.

The Fates clearly thought she needed a little more time.

It was not news about Daisy but an email from Simone, who was in a bit of a flap about losing the diary she'd been writing all through her trip. Confessing that towards the end it had become more an emotional than physical record of her journey, containing the secrets that had spilled out in the clear quiet of the mountains.

If anyone had found it they all risked exposure.

Maybe it was disappointment, or that she was still aching from the encounter with Ivo, but she couldn't bring herself to get worked up about it. But Simone was anxious, full of remorse, and Belle responded with reassurance—the diary was undoubtedly in some airport trash compactor and on the way to landfill by now. Then, because the contact restored her, renewed her conviction in the rightness of what she was doing, she scanned one of the pictures from the strip she'd taken in the photo booth, adding:

I'm attaching a picture of the 'new' me. As you can see, I'm now a little less Monroe, rather more, well, me, I suppose. And not before time. I spent the weekend shopping for new clothes too and not an image consultant in sight. The combination had a blissfully jaw-dropping effect when I walked into the studio at the crack of dawn this morning, an effect that was considerably enhanced when I announced that I wouldn't be renewing my contract.

Ivo dropped by and nearly had a conniption when I told him I'd bought a car…

On the point of telling them about how she'd teased him, she stopped herself. She'd told Claire and Simone that they were separated. To use them to talk about him would be self-indulgence of the worst kind. She had to excise him from her thoughts.

Difficult. Maybe impossible. But she could excise him from her emails… She continued:

But that's just the cosmetic stuff.

My big news is that I've registered with the Adoption Register. If Daisy has done the same, I should be in contact very quickly. If not…

If not, tracking her down could take weeks, months, years… Simone had urged her to ask Ivo for help.

She glanced automatically towards the door, as if half expecting to see him still there, waiting for an answer to his question.

'If you need *anything*…?'

A million things. Help her find Daisy. With his contacts he could probably do it in a second. But truly there was only one thing she wanted from him. His love. But that had never been on offer.

Turning back to the email, she deleted, *If not*…

She would not, must not, allow herself to be sucked in by negative thoughts. Or transmit them to Claire and Simone, who had their own demons to face. Instead she asked how their own plans were going, prompting Claire, in whom she sensed hesitation, not to delay her own search, before signing off, with love.

Then she returned to the adoption website, obsessively reading the stories of people who had been adopted with both wonderful and tragic results. Mothers who had parted with their children. Children hunting for their roots. Stories full of loss, joy, experiences that covered the entire spectrum of emotion. Looking for something that would give her hope, using it to stuff her mind against thoughts of Ivo that, no matter how hard she tried to block them, would seep in and fill her head.

*Ivo, on the day they'd stood on a tropical beach, her hand in his as she'd repeated their not to be taken too literally till-death-us-do-part vows. Maybe her heart had known then what her brain had refused to admit.*

*Ivo, turning away from some close discussion about a major business deal to seek her out, find her at the far end of the dinner table.*

*Ivo, in a rare moment when he'd fallen asleep in her arms and was, for a brief, blissful moment, entirely hers.*

It was late when Ivo finally got home.

'Your secretary rang,' Manda said, her irritation driven, he knew, by anxiety. 'You missed a meeting.'

'I know. I sent my apologies.'

'That's not the point! No one knew where you were.'

'Will I get detention?' he asked.

'Ivo…'

Belle would have laughed. She might have been angry with him, but she wouldn't have been able to help herself. He'd tried so hard not to take more than she had signed up for—the sex and security deal—but she'd drained the tension from him with a smile, a touch.

'You've been to see her, haven't you?' Adding, 'Belle.' As if she could have meant anyone else.

'There were things we needed to talk about.'

Not that they had. Talked. At least not about anything that mattered. But it had been informative, nonetheless. Belle hadn't wanted him looking at her laptop. Had twitched to close it. Hide what she was doing. And she had positively jumped when an email had dropped into her inbox. She was hiding something—not another man, she wouldn't have been able to hide that. Wouldn't have tried to.

He wished he'd taken more notice of what had been on the screen…

'Ivo?'

He realised that his sister was waiting, expecting more, but he shook his head. 'Belle will be in touch about picking up her things.'

'Oh, right, and I'm supposed to snap to attention, I suppose, and run around organising one of the staff to help her pack. Sort out transport to shift it all.'

'I thought you'd relish the moment. Isn't it what you've been waiting for?'

'I... I always knew this would happen.'

'Yes, well, I'm sure you weren't alone.'

'Ivo...'

He turned away from her sympathy, cutting in sharply with, 'If Belle chooses to call ahead as a matter of courtesy it's because she has the instincts of a lady, even if she didn't have the benefit of the most expensive education money can buy.' Then, 'She is my wife, Manda. This is her home.'

'So where is she, hmm?' She made a single sweeping gesture to indicate her absence. As if he needed reminding. 'What is it about her?' she demanded. 'How does she do it? Reduce everyone to drooling mush. She floats about on a cloud of sweetness and light doing absolutely nothing except look glamorous and yet she has the entire world at her feet.'

'If that's all you see, Miranda, then you're not nearly as clever as you think you are,' he said, too angry to use her childhood name.

'Even now, when she's walked out on you, you're defending her.'

'She doesn't need me to defend her.'

Didn't need him for anything. Was that what she'd learned on the mountains? That she was strong enough to stand alone?

'As for the sweetness and light thing,' he added, 'you could, with benefit, try it yourself once in a while.'

His sister flamed, then shrugged, an oddly awkward gesture. 'It's not my style, Ivo.' She lifted her hands in an out of character gesture of helplessness. 'I can't...' Then, 'She makes me feel so...inadequate. As a woman,' she added quickly, in case he thought she meant in any way that was really important. 'The minute she walks into a room I feel as if I've suddenly become invisible...'

'Manda...'

She shook off the moment of weakness, straightened. 'I'll do whatever I can to help,' she said, making an effort to be helpful, 'but wouldn't it be more sensible for Belle to wait until she's moved before collecting more than her basic needs?'

'Moved?'

'You're not going to let her stay in that poky little flat in Camden?'

'I don't appear to have a say in the matter.'

'Oh, I see. She's going to stay put and play poverty to jack up the settlement she'll wring out of you.'

He sighed. That hadn't lasted long.

'Belle will have trouble pleading poverty,' he pointed out. The one thing he had been able to do for her was ensure that her considerable earnings had been well-managed. Maybe that had been his mistake. If her investments had been bungled she would still need the security she craved. That he could offer. 'Wringing will not be necessary, however. Everything I have is hers for the asking.'

'Including this house?'

Unlikely. The one possession of his that Belle would not want, he suspected, would be this house. But he wasn't feeling kind. 'Maybe you'd better start house-hunting yourself,' he advised. 'Just in case. I'm told Camden is going up in the world. Maybe Belle will do a swap. Her flat isn't that poky.'

Not poky at all. It was small in comparison with this house—anything would be small in comparison with it—and shabby, but it had a welcoming warmth which, despite every imaginable luxury, was totally absent from the pile of masonry he called home whenever Belle was absent. And of course that was the point. It was Belle who made the difference.

'Once it's redecorated,' he added, recalling the colour cards and fabric swatches he'd seen lying on the table beside her laptop…

Adoption.

It had been a website about adoption. And suddenly everything fell into place.

'…it'll be fine,' he finished.

* * *

The email she'd been waiting for came the next day. Daisy Porter had registered with the agency and had been informed that a family member was looking for her. If she wanted to send a letter they would forward it...

Belle wrote a dozen letters. Long. Short. Every length in between. Finally she summoned a courier—she couldn't wait an extra day for the post—and sent one that contained the bare essentials. No excuses. No apologies. Asking her to write or ring. Giving her address. Her phone number. Her mobile phone number. And, at the last moment, she clipped one of the photographs from the strip she had taken at the photo booth and enclosed that too.

And, because the waiting was unbearable, because she had to do something, she stripped the wallpaper from the living room walls.

By the weekend she wasn't stripping the walls, she was climbing them, so she bought a stepladder and started painting the ceiling. She was working on a fiddly bit of the cornice that decorated her high ceiling when the phone rang, shatteringly loud in a room stripped of curtains and carpet.

She grabbed the handle at the top of the ladder and steadied herself.

She'd expected an instant response from Daisy but, after days of rushing to answer every call, she forced herself to ignore it. Racing up and down a stepladder was just asking for trouble.

It was more likely to be someone from the media who'd finally tracked her down, she told herself, still doing her best to appease the Fates.

So far the studio had managed to keep a lid on the fact that she wasn't renewing her contract. That two weeks from now—unless they could persuade her to change her mind—there would be a new face to go with the cornflakes. And the newspapers and gossip magazines, totally obsessed with her new look—her face ached with smiling at photo sessions—had somehow missed the really big story, that she'd moved out of the marital home. That the smile was not the real thing, but something she had to coax her muscles to do. That it had taken all the make-up artist's skill to cover the dark hollows under her eyes. That her mascara had to be waterproof.

It couldn't last and when the story broke the phone would be her enemy, not her friend.

She should have just given Daisy her cellphone number. Bought a special phone with a number that only she would know. Too late…

The machine picked up, the message played. She'd left the pre-recorded response until she'd heard that Daisy had registered to look for her. Once she'd given her the number, she'd recorded a message in her own voice. Probably a mistake. If it was some gossip columnist hoping to confirm a suspicion, he'd just done it.

She glanced out of the curtainless window, but there were no photographers with long lenses pointed in her direction. No, well—easing her aching shoulder while the message played, hoping against hope that it would be the one call she was waiting for—she still didn't really believe it herself.

The caller hung up without leaving a message.

She dipped her brush into the paint. Her nails, her fingers, were coated in the stuff. More work for her manicurist who had taken to joking that she was going to finance a Christmas holiday in the Caribbean with all the extra money she was making.

The phone began to ring again. She dropped the brush, slid down the stepladder, grabbed the phone before the machine could pick up.

'Yes?' she gasped breathlessly. 'I'm here.' There was the briefest silence. Then once again the caller hung up.

Fingers shaking, she punched in 1471. Listened to the recording telling her that '…we do not have the caller's number…'

She rubbed briskly at her arms, stippled with gooseflesh. Of course she was cold. She'd opened the windows… What she needed was a warm drink, a hot mug to wrap her fingers around.

She'd just reached the kettle when the phone rang again. She grabbed the receiver fastened to the kitchen wall and said, 'Please don't hang up!'

'Belle?'

Ivo.

'Oh...'

'Not who you were expecting, evidently.'

'No... Yes...' She shook her head, which was pretty pointless since he couldn't see.

She should have guessed he'd ring.

He'd called at the flat earlier: she'd looked out of the window and seen his car—not the work day Rolls with Paul at the wheel, but the big BMW he drove himself—and had resolutely ignored the doorbell.

This was hard enough without these constant reminders of everything she was missing. Not just the scent of him that nothing seemed to eradicate, but the way he loosened his tie, undid the top button of his shirt, without even realising what he was doing. The way his hair slid across his forehead, evoking memories of it damp, tousled from the shower...

'Are you still there?'

'Yes. Sorry. I'm waiting for someone to ring,' she said helplessly.

'I got that bit.' He didn't wait for her to reply but said, 'You sound as if you've just run a marathon.'

'Nothing that easy,' she said. Then, a touch desperately, 'Can this wait?'

'It's okay, I won't stop you working. If you'll just buzz me up...'

Buzz him up? She looked at the phone, then put it back to her ear. 'Where exactly are you?'

'Right this minute? Standing on your doorstep.'

She crossed to the tall French windows, standing open to the small balcony to let out the smell of paint, and looked down. There was no BMW parked at the kerb behind her own smart little convertible. Only a van.

Clearly he'd guessed she was lying doggo earlier so this time he'd stopped further down the street and used his cellphone to establish that they both knew she was in before he revealed his presence. Smart.

'I'm really busy,' she said. 'Can't you just push the post through the letterbox?'

'The stuff I've got here won't go through the slot.'

Which was why he'd had to come back. Now she just felt bad and, out of excuses, she buzzed him up, but, having left the flat door open, she abandoned all thoughts of making a hot drink and retired to the top of the stepladder, ensuring a safe distance between them. If he saw she was working, he'd get the message and wouldn't linger.

She heard him walking across the bare boards in the hall. 'Just dump it there,' she called, hoping he'd take the hint.

'One more load.'

What?

She frowned, turned, too late. She could hear him taking the stairs two at a time.

One more load of what?

Had he got tired of waiting for her to pick up her belongings and decided to bring them over?

She swallowed down the painful lump in her throat. This was her decision. She should be grateful, she thought, jabbing at the cornice with her paintbrush. He was saving her a job.

She heard him put something down. 'That's it.'

'Could you leave it in the hall?' she said, aware that he was watching her but resolute in her determination not to get drawn into conversation. To even look at him.

'It won't be much use there.'

And he had her. Curiosity…

Ivo had a weekend wardrobe to go with his weekend car. Expensive casuals, cashmere sweaters. He might carry on working at the weekend, but he didn't consider it necessary to wear a suit when he was at home. Mostly.

Today he was wearing stuff she'd never seen before.

Really old form-hugging jeans that clung to his thighs and

sent a whisper of heat whiffling down her spine. And, under a rubbed to the nap leather bomber jacket, a T-shirt that had once been black but was now so faded that even the logo promoting some eighties' rock group was barely discernible.

She tore her gaze away from his body to look at the box he'd set on the floor. It contained not post, not clothes, but paint-brushes, brush cleaners, sandpaper—tools a decorator might use.

Startled, she said, 'What on earth do you think you're doing?'

'The ceiling will take half the time with two of us doing it. I've brought my own stepladder,' he added, before she could tell him that he wasn't sharing hers.

While she balanced, open-mouthed, inches from the ceiling, he fetched it from the hall and set it up in the far corner of the room. Then he took a paint kettle from the box, helped himself to paint from the tin she was using and, without waiting for her to thank him, or tell him to get lost, he set to work.

'No,' she said, when her mouth and brain finally recon-nected. 'Stop.'

He paused. Glanced across at her.

This was too weird. Ivo didn't do this stuff. If something needed fixing, Miranda summoned someone from her list of 're-liable little men' to deal with it.

'Haven't you got more important things to organise? A take-over, a company launch or something,' she added a little des-perately.

He almost smiled. 'All of the above, but I can spare a couple of hours to give you a hand with this,' he said, then carried on with what he was doing.

No doubt. Leaving some CEO to sweat out his future while he calmly painted her ceiling as if he had nothing more on his mind than…painting her ceiling.

'No,' she repeated, putting down her paintbrush and climbing down the ladder. If he had time to spare he could go 'spare' it somewhere else.

She didn't want him turning up, taking over. This was like the thing with the car. Treating her as if she didn't know what she was doing. This was her life and she could handle it.

He took no notice, carrying on as if she hadn't spoken. For a moment she stood beneath him, watching as he stretched to stroke the brush across the ceiling, apparently hypnotised by the bunching and lengthening of the muscles in his arm. The low autumn sun slanting in through the window gilding the fine sprinkling of dark hairs on his forearm.

'If you've got an hour or two to spare,' she said, dragging herself back to reality, 'world peace could do with some attention.'

'I can do a lot more with ethical company practice than I could ever manage with political hot air.'

'Can you?' Then, because getting into a debate with him was not her intention, 'How did you know I'd be decorating?'

He stopped, looked down at her.

'I noticed the colour cards on Monday and when I came by earlier you'd taken down the curtains.' He dipped the brush into the paint. 'It seemed like a reasonable assumption.'

'I might have had decorators in.'

'You have,' he agreed. 'Grenville and Davenport. No job too small.'

How easy it would be to let that go. Just shut up and let him get on with it. Working towards each other. A team. This was, after all, what she had always wanted. The two of them getting close over the ordinary things that other people did.

People, courtesy of the gossip magazines, thought she had the perfect life with Ivo, but she would have willingly surrendered the luxury just to fall into bed with him at the end of a hard day, too tired to do anything but sleep.

'If you want to set up in the decorating business, Ivo, you're going to have to find another partner. And somewhere else to practise.'

Ivo, who had relied on speed and determination—skills that had served him well in the past—to override her initial objections, certain that in retrospect she'd be glad of his help, stopped what he was doing, finally listened to her.

'You really mean that, don't you?'

'I really mean it.'

'You don't want my help?'

'I don't want anyone's help. I want… I need to do this myself.'

He didn't just listen to her, but heard what she was saying. Understood that she wasn't rejecting him. She just wanted to do it herself. To prove something to both of them.

It was a light bulb moment.

'You'll be sorry,' he said. He was sorry too, but only for himself. There was something about Belle's new determination, new independence that made him intensely proud of her.

He climbed down the ladder, looked around. 'This is a lovely room. Good proportions.'

'It will be when I've finished. When the new carpet is down.'

He looked at the tacks and staples, the junk left behind by earlier floor coverings. 'These should come up.'

'It's on the list.'

'Do you want me to leave the tools?'

Belle, looking down, caught a glimmer of something in Ivo's grey eyes. Need? Could it really be need? It was so swift that she couldn't be sure, only that it made her regret her swift rejection. To be needed by him was all she had ever really wanted.

And she'd made her point, she rationalised.

That if he stayed it would be on her terms, not because she couldn't cope. Not even because he thought she couldn't cope. And, as he sorted out pliers, a small hammer, a screwdriver, she said, 'On the other hand, I suspect it's going to be a tedious and painful job. Nail hell.'

'Painting a ceiling isn't much fun,' he pointed out. But he left her to it while he began to tackle the floor.

The phone rang three more times while they were working.

The first time Ivo looked, but made no effort to get up. The caller hung up without leaving a message.

The second time it rang he said, 'Do you want me to get that?'

'No, thanks,' she said. It was another hang-up.

The third time they both studiously ignored it.

When she was done, she climbed down the ladder, her fingers so stiff she could barely move them. He didn't say a word, simply took her brush and the one he'd briefly used and washed them out under the tap. She didn't protest since the alternative was standing shoulder to shoulder with him at the sink. That was when the phone rang for the fourth time.

'Do you get a lot of hang-ups?' he asked, turning to her. 'This is an unlisted number?'

'It's nothing. One of those computer things,' she said. 'A silent call. I'll contact the phone people. You can register to put a stop to them.'

'Silent calls don't listen to the answering machine message,' he pointed out. 'They hang up as soon as the phone is answered.'

'Do they?'

'It sounds to me as if someone likes listening to your voice.'

'What?' Then, blushing, 'What are you suggesting?' she demanded.

'Nothing.' He squished more soap on to the bristles. 'Only that you might consider changing your number.'

'I can't...' she began. Too vehemently. 'I can't be bothered. It's too much trouble to let everyone know.'

'Well, so long as it stops at hang-ups. Nuisance calls can get nasty. Who knows you're living here on your own?'

She shrugged. 'Not many people. My agent. You.'

Daisy...

Could it be Daisy calling just to listen to her voice? Building up courage to get in touch...

'And someone else,' he suggested, working the soap into the bristles with his long fingers, although the brush looked pretty clean to her. 'I've been expecting to read all about this...' he made a gesture with his head that indicated the flat '...in the newspapers.'

'Have you? Yes, well, it's a smoke and mirrors thing. The new image has distracted them for the moment.'

That and the fact that the split had all been so unbelievably civilised. There had been no drama. No tears. No sordid triangle spilling out into the public arena. Nothing to draw attention to what had happened.

The flat below her was between tenants and her ground floor neighbours, if they had actually noticed her comings and goings, presumably thought she was just doing some work on her empty flat.

It was almost as if the idea of her leaving Ivo was so unbelievable that while the world, if it looked, must plainly see what had happened, it collectively refused to believe its own eyes.

'Better make the most of the breathing space,' she advised him. 'It'll happen soon enough.' Then, because he had to find out sooner or later, 'With luck my other news will save you from the worst of it.'

He stilled.

'Other news?'

'My departure from breakfast television.'

*'What?'*

'Welcome to the club.' He raised his eyebrows. 'The "What?" club,' she said, making little quote marks with her fingers, although he'd sounded surprised rather than shocked, which had been the standard response. As if he'd been anticipating something different, although if he really thought she was having an affair why would he be here today, helping her decorate? Presumably that would be the 'lover's' prerogative. 'So far the membership is pretty exclusive. The network executives. My agent. When the news breaks I imagine it'll be standing room only.'

'Undoubtedly. Breakfast will never be the same again. Have they got anyone else lined up?'

Was that it? Mild surprise and who's taking over from you?

'For the moment they're refusing to believe it,' she said.

Rather like his response to the fact that she'd left him. 'They think I'm angling for more money.'

'And are they offering it?'

'I'm getting the impression that I can pretty much fill in the blank, which is ridiculous. No one is irreplaceable.'

'You think?' For a moment she thought he was going to say more, but he let it go. 'Do you have anything else lined up?'

'I'm taking a break. It's not for the want of offers,' she added. Pride talking. 'Including a six-figure advance for my biography.' It would be ghost-written, Jace Sutton, her agent, had assured her, assuming that her horrified response was due to the thought of having to put pen to paper herself.

'I'd save that one for the pension fund.'

'Don't panic; I have no intention of washing my dirty linen in public.'

'What dirty linen would that be?'

'Nothing,' she said quickly. 'It's just an expression. Neither do I see myself as the host of a daytime game show.'

'What about that project you're working on?'

'Project?'

'Something about adoption?' he prompted, regarding her with a look that left her floundering.

How did he know?

'You were researching the subject the other day.'

'Oh, right. Yes.' She cleared her throat. 'It's in the very early stages.'

Actually not such a bad idea, she thought, recalling some of the stories she'd read. The desperate searches. The joyful reunions. The heartbreak of a second rejection. Maybe she could put together something that would really help people like her, like Daisy.

Realising that Ivo was expecting more, she said, 'Perhaps I should make producing my own documentary a condition of staying on. That would really test the network's resolve.'

He frowned. 'You're joking, surely?'

'Well, yes, obviously…'

'Unless they're complete fools, they'd jump at it.'

He thought that? Really?

'But why bother?' he went on.

Obviously not.

'If it's something that you're passionate about, you should set up your own production company.'

She stared at him.

'My own company?'

'If you're moving on, it's the next logical step. You could do what you wanted without the bean counters pulling the strings. If you're interested I'm sure Jace would know who to approach for finance.'

'No.'

She wasn't one of those high-flying women with a first from Oxford.

'Making television programmes is expensive,' he said, misunderstanding her response.

'I know, but who on earth would risk money on me?'

'People trust you, Belle. The public love you. I…'

His voice faltered and in a second the atmosphere had slipped from a relaxed working relationship to something else as heat, like the opening of an oven door, flared between them.

'You?'

'I should be going.'

# CHAPTER FIVE

HE'D nearly blown it. Ambushed by a four-letter word that he didn't know the meaning of.

After her initial rejection of his help, he'd been so careful to keep it casual. Didn't even know what was driving him to hang in there when he understood only too well why she'd left him. He had, after all, been waiting for the moment ever since he'd fled their honeymoon in an attempt to right the wrong he'd done her, intending to tell her the truth when he'd put it right. But there were some mistakes that were beyond repair.

Belle had been right to leave him.

It was just that he couldn't let her go. Winning her back was never going to be easy. He knew her; it would have taken far more than a fit of pique to screw her to the point that she could walk away from a marriage that, by her own admission, had given her everything she'd ever wanted. Bar one.

Marriage should have been the last thing on their minds. Somehow it had been the only thing on his and her terms had made it so easy for him.

*'Marriage?' She'd laughed at the very idea. 'The only reaon I'd marry is for security. A man so rich that I'd never have to think about money for the rest of my life. Never have to worry about whether the network were going to renew my contract...'*

*And he'd said, 'So, what's your problem? Just say the word and I'll buy the network.'*

*'What about love? Don't you...?'*

*'We're adults, Belle. Love is for adolescents.'*

*'But why marriage?' she'd pushed.*

*'It keeps the taxman at bay.'*

It had been that easy. Too easy...

He should have known that nothing good was ever won that lightly and now he was going to have to put in the hard work.

Easier said than done. He was so bad at the emotional stuff.

It was second nature to Belle. She could reach out, touch people. She'd done it to an entire country for heaven's sake; he'd turned to look at her out of curiosity, never suspecting the danger. Certain that he was immune.

Ivo had always prided himself on total honesty in business, but obsessed with her, with the need to own her, keep her for himself, he'd behaved like the worst kind of corporate raider, taking advantage of her vulnerability, her insecurity, instead of digging for its cause. Sweeping her away on the promise, the one thing that he could offer her, that, as his wife, she'd be safe from the vagaries of an uncertain business.

He'd just thanked his lucky stars that she hadn't asked for more and for a whole week had lived in the bliss of a happiness he'd thought beyond him. Bliss that had been shattered when, in the sleepy aftermath of intimacy, she'd babbled happily about a future that he'd never envisaged. A rose-coloured picture of family life that he knew did not exist.

He should have told her the truth then. Given her the choice of walking away. But he couldn't risk losing her. Any more than he could let her walk away now.

Useless at emotion, he'd utterly blown his first attempt to keep her from leaving him. Now he was using what he knew, the techniques he'd learned in the boardroom, in an attempt to save his marriage. It was, he'd rationalised, not that different from planning a takeover, albeit one that might turn hostile at any moment.

The first requirement was information. He needed to know what she was thinking. What was driving her.

Had she, out there in the Himalayas, pushing her body to the limit, reached deep and found a hitherto unsuspected inner strength? Was that why he'd felt so threatened by the trip? Why, from the first moment it had been mooted, he'd behaved like some Victorian husband demanding obedience from his wife.

Too late to see that he should have abandoned business and gone with her. Right now, all he could do was hang in there, show her that she needed him, whether she knew it or not.

Decorating, for instance. What on earth did she know about decorating? How hard it was?

He'd banked on the fact that she'd be grateful for the help and when he'd seen that she'd opted to the safer distance at the top of the ladder, knew that short of coming down and throwing him out this morning, she was stuck with him.

His first mistake.

But then, almost as if she'd taken pity on him, he'd got an unexpected reprieve and since then it had gone as well as he could have hoped. Better…

In fact it was just as well that his hands were still under cold running water. It would have been so easy to go with the moment, take it from there.

He had felt the reciprocal heat in that exchange, a charge that on any other occasion would have carried them to bed. This time, he knew, that wouldn't be enough.

A company, its directors, staff had to be courted, won over, to want what he was offering. He'd never courted Belle. What had happened between them had been instant, a conflagration.

Now, he sensed, he needed to go back to the beginning, do what he hadn't been able to do then. Keep his head. Be patient. Somehow make himself say a word that had been deleted from his dictionary. That he wasn't sure he understood. Except if the pain he was feeling, if the emptiness in his life had a word, then it could only be filled by Belle.

Easier said than done. It took a supreme effort of will to keep his hands from reaching out to her, keep them from cradling her face, from holding her as he slipped the buttons on her jeans. Stopping her protests with his mouth as he dipped his fingers into her warmth, watching as her eyes darkened until the only thing on her mind was him, buried deep inside her.

Not this time.

Patience…

After what felt like a year but was probably no more than a couple of seconds, Belle looked away, took a step back and, before she could put into words what she was plainly thinking—that he should go—he said, 'I'll put together a package for you to think about.'

And, instead of suggesting he pick up some sandwiches and coffee from the café across the road, he stuck to the practicalities.

'Do you know how to prepare the woodwork?' he asked.

'Pre…prepare…' She took a breath and the fact that she was forced to swallow before she could speak gave him hope that she had felt the same urgency, the same need. 'Wash with soft soap, sandpaper, undercoat, gloss,' she said quickly.

'You always were hot on preparation.'

People thought that she winged it on her programme every morning, that the apparently off-the-cuff chatter came easily. He knew the hours she put in every day, studying the people she was going to interview, the subjects she was going to cover, so that it looked that way.

'The woman in the shop gave me a leaflet explaining it all.'

'Right. Well, I'd better be going.'

'Thank you for your time. My manicurist will be eternally grateful,' she said, easing her neck.

He clenched his fingers into his palms to stop himself reaching out to knead out the creases. Patience…

'If you need anything—'

'I can manage.'

'I can see that.' Then, 'You've got an awards dinner on Tuesday?'

'Yes.' She pulled a face. 'I didn't think you'd remember.'

'It's in my diary. I've told Manda you'll be picking up some of your stuff. Or is there going to be a new dress to go with your new look?'

'I've already invested in a very old one. I'll pick it up after work on Monday, if that's convenient?'

While he was at the office. 'Manda should be home. If not, you've got your key.' Then, fighting the urge to offer himself, 'You have an escort?'

'Jace offered…'

He nodded. Her agent's presence at her side at the biggest industry event of the year wouldn't raise any eyebrows. 'Paul is free for the evening so if you'd like him to drive you—'

'No,' she said quickly. 'Thank you. I've made my own arrangements.'

He dug in his pocket for his keys, just about managing to stop himself from saying any of the things that were fighting to trip from his tongue. Keep it to a casual, 'Fine. Well, good luck.'

'Thank you.'

So formal. So distant. And, before he knew it, he was standing beside the van he'd borrowed from the office janitor.

He glared at her convertible. It was a declaration of independence. Of separation. He wanted to have it towed away, put in a crusher, reduced to a cube of metal. But what good would that do? Belle had made it very clear that it was her business, not his and maybe he should be taking notice of that. Give her space to stretch her wings. Test herself. Doing what his sister had been so incapable of. It occurred to him that he should be helping her find her feet, not trying to knock her off them, keep her dependent upon him.

He had intended to turn up tomorrow, find something else to do. Maybe he needed to wait for her to ask for his help.

As he rounded the van to the driver's door, he realised he wasn't the only one looking at it as if it were a hate object. A girl, stick-thin, her fair hair streaked with green and wearing clothes a charity shop would shun, was glaring at it too. It undoubtedly represented everything she didn't have and he wondered if she was planning to break in or just take out her envy on the immaculate bodywork.

'What are you staring at?' she shouted when she saw him looking at her.

'My wife's car.'

Belatedly he realised how possessive that sounded. Belle did not belong to him. He did not own her.

He transferred his feelings of protection to her car.

'If you were thinking of breaking into it, I'd advise you to think again,' he said.

For a moment the girl defiantly stood her ground before, quite deliberately placing a hand on the door and setting off the alarm. Only then did she turn and flounce away.

Belle appeared at the window. She said something but, although her mouth was moving, the words were obliterated.

He mimed an instruction to toss down her keys so that he could kill the alarm and, by the time she'd joined him, it was all over.

'I hope that isn't going to happen every time someone gets within breathing distance,' she said.

'No. It was just some girl with green hair wanting to make an impression,' he said. He reset the alarm, locked up and handed back her keys.

'Take care, Belle,' he said, then, with the briefest touch to her arm, he climbed into the van. He drove around for a while, hoping to spot the girl. There had been something about that little scene that had seemed...staged. He didn't believe in it any more than he believed in Belle's documentary.

Her twitchiness when she'd thought he was looking at her laptop last week, the way she'd jumped when an email arrived, had suggested something else entirely.

Something that might explain everything. That could offer him a measure of hope.

She'd been looking at adoption sites and one answer had leapt into his mind and refused to go away. If Belle had been a teenage mother, had given her baby up for adoption, the child could well be coming up to an age where it was possible to search for, contact his or her birth mother.

Was that what this was all about? Was she waiting, hoping for a call from a child she'd surrendered to a couple who couldn't have one of their own? How ironic that would be.

And he wondered too about those silent calls.

Her stiff back as she'd determinedly ignored them, the way her brush had stopped working as her invitation to leave a message came to an end, the beep. The slump in her shoulders as there was yet another hang-up.

Had her family disowned her? Did people still do that? It would explain why she never talked about them.

It would explain so much more than that.

But why she'd married him was not the issue.

It was the fact that she'd assumed he would disown her too, once he knew the truth, that she didn't trust him enough to share her secret, her loss, that was painful beyond imagining.

Awards dinners were not a new experience for Belle. She'd even been nominated before, although admittedly not for the top honour. But arriving on her own, walking down the red carpet into a barrage of flashlights without Ivo at her side was a very new, very lonely experience. One that her agent's presence did nothing to assuage.

Thank goodness for the dress. Strapless cream silk, worn with a bronze lace evening coat that hung from her shoulders to spread in a demi-train, brought gasps from the crowds gathered on the pavement to see their favourites arrive.

And at her throat she wore the choker of large freshwater pearls, each nestling in its own crumpled gold and diamond cup, that Ivo had bought for her birthday the year before. It was stunningly modern and yet as ageless as the dress she was wearing. She'd forgotten about jewels, would have gone without rather than call Ivo, but he forgot nothing and had sent his chauffeur over on Monday night with the contents of the safe. He clearly expected her to keep them, but she'd picked out what she'd needed for the dinner and sent the rest back, citing security.

The dress, the jewels, were not enough.

In front of the cameras she was fine. It was easy to reduce her audience to one imaginary old lady, nodding off in an armchair. In public, faced with real people, she always expected someone to shout, 'Fake!' To expose her. Show her up for what she really was.

Without Ivo's steadying hand beneath her elbow, Belle had to fight down the urge to run, to escape all those eyes, all those cameras, reach deep for a smile as she forced herself to walk slowly along the carpet, stop to exchange a word with someone she recognised, respond to the calls of the photographers and wave in response to the calls of 'good luck'.

Call back, 'Thank you', when someone shouted, 'Great hair!'

She even managed to blow a kiss directly into the lens of her own network's news camera as it tracked her progress.

She told herself that Daisy might be watching.

Ivo, she knew, would not be. Beyond the financial and political news, he had no interest in television.

He had, however, sent her creamy hothouse freesias with a card inscribed simply with his name.

Just 'Ivo'. Not 'Love…', or 'Thinking of you…'. Not his style. He had, however, written it himself. Had spoken to the florist personally. His PA would have sent a basket of red roses. Miranda, more imaginative, would have scoured the hedgerows for deadly nightshade—but they would have been exquisitely arranged.

Ivo had sent her freesias the morning after their first night together, when they'd made love as if the world were about to end. An odd choice—they were the flowers a man might have sent to his bride—but exotic hothouse blooms would have been too obvious and he had never been that.

She slammed a door shut on that thought.

It wasn't a romantic gesture she told herself. It was the gesture of a man who, when he wanted something, was prepared to take infinite trouble to acquire it. Knew how to make surrender feel like triumph.

She thought he'd let her walk away, maybe even be glad that she'd taken the decision, but he was there every minute of the day, not just crowding her thoughts, but physically present. Checking that she was coping. Turning up to help her decorate, even. And that confused her too. It was as if he was saying, 'I'm fine with this…', 'I'm just helping you move on…'

It didn't feel like that, though.

Or maybe it was just that she didn't want it to be like that.

Bad enough that she'd rushed home on Monday. She might have fooled herself into believing that it was Daisy she was desperate to hear from, but the disappointment when Ivo had not dropped by with her post, when he'd sent Paul with her jewels instead of coming himself, had been just as keen as the lack of a response from her sister.

Ivo was watching the news, knowing that after the serious stuff they'd show the celebrities arriving earlier that evening for the awards dinner. As Belle took Jace Sutton's hand and stepped from the car, looked up, smiled into a barrage of flashlights, he could scarcely breathe.

Had he expected, hoped that she might look a little lost? As if she was missing him? On the contrary, she looked utterly self-possessed. Stunning. And, as she turned to the camera, blew a kiss, he was the one who was lost…

There was a tap at the library door and, as he flicked off the television, his housekeeper said, 'I'm sorry to disturb you, Mr Grenville, but there's a police officer looking for Mrs Grenville.'

The evening was interminable. Ivo's absence was not remarked upon; in the self-absorbed world of television, Jace Sutton, full of industry gossip, secrets, made a much more entertaining, and useful, contact.

Dinner, endless awards, gushing speeches, washed over her in a blur. When the man who'd given her that first chance—setting her on the path that ended here—at last read out the list of nominees for the final award of the evening—Television Personality of the Year—then opened the gold envelope and smiled as he read out the winner's name, it took a moment for her to realise that the name he'd read out was 'Belle Davenport'.

That it was her.

That she would have to walk up to the stage and somehow thank everyone who'd ever so much as made her a cup of tea for making her success possible.

Far too late to regret wanting to prove to herself that she could do this on her own and wish she'd pulled a sickie.

It took a while to make it to the stage. So many hands reached out to her that could not be ignored. Eventually she mounted the steps, took the trophy, turned to acknowledge her audience and the room stilled.

She looked down at the trophy in her hand and blinked back tears that she'd been fighting all evening. 'This trophy has my name on it, but it isn't really mine. It belongs to everyone who makes Breakfast With Belle the kind of programme people switch on every day. Susan, who meets me at four-thirty with a cup of Earl Grey and a smile. Elaine, who works magic with make-up. No, honestly, it's true. I do wear make-up…' There was laughter. 'It's unfair to pick out names, but look at the list tomorrow morning when the titles roll. Every one of them should have their name inscribed on this award, because it takes every one of those people, doing their job behind the scenes to make me look good. It belongs to the people they live with too, their partners who are disturbed at four o'clock every morning and who never get a decent night out because we have to be in bed by nine o'clock every evening.'

'Lucky Ivo Grenville,' someone shouted and everyone laughed, giving her a moment to recover.

Ivo, standing unnoticed in the doorway watching her, saw her smile, too.

'Lucky Belle Davenport,' she said with feeling when the laughter subsided.

For a moment he thought she'd seen him, but then he realised that she was seeing no one. That she wasn't speaking for effect, but from the heart.

'Oh, Belle. What have I done to you?' he murmured. A waitress was standing within touching distance, but she didn't hear; she was totally enraptured by the woman standing on the stage.

'Some of you already know that this next week will be my last "on the sofa".'

There was a rustle, whispers, a shocked 'No…'

'It's time to move on, but I want to thank all of you for watching, for supporting me over the years. Please be as kind to whoever takes my place.'

Belle, unable to say another word, simply raised her trophy in acknowledgement of the applause. In front of her was a sea of faces but there was only one who would have made this moment memorable.

And as if the need, so powerful, called up the man, she saw Ivo standing by the door, looking at her. The only person in the room not smiling. Not applauding.

She walked down the steps and, ignoring the outstretched hands, she walked towards him until the applause died away to silence and she was close enough to touch him.

Not an illusion conjured up out of her need, but real, solid.

He wasn't in evening dress. Fine rain misted his hair, the shoulders of his long overcoat, and belatedly she realised that he hadn't turned up to witness her big moment. That he was here because there was something wrong.

'What is it?' she said. 'What's happened?'

'Not here.'

And her stomach lurched as, face set, he took her gently by the arm and led her out of the banqueting hall, down the stairs and into the lobby, past photographers caught with their lens caps on. The doorman was waiting by his car and she was in her seat before they recovered.

'What is it?' she demanded again as Ivo slid in beside her behind the wheel. 'What's wrong?'

'The police are looking for you. For Belinda Porter. They went to the flat and a neighbour explained who you are, that you were probably at home with me.'

'I'm sorry…'

'No. I'm sorry to have ruined your evening.'

He was looking at her as if he knew, she thought. Knew that all evening she'd been fighting the need to reach out, find his hand. Then she realised that it wasn't his absence he was apologising for, but dragging her away from the celebrations for the award she was still clutching.

Breaking away from a look that seemed to sear her soul, she turned away, tossing the thing on to the back seat.

'Has there been a break-in?' she asked as he pulled away from the kerb, into the busy late-evening traffic.

'No. The flat is fine,' he said, concentrating on the road as he eased his way across the lanes.

Of course it was. If it had been something that simple he wouldn't have bothered her; he'd have dealt with it himself. Or had Miranda do it for him.

'I don't understand. Nobody knows I'm living there.'

Only Simone and Claire. Simone's lost diary flashed through her head but she dismissed it. The address of the flat couldn't possibly have been in her diary…

'Just you, my agent…'

Daisy.

She felt the blood drain from her face.

Daisy was in trouble. 'What is it? What's happened?'

'They wouldn't give me any details, Belle. Just that someone admitted to A&E earlier this evening was carrying a letter with your name, your address and they didn't know who else to contact.'

'Hospital? But…' She moved her lips, did everything right, but no sound emerged. 'She's unconscious?'

'Apparently she collapsed in the street. They wouldn't tell me any more.'

'No…' She cleared her throat, tried again. 'No.' Then, 'I'm sorry you were bothered. I didn't want you…'

'Bothered.' He finished the sentence when she faltered.

Belle heard the dead sound in his voice. Well, what had she expected? 'I'm sorry.'

'So am I, Belle. So am I.'

Ivo steered the big car across the city with only the intermittent slap of the wipers clearing the icy drizzle breaking the silence. She.

He hadn't said whether the person was male or female, but Belle had known. So it was true. She had a daughter.

He waited, hoping that she would tell him, trust him. Then, glancing at her as he pulled up in front of the hospital, he realised that she was beyond that. That she was taut with anxiety, with something else. Fear?

He reached across, briefly touched her hands, which were clenched together in her lap, and when she looked up he said, 'We'll take care of her, Belle.'

For a moment he saw something flicker in the depths of her eyes, something that gave him hope, then, quite deliberately, she shook her head, moved her hands.

'There is no we. Thank you for coming to fetch me, for the lift.' She opened the door before he could get out and do it for her. 'I can handle it from here.'

'You may not want to live with me, Belle, but I'm still your husband,' he said, doing his best to keep the desperation from his voice. To stop her from shutting him out. This was not like buying a car. Painting a ceiling. He'd spoken to the policeman. He knew how hard this was going to be. 'I am still your friend.'

She did not look at him as she said, 'We've never been friends, Ivo.'

And with that she swung her legs from the car and walked away from him, picking up her gown as she climbed the steps to the entrance.

For a moment he stayed where he was, pinned to his seat by her words. Knowing that he should go after her, that she would need him, no matter what she said.

*We've never been friends...*

Was that the truth?

He'd wanted her body. Had wanted the warmth she'd brought to his life.

What, apart from a sense of security that she no longer needed, had he ever given her in return?

Even now, when she'd left him, when she'd plainly said that there was nothing in their marriage, nothing in him, to hold her, he was plotting and planning as if she were some company, some *thing* he wanted to possess, control.

Not a woman who, with each passing day, he admired more, understood more, missed more. Who he knew he would not want to live without.

*We've never been friends...*

Her words dripped into his mind like acid, peeling away the layers of scar tissue that had built up since his earliest years, protecting him from pain, letting in light so that he could see that he'd been asking the wrong question. It wasn't what, how much, he could give her to bring her back that he should be asking himself; he already knew that there weren't enough diamonds in the world, or flowers, no penthouse apartment built that would do it for him.

She didn't want, need, possessions; she had all she'd ever need without him. But security wasn't just a well-stocked portfolio. There was a deeper psychological dimension to it, a need that transcended physical comfort, one which no amount of money could provide; that was the security she'd sought from him and which he'd failed so miserably to give her. Because for all his wealth, he knew his own emotional piggy bank was empty.

How did you fill a dry well?

Where did you go for something you could not buy?

The dilemma of a thousand fairy tales. What did he have to barter that was worth the heart of Belle Davenport?

As if on cue the phone rang, offering, if not an answer, another chance.

Belle ignored the ripple of interest that her arrival in A&E provoked.

She made herself known at reception, was taken through to one of the treatment rooms where a scarecrow of a girl was lying on the examination table. Thin, pale, wearing nothing more than a T-shirt, a pair of black jeans. Belle tried not to react, betray her shock, horror, but forced herself to reach out.

'Daisy?' she said.

The girl did not respond to her touch, refused to meet her eyes. She was nineteen, nearly twenty, but she looked so young, so pathetic, so thin…

She'd had this picture in her head of Daisy as a grown-up version of the little girl she remembered. Blonde, pretty. Happy. A young woman with a family. Someone she could love. Who would love her. Not this sorry creature.

'Is she hurt?' she asked, turning to the nurse.

'The doctor couldn't find anything. No bumps, no bruises, no sign of self-harm.'

Self-harm? She swallowed.

'Is she anorexic?' She could hardly bring herself to say the word, but she needed to know the worst.

'She's pregnant, Miss Davenport.'

'Pregnant!'

'She just passed out. It happens, although it would be less likely if she was eating regularly, had a little TLC.' Then, 'I thought you knew her?'

'Yes,' she said. 'I know her.'

At least she thought she did, but there was no connection, no instant bonding, none of the emotional attachment that she'd anticipated, hoped for. But then, why would Daisy have any reason to feel that way about her?

'It's been a very long time since I've seen her,' she added, when the nurse continued to look at her, clearly expecting a little more. 'Are you admitting her?'

'This is a hospital, not a B&B.'

B&B? Bed and breakfast… 'She can't wait until morning for something to eat!'

'We're not an all night café, either.'

'No.' Belle flushed with embarrassment. 'I'm sorry. I can see you're rushed off your feet. I'll go and organise some transport, get out of your way.' She glanced at Daisy, but there was no reaction, no pleasure, no rejection, just a blank stare. 'If that's all right?'

'If you want her, she's all yours.' She turned to the girl, who had not moved, and said, 'It seems as if it's your lucky day.'

That earned the nurse a glare. She was clearly immune because she just said, 'Take it or leave it, but I need this room for someone who's actually sick.'

Daisy sat up slowly, lowered feet encased in a pair of scarred and muddy black sports shoes, then slid to the floor, picked up her coat and headed for the door without a word.

The nurse raised a rather-you-than-me eyebrow in Belle's direction. Belle shrugged and then, realising that she was in danger of losing her sister all over again, hurried after her.

'Wait.' Then, when she kept going, head down as she strode towards the door, 'Daisy. Please…'

'I didn't ask them to call you,' she said, without stopping.

'I know.' Belle hurried alongside her, struggling to keep up in her high heels and long dress. 'But I'm here. Look, just wait while I call a cab.' Daisy finally stopped, but still did not look at her. 'Sit down. Or get a cup of something hot from the machine. Chocolate. That will warm you…'

'I haven't got any money.'

'Take this.'

Belle turned. Ivo was standing behind her, extending a handful of change in Daisy's direction, but he was looking at her. After what she'd said to him, she hadn't expected to see him ever again.

Maybe that had been her intention. To drive him away.

'You left your bag behind,' he said, before she could ask. 'Jace came after you, but we'd already gone so he dropped it off at the house. Manda phoned me. She knew you'd need your keys.'

'I…yes.'

Only then did he turn to Daisy. 'We've met before.'

She didn't reply, just stalked off towards the door.

'When?' Belle demanded. 'When have you seen her before?'

'She's the girl who set off your car alarm the other day.'

So close. She'd been so close… 'You said she had green hair.'

'That was four days ago. And actually I think I prefer the blue,' he said. 'It goes with her eyes.'

'What do you mean by that?'

'Nothing.' Then, 'Hadn't we better go after her?'

# CHAPTER SIX

*THERE is no we...*

She'd said the words in an attempt to drive him away and she suspected that he was using 'we' now in an attempt to show her how wrong she was.

He needn't have bothered.

Whatever happened they would always, in her mind, her heart, be connected for eternity—in the memory of every touch, kiss, the sweet caresses that drove every other thought from her mind. In those moments when nothing else existed.

'Belle?'

'Yes,' she said, catching her breath. Then, as they emerged through the sliding doors, 'Where's she gone?'

'Not far,' Ivo said with certainty.

Belle ignored the cynical undertone—he didn't understand, how could he?—and said, 'We've got to find her. It's cold. She's hungry...' She couldn't quite bring herself to say what else she was.

'She's there, look. On the other side of the road.'

Wishing she was wearing something more sensible on her feet, something more sensible full stop, Belle ran down the steps. Ivo was there before her. 'Get in the car.'

She took no notice, side-stepping him, lifted her skirts as she began to run.

'Daisy, wait...Where are you going?' she demanded breathlessly, dodging cars to cross the road. Just wanting to hold her, keep her safe.

Then, as Daisy paused and turned, instead of reaching for her, she found herself held back by a force field of anger so powerful that she took a step back.

'Why did it have to be you? You abandoned me!' Then, pitiably, 'I wasn't looking for you. I was looking for my father.'

'Why?' The word was shocked out of her. 'Why would you want to find him? He didn't just abandon Mum and me, he abandoned you too. Everything that happened was his fault...'

'Liar!'

'It's true!' And then, seeing Daisy's face crumple, Belle would have done anything to call the bitter words back. She'd been a baby when it had happened. She didn't have a clue. How could she? All she knew was that her mother had died, her sister had abandoned her. Who else was there for her but some fantasy figure of a father? What other hope did she have?

The rain had stopped but a raw wind was whistling down the narrow street and, shivering, desperate to make it right, call the words back, Belle fought back all the bad memories. If that was what Daisy wanted, if that was what she needed, then she'd find her father for her.

'We'd have a better chance of finding him together, Daisy.'

'Oh, right. Like you want that.'

'It's what you want that matters to me.'

Ivo pulled up alongside them, got out of the car and took off his coat, wrapping it, warm from his body, around her shoulders, as if she were the one who needed looking after. As if he were the only person in the world capable of doing it.

Maybe he was.

And she heard Simone's voice saying, 'Ivo could help you...'

She had no doubt that finding Daisy's father would be a lot more difficult than finding Daisy. That if anyone could do it, he could.

She shook her head. She had to do this on her own. Stand on

her own two feet and, shrugging off his coat, she draped it around her sister.

'I'll help you, Daisy,' she said. 'Whatever you want. There are agencies who can help, who specialize in searching for people. Family members.'

'Family? You're not my family!'

Ivo saw Belle flinch as if struck. Open her mouth as if to speak but unable to find words to express her feelings, and he felt her pain to the bone.

'Belle… Please,' Ivo said, impatiently. 'Both of you. Daisy? Why don't you get in the car?'

Daisy told him in words of one syllable, just what he could do with his car.

'There's no point in standing here getting soaked,' he said, letting it go. There was enough raw emotion flying about without him adding to the mix. Belle had made it more than clear that she wanted to deal with this herself, didn't want him involved. 'I'll leave you to talk.'

'Why would I want to talk to her? She abandoned me, left me, didn't want to know!'

'No!'

Belle's cry tore at him. He'd heard enough and cutting off the torrent of abuse that Daisy unleashed upon Belle, he said, 'That's it. Enough. I'll give you money for food, but I'm not going to allow Belle to stand here in the rain listening to your self-pitying rant—'

'Allow me?' Belle turned on him, blazing with fury. 'Allow me?'

'You won't be use or ornament with pneumonia,' he pointed out, doing his best to keep things on an even keel, but aware that sympathy would only fuel whatever was driving Daisy's misery.

'Don't you understand? I don't care about myself. I only care about her.'

'I know, Belle. Believe me, I know.'

'This isn't about you. About us,' she said, misunderstanding his meaning. Assuming he was referring to the fact that she'd left him for this. 'If I walk away, where will she go?'

'The same place she stayed last night, I imagine,' he said, as gently as he could. 'And the night before that. Why don't you ask her?'

'No.' Belle felt the rain soaking through the lace and silk to her skin. Freezing rain. She'd been here before. Cold, wet, hungry. She knew all the dark places where frightened women hid from the night. 'No,' she said, talking to herself as much as Ivo, 'I can't take that risk.'

'What risk?' He turned his attention to Daisy. 'She's been hanging around your flat, ringing your number. Do you imagine it was a coincidence that she conveniently passed out in the street with your address in her pocket on the biggest night of your year? She's making you run, Belle, making you chase her. She's not going anywhere you won't find her.'

'What made you such a cynic, Ivo?' she demanded.

Ivo was desperate. The rain was coming down steadily now, soaking into the sweater he was wearing, soaking into the girl's miserable clothes, plastering Belle's beautiful dress to her skin and her hair to her cheeks, her neck. She said she didn't care about herself but *he* did and, despite everything, he cared more than he would ever have believed possible about her daughter too, simply because she was Belle's flesh and blood.

'I'm not a cynic, Belle,' he said, but he knew what he was dealing with here and if he had to be the bad guy to get them somewhere safe and warm, he was prepared to do that for them both. 'I'm a realist.' He opened the rear passenger door and said, 'What do you say, Daisy? A hot bath, a warm bed, good food. It's got to be better than this.'

'Stuff your hot bath. I don't need her and I certainly don't need you.'

'You don't get me,' he assured her, hoping that humour might work where an appeal to sense had not. She didn't move. 'Suppose I throw in a hundred pounds?' he offered. Money was the only inducement he had left. Money always talked.

'Ivo!'

'No? A thousand pounds?' he persisted, ignoring Belle's outrage.

'I hate you,' Daisy said, glaring at him. Then, sticking her chin out, 'Five thousand pounds.'

He saw Belle's face and something inside him broke. She didn't deserve this. She didn't deserve any of this...

'I hate both of you,' Daisy shouted, tossing off his coat, flinging it at Belle. It happened so quickly that while Belle was caught up in the coat and he was momentarily distracted, the girl disappeared. It was as if she'd melted away. Thin as she was, that clearly couldn't be the case; obviously she'd ducked down one of the barely lit alleyways between the buildings.

He swore, furious with her, furious with himself. It wasn't supposed to be like this. It wasn't how he'd imagined it. He'd been sure that when Belle had connected with her lost child, had that need fulfilled, he would be able to tell her the truth. From the time the policeman had arrived on his doorstep he'd known it wasn't going to be that easy but, with all his experience with Manda, he should have done better than this.

It was as if he'd turned into his father overnight.

'I'm so sorry, Belle.'

She shook her head. 'Help me, Ivo,' she begged. 'Help me to find her...'

Her words should have made him the happiest man alive, but life was never that simple. All he had to be grateful for was that he was there, that she was still speaking to him.

They searched the nearest alleyway, then the rest of the street, calling her name, Belle alternately pleading with her and yelling at her to come back.

It was only when her teeth were chattering so badly that she could scarcely form the words that she finally gave in, allowed him to take her back to the car. Even then she insisted on driving around very slowly so that she could peer into shop doorways, hoping for a glimpse of Daisy. She didn't bother to reproach him. She didn't need to say the words.

They both hated him.

Which made three of them.

He'd wanted to protect Belle, but all he'd done was hurt her.

It was the early hours before he insisted on calling a halt, not because he was ready to give up, but because she couldn't take any more.

'It's no good. I'm willing to search all night but if she doesn't want to be found we haven't got a chance.'

'You said that she wanted to be found.'

'She does, Belle. But maybe she doesn't know it yet.'

Belle's only answer was a long, painful shiver.

'I'll take you home,' he said, far more concerned about her than the girl who was causing her so much pain. 'I'll carry on looking. I promise I won't give up—'

'No, you're right. There's no point. She knows where I am.'

He didn't quite trust her quiescence but she waited patiently in the car while he fetched her bag from his house and, when they reached Camden, since she was shaking too much to connect key to lock, she surrendered it to him. He didn't wait for an invitation, but followed her upstairs, turned up the heating and put on the kettle while Belle got out of her finery, now damp and muddied around the hem, and into a warm dressing gown.

'Heat, a hot drink,' she said as she curled up on the sofa and he placed a warm mug of chocolate liberally laced with brandy into her hands. 'Daisy won't have that.'

'Her choice. She could have been here, Belle, but she wants to punish you. Wants to make you suffer,' he said, kneeling in front of her so that he could wrap his own hands around hers on the mug to stop them from shaking. Holding it while she sipped from it, not allowing her to push it away even when she pulled a face.

'She's not the only one. What did you put in this?'

'It'll warm you. Drink it.' Then, because he had to make her understand, 'She believes that hurting herself will cause you more pain than anything else.'

'How do you know that?'

'It's true, isn't it?' he said, avoiding a direct answer. She nodded. 'She'll come back when she thinks you've suffered enough. Tomorrow. The next day.'

'And if tomorrow is too late?'

She looked up, all colour had been leached from her face but she was still holding everything in. There were no tears, no outward display of anger. Coming from a family where emotion was repressed to the point of destruction, it had never occurred to him to wonder before at the way she held everything tight within herself—only to be grateful that she didn't indulge in tears and hysterics.

Now he understood where that restraint came from he would have welcomed a little hysteria, would have been glad to see the dam break, tears flow.

'She's so thin, Ivo...' He waited, hoping she'd let it all out. 'If I could just have given her something to eat. She needs care. Looking after. I don't have the first clue about where to find her.'

'What exactly do you know, Belle?' Then, because she was famous and wealthy and there were people out there who would use any vulnerability to take advantage of her, to cheat her, 'Are you even sure she's the girl you're looking for?'

'She had my letter. She'd registered with the adoption search agency and I wrote to her. How else would she know where to find me? My phone number...'

'You believed that was her calling, didn't you? The hang-ups?'

'I don't know. I suppose so. At least I hoped...'

'I'm sure you're right,' he said, rescuing the mug, placing it on a low table before moving to her side, encouraging her to lean into him, offering his own warmth as comfort. Doing his best not to think about the softness of her hair against his cheek, her scent seeping into his head, a yearning to draw her close and never let her out of his arms again. This was not about him.

This was about the woman he would do anything for. A woman who brightened every room with her presence. A woman he...loved. The word slipped into his mind, filling a vast empty space.

Belle, exhausted, let her head rest against Ivo's chest. Just for a minute. While she gathered herself.

He'd been so strange tonight. Loving, caring, awful. All mixed up. Like her. There had been that moment when she'd been so angry with Daisy for wanting her father. Proud of her when she'd challenged Ivo. Five thousand pounds? What was all that about?

'How many letters did you write?' he asked.

She caught a yawn. 'Letters? To Daisy? Just one.'

'I'm not talking about how many you sent. How many did you write?'

'Oh, I see. A few,' she admitted, remembering all the drafts.

'And what did you do with them? Have you got a shredder here? Or did you put them into the rubbish where anyone could find them?'

'No…' Then, 'No!'

Not 'no' to the questions, but 'no' to what the question implied. That this was a set-up, that someone had been through her trash, had found one of the drafts and was using it.

Ivo tightened his arm around Belle's shoulder as she pulled away, recognising in that cry of anguish a need that he couldn't fulfil.

All he could do was hold her, say, 'I know.' Be there for her. 'I know what you hoped for,' he said as her head fell back against his shoulder. 'It took me a while, but I knew there was something bothering you. Something that you didn't think you could share with me…My fault, not yours,' he said quickly. 'Then, when I remembered that you were searching for adoption websites, it all fell into place…'

'Ivo—'

'Tonight,' he said, before she could deny it, 'when I told you that someone had collapsed, you didn't ask who. You knew. You said "she". So…' Her eyes were wide, anxious. 'So I'm telling you that I know. You had a baby girl. Gave her up for adoption…'

'Daisy?' The colour had returned to her cheeks, she'd stopped shivering. 'You think that I...that she...'

She was finding it so difficult to speak that he said it for her. 'You've been looking for her. Tonight you believed you've found her.'

'Believed?' A sound, something between a shudder and a sigh, escaped her and she closed her eyes as if to blot out pictures in her head that were too painful to bear.

Dark smudges were imprinted beneath her eyes. How long had it been since she'd slept properly? he wondered. How long had she been searching? Longing? Why hadn't she come to him, asked him to help?

No, scrub that last question.

This was a marriage without emotional baggage.

They could have just stayed with the hot sex, two individuals who shared a bed, no strings attached. But Belle had wanted security and he'd just wanted her so they'd made a deal, formed a mutually beneficial partnership. Quite possibly the perfect match. They both had got what they'd wanted and, without any of those messy emotions, who was there to get hurt?

Too late to whine when he'd discovered he didn't like the answer.

'I know this is not what you want to hear now, but I have to ask if you're absolutely sure she's the girl you're looking for.'

He anticipated an angry reaction, expected her to shout at him, tell him that he didn't know what he was talking about, but, although her lips parted, the words didn't make it. She just pulled away from him as if touching him would contaminate her with the same vile suspicions.

It hadn't even occurred to her to doubt the girl, he realised. She wouldn't have checked or run any tests.

Maybe that made her a better person than him. It also made her vulnerable, at the mercy of the unscrupulous.

Right now it was more important that she trusted him and he gripped her shoulders, turned her to face him. 'Look at me, Belle.'

For a moment she resisted.

'Belle…'

Slowly, reluctantly, she raised her lashes. Her eyes were glistening liquid bronze, but still the tears did not fall.

'She didn't want me,' she said, as if that answered all his questions, all his doubts. 'It was her father she was looking for, hoping for…'

And that hurt more than he'd believed possible too. That out there somewhere was a man who'd given her what he was unable to—a child. A fool of a man who didn't know how lucky he was…

'We'll find her, Belle. I'll find her for you. I'll find him too, if that's what she wants. If she's really your daughter…' And suddenly he was the one having trouble getting the words out. 'If she's really your daughter, then that makes her mine too.'

'No!' Belle pulled away from him, wrenched herself from his arms. 'No, Ivo—'

No. Of course not. What kind of fool was he to imagine…? 'My responsibility, then,' he said, before she could tell him that it was nothing to do with him. None of his business. Said the words that excluded him for ever.

'No! Ivo, you've got this—'

'I've seen her, Belle. It's not going to be easy. You're going to need support. That's something I can do for you. I can help you both if—'

Her eyes widened a little at that, and this time all she could do was shake her head.

His fault. Exhausted though she was, she'd picked up on his hesitation. That word 'if'. *If* she's your daughter. If she wasn't some con artist homing in on a desperate woman. For her sake he wanted it to be so. For his own too…

But someone had to be responding with their head rather than their heart and it was so much easier for him. He'd never clogged his up with the silt of emotional cholesterol.

Hard though it was, as little as she'd thank him, as her husband, her friend, he was the one who had to lay it on the line for her. Even if she never forgave him. That was what you did for the woman you loved.

'She doesn't look much like you,' he said.

Belle blinked. 'Oh, I see. Yes, well, it's true that I haven't got blue hair.'

'Or blue eyes,' he persisted, knowing that she didn't want to hear this, that she wouldn't thank him for pressing this. Not now. Maybe later, when she'd had time to think, when her emotions weren't in a turmoil. 'It's not impossible, I know…'

'But you're suggesting that it's genetically unlikely?'

She was too calm.

'I'm sorry.'

'Why should you be sorry for pointing out the truth, Ivo? You're absolutely right.'

He frowned. The fact that she was agreeing with him did not fill him with optimism.

'But, then again, you're completely wrong.'

'Sweetheart…' The rare endearment slipped out. For a moment he thought she'd got it, understood the danger…

'Daisy is not my daughter, Ivo. She's waif-thin, looks like a kid, but she's only ten years younger than me. She's my sister. Half-sister, anyway. We had different fathers. Mine died, hers deserted. Same result.'

And for a moment he was the one momentarily bereft of words.

Not?

Not her daughter?

He'd been so sure. And, without warning, there was a gap where some unrecognised emotion had briefly flared, lodged. An emptiness that had been briefly filled…

'She's your sister?'

'You sound almost more shocked,' she said.

'No…' He shook his head. It wasn't shock. It was far worse than that. 'No. I…' The words died.

'Don't feel bad, Ivo. You have every right to be shocked. She was all I had and I turned my back on her.'

He'd been so sure; now he was struggling to get to grips with this unexpected twist. 'But you were searching for her. I saw the adoption website.'

'She was adopted. I wasn't.'

'What? They separated you?'

'She was four. The perfect little girl. White-blonde curls, blue eyes. A smile that could light up a room. I was fourteen. An angry teenager who'd lived rough for the best part of three years, on the run from my mother's demons, from Social Services. Scavenging to live, seeing things that no child...' She shivered, did not resist when he pulled her back into his arms, rocking her as if she were the child. 'Daisy was whisked off to a foster family. I was admitted to hospital with the same chest infection that killed my mother. A cough that a smoker would have been proud of. Hence the husky voice.'

He let slip a rare expletive as his imagination filled in the gaps. The reality of what she'd suffered.

'How did Daisy escape? The infection?'

'My mother gave what little food she had to us. I gave most of mine to Daisy. She was always warm. Always fed. Always came first.'

'And you did what you thought was best for her.' Not a question. More to himself than her. How could he doubt it? He'd seen the fervour with which she'd embraced her chance to do something for other children in that position. Understood now why the charity trip had been so important.

He'd always known that there was something in her past. It was too much of a blank; there were no links that went back beyond her time in television. No emotional ties. He'd thought that made them equal, but it didn't. She'd been loved once. Had been part of a family who took care of each other, made sacrifices to keep each other from harm.

He'd lived with her for three years and didn't know a thing about her, he realised, as the questions crowded into his head.

What had her mother been running from? Three years with

two children, one little more than a baby. How on earth had they survived?

The only question he didn't have to ask himself was why she'd never told him.

But all that would wait. Some things wouldn't—not if he was going to find out if this girl was genuine. What had happened to her.

'The authorities separated you when your mother died?'

'Poor Mum. She was so afraid of Social Services. She knew that she'd lose us if they took us into care. Even when she was too sick to stand, she wouldn't let me get help. Then one morning I couldn't wake her. I knew she'd yell at me, tell me I was a fool, but I panicked, called an ambulance. I didn't want her to die.'

'You did the right thing.'

'No, Ivo. I should have done it a week before, when there might have been a chance. I wouldn't have cared how much she shouted at me. I would have run away from care to be with her.'

'You blame yourself?'

She roused herself, turned on him. 'Wouldn't you?' she demanded. Her lovely eyes, usually so full of warmth, life, were bleak with exhaustion. Something more.

He shook his head, unable to express what he was feeling, imagine what she'd been through. 'They shouldn't have separated you.'

'Years ago they used to routinely split up entire families. Twins even. I've read some heart-rending stories, Ivo. Brothers, sisters reunited after half a century. It wouldn't happen now,' she said, reaching out as if to reassure him. As if he was the one who needed comfort. This was the warmth that her viewers responded to. She genuinely cared for people, even him, and he used that now, shamelessly, to draw her close, bring her back within the compass of his arms, as if he was the one in need of comfort. 'It probably wouldn't have happened then if there hadn't been such an age gap,' she said. 'Daisy was young enough to forget, have the chance of a decent life, Ivo. A real family. It was already too late for me.'

'It's never too late,' he said as another yawn caught her by surprise. She'd been on the go since before dawn and the warmth of the flat, the brandy-laced chocolate was seeping into her system, doing its job. She was both mentally and physically exhausted and soon she'd sleep, but she fought it, needing, he suspected, to get it all off her chest. 'I was so angry,' she said. Then shook her head, so that her short tawny hair, corkscrewed by the rain, brushed against his cheek. 'No. That's too clean a word. It wasn't anger; it was jealousy. I was jealous of a little girl who still knew how to smile. Knew how to make people love her. I couldn't forgive her for that so I walked away.' She sighed. 'Clever Ivo,' she said. 'You're always right.'

'No…'

'Oh, yes. You said she wanted to punish me and tonight she did it in the only way she knew how, the way I taught her, by turning her back on me and walking away.'

'She'll come back.'

'Will she?' She looked up, seeking assurance. 'She said she was looking for her father.'

'You could help her. She knows that.' She shook her head just once. 'She had your address in her pocket, Belle. If she didn't want to know you, why did she keep it?'

Belle didn't answer, but closed her eyes as if to blot out a world of pain.

Ivo wanted to move mountains, change the world for her. Wanted to crush her to him, take that pain into himself, but he knew she would not, could not surrender it. That she was living in a world of guilt that only she could work through.

Power, wealth meant nothing here. For the moment all he could do was hold her, be there for her, no matter how many times she pushed him away.

Maybe, in the end, that was all anyone could do.

Maybe, for now, that was enough, he thought, as the tension finally melted from her limbs and, finally claimed by exhaustion, she softened into him, dropping away into sleep.

It had been weeks since she'd lain against him like this when, all passion spent, she'd fallen asleep in his arms. It was a moment he'd always treasured.

There was an almost unbearable sweetness in the way she surrendered consciousness to him and he felt a selfish joy in the moment—to be, if only for a moment, this close, this trusted.

'It will be okay, my love,' he said softly. Brushed his lips against her forehead. 'I'll make it okay.'

She didn't stir. His arm went to sleep. A muscle in his back began to niggle. He welcomed the pain.

# CHAPTER SEVEN

SOMETHING hard and sharp was digging into Belle's cheek. She turned her head, reaching up to grab the pillow, turn it to the cool side.

Her hand encountered something—warm, firm. Not smooth cotton, but soft to the touch. Cashmere...

She'd fallen asleep on the sofa?

There was a blank moment as she groped for memory, then, as she shifted to a more comfortable position and a dozen niggles from back, arm, neck brought the hideous events of the night back to her in a rush, she opened her eyes, only to be distracted by the thought that the pashmina she'd draped over her sofa to disguise its age was not grey.

But then, as the fog of sleep cleared, it became obvious that she was not alone on the sofa.

She raised her head. Ivo, unusually rumpled, with a shadow several hours past five o'clock darkening his chin, was regarding her with sleepy eyes and she felt herself blush.

She'd slept all night on the sofa with Ivo, her head on his chest, her arm around his waist, their limbs tangled together and somehow the fact that they were both covered from neck to ankle in several layers didn't make it any less intimate.

Any less awkward.

She'd left him. She'd cut him out of this part of her life, had told him, more than once, that she didn't need him. But last night, despite the cruel way she'd rejected his offer of friendship, had walked away from him, he hadn't left her stranded without money or keys—which plainly she'd deserved—but had come to find her. Even when she'd turned on him, had blamed him when Daisy had run off, he'd spent hours patiently searching with her.

And when, finally, she'd told him the truth about her life, he'd stayed.

All night.

Of course the fact that she was lying on top of him, that he couldn't escape without waking her, might account for that. But he hadn't had to lie there and hold her as she'd finally succumbed to sleep. Hold her, whisper comfort in her ear. Call her 'my love'…

No. She'd imagined that. He didn't do those words. He was a minimalist husband. Beautiful to look at. Perfect in every detail. But cold…

'I'm sorry,' she said.

'What for?'

'Everything.'

For the fact that she didn't want to move, ever, but to stay pressed up against his warm body.

That she'd lied to him.

'For falling asleep on you,' she said, picking on the smallest reason. The one that wouldn't embarrass either of them.

'You'd have been more comfortable in bed, but I didn't want to disturb you,' he said, stroking a thumb beneath one of her eyes. Last night there had been dark smudges that it had taken some very expensive concealer to disguise. 'How long is it since you really slept?'

'I looked that bad?'

The phone rescued him—rescued both of them—jolting her out of a desperate longing to just stay where she was, in Ivo's arms, to forget everything else.

'What's the time?'

'Does it matter?'

'Yes.'

No…

She lifted Ivo's fingers from her face and for a moment just held them. How easy it would be to turn his hand, trail her lips along his fingers, enticing a response, a touch, a kiss, the slow peeling back of her robe, Ivo's mouth on her neck, his fingers trailing over her skin in a slow prelude to the closeness, the precious intimacy her body craved.

She'd missed him so much…

Realising that she was still holding his fingers, she twisted her head to look at his wristwatch. 'No,' she said. 'That can't be right. My alarm…'

'You might have forgotten to set it.'

'The studio! I should have been there hours ago. Why didn't someone call? Where's my BlackBerry?' she wailed, attempting to disentangle arms, legs.

'Still in your bag, switched off, I imagine.' She stared at him blankly. 'The award ceremony?' he prompted.

She groaned and, finally free, she jerked away from him, only to find herself hurtling back into Ivo's arms.

'Let me go!' she demanded.

He held up his hands. 'I didn't do a thing.'

'What?' She eased up, discovered it was her dressing gown trapped between Ivo and the sofa. 'Well, move!'

'My leg's gone to sleep.' He caught her arms, holding her. 'Calm down; whoever it is will leave a message.'

'No…' Didn't he see? Didn't he understand? 'It's Daisy! It's got to be Daisy—'

The machine picked up, her brief message played. The caller hung up.

'She was always going to hang up,' Ivo said as, not looking at him, she carefully extracted herself from the sofa.

She knew it, but it didn't help.

'It's a game, Belle.'

'No…'

A long, insistent peal on the front door-bell cut her off and, heedless of Ivo's warning, 'No!', she didn't stop to use the entry phone, but raced down the stairs in her bare feet, wrenching open the front door.

'Good grief, Belle, you look as if you've had a rough night,' Manda said, immaculate from the top of her sleek dark hair to the toes of the Manolos she was wearing on her narrow feet. 'It's just as well Ivo asked me to call the studio and warn them not to expect you this morning.'

He had?

'He did?'

When?

'Didn't he tell you?' Manda shrugged. 'He is here? I've brought him a change of clothes,' she said, lifting one hand, in which she was carrying a suit carrier and a document case. 'I'm sure your problems are much more pressing, but I've been apologising for cancelled engagements ever since you arrived home and since this one is with the PM—'

'I didn't ask him to stay,' Belle snapped, disappointment sharpening her tongue. Then, 'What are you talking about? What cancelled engagements?'

'Nothing important,' Ivo said, placing his hand on her shoulder, 'but you're right, Manda, I can't expect the PM to re-schedule.' Then, regarding the paper carrier she was holding in the other hand, 'Please tell me that's coffee you've got in that bag.'

'Coffee and a muffin,' she said. 'Less messy than a croissant. You can eat while I'm briefing you on the way to Downing Street. I'll wait in the car.'

'There's no need,' he said, relieving her of the bag and the suit carrier. 'Save time and tell the PM yourself.'

'Ivo…' Miranda was, for once, the one left doing an impression of a goldfish.

'Do you have a problem with that?'

'You want me to go to Downing Street in your place?'

'He wants my help with some overseas aid project. If it goes ahead you'll be doing all the work. I'm just cutting out the middle man.'

'Yes, but…'

'I need you to do this for me, Manda.'

Belle sensed that this was important. That this kind of trust was something major. Something new.

'But…' Manda struggled for a moment with the idea, then said, 'Right…' She took a step back and Belle could almost see her giving herself a mental shake. 'I'd better, um, go, then.' Miranda glanced at her, then back at Ivo and said, 'I'll see you later?'

'Later,' he agreed.

She nodded once, turned, then, as she ducked into the back of the car Belle instinctively followed, stepping out on to the path to look up and down the street, hoping against hope to catch a glimpse of her sister loitering somewhere near.

'Don't,' Ivo said, taking her arm, drawing her back inside so that he could close the door. Then, presumably to distract her, he lifted the hand holding both his suit and the paper carrier and said, 'Coffee?'

'I don't think Miranda included me in the breakfast invitation,' she said, taking the carrier, looking inside. 'No, I thought not.'

'We can share.'

'The only thing we've ever shared is a shower and a bed.' And, last night, a sofa…

She turned away to run back up the stairs, into her flat, into the kitchen.

Damn, damn, damn!

Why hadn't he just gone with Miranda?

She'd left him. Didn't he understand? This wasn't his concern. And even when they'd lived together they didn't do this cosy breakfast stuff.

Then, as he followed, favouring his left leg, she forgot that and said, 'How is it? Can I do anything?'

For a moment their eyes locked and her mouth dried at the

rush of memory. His thigh beneath her fingers. The warmth of his skin. The power-packed muscles beneath it.

'No,' he said abruptly. 'It's fine.'

'Right.' Then, as the silence stretched to snapping-point, 'I can't believe you just did that.'

'What?'

'Sent Miranda to see the PM in your place. You do realise that you've probably just thrown away a knighthood? Maybe even a seat in the Lords.'

'Do you think I give a damn?' he asked, taking the lid off the coffee, reaching for a couple of mugs, sharing the contents between them.

'To be honest, Ivo, beyond the bedroom I haven't a clue what you think.'

'About a knighthood?'

'About anything.'

'Then let me enlighten you about one thing. A couple of days ago I told Manda that she underestimated you.'

He did? No, no... 'I won't embarrass you by asking what she said in reply to that.'

'It wouldn't embarrass me, but I suspect Manda would never forgive me for telling you that you make her feel inadequate.'

Inadequate? 'I don't believe that.'

'As a woman.'

'They can do wonders with silicone these days.'

'It has nothing to do with the way you look. It's the way people respond to you. Your natural empathy,' he said. 'Which is why I did you the courtesy of assuming you wouldn't make the same mistake about her.'

It took a moment for Belle, momentarily floundering, to backtrack. 'Oh, I don't underestimate her. I just think she'll scare the pants off the man.'

He looked up. Ivo was a man so contained that she sometimes thought she must have imagined the passionate midnight lover who came to her bed, who haunted her dreams. But here, in her tiny kitchen, unshaven, his hair, his collar, rumpled, the suspicion of a smile creasing the skin around his eyes, she caught a glimpse of the man who had laid siege to her, who had refused to take no for an answer and had flown her away to his paradise island for a sunset wedding for two at the edge of the sea.

'And your problem with that is?' he asked.

She shook her head and, ambushed by the need to respond with a smile of her own, ducked her head. 'No. You've got me.'

He took her chin in his hand, lifted her face and backed her up against the kitchen island, there was no escape. 'Have I?' he asked.

His fingers were cool against her skin. She shivered and somewhere deep in her throat a sound struggled to escape. She didn't know what it was. Yes or no, it would be wrong and she swallowed it down, shook her head, keeping her lashes lowered so that he should not see her eyes, read there what she could not disguise.

If he saw them, he'd know, as he'd known before when, across a room packed with people, he'd somehow forced her to turn and look at him.

Then his weapons had been flowers, tiny treasures, glimpses into his world.

But a man did not reach his heights without being intelligent, adaptable.

He'd seemed to accept her decision, but she should have known he would not, could not let her go that easily. This was now about much more than an unquenchable passion; his pride demanded that he win her back, restore his life to its ordered routine. Tempt her back in the gilded cage she'd stepped into so willingly. And he was prepared to go to any lengths to make that happen. Even using the infinitely more precious gift of his time, if that was what it took.

Even as she held her breath, there was a touch to her mouth so light that she thought she might have imagined it, that her lips, of their own volition, sought to confirm.

They met nothing but air and her eyes flew open but Ivo had already turned away to retrieve the muffin from the bag. He broke it in two, offered her half. Eve's apple, she thought. Persephone's pomegranate seeds. Like the touch of his lips, irresistibly sweet temptation…

'No…' Then, 'Thank you. I need to get dressed. I have to call the studio, make my apologies. Call my PR people.' She pulled a face. 'Heaven alone knows what the redtops will make of my rather sudden exit…'

'I'm sure Jace fed them some plausible story that will hold them off for the time being.'

'No doubt. It's what they'll do with it that bothers me.' Then, 'You asked Miranda to call the studio last night? What did she tell them?'

'That you had a family crisis. Jace and I both thought it would be better coming from her.'

'Of course. Who would dare question Miranda?' Before he could answer, she said, 'My life is about to get very messy, Ivo. You should step back.'

'On the contrary. You should come home so that you'll get some peace.' Then, with a frown, 'Is that what this is all about?' He made a circular gesture with half a muffin, taking in the apartment. 'Protecting me from tabloid splatter?'

'No.'

'You said that too quickly.'

'It wasn't something I had to think about.' If they'd had a real marriage there would have been no secrets and they could have taken 'messy' in their stride. 'You signed up for "perfect", Ivo.' For as long as perfect lasted. 'This was never going to be for ever.'

'No?'

She managed to pick up her coffee—it was a good thing that it was only half a mug or she'd have been in trouble—and tried to think of something to say. Nothing came and she had a momentary flash of sympathy with Ivo when, faced with her bald announcement that she was leaving him, he'd been monosyllabic.

Like him, she discovered, she didn't have the vocabulary to cover this situation, so she said, 'Help yourself to the shower in the guest room,' before retreating to the bathroom.

Ivo, left alone in the tiny kitchen, looked at the muffin he'd torn in half. It was in much the same state as his marriage. He fitted the two pieces back together, but there were bits missing and the join wasn't perfect; it jarred the eye.

But perfection was an illusion. Life had to be lived as it came with all its flaws and risks. Without the grit, there could be no pearl.

Belle was right. This marriage—this perfect marriage—was over. It was time to stop trying to fix it back together. What he had to do was work on rebuilding it from the foundations up.

Belle briefly recoiled from her puffy-eyed, bird's-nest-hair reflection, but had no time to worry about it. She certainly didn't waste time blow-drying her hair into her new style, just fingered it into place and left it to look after itself.

Her evening bag was on her bed where she'd thrown it last night when she'd stripped off her dress. She dug out her BlackBerry and switched it on, scrolling swiftly through a load of texts, all of them congratulations on her award. There were voice mails too. And a couple of emails.

Nothing from Daisy.

Well, what had she expected?

She opened the next best thing, an email from Claire. They'd had a lively exchange of text messages at the weekend; Claire had been putting off the moment when she faced her own demons and Belle had applied the cyber equivalent of a boot to her backside. She was hoping this would be good news.

It wasn't.

It was an email to Simone, copied to her:

I can't say I'm happy that my dirty laundry will soon be hanging out to dry in public...

What?

She flipped to Simone's email and she let slip a word she hadn't used in years. The lost diary had been picked up by a Sydney-based journalist who'd had no trouble in identifying all of them and had called Simone, inviting her to meet him. No chance that he hadn't read it, then. Every word.

She sat down, quickly thumbed in:

Simone, I've just picked up your email and can scarcely comprehend how difficult this must be for you. I'm with Claire—you can tell Mr Tanner from me that Belle Davenport thinks he's lower than a worm's belly—as if he'd care! As for me, Ivo knows pretty much everything so, as far as I'm concerned, you can tell him to publish and be damned. Not so easy for you...

She thought about mentioning Daisy. Decided against it.

Then she returned the call from her agent. She owed him for taking the trouble to leave the celebrations to deliver her bag to Belgravia.

'Babe!' He was mellow. 'Anything for my favourite client. I had a couple of calls from the diarists, but they bought the family crisis. One of the benefits of being a good-living girl. If anyone else had pulled a stunt like that, the press would be staking out The Priory even as we speak. You might want to think up something credible for public consumption, though. The press being what they are.'

'I've got credible. Whether you'll like it is something else.'

'Well, that depends. If it's something really shocking, I could squeeze the publishers for another one hundred advance on your biography,' he offered hopefully, 'and the papers would be fighting for serial rights.'

'My financial adviser said I should keep that as the pension plan,' she said.

'What about *my* pension? Thirty years from now I'll probably be pushing up daisies. And celebrity biographies might not be big business then. In fact, thirty years from now, if you don't make a decision on some of these offers I've got lined up—or, better still, sign that lovely new contract for your breakfast show—no one will remember your name.'

'That's a risk I'm prepared to take. Look, I've got to go. I'll call you later to fix up a meeting—'

'Come over now and we'll have lunch at The Ivy. Celebrate the award. Better still, bring your financial adviser. He can pay.'

She laughed. 'I'll call you later, Jace.'

She was still smiling when she walked into the living room. Ivo, hair damp, was standing back from the window, looking down into the street.

'You're still here? Haven't you got a corporation to run?'

'The shower was on a go slow.'

'Sorry. It's on my list of improvements.'

'It doesn't matter. I don't suppose it will collapse if I miss a morning.' Then, 'You might want to get your car keys.'

'What?'

He indicated the street below and she crossed to the window, standing beside him. Below her, on the pavement, standing next to her convertible, stood Daisy.

'Purple hair today. Oh, right, here we go,' he said as she looked up, and realising that she was being watched, took hold of the door handle and gave it a shake.

Belle was already running for the door when the klaxon sound of the car alarm rent the air. Was at the bottom of the stairs when Ivo caught up with her.

'Don't!' she warned, arm extended, palm face up as she held him off. 'Stay away. I want to do this.'

'You forgot the car keys,' he said, taking her hand, turning it over and placing them in her palm, wrapping her shaking fingers around them so that she wouldn't drop them.

'Oh…'

'She came back, Belle. She wants to see you. Needs to talk to you.'

'I…Yes…'

'Do you need me to stay?'

'I…' Despite her warning for him to stay away, she was suddenly scared.

He laid his hand briefly on her arm, then leaned forward, touched his lips to hers. Barely a kiss and yet it fizzed through her like electricity—pure energy—and for a moment all she wanted to do was reach out and grab him by the lapels of his jacket, pull him close, bury herself in his warmth until the world outside went away. 'You'll be fine.'

'Yes. Of course I will.'

'Call me if you need anything. You'll need someone to talk to. Someone you can trust.'

'Ivo, about last night…' As he opened the door, her words were drowned out by the car alarm and he turned to look at her. 'Thank you,' she said. He nodded once, stepped out on to the footpath, left her.

*Goodbye*…she thought.

Then, drawing in a deep, shuddering breath, she followed him out into the street where Daisy was leaning on the car, all aggressive angles as she watched Ivo remove a parking ticket from his windscreen—he'd overstayed the night-time parking limit—climb into his car and drive away.

The noise from the car alarm was deafening and Belle didn't attempt to speak above it, but unlocked the car, turned off the alarm, then relocked it.

'Neat car,' Daisy said. 'Can I drive it?'

'Have you got a licence?'

'Oh, forget it,' she said, stuffing her hands deep into her pockets and turning to walk away.

Belle, instinctively taking a step after her, was brought up short by Ivo's voice in her head.

*It's a game. She wants you to chase her…*

'I'm going to make breakfast,' she said and, hard as it was, she turned around and walked back inside, holding the door open. Then, 'A bacon sandwich.'

Bacon sandwiches had been dream food. Thick white bread, layers of bacon, ketchup… She'd been drawn by the scent to a small café that made sandwiches for office workers. Her mother wouldn't beg, but Daisy had been hungry and she'd picked a place, just out of sight of the café staff where she could lie in wait for customers, carriers stuffed with expensive calorie-laden sandwiches, coffee or hot chocolate in cartons with lids, huge muffins. Had learned to hit them for change while they still had it in their hands.

Guilt had done the rest.

It had been a great pitch, but it hadn't lasted long.

Someone had called Social Services. Or complained to the café staff. Only her street-sharpened survival instincts had stopped them from being picked up but, even now, when she caught the scent of bacon cooking she felt something very close to pain in the pit of her stomach.

After a pause that felt like a lifetime, Daisy turned around and walked right by her and up the stairs without a word and was already standing in the centre of the living room looking around by the time her own shaky legs had carried her up.

'This is a mess,' Daisy said, looking around.

'I'm decorating.' The ceiling, one wall and the French windows so far—she'd needed to get the curtains back up—but all her own work. 'It'll look better when the new curtains and carpet arrive.'

'Are they beige and white too?'

'Please! The walls, when they're finished, will be Velvet Latte, the paintwork Silk Frost,' Belle said, hoping to raise a smile. Light, uncluttered after three years living in the Grenville family museum. 'It's minimalist.'

Like her marriage. Maybe it hadn't been such a good choice of look.

'It's boring. And no one has carpets now. It's all hardwood floors.'

'Not exactly neighbour friendly when you're in the top floor apartment.'

'I suppose.' Then, 'Your furniture is junk.'

'I'm going shopping for a new sofa this afternoon.' She'd picked out something ultra-modern in brown suede but she'd suddenly gone right off it. 'Do you want to come with me? Clearly I could do with some help.'

Daisy shrugged her skinny shoulders without taking her hands out of her pockets. 'Like I care what sofa you buy. You said you'd help me look for my dad.'

'We can do both. If that's really what you want.'

'You knew your father,' Daisy said, picking up the negativity of the question in her voice, turning on her. 'I never…' She broke off. Then, 'I never had anyone.'

'Mum loved you, Daisy.'

'She died.'

Belle swallowed down the words that leapt to her lips. Blaming Daisy's father for what had happened to them wouldn't help. They'd all abandoned her, one way or another.

'What about the people who adopted you? Didn't they love you?'

'They lied to me! I waited and waited and they said you'd come but you didn't. I wanted you, Bella, and you weren't there!'

Bella.

Daisy, only Daisy, unable to manage 'Belinda' had ever called her that.

'Where did you go?' she demanded and Belle, jolted out of memory, shook her head. 'Nowhere. A care home. Nowhere…' She shook her head. There was nothing to be gained from telling Daisy that her new family had only wanted her. That everyone had said it would be easier for her to settle down without disturbing memories of her previous life. She had known they were wrong, but no one would listen to her. And she'd been hurt and angry and grieving too.

She knew what Daisy was feeling now because she'd lived it.

'What happened to you, Daisy? Why are you living like this?'

'Like what?' Then, abruptly, 'I thought you were going to make breakfast.'

'I am. Do you want to come through to the kitchen while I cook?'

If she'd ever imagined this was going to be a joyful reunion, then last night had crushed that hope beyond recovery, but this was more difficult than anything she could have imagined.

Simone, Claire, she thought, I really hope, wherever you are, it's going better for you.

She took a pack of bacon from the fridge, turned just as Daisy swept something into her pocket. What? There was nothing on the counter top but a couple of mugs, the empty carton of coffee.

The muffin…

She bit down hard to keep the pain in, began to lay strips of bacon on the grill. 'Do you want to take off your coat?'

Daisy's only response was to wrap it around her more tightly and Belle didn't press it, but it took her a moment to compose herself. 'I'll find your father, Daisy.'

She just hoped the reality wouldn't hurt her sister too badly.

'Whatever. Can I use your bathroom?'

'Of course. Use the *en suite* in my bedroom.' The one in the spare bedroom was a bit bleak. Definitely on her list of improvements. 'First door on the left.'

# CHAPTER EIGHT

Ivo, uneasy, drove round the block, parked out of sight of Belle's apartment, bought a paper and walked into the small café on the far side of the street, ordered coffee and settled down to wait.

Belle had taken the unilateral decision that her past and their future were incompatible. That finding Daisy meant she had to lose him. That once the truth about her past became common knowledge—and the press, once they got a sniff of a story, would be digging around for every grubby detail—he wouldn't want to know.

That she felt that way shamed him.

Maybe she had wanted the security he could offer, but she'd wanted more than that. A real marriage. A family.

She wasn't the one lacking the courage to confront what that meant. He was the one who'd been incapable of embracing life with all its messiness.

He didn't blame her for leaving him—there wasn't a day in his life when he hadn't wished he could leave himself. On the contrary, he was grateful to her. He felt like a man who'd had his head yanked out of the sand. And Belle, still touchingly vulnerable, unsure, beneath the surface skim of professional polish, had broken out of her own shell. She was still vulnerable, still believed that her success was a fluke, the result of good PR, but she was making an effort to stand on her own feet, to do things for herself. Had been prepared to tell him that she no longer needed him as a prop.

In doing that, she'd kicked the legs out from under him. As they untangled themselves he had to make sure their feet were pointing in the same direction and somehow, he knew, Daisy was the key.

Daisy was gone for so long that Belle was afraid that she'd slipped out, disappeared again. Had to force herself to stay in the kitchen, watching the grill, sensing it was a trust thing. That she was being tested.

Her reward came when Daisy finally sauntered back in to the kitchen, smelling sweetly of vanilla-scented shower gel, her damp hair minus the purple streaks.

'Does he live here?' she asked, sliding back onto the stool, her look daring her to say one word about using the shower.

'Ivo?'

'*Ivo*! What kind of name is that?'

'It's a diminutive of Ivan. He was named for his Russian great-grandfather.'

'Lucky him. We don't even have a father between us.' Then, 'He said he was your husband, but there's no men's stuff in the bathroom.'

'He did? When?'

He'd said he'd seen Daisy outside the flat, but he hadn't said he'd spoken to her.

'He got all protective when I got too close to your car.'

'Oh.' She found herself smiling. Then, catching Daisy's 'yuck' look, said, 'He is. But we're separated.'

'Not that separated. He was here at the weekend helping you decorate. And he hadn't shaved this morning so I'm guessing he stayed all night.'

'Yes…' She could still feel the warmth of his kiss. Hear his soft, 'Call me…' 'Your fault. It was the early hours before we got back here last night,' she said, 'so he slept on the sofa.'

He'd got it so wrong! Thinking that Daisy was her daughter. But he hadn't been judgemental. Far from it. He'd said a child of hers would be his responsibility too. He'd hung in there, been there for her, even when she had been horrible to him. Would have gone out to continue looking if she hadn't stopped him. Then, when she'd fallen asleep on him, he'd stayed with her, holding her. All night. It must have been the first time they'd just slept together. Without getting naked.

Just like a real husband and wife.

She poured mugs of coffee, leaving the sugar and milk for Daisy to help herself.

'What about you?' she asked, pushing away the desire to do it again. Very soon. 'Are you living with your baby's father?'

'No.'

'Do you love him?'

'Oh, please!'

'You had unprotected sex.'

'There's no other way to get a baby.'

'You wanted…' She swallowed. Of course she did. Someone who would love her without reservation.

'She shouldn't have told you I was pregnant. That nurse. That kind of stuff is confidential.'

'She wanted me to understand why you'd passed out.' Wanted to be sure that someone responsible knew. Someone who would take care of her. 'Are you booked into an antenatal clinic? Getting vitamins? Have you been tested?'

'What is this? The Inquisition?'

'Your baby needs you to protect her. Keep her safe.'

'Like you would know all about that.' Then, 'I'll sort it, all right? I'm still getting my head around the idea.'

'How pregnant are you?'

'Totally. It's the only way.'

Her sister had a sense of humour. Things were looking up. 'I'll rephrase the question. When can I plan on being an aunt?'

'I didn't know I was pregnant until last night. I'm about six weeks gone, so somewhere between seven and eight months, I suppose.' Then, 'I didn't pass out on purpose, despite what Ivan the Terrible thinks.'

Belle struggled to hold back a smile. 'He's not so terrible. In fact he offered you five thousand pounds. Why didn't you take it?'

'He just wanted to get rid of me.'

'No…' The word had been an automatic response, but having thought about it, she said it again. 'No. He was just testing you.'

Protecting her. Treating her like some idiot who didn't know what she was doing.

'Then I guess I passed,' Daisy said.

'You don't have to prove anything to me,' Belle snapped. Then, 'Sorry. Late night.' And, changing the subject, she said, 'Okay. We can fix you up with a clinic. Go to classes together, if you like.'

'I don't need you.'

'Everyone needs someone,' she said. Someone to reach out a hand, to say '…Call me…'. Someone who you know will be there. Who cares how you're feeling.

How *was* Ivo feeling?

How had he felt when she'd told him she was leaving? Really?

She buttered bread, keeping her hands busy, but her mind needed total distraction. 'What about a job?' she asked. 'Or are you at college?'

'No.'

This was not going well.

She was paid ridiculous amounts of money to chat to total strangers every morning. She put them at their ease, made them laugh, drew them out with open-ended questions. The difference being that she'd done her homework on the people she interviewed. Knew the answers before she asked the questions, mostly. The trick was to avoid the obvious, get them to open up, forget the answers they'd prepared ahead of time and relax.

There was only one rule. Never ask a question that could be answered with a simple yes or no.

It hadn't occurred to her that it was a rule she would need when she finally came face to face with her sister. That a shortage of words would be a problem. On the contrary, she'd imagined that all the feelings would just come tumbling out. The anger, yes, she'd expected that, but had believed that the early years when they had been everything to each other, when she'd taken care of Daisy, looked out for her, would mean enough to override the years they'd spent apart.

It wasn't going to be that way. The wound had gone too deep and despite the fact that it would probably choke her, she bit into her own sandwich simply to stop herself from blurting out needy questions about her sister's life, the people who'd adopted her, knowing that she was just longing for answers that would absolve her of guilt, somehow justify what she'd done.

'Thanks for the sandwich.'

While she was still chewing through her first mouthful, Daisy had finished and she slid off the stool.

*'You're leaving?'*

Let her go. She'll come back.

That would be Ivo's advice, she knew. But then, detached, emotionally disengaged, that was easy for him to say. Much harder for her.

'Don't you want to stay and help me search for your dad on the Internet?'

'You think I haven't done that?' Daisy said, heading for the door. 'I'm not dumb.'

'I was going to contact an agency who specialise in finding people.'

For a moment she hesitated. Tempted. Then she said, 'What's the point? If he wanted to know, he'd be looking for me.' And she kept walking.

'Maybe he's scared, Daisy. Maybe he thinks you wouldn't want to know. Have you any idea of the courage it takes to seek out someone you've hurt? Let down?'

Her sister paused, glanced back from the doorway, her thin face wreathed in sudden doubt. But she rallied, said, 'Maybe he just doesn't care. Maybe he's just a…' She stopped, apparently unable, despite her defiance, to say the word.

'Say it, Daisy. It won't be anything I haven't heard before.'

'Babies can hear, can't they?'

Belle tried not to smile at this unexpected evidence of maternal care. 'So I understand.'

'You don't have any kids?'

She shook her head just once.

'Men are a waste of space.'

'Not all of them,' Belle said. Then, trying to keep the need from her voice, 'You can stay here, Daisy. There's a spare room. All the hot water you can use.'

'I've got a place.'

'Somewhere suitable for a baby?'

'I lived in worse when I was a kid,' she said.

'Then you know enough not to inflict it on your own child.'

'I was happy…' She snapped her lips shut, her lips a thin tight line.

Happy *then*? Was that what she'd been about to say? If that was her yardstick for happiness, what horror had she lived through since?

Belle shivered, but managed to hold in her concern. 'The offer's open. Any time.' Then, 'Do you need anything?'

'From my glamorous, famous big sister who couldn't be bothered with me all these years?' Belle caught the telltale sparkle of tears before Daisy blinked them away. Not so tough, then… 'I worshipped you.' Then, 'Not *you*. Belle Davenport. She was everything a big sister should be. Fun, warm, smart, caring and just so lovely. I used to watch her every morning and think if my sister had been anything like her I'd have been the luckiest girl in the entire world. Big mistake, huh?'

'It wasn't… That wasn't me.'

'Absolutely right. You're both fakes.'

'Daisy, please—'

'Please what? Fifteen years and all I get is a three-line letter and a photograph; what was I supposed to do, Bella…sorry, *Belle*? Fall at your feet in gratitude because you'd finally found time out of your busy life to remember that you had a little sister?'

'I never forgot you.' Belle stopped. What was the point? How could she expect Daisy to understand when she didn't understand herself. 'It wasn't your mistake, Daisy. It was mine.' Then, 'I'll see what I can find out about your dad, so next time you ring…don't hang up, hmm?'

'Who says I'll ring again?' she demanded, then flung open the door and ran down the stairs.

Belle fought the impulse to go after her, to go to the window to see which way she went. She didn't have any right to know where Daisy went, who she was with. What her life was like.

She'd forfeited that when she'd walked away and now she was going to have to earn Daisy's trust by being there for her. By never, ever, no matter what, letting her down again.

Then, seized by a flash of inspiration, she ran to the window, flung it open. 'Daisy! We can get a licence and I'll teach you to drive.'

Her sister didn't stop or look up, just scrunched down deeper into her thin coat.

Ivo, seeing Belle's front door open, folded up his newspaper, stood up and made for the door. Daisy was always going to leave. Assert her independence. Keep her sister guessing. Hurting.

He stepped back into the doorway when Belle flung open the window, smiled to himself at her smart bid to grab the girl's attention. Not that Daisy responded. He'd have expected a self-satisfied little grin, but instead she seemed to shrink.

He waited until Belle closed the window and then, keeping to the far side of the road, set off after Daisy.

Belle, her own shoulders not exactly bouncing to her ears with excitement, turned to her laptop and logged on to one of the agencies that specialised in tracking down family members. Somehow just filling in a form and pressing buttons seemed depressingly impersonal; she needed to talk to someone…

Everyone needs someone.

*'Call me…'*

No. It was over. Not that he wouldn't help her on a practical level. He was a man who could cut through red tape, make things happen. But the cost was too high. Being with him was too painful. She'd played the role assigned for three years, hiding her feelings, because the one thing Ivo Grenville had made clear from day one was that he never used four-letter words.

For a few brief days on that honeymoon idyll, she'd thought it didn't matter. That even if he never said the word, he lived it. Her mistake had been to let her guard down in the sweet, golden aftermath of love, when he'd been half asleep, when she'd been dreaming of a family of her own.

If his face hadn't been enough to bring her back to earth, the next day he'd left her to deal with some business problem that wouldn't keep—a sharp reminder of the status of honeymoons, of her, in his life.

She snatched her hand back from the phone.

She'd lived a half-marriage for three years and, while Ivo's passion hadn't dimmed, he had, if anything grown more distant, at least until these last few days. She loved him, had loved him since the day she'd turned to meet his gaze, fallen into those ocean-deep eyes. Would never love anyone else with the same wholehearted, body and soul commitment, but she'd take nothing rather than go back to the way things had been.

And she had Daisy to think of now.

She made a note of the agency's telephone number, then called, talked to an adviser who took all the details she had, somehow managing to tease stuff out of her memory that she didn't know she remembered. Or had, maybe, striven to forget. Promised to get back to her with something, even if it was to say that she'd found nothing, by the end of the next day.

That done, she poured out her heart to Simone and Claire in an email.

As she typed, she could hear their voices in her head asking all the right questions, posing ideas, offering suggestions. It was exactly what she needed to clear her head and she didn't bother to send the email.

There was nothing more they could do except offer sympathy—something she neither deserved nor needed. In fact, much as it pained her to admit it, what she could really do with just at that moment was a little of Ivo's detachment. His ability to distance himself from the emotional response.

Not that he was behaving in a wholly predictable way.

Turning up to decorate her flat had been completely out of character for a start. Calling in a professional—no, asking Miranda to call in a professional to do the job—that was more his style.

And cancelling business appointments? What was that all about?

*Call me if you need anything…*

She picked up her phone, flipped it open and called her insurance company and had Daisy's name added to her policy as a named driver.

Then she set about responding to all the messages.

Practical, unemotional. Ivo would be proud of her, she thought, except that his kiss had felt totally emotional.

Not in a big dramatic way. It wasn't a you're-hot-I'm-horny-come-to-bed kiss. It was an I'm-here-for-you kiss. A tender I-care-for-you kiss. She could almost have fooled herself that it was an I-love-you kiss.

If it had been anyone else.

She really should warn him about Simone's diary, she rationalised. There wasn't a thing they could do about it, but he'd at least be prepared for the fallout, the never-ending phone calls. Take action to avoid either him or Miranda being door-stepped by the press. Although, actually, she pitied any journalist who decided to take on Miranda.

She'd meant to tell him, but then Daisy had turned up and put it right out of her head.

It was time to bring Jace and her PR people into the loop too. Prepare a statement…

She flipped open the phone again and called up the address

book. Then decided that Ivo had done enough chasing after her. It was time she went to the house, went through her things and sorted out what she was going to keep, what could go to a charity shop.

It was only when she stopped for petrol, to pick up a pair of L plates, that she discovered that her purse had been filleted like a kipper.

But for bones, read credit cards and cash.

*Call me…*

It seemed that she didn't have much choice.

'I'm sorry, Ivo. I'm so sorry.' Belle had said it a dozen times. 'I should have cut them up.'

She'd called him on his mobile and he'd come and bailed her out at the garage, then followed her back to the flat and was now sitting on the end of her bed, waiting for the call centre to answer while she checked to see what else was missing.

The only jewellery she'd had in the flat had been the choker and earrings she'd worn to the awards ceremony—precious only because Ivo had given them to her.

She'd abandoned them on the dressing table last night, not bothering to put them away.

Tempting glitter.

Her antique wedding ring was safe. Please let it be safe…

She opened the drawer in the base of her mirror, clutched at her stomach.

'Belle?'

She shook her head. It was too awful. She couldn't tell him…

'I meant to cut them up,' she repeated, just a little desperately. If she concentrated on the credit cards, she could blot out this, more painful, loss. 'Your cards.' She rarely used them. 'I should have left them at the house. If I'd been more organised—'

'I'm grateful that you weren't,' he said, hanging on, waiting in an apparently endless queue for his call to be answered so that he could cancel the cards.

'Grateful?'

'You wouldn't have called me if the only stuff she'd taken was yours.' She neither confirmed nor denied it. 'Would you?' he persisted.

'She's my sister.' Confronted with his impassive face, she said, 'Really.' It wasn't just that she'd called her Bella. 'There are things she said to me that no one else…' She raised her hand to her mouth, unable to say the words.

'Hush…' He reached out. Took it, kissed it, then held it, as he'd hold a child's hand, for comfort. 'It's okay. We'll get your stuff back, but I have to do this first. One call…'

'Get it back?' She tried to pull away but he closed his hand around hers, holding her a little more firmly, keeping her close. 'You aren't going to call the police! Please, Ivo!'

The call centre finally answered and she was forced to wait while he gave the details of the cards.

'Okay, all done. We'll get the new ones in a couple of days.'

'I don't want new cards. Ivo, promise me you won't go to the police!'

'Not this time.'

It was all she could ask for.

'Thank you.' She frowned. 'Then how…?'

'You're the sweet one in this partnership, I'm the cynical one. When I left this morning … Well, I didn't. I just parked around the corner and waited until your sister left, followed her back to the squat she's living in.'

'But that's…'

'Appalling?' He filled in the word for her. 'An invasion of privacy?'

She shook her head once, her thoughts a confused jumble of anger that he'd assumed her sister would steal from her. Gratitude that he'd had the foresight to take action. But then that was what Ivo did. He didn't wait for things to happen. He made them happen.

'No,' she managed. 'You were right.'

'I didn't do it because I thought she was going to steal from you, Belle. I did it so that you'd know where she was. In case she didn't come back.'

'Oh…' She was nearer to crying at that moment than she had been in years. He'd spent his morning hanging around, wasting time—something he never did—and he'd done it for her. 'Thank you.'

'Unless she's an experienced thief, she'll still have the stuff with her.'

'I can't believe…'

*Won't* was probably a better word, she thought. Didn't want to believe her sister was a thief. Only, perhaps, desperate…

'To be honest, neither do I,' Ivo said, taking her by surprise. 'I suspect it's a lot more complicated than that.'

'I'm not sure I can handle anything much more complicated.'

'I believe you can handle just about anything you set your mind to.' He regarded her steadily. 'I know you, Belle. You'd never give up on anything you really cared about.'

More question than statement, she thought. What was he asking?

'Can you lend me a little of that confidence?' she asked shakily.

'You don't need me, Belle. If I tell you where she is, you could handle it.'

Under his steady gaze she realised that it was true. That she'd faced the worst that could happen to her—leaving Ivo—and had survived.

She'd found the courage to walk away from a job that no longer interested her.

She'd shed a look that she'd outgrown.

'Maybe I could,' she said. 'But I'd like you to come with me.'

The squat was a five-storey Edwardian town house in the poor part of the area, boarded up, like its neighbours, waiting for the tide of gentrification to reach it.

Ivo had followed the girl on foot. She'd had her head down, barely looking up even when she'd crossed the road, only giving a cursory look around as she'd slipped round the back.

He'd held back then, giving her time to get under cover, before following her. It had been easy enough to pick out which house she was living in. A path had been worn across the overgrown backyard, half the board missing from an upstairs window.

He'd been prepared to step back, let Belle do this on her own, but he was relieved she'd asked him along. Was oddly grateful to Daisy for, unwittingly, bringing them together. For that alone, he'd do everything he could for the girl.

He led the way, testing the boards covering the rear door, the windows, until he found the loose one, slid it aside, climbed in.

'Maybe you should wait here,' he suggested as Belle made to follow him. Who knew what they'd find?

'I want to go to Daisy,' she said, climbing in after him. He didn't bother to argue. Instead he offered her his hand, pulling her up after him, steadying her as she dropped to the floor. 'Ugh! This is horrible.'

'Watch your step,' he warned as, hand still firmly grasping hers, he switched on the torch he'd brought from the car and shone it around the floor, checking for gaps. It looked sound enough, but looks could be deceptive. 'I don't imagine the boards are in that great a shape.'

'She can't stay here, Ivo!' Belle, responding to the dark, whispered. 'I can't leave her here. It's freezing. Damp. What *is* that smell?'

'Dry rot.' It was a smell the owner of every listed property dreaded. Then, 'You know if she wants to stay here there's nothing you can do about it.'

'You want to bet?'

'If we take this from her, she'll just move on somewhere else and we won't know where to find her.'

'According to you she'd come back.'

'Not now,' he said. Not now she'd stolen from her.

'We've got to do something,' she said. Then, almost reluctantly, 'She's pregnant, Ivo.'

There was something in her voice, something more than the loss of her sister—a transparent yearning that went straight to his gut.

'She told you that?' he asked, hoping that it was just another tug on vulnerable heartstrings. 'She looks anorexic to me.' She turned to stare at him and he realised he'd said too much. Well, she wasn't the only one with her emotions being ripped raw, exposed… 'Miranda,' he said, by way of explanation.

'Oh.' Then, as if everything had fallen into place, 'Oh.'

He'd never told her, had never shared that nightmare with her. It was his sister's secret, not his. Belle nodded as if it was all the explanation she needed. It wasn't. They'd started their marriage with a blank sheet. No baggage. That was the way he'd wanted it. But life wasn't like that. You were made by your family, your experiences.

You couldn't escape who you were.

'The nurse in the hospital told me that Daisy's pregnant,' Belle said, after a moment. 'That's why she passed out. She needs to be somewhere safe. She needs to be with me.'

'You asked her to stay?'

'Of course I did.' She shivered again. 'I've got to persuade her to come home with me, Ivo. Anything could happen to her here.'

'Don't worry. I'll issue an invitation that she won't be able to refuse.'

'What are you going to do?' Then, 'Not money!'

'Trust me, Belle. I won't repeat last night's mistake.' He tightened his grip on her hand. 'Come on.'

They picked their way across the rubbish-strewn floor, a safe path clearly marked by a passage in the dust made by wet footprints, leading upstairs.

Daisy had made one of the rooms at the back into a comfortable nest, using old furniture and bits of carpet scavenged from heaven alone knew where.

There was no electricity, but a little light filtered in through the filth on the window. Enough to see her sitting on the floor surrounded by credit cards, cash, the jewellery Belle had been wearing last night.

The wedding ring he'd placed on her finger.

She hadn't told him that Daisy had taken her ring, but he knew exactly when she'd discovered it was missing. That moment when she'd checked a drawer, clutched at her stomach as if in pain.

Pulling away from him, she reached for Daisy. 'Come home,' she said. 'Come home with me.'

'Go away.' Daisy pushed her away. 'I don't need you!'

'Please, Daisy. Let me take care of you. For your baby's sake.'

'I don't need you,' she repeated stubbornly. 'I don't want you.'

The words were vehement enough, but Ivo recognized the desperate need underlying Daisy's rejection. The girl had stolen from Belle, putting herself beyond her sister's love. If she was the one instigating rejection, then she remained in control.

He'd been through this when Miranda had been bent on the same course of self-destruction and knew how desperately hard it must be for Belle. It was hard for him to see her in so much pain.

'It's your choice,' he said, bending down to pick up one of the cards. 'You go with Belle, or you go with the police.'

He heard Belle's sharp intake of breath, but she caught his warning look, instantly understood what he was doing and said, 'I'm sorry, Daisy. You didn't just take my things. Some of the cards were issued on Ivo's accounts so I had to call him.'

'I didn't do anything with them,' she said sullenly, to him rather than Belle.

'Go home with Belle, now, and I'll forget it ever happened.'

She got to her feet, stuffed her hands in her pockets and headed for the door. Then, when they didn't follow, she stopped, looked back. 'What?'

He indicated the loot, scattered over the floor. 'Haven't you forgotten something?'

She stomped back, picked up the cards, the necklace, the earrings. Then began to search frantically. 'There was a ring. It was here. I know it was here.'

He felt almost proud of her. He'd expected her to brush over the fact that it wasn't there, deny she'd ever taken it. Maybe even believe she could come back and look for it later, if she needed a way out.

'I have it,' he said, opening his hand. And, taking Belle's left hand, he slipped it back on to her finger, holding it there for a moment. 'Maybe it's safer there.'

Belle felt the weight of the ring. Remembered the moment Ivo had placed it on her finger. How right it had felt, how happy she'd been. She tightened her hand as if she could recapture that precious memory.

'I won't lose it again,' she promised, her voice little more than a whisper. And for a moment it was as if they were back on that beach with a lifetime of possibilities ahead of them. Then, briskly, she turned away from him. You could never go back. 'Well,' she asked, 'what are we waiting for?'

'Don't you want these?' Daisy held out her hands, full of the things she'd picked up.

Belle glanced at them. 'Just stick it all in your pocket. We'll sort it all out when we get home.'

Ivo squeezed her hand, then released it. 'Come on, I'll take you home.'

'No…' Then, more firmly, 'No.' His approval meant a lot to her, but she wanted, needed to stand on her own feet. 'Daisy and I are going to walk home through the market.'

'Are you sure?'

Her wedding ring warmed against her finger. 'Quite sure. Thank you, Ivo.' Then she reached out, touched his arm. 'Call me.'

# CHAPTER NINE

'WHERE is she today?'

Belle was saved from answering by the appearance of the waiter, bringing them water, taking their order.

'Daisy,' Ivo prompted, when he'd gone. Picking up as if they hadn't been interrupted. As if there was any other 'she'.

'I don't know,' she finally admitted. 'Don't look at me like that, Ivo...' frustrated, angry '...she was gone when I got home from the studio this morning.'

'Punishing you for putting work before her too?'

'She knows it's just until the end of the week.'

'Not like...' He stopped himself from saying the words. *Not like a marriage.* Then, 'She didn't leave a note?'

'She's an adult. She doesn't have to account for her time.' Then, a touch desperately, seeking reassurance. 'I have to trust her.'

He reached out, covered her hand with his own. 'I know. It's the hardest part.' He sat back, taking his hand with him. 'I'm not complaining. Having you to myself is more than I'd hoped for.'

Ivo had brought her a package that had been delivered to the Belgravia house, the first time in a week that he'd come to the flat, although, taking advantage of her invitation, he had called her every day just to chat. Ask how things were going. Supportive. Offering advice only when it was requested. There for her, but giving her space too. Giving her...respect.

But the truth was that she'd been going out of her mind with worry when she'd got home and Daisy wasn't there. Had practically fallen on his neck in gratitude when he'd suggested lunch. When he hadn't insisted on one of their usual fashionable haunts, the kind of place where everyone would know them, but agreed to her choice of this tiny Italian trattoria on the other side of Camden Market.

'How is it? Really?' he asked.

'Not easy,' she admitted. 'Apparently the adoption broke down after a couple of years and Daisy's been in more foster homes than she can count, then a halfway house. That's where she met this boy whose baby she's expecting.'

'Is he still in the picture?'

Belle shook her head. 'Daisy just wanted a baby.'

'He has the right to know.'

She looked up, surprised by the fierceness of Ivo's response. 'One step at a time, Ivo,' she said.

'Yes, of course. I'm sorry. I wasn't criticising. You're doing amazingly well.'

'Am I? The mood swings are difficult,' she admitted. 'She's up and down. Prickly one minute, loving the next.'

'Maybe it's her hormones.'

'It can't be helping. The doc's given her a clean bill of health at least and she's looking better. There's nothing wrong with her appetite.'

'So what's bothering you?'

She shook her head.

'There's something.'

'Nothing that can be solved with a new coat or a vitamin pill.' He waited. 'It's nothing at all. Stupid. She just hates that it's all one way. Seems to think she's a charity case. I can't get her to understand how much it means to me to be able to do stuff for her.'

'She thinks you're going to lose interest. That she daren't care too much in case you dump her like everyone else in her life.'

'But that's…' About to say ridiculous, she realised that it wasn't. That somehow Ivo knew exactly how Daisy was feeling. She realised just how little she knew about his past beyond the privileged lifestyle, the fact that his parents had been killed just after he'd graduated. 'If I didn't know better, I'd think you'd read Psychology at Uni, instead of Economics. How come you understand her better than I do?'

'You're doing fine.'

An evasion.

'Maybe what she needs is a job. Something to make her feel useful. Give her something of her own so that her entire life isn't invested in you.'

'Or make her think I'm getting ready to pitch her back out into the big wide world. Especially if she thinks the idea has come from you.'

'She thinks I'm some kind of threat to her?'

Ivo sensed rather than heard Belle's sigh and it provoked mixed feelings. The fact that Belle was still wearing her wedding ring had given him hope. And if Daisy sensed a threat, then it meant that Belle talked about him.

'She's fragile, Ivo. Needs to be the sole focus of attention.'

She didn't have to tell him. He knew how needy, how self-centered, how destructive the damaged psyche could be.

'Maybe it would be better if I left Manda to suggest it.'

'Manda!'

He smiled at her horrified response. 'Trust me. She knows what she's doing.'

He understood her lack of enthusiasm; Manda had given her a hard time, he knew. 'Really,' he assured her. 'In fact, I suspect you have a new fan.'

'Now I'm really worried. What exactly have you told her, Ivo?'

'Just enough, so that when this hits the headlines she'll be prepared to be door-stepped by the press.' He glanced at her. 'Any news from your Aussie friend?' She shook her head. 'It's like waiting for the other shoe to drop, isn't it?'

'A bit.' She regarded him curiously. 'You're good at this, aren't you?'

'It's easier for me. My responses aren't muddied by emotion.'

About to say that was because he didn't do 'emotion' she stopped herself. She was beginning to suspect that it wasn't a lack of emotion that kept him buttoned up, but a fear of letting it spill out.

'It's more than that, Ivo. You seem to know just what Daisy's feeling.'

'I have a sister.'

'That's it?' On the point of laughing at the idea of Miranda being an angsty teen, she thought better of it. Ivo had told her a little of what his sister had been through. 'I'm trying to focus on the early days with Daisy. It's when we were together,' she explained. 'A family.'

'You don't blame her, do you? Your mother?'

'She was trying to protect us,' she said. 'And she was my mum. Unconditional love is a parent/child thing.'

Something she'd longed for too. Something a child would have given her. That she'd believed her sister, in her new home, would be able to give, to receive—something precious that would blot out everything else.

'Daisy's father was a gambler, Ivo. He ran up debts, mortgaged my mother's house with three different companies, borrowed money from loan sharks and then disappeared. Mum never saw the letters from the bank or the finance people. I imagine he'd lain in wait for the postman and siphoned them off. The first she knew anything was wrong was when the bailiffs turned up.'

'That's fraud. He could have gone to prison.'

'Yes, well, first you had to catch him. Then you had to prove that he'd done it. All academic, because a couple of loan shark heavies threatened Daisy, held a knife to her throat until my mother handed over her child allowance, issued an instruction to be there every Monday morning for a repeat performance.'

He swore, something he did so rarely that Belle's eyes widened in shock. 'Why didn't she go to the police?' he demanded.

'The graphic description of what would happen to both her children if she did?'

He let slip another expletive, betraying just how deeply affected he was. 'I'm sorry…'

'No, that describes him perfectly. Mum got us home, packed what she could carry and ran.'

'Four years? You lived like that for four years?'

'Something inside her broke, Ivo. My dad was supposed to be the bad one. He drank, he knocked her about, fell into the canal one night—or was pushed—and drowned. Daisy's dad looked and acted like a gentleman. She thought the sun shone out of his eyes. He told her he was going away on business for a few days and while she was ironing and packing for him, he was emptying her purse. When her world fell apart, she wasn't capable of putting her life back together. There were people who could have helped; she was just too broken to see it.'

'And still Daisy wants to find this man? Acknowledge him as her father?'

'Unconditional love,' she repeated. 'It's given to bad parents as well as good ones.'

'Not always,' he said. 'Not if you don't know what love is. Not if you've never known it.'

Ivo knew that to compare the misery of his childhood with what she'd been through was beyond pathetic. But she'd bared her soul to him. Had told him things that she hadn't told anyone. She deserved as much from him. The truth; the whole truth. Because, like her, he'd lived a lie, had hidden behind a façade of the perfect life. The man who had everything, including the country's sweetheart, Belle Davenport. Except that had all been a lie too.

Well, he was done with lies. Belle had been brave enough to confront her past; he could do no less. And if anyone was capable of understanding, it was Belle.

'My parents didn't love each other and they sure as hell didn't love us.'

Belle was frowning, clearly confused. 'But I thought…you had everything. The wonderful holidays in France, Italy. I've heard you and Miranda talk about them.'

'Did you ever hear either of us mention our parents?'

She thought about it. 'Well, no.' She sat back. 'No, I suppose not.'

'We barely knew them. Neither of them wanted to be bothered with us, even with a nanny to do the dirty work. We were shunted off to boarding school at the earliest possible age. Learned behaviour. Our grandparents were no different. Forget seen but not heard. We weren't even wanted for decoration.'

'I had no idea.'

'No, well, maybe we both had stuff we didn't want to talk about, Belle. Didn't want to remember.'

'Only the holidays. Who did you spend them with?'

'Every year we were dumped with some family who took in kids for the summer while they went off on their own affairs. And I do mean affairs. We were just getting to the age when we might have been interesting enough for them to notice when they were drowned. What they were doing on the same yacht has always been something of a mystery to me.'

'I'm so sorry.'

'Don't be. And some of the families were wonderful. Some summers. Those are the ones we remember, talk about.'

'And the rest?'

'We survived until a universal aunt arrived to take us back to school.'

'And you hated that too?'

'Hate would be too strong a word. It was just all a bit unrelenting. There was never any warmth. No one to give you a hug.'

He realised he was gripping her hand, clinging on to it as if to stop himself from drowning. He forced himself to release it but, before he could lift it away, she caught it, held it, then pushed her chair back.

He rose automatically as she got to her feet, held his breath as she came round the table. 'No…' The word, wrenched from him as she put her arms around him, pulled him close, was scarcely audible.

She was soft, warm, against him. He'd tried so hard not to

admit to feelings that he knew would break him. Had built a barrier to protect himself. Had not allowed himself to get too close because he knew that one day she would give up waiting for what he could not give her.

Himself. A child…

And with one hug she had brought the whole edifice tumbling down so that he clung to her, held her, felt something that could only be tears stinging his eyes.

Belle leaned back, looked at him, then reached up, wiped her fingers over his cheek. 'Let's go home, Ivo,' she said softly.

Her scent filled him like a warm balm to the spirit and the temptation to accept the comfort that she was offering was almost beyond enduring. The only thing that would be worse would be the aftermath.

'I can't.'

He was scarcely able to believe he'd said the words. This was what he'd wanted. Her back in his arms, warming the ice. But he couldn't do it to her. Not again. He thought he'd loved her too much to let her go. Now he understand the difference between need and love. He'd seen real love in action. It wasn't about need, about self; it was about giving, about sacrifice, about doing what was best for the person you cared for.

'I can't,' he repeated.

He lowered her into her chair, carefully placed himself on the far side of the table, tried to blot out that confused look of rejection confronting him, a look that he knew from the inside.

'I thought I could,' he said. 'I thought I had it all worked out. You were restless. You'd been thrown out of the groove by your Himalayan trip and you were tired of what you were doing. I thought all I had to do was stick around, point you in the direction of something that would grab your attention, distract you from the emptiness in our lives—'

'Ivo…'

'No. Don't stop me, Belle. I have to say this. Have to tell you the truth.'

She made as if to say something, swallowed, waited, her face set and white.

The waiter arrived with a platter of antipasto. Did something fancy with a pepper mill. Finally left them alone.

They shouldn't be here, he thought. They should be somewhere quiet. Somewhere private. And yet maybe this was best. A public place where emotion had to be kept on a tight rein.

'I thought—believed,' he said, carrying on as if they had not been interrupted, 'that if you found something new to fill your life, then you'd be able to forget, that a moment would come when you'd slip back into your place in my life and then everything would be as it should be. Ordered. Tidy.'

'Forget what, Ivo?'

'That you'd made a bad deal. That security without love, without a family, without…without children, was never going to be enough for someone like you. I wanted you so much…' He closed his ears to her gasp of something very like pain, forced himself to continue. 'Needed you. Beyond reason. Maybe, if I'd known, understood that you wanted more, needed more, I would have found the strength to walk away.' He would have been abandoning all that was vital, alive in him, but he'd have been in control. 'I believed you when you said you only wanted the security of marriage. None of the emotional trappings. Or maybe I was grasping at straws, desperate to believe you because that way I didn't have to address my conscience. Tell you the truth.'

'What truth?' A tiny crease furrowed the space between her eyes. 'Tell me, Ivo.'

'In those few precious days we spent together after the wedding, you began talking about the future as if it was real. About having children.' He looked up, faced her. 'I can't go home with you, Belle. I can't be the husband you need—you deserve. I know, I've always known, that I can never give you children.'

He saw the confusion, the frown deepen as she struggled to comprehend the magnitude of what he had told her.

'Is that…' She stopped. 'Is that why we came home from our

honeymoon early?' She struggled to say more. 'Is that why you chose to sleep separately? Because you thought I wouldn't stay. If I knew.'

He nodded, just once. 'I should have told you.'

'Yes, you should. But then we should have told one another a lot of things, Ivo, but if I'd married you simply for children, I wouldn't have stayed after I saw…' She was struggling with the words. Paused to gather herself. 'I couldn't have stayed when you left me alone on the pretext of flying off to deal with some business crisis.'

'How did you know?'

'That it was a lie? You didn't have to say anything, Ivo. You're good at hiding your feelings, but that day I could read you like a book. I knew that you didn't love me, that I was always going to be a temporary wife, but when we were alone, after the wedding, I glimpsed a sight of some fairy tale happy ever after. Made the mistake of sharing it. One look at your face told me I was on my own…'

'So why didn't you leave then?' He dragged a hand over his face, struggling to understand what she was telling him.

Belle swallowed. She'd got it so wrong. Right from the beginning she should have fought for her marriage. Fought to hold on to something precious. She'd been so afraid to show him how she felt. Overwhelmed by that horrible house. Intimidated by his sister…

'I was afraid,' she said. 'Afraid I'd lose you.'

'Then, why now?'

She looked at him. She'd been so afraid, but she wasn't now. She was struggling, but she was winning—a new life, a sister. Maybe, if she was brave enough, she could even have the marriage she'd always wanted.

'I left because I hated myself for compromising. For hoping and hoping that one day you'd wake up and…' she made a helpless gesture as if the words were too difficult '…*see* me. Be the man I'd glimpsed on our honeymoon. Relaxed, happy…'

'They were the happiest days I've ever spent.'

'Then why? Why couldn't you talk to me?'

'You were not the only one who was afraid. You were the most beautiful woman I'd ever met. No!' he said, when her dismissive gesture suggested that she'd made her point.

That she was no more than a temporary trophy wife.

'I'm not talking about your looks, although that's true too. You are lovely. It was your warmth, your vitality, a smile that could melt permafrost that drew me to you. I always knew you wouldn't stay.'

'Permafrost? You appear to have overestimated its power.'

'No. If you hadn't melted it, why would I care?'

'I didn't leave you because you so plainly didn't want children, Ivo. I left you because I couldn't stand the coldness. The distance. Couldn't bear the thought of waking up alone one more day.' And then, as if everything had suddenly fallen into place. 'That's what you've been doing, isn't it?'

He didn't ask her what she was talking about. In the last week he'd talked to her about Daisy. And about Miranda.

His sister's desperate need for love had driven her into a series of disastrous relationships. Too needy, too desperate. When, over and over again, everyone she loved, in whom she had invested her emotions, rejected her, she'd spiralled down into a destructive phase of anorexia. Rejecting herself.

Stealing from Belle, he knew, had been prompted by the same self-destruct response in Daisy. Anticipating rejection, she'd provoked it.

He'd been there himself. Had fought his own demons in his own way. Self-destruction came with the territory.

'You were waiting for me to reject you,' Belle said, slowly, wonderingly. 'Protecting yourself from being hurt.'

'It didn't work.'

'You held me at such a distance, Ivo—'

'I meant about the hurt.' Living with himself had been a world of hurt. The only relief had been in her arms and selfishly he'd sought to win her back. Keep her. 'I cheated you. Lied to you. You were right to leave. You deserve better.'

'Life isn't about what we deserve, Ivo.' She raised her hands in a helpless gesture. 'If it was about what we deserved then there wouldn't be any kids on their own, cold and hungry. Scared women. Men for whom fatherhood is an unfulfilled dream.'

'Leave me out of your list of deserving souls.'

'Why? You've suffered too.' Then, with a sudden frown, 'What happened to you, Ivo?' she demanded, the bit between her teeth now, fearless in her refusal to accept anything less than the whole truth. 'Were you sick as a child? How do you know that you can't have children?'

He'd hoped she wouldn't think to ask him that. Unlikely. What man, unless he'd attempted to father a child and failed, would know he was infertile?

He had none of the pity-inducing excuses to offer. No mumps or childhood fever to blame. Only himself.

'I know,' he said, 'because ten years ago I had a vasectomy.'

A vasectomy.

The word filled her head, swelling until she thought it would explode.

Belle looked at the food laid out temptingly on a platter for them to help themselves. Grilled baby aubergines, olives, sun-dried tomatoes, paper thin slices of meat. All of them untouched.

She made a helpless gesture, then, covering her hand with her mouth to hold in the cry of pain, she scrambled to her feet, rushed outside, desperate for air.

Just desperate.

Neither of them said a word when Ivo emerged in a rush a few moments later, catching up with her as she walked blindly through the lunchtime crowds of the market, draping her abandoned coat around her shoulders.

The tenderness of the gesture caught her unawares. Without warning, the strength went out of her legs and she subsided on to a bench, sat, bent double, her face pressed against her knees.

The awful thing was that she didn't have to ask why he'd done it. She knew. Understood. The sins of the father. His grandparents, his parents, the fear that he too would follow the genetic imprint—become another cold, distant parent of unhappy children.

Understood why he was so driven—the relentless pursuit of wealth and power filling a bottomless void.

He sat beside her, not touching her, said, as much to himself as to her, 'At the time it seemed so rational.'

She didn't look up, just reached out a hand. There was an endless space of time before his fingers made contact with hers; maybe he thought that she was the one who needed comfort. He wasn't a man who knew how to ask for it.

'I suspect I was on the edge of a breakdown. Miranda was already there. I'd just signed the papers to keep her in hospital for her own protection…'

'You don't have to explain.' She risked an attempt to sit up. The world tilted, then steadied. 'Really,' she said, 'I understand.'

'Do you?'

Oh, yes. He'd thought he was protecting some unborn child from what he'd been through. He was, like Miranda, like her sister, like her when she'd been too scared to tell him that she was marrying him not because of his millions, but because she couldn't imagine living without him—like most people faced with the prospect of pain—just doing what he had to in order to protect himself.

Not self-destruction, but self-preservation.

'I tried to have it reversed. When I realised what I'd done. What I'd done to you.'

She turned to look at him then. 'You'd have done that for me?'

'I…' He faltered. 'Yes, I'd have done that. Done anything.'

'Except say the words.'

'I…I didn't know how to.'

'There is more than one way of showing love, Ivo. Words are the least of them.'

The fact was he hadn't left her on their honeymoon, left her to return home and face Miranda's cold welcome by herself simply to chase down some deal, but to try and have the vasec-tomy reversed.

'I'd been able to justify what I'd done, marrying you, not telling you, because…' He broke off.

'Because I said that the only reason I'd marry you, marry anyone was for security.'

'Sex and money. I thought we'd both got what we wanted and then you started talking about a future, a real future, children, and I knew—'

She tightened her grip on his hand to stop him.

'—I knew that's what I wanted too,' he persisted. 'I'd just been too afraid to admit it to you, to myself. I thought I could fix it. That I could come back and we could begin again. But you didn't wait.'

No. He'd said he would come back once he'd dealt with 'business' but there had seemed no point. They had been in paradise and she had wanted more. Had destroyed it.

'Don't,' she said. 'Please don't blame yourself. Neither of us were brave enough to risk everything for something as danger-ous as love.'

'No.' Then again, 'No.' And, almost to himself, '"…*the coward does it with a kiss*…"' He sighed. 'Confronted with what I'd done to you, I knew I had to get home to see the doctor who'd performed the original surgery. Beg him for a miracle.'

'I'm so sorry…'

He shook his head, rejecting her pity. Never had she felt so helpless. Felt the lack of words to express the way she ached for him.

'I can't say I wasn't warned when I first went to him. He hadn't wanted to do it. Had advised me against it, suggested some kind of counselling. He only relented when I made it clear that if he wouldn't do it there and then, I'd find someone who would, even if it meant going abroad. He was kind enough not to remind me of that.'

He looked down at their locked hands.

'When I thought Daisy was your daughter, when I thought that you had a chance to be a mother, it seemed like a gift. The miracle I'd hoped for.'

'A difficult teenager?' She managed a smile. 'Not everyone's idea of a miracle.'

'She'd have been *your* difficult teenager. Our difficult teenager,' he said, and she thought her heart would break for him. Almost wished she had been a teenage mum with a kid out there somewhere just waiting for her to get in touch.

'She's not my daughter, Ivo, but she still needs us. If it hadn't been for you…' She looked at him. 'Did I ever say thank you for what you did?'

'Don't…' He shook his head. 'Don't ever thank me.'

She owed him more than thanks, but she let it go and said, 'Daisy needs us, Ivo. Not just me, but you. A decent man in her life. And there's her baby. Seven months from now there'll be a little one who'll need an aunt and uncle to spoil him or her rotten.'

'Don't be kind, Belle. Don't pretend that it doesn't matter. I saw your face when you told me that Daisy is expecting a baby.'

'Still jealous of my little sister? Not a very attractive picture, is it? Especially from someone as lucky as I've been.'

'Luck had nothing to do with it. You radiate warmth, Belle. It was there from the first moment you looked up from the telethon switchboard, smiled into the camera, said "Call me" in that sweet, sexy voice. Half the country reached for their phones.'

'Sex sells,' she said dismissively. 'I got my break because it was hot and I'd undone one too many buttons.'

'Do you really think that's why the network is so desperate to hang on to you that they'd pay you any amount of money? Because of your cleavage?' He finally smiled. 'Lovely though it is.'

'No. They're offering me big money because it's easier— cheaper—than finding someone to take my place. Go through all the time-consuming, expensive, image-building hoops with someone new.'

He breathed out another uncharacteristic expletive and said, 'You haven't got an egotistical bone in your body, have you?'

'What have I got to be vain about? Other people put me together, made me what I am.'

'You really don't get it, do you?' he said, not bothering to hide the fact that he was angry with her.

'Ivo…' she protested uncertainly. He didn't lose his temper, didn't get angry.

'What you are, Belle, what makes you a star, won you that award, has nothing to do with image consultants or PR. The viewers adored you from that first husky giggle, a fact the network wasted no time in taking advantage of. All the professionals did was put the polish on a very rare diamond.'

'Oh, please!' Belle knew she was blushing. It was ridiculous… Then, 'I have to get back,' she said. 'Daisy will be wondering where I am.'

'You're an adult, Belle,' he replied, refusing to back off. 'Daisy has to learn to trust you when you're out on a date.'

And without warning the whole tenor of the conversation shifted. One moment he'd been angry with her, the next his eyes were a soft hazy blue-grey that she knew was for her alone. That never failed to stir an echo from somewhere deep inside her.

She swallowed. 'This is a date?'

'We're sitting on a bench holding hands. The last time we did that…'

He stopped, but her memory filled in the rest. The last time had been the first time. She'd been talking to someone about the charity they were all supporting that night when something had made her turn. It was all the invitation he'd needed and a path had seemed to open up before him as he'd walked across the Serpentine Gallery, offered her his hand and said, 'Ivo Grenville.'

And she'd said, 'Belle Davenport.' And took it.

And that was all. He was a workaholic millionaire, she was a television celebrity, their histories were public knowledge and words weren't necessary. And when she placed her hand in his, he tucked it beneath his arm and walked out of the gallery with her, through the dusky park, along the side of the lake until, eventually, they'd reached a bench set in the perfect spot. And they'd sat on it, her arm tucked beneath his, his hand holding hers.

'I remember,' she said, her voice thick with regret for all the wasted years. Was it too late? Could they go back to that moment? Start again? 'Do you remember what comes next?'

Around them the market was a blur of noise and colour but Ivo was back in another time—another place; in the warmth, the stillness of a summer's evening with a beautiful woman who, like him, had recognised the moment for what it was. For whom words were an irrelevance.

'Do you remember?' she asked again.

Ivo rubbed his thumb over the ring he'd placed on her finger.

He remembered. Every touch, every look. Eyes like warm butterscotch, hair gleaming pale as silver, a soft, inviting mouth waiting for him to take a step outside the emotional vacuum in which he'd imprisoned himself. Waiting now, for him to find the courage to finally break free.

He stood up, his hand beneath hers inviting her to do the same. She rose at his touch, waited.

He lifted a hand to her hair, as he had then.

'Did I tell you that I like this new style?' he said. 'That you look wonderful?'

She didn't answer, seeming to know that he was talking to himself rather than her.

He laid his palm against her cheek and she leaned into it, nestling against his hand, closing her eyes.

'Look at me,' he said.

And when she raised her head, lifted heavy lashes, he kissed her—no more than the touching of lips, it was deeper, more meaningful than any exchanged in hot passion. It said, as it had said then, everything he could never put into words. Say out loud. Admit to.

'You remembered,' she said, her sweet mouth widening into a smile.

'How could I ever forget?'

A kiss. A cab ride. The slow sensual dance of a man and woman making love for the first time. Each touch something rare and new. Each kiss a promise.

'You took me home,' she said, tucking her arm beneath his and turning to walk the short distance to her flat. 'And stayed to be dragged out of sleep by my four o'clock alarm call.'

'I remember.' Then, 'That's not why—'

'I know,' she said quickly. 'I understand now why you wanted separate rooms. Why you left my bed.'

'Because the kiss was a lie. If I'd loved you, truly loved you, I'd have walked away then.'

Instead he'd deceived her. Deceived himself. Fooling himself that he was taking no more than the minimum.

Protecting himself from the moment when she'd see their marriage for what it was—a hollow sham. And then, when she'd done just that, driven away by his coldness, he'd discovered that there was no way of protecting himself from loving Belle Davenport. That he couldn't live without her.

'Don't be so hard on yourself, Ivo.'

'Why not?'

She didn't answer, but as they reached her front door, she handed him the keys and he unlocked it, remained on the step. She didn't take them from him, but walked up the stairs, leaving him with no choice but to follow.

She'd already tapped on the flat door by the time he joined her. 'No answer. Daisy's still out,' she said, standing back so that he could open that door too, dropping her bag on the hall table before sliding her hands around his neck.

'Belle…'

He'd said her name in just that way too, that first time. Then it had been a warning that once he'd stepped over the threshold there would be no turning back. Now it was more complex.

He wanted her and right at this moment he was sure she wanted him, but it was simple need, comfort they both craved. Afterwards, nothing would have changed.

'I can't,' he said. 'It wouldn't be right.'

'Just lie with me, Ivo. Hold me.' And, for the first time since he'd known her, the tears that brimmed in her eyes spilled over and ran, unchecked, down her cheeks. 'Please. I'm so tired. I can't sleep. But if you held me, just for a little while…'

Denying her was beyond him and he took her coat from her shoulders, hung it, alongside his own, on the stand, then took her hand and led her to her bedroom, undressing her slowly, as he had time without number, each button, hook, zip, each brush of his fingers against warm skin sweet torture. When she was naked, utterly defenceless, he lifted back the soft down quilt, settled her beneath it. Then he, understanding her need for closeness, began to undress.

This was new.

This was new, different, important beyond imagining.

For the first time in three years he was about to share a bed with his wife and not make love to her.

Or maybe he was. Because that was what this was, he thought as he slid in beside her, put his arms around her and pulled her back against him, fitting her to his body like a spoon. Gently kissed her shoulder, whispering soft words of reassurance, words of love that spilled out of some locker where they'd been stored away, not needed in this life.

This was the love, comfort, sharing, being there for someone that he'd been running from all his adult life. He nestled his face into the back of her neck, breathed in her familiar scent. Vanilla. Rose. Something darker, more potent that stirred the passions.

He'd imagined having to fight down his body's aching need for her, do quadratic equations in his head to distract himself, but it wasn't like that. This wasn't about him; it was about Belle. Giving back all he'd taken.

And conversely feeding his desire on a completely different

level, transcending the purely physical; this closeness, just holding her, met his needs, fulfilled them in every way that mattered. And he closed his eyes.

# CHAPTER TEN

BELLE stirred, turned over and found that she was still lying in Ivo's arms. She'd slept—not surprising; she rose at four every morning to go to the studio.

But it wasn't her brief nap that made her feel brand-new. It was Ivo, holding her, being there.

She'd slept and he hadn't left her.

All her dreams rolled into one. Or as near as they could be and she grinned, madly, stupidly happy.

'This brings a whole new meaning to the expression "they slept together",' she said.

Then, because this felt like the start of something new, something different, rather than an ending, she reached out to lay her hand against his heart.

He caught her wrist, held her an inch away from his skin.

'Belle…'

She ignored the warning. He believed she wanted more than he could give her and because of that had kept her at a distance. Kept himself at a distance.

He was wrong.

Now she knew the truth a world of possibilities opened up before them. Before her. There were countless children for whom she could make a difference, with her time, her love, her money. There was only one man. And with one arm trapped beneath her, one hand occupied keeping hers captive, he was at her mercy.

With her hand neutralised she did what any woman would do and used her mouth to break down his resistance.

She heard the hiss of agony as she laid her lips against his heart, feeling the hammer of it. His skin was warm, like silk beneath her tongue.

He tried to speak, caught his breath as she curled her tongue around his nipple, tasting him, savouring him as it responded, tightening to her touch. The power was all hers and she used it, taking her mouth across his chest to the concave space beneath his ribs. He gathered himself then, made an effort to put an end to this raid on his senses, but he'd left it too late and the soft twirl of her tongue around his navel wrung a groan, more pain than pleasure, from him.

He was a strong-minded man, but his body betrayed him, rising to meet her. She welcomed it with open mouth.

Ivo had swiftly discovered that quadratic equations were no match for his wife when she was set upon seduction. That when he should have been saying 'No...', the only word he seemed capable of saying was 'Yes...' That when she straddled him, leaned forward so that her luscious breasts stroked against his chest, sheathed herself on him, as she said, 'I love you. Love me, Ivo...' that the small warning voice hammering away somewhere inside his head was wasting its time.

Afterwards, when they'd made love with no secrets, no barriers between them, she cried. He wrapped his arms around her and held her close.

'I'm sorry,' she said, dashing her tears away with the back of her hand. 'I don't do this...' Then, smiling, if somewhat shakily, 'You didn't bargain on this when you dropped by with that package, did you?'

'I might start sending them to you myself if this is the welcome I get,' he said. Then, 'Or you could just come home.'

She stiffened. 'I can't. I can't go back there...' Then, 'Did you hear something?'

A crash, then the sound of the front door being slammed, the feet pounding down the stairs, made denial impossible and Belle catapulted out of his arms, grabbed a dressing gown, clutching it around herself as she wrenched open the door.

'Oh…'

She sounded as if she'd been punched, as if the air had been driven from her and he didn't stop to pull on his pants, but followed, coming to an abrupt halt in the doorway of the small third bedroom that Belle had converted to a wardrobe and dressing room.

The dress that she'd worn for the awards ceremony, the lace evening coat, had been reduced to litter. Mere shreds of material.

Daisy.

How long must it have taken her? How long had she been home? Seeing his coat hanging beside Belle's, the shut bedroom door, standing there, listening to the sounds made by two people lost to the world as they made love.

He looked up and saw that the scissors she'd used had been flung at the mirror.

His instinct was to reach for Belle, protect her from this, but she twitched away from him, rejecting a gesture of comfort that an hour before she'd begged for, the kind of gesture that was fast becoming second nature to him.

'Something's happened,' she said. 'Something bad.' She turned on him. 'She needed me, Ivo, and I wasn't there for her.'

He drew in a breath, hunting for something to say, anything to help reassure her. To reassure himself. The painful reality was that sometimes there were no words.

'She'll have gone to the squat.'

'Why would she do that? She knows it's the first place I'll look for her.'

He wondered if the switch from 'we' to 'I' was conscious, or whether Belle had slipped instinctively into self-preservation mode in anticipation of what was to come, already anticipating the worst.

'She wants you to find her, Belle.' He indicated the coat stand where she'd hung the expensive quilted jacket that her sister had bought her alongside his overcoat. 'She didn't take a coat.'

Because she wanted to punish her sister, but he kept his thoughts to himself.

'She'll be freezing.'

'Come on, I'll drive you—'

'No!' Then, more firmly, 'No.'

Daisy had helped to bring them closer, to open up, let light and air into the dark core of suffering that they'd chosen to bury, but she was a loose cannon and, in her need, was just as capable of driving them apart.

Forced to choose between them—and Daisy would make her choose—Belle, driven by guilt, would sacrifice anything to convince her sister that she was loved. Him. Her own happiness.

All he could do was hang in there. Do whatever he could to make it easy for her. Starting now.

'She'll want to shout at someone. Blame someone for the fact that when she needed you, you were in bed with me. If I'm there she can use me as her verbal punch bag,' he said.

'I wanted you, Ivo. This isn't your fault.'

'This isn't about us. She needs you, Belle. I'm dispensable.'

The squat had been secured against intruders—he'd called the property developers himself to make sure it was done quickly and they'd made a solid job of it.

Daisy had clearly tried to kick her way in—there were footprints on the new board—but, beaten, she was now sitting, hunched up, shivering, her hands stuffed into her sleeves, on a low wall.

Belle said nothing, just handed her the coat she'd left behind and was invited, in the most basic of terms, to go away. Her response was to take off her own coat, lay the two of them side by side on the wall and sit down beside her.

'Do you want to tell me what happened?' she asked matter-of-factly.

'Like you care.'

'If I didn't care I wouldn't be here. What happened?' she repeated quietly.

'You *weren't* there!'

Daisy sounded more like a petulant child than a grown woman, Ivo thought, but she'd been through a lot. Would need a great deal of help, counselling, endless amounts of that unconditional love that Belle talked about, to build up her self-esteem. He knew from experience that it was a full-time job.

'When wasn't I there?' Belle asked patiently.

'This morning when the agency phoned.'

'I was at work, Daisy. You know that.' Calm, steady. He knew how hard that was and he was desperately proud of her. 'What did they want?'

'They found my dad.'

'What?'

Belle, doing her best to remain calm, composed, controlled, was shaken to her foundations and Daisy finally looked at her.

'They called this morning to tell me that they'd found him.'

'But they shouldn't have…' She'd given express instructions to the agency.

'What? Told me? Why? He was *my* dad.'

'I know, but… I wanted to be there when they talked to you. You shouldn't have been on your own.'

'It's nothing new.'

'That was then. This is now.'

'Right.' Disbelief. A glance in Ivo's direction that said it all.

'I can't believe they told you. Wait until—'

'They thought I was you. One Miss Porter is pretty much like another on the telephone. They had news; I wasn't going to say call back when my big sister's home, was I?' And, without warning, her face crumpled. 'He's dead, Bella. My dad died six months ago. I went to see his grave. I took flowers. It was horrible. There was no headstone. No name. Just a number.'

'Oh, darling,' Belle said, putting her arms around her. 'You shouldn't have been alone.' And she never would be again. This afternoon she'd seen a different Ivo—someone caring, someone capable of immense feeling, the man she'd glimpsed in those first heady days, the man she'd fallen in love with and she'd wanted him, had pushed him into something he knew was a mistake. Selfish, selfish, selfish… 'I'm so sorry.'

'Oh, please!' She shook her off. 'You don't care. You hated him, blamed him for everything.' Belle, Ivo could see, was struggling to find a response that wasn't going to curdle in her mouth, something to comfort Daisy, but her sister didn't wait. 'You hated him and you don't give a damn about me.' She looked up, glared at him over Belle's shoulder and said, 'He's the only person you ever think about.'

'No…'

'It's true. He's always calling you. When you talk to him your face goes all soft and gooey and when I came home he was there, in your room. I heard you! You're supposed to be separated, getting a divorce, not having sex in the middle of the afternoon!'

Her youthful outrage would have been funny, Ivo thought, but he felt no urge to laugh. Belle's desperate 'No…' had chilled him to the bone. He'd known it would be bad—the destruction of the dress was not the work of a girl mildly irritated with her sister— but this was worse than he could ever have imagined.

And when Belle turned and looked at him, he knew he was right. Knew that she would sacrifice her own happiness, this tender shoot that promised a new beginning to their marriage— anything to make up to her sister for a mistake she'd made when she was fourteen years old. A decision she'd made for the best of reasons. The truth was that Daisy needed one hundred per cent of her sister right now and that was what she'd get.

There was nothing he could do or say to change Belle's mind. That to even try would be to hurt her more than she was already hurting.

He knew because he'd have done the same for Miranda. Would have sacrificed anything to make her well, make her whole; but her words, as she continued to look at him, still tore his heart from his body.

'Today was just one of those things that sometimes happens when something important is over, Daisy. Revisiting the might-have-beens. The very-nearlys. But we can never go back.'

Her words were telling him that waiting was not an option, that she had made her decision, that today had meant nothing. But her eyes, begging him to understand, to forgive her for putting Daisy first, were saying something else and, as if she knew that they betrayed her, she closed them, turned away, drew Daisy close as if she were a child.

'You're more important to me than anyone in the world, Daisy Porter. No one can ever come between us. You have to believe that.'

There were tears in her eyes as she said it, but Daisy, sobbing out her own grief, for a man she'd never known, who'd never loved her, who'd robbed them both of the life they should have had, didn't see them.

Life had a way of calling you on bad decisions, Ivo knew. He hadn't walked away three years ago, hadn't had Belle's heart, her capacity for sacrifice. This time, though, things were different. Belle had taught him the power of love, its enduring nature.

She needed this time alone with her sister and he was strong enough to give her the space she needed, for as long as she needed.

'For as long as we both shall live.'

He repeated the words from the marriage service under his breath, the difference being that this time he understood what they meant. And, more importantly, he believed them.

'You should have an early night,' Belle said.

Daisy had her feet up on the sofa she'd chosen—fuchsia-pink velvet, not as practical, but a lot more exciting than the brown suede she'd picked out—watching television.

'An early night?' She'd got over her tears, had a bath and a slice of pizza, which was all she seemed to want to eat. 'I'm not a kid.'

Then stop acting like one, she wanted to yell at her. Grow up. I had to. Ivo had to...

She held it in. This was her fault. If she'd been there, if she'd fought with the social workers for access, visiting rights, maybe it would have all worked out.

If she hadn't lost all sense today, hadn't been thinking solely of herself, then maybe, gradually, she could have slowly built on this brand-new fledgling relationship with Ivo.

Instead Daisy, selfish, needy, desperate, had forced her to choose between her sister and her marriage. She didn't know that she'd already chosen Daisy when she'd left Ivo.

For a moment she'd believed that he could be a part of their lives. But he understood the problems, the sacrifice involved in taking care of someone who had been emotionally damaged, broken by circumstance.

There had been no need for words. He'd made it easy for her, making it clear, when he'd dropped them back at the flat that he wouldn't be around for a while. Offering some excuse about pressure of business…

She dragged her mind back to her life, said, 'I didn't say you were a kid, but it's my last day on the breakfast sofa tomorrow, Daisy. I'd like you to be there with me.'

'What?' For a moment she looked excited, then just plain scared. 'Oh, no…' Then she bounced back. 'My hair!'

'The make-up girls will fix it for you.'

'But what will I wear? Can I borrow your…?' she began. Then, as quickly as it had bubbled up, her excitement evaporated and she sank back into the sofa. 'Forget it. You don't want me there.'

'I wouldn't have asked if I didn't want you there. I want the world to know I have a sister.'

'Parade me as your charity case? No thanks.'

She was doing it deliberately. For a moment she'd forgotten about the dress. What she'd done to it.

'You don't have to punish yourself over the dress, Daisy,' she said. 'You did it. It happened. You apologised. Now move on.' She didn't move. 'Okay. Let's deal with this. Come on.'

'What?' But Belle had her by the hand and, before she knew

what was happening, they were in the room where all her gowns were hanging on rails, waiting for a carpenter to find time to start work on fitted wardrobes.

Nothing had been touched since Daisy's attack on her dress. She'd simply shut the door on it, unable to face what it meant. For a brief shining moment it had seemed that she'd been offered a second chance, not just with her sister, but with Ivo. Life, however, wasn't that simple.

She'd never forgive herself for what she'd done to Ivo, for overriding his natural reserve, common sense, with a promise of something that was not hers to give.

Wanting it all.

She, more than anyone, should know how impossible that was. She'd found her sister. Eventually she'd find herself. And Ivo would, now the barriers had been broken down, find someone else.

Now, like her sister, she needed to live with what she'd done, move on, and she walked along the dress rail, running a finger over the hangers.

She'd cleared out a lot of her clothes, sent them to a charity shop. She was already building a new wardrobe for the different woman she was becoming and had only kept those that she needed for work, the ones that meant something special to her.

Her finger stopped at random and she took the dress from the rail, held it up for Daisy, hanging back in the doorway, to see. It was black, a sizzling strapless gown. She'd never wear it again. Had kept it out of sentimentality.

'I wore this dress to my first awards dinner years ago,' she said. Remembering the night. How nervous she'd been. How startled she'd been when she'd seen the glamorous photographs in the gossip mags the following week. Thinking it couldn't be her. It wasn't *her*... She turned to look at her sister. 'I wasn't nominated for anything. I was just a B-list celebrity there to make up the numbers. I can remember waiting for someone to call me on it. Ask me what the heck I thought I was doing there.'

She picked up the scissors, still lying where they'd fallen, gouging a lump out of the surface of the dressing table, and hacked it in two, discarding the pieces so that they fell to the floor to lie with the shreds of cream and gold. Ignored Daisy's gasp of horror as she continued running her finger along the rail.

'Now this one,' she said matter-of-factly, picking out a low-cut scarlet gown, 'was the dress I wore to some fancy affair involving bankers.'

Newly married, she'd been planning to wear something sedate in black, but then Manda had stuck her oar in, warning her not to make an exhibition of herself and what was a girl to do? Ivo hadn't said a word. His eyes had done the talking and, later, his fingers had done the walking.

'Billionaires, Daisy, drool just like normal men.'

Her sister whimpered as the scissors flashed and it joined the black dress on the floor.

Moving on.

She worked her way along the rail, picking out special favourites from these treasured gowns, recalling for her sister the special occasions on which she'd worn them. Birthdays, anniversaries, galas. Shutting her mind against the afterwards, when Ivo had unzipped, unhooked, unbuttoned each one, sometimes slowly, sometimes impatiently, always with passion.

By the time she reached the end of the rail Daisy was in tears and she was very close to them, her eyes swimming as she reached for the last gown.

A simple pleated column of grey silk, it was the first vintage gown she'd bought. Chanel at her most perfect. It was the gown she'd been wearing on that evening in the Serpentine Gallery.

Cutting this one would be hardest of all and yet it would be a symbol, a promise to her sister, even though it was one that Daisy would not understand. A promise to her sister, a demonstration that none of this mattered. That nothing would come between them ever again.

As she raised the scissors, Daisy caught her arm.

'Don't,' she sobbed. 'Please don't.' Then she sank to her knees, picking up tiny pieces of gold lace, holding them together as if she could undo the destruction. 'I'm sorry, Bella. So sorry.'

'It's only a dress, Daisy,' she said, letting the scissors fall to her side, almost faint with relief, sinking down beside her. 'It's not important. I just wanted you to understand that there is nothing more important to me than you.' She lifted her chin, forcing Daisy to look at her. 'You do believe me?'

'You looked like a princess that night,' she said, wiping her cheek with the palm of her hand. 'I was in the crowd outside the hotel, waiting for you to arrive. I wasn't going to ever come to you, mess up your life, but I wanted to see you and when you got out of the car everyone just sighed.'

'I was shaking with nerves.'

'Shaking? No! You were so beautiful. So perfect. And then you looked right at me and blew a kiss. Silly, you didn't know I was there…'

'I was thinking of you.'

She looked up. 'Were you?'

And Ivo…

No. She wouldn't, mustn't think of him. She'd never forgive herself for what she'd done to him, but he was a man. Strong. He'd be hurting, she knew that, but he'd survive without her.

Daisy would not.

'I thought you might be watching,' she said, pushing the thoughts away, concentrating on the girl in front of her. The future. 'I hoped, if you were, that you'd know it was just for you.'

'I should have trusted you. I thought…'

'I know what you thought. I let you down, wasn't there when you really needed me, but that will never happen again. Whatever happens, whatever you do, I will love you, be there for you.' Then, 'Tomorrow we'll see about getting a headstone for your Dad, hmm?'

For a minute they held each other, clinging on to each other amidst the wreckage of their lives, and Belle knew that a crisis had passed. Not the last crisis, but perhaps the biggest.

Ivo stayed at home to watch Belle's last morning. Every minute of it: the news, the papers, a celebrity interview, a fifty-year-old cab driver who'd written a book, a woman with cancer who was campaigning for some new treatment, the weather.

All the usual ingredients, Belle the glue that held it all together with her warmth, her charm, a little touch of steel that he'd somehow overlooked. Or maybe that was new. Something she'd found in the Himalayas. Something that made him love her all the more. He just hoped her wretched sister understood how lucky she was.

Today, her last day, the editors had put together a montage of her 'best bits' to end the programme. Her famous 'telethon' moment of discovery. Her first day on the set, making a hash of the weather. An interview that had gone hilariously wrong. Belle, eyes wide with excitement, at the wheel of a double-decker bus on the skid pad.

There was a shot of her interviewing the Director of the United Nations too. One of her with a much loved actor a few weeks before he died. That report to camera from the Himalayas with blood trickling down her face.

He'd expected it to end there with the credits rolling over that image, but instead the camera focused on her again.

Belle had a rare stillness, a presence in front of the camera, but today there was something new, something more. A maturity that had nothing to do with her grown-up haircut, more casual clothes. She had, he realised, finally learned to believe in herself and, despite everything, he found himself smiling. Urging her on to new heights, new challenges…

'I've been part of this programme one way and another for nine years,' she began, 'and, despite what you've just seen, the one thing I've learned is that it's not about me, but about you, the people who take time to tune in each busy morning, whether for a few minutes or an hour. It's about you, your lives, your news.' The camera went in close. 'Today, as you all know, is my last day on this sofa so I'm going to beg your indulgence and use these last few minutes to talk about myself.' She smiled. 'Actually, not just about me. I'm going to tell you the story of two little girls…'

He stood and watched as she told the world the story of her life. Of the horrors, but of the love too. And of a sister who she'd lost and had now found.

As she finished, she turned to smile at someone and the camera pulled back to reveal Daisy sitting beside her, sharing her sofa. Skinny as she was, lacking her sister's curves, she looked, at first glance, amazingly like Belle the day she'd smiled uncertainly up into a handheld camera. No doubt the studio make-up had emphasised the similarities and yet there was something…

For a moment there was complete silence and then the entire crew walked into the shot, applauding Belle, hugging them both.

He couldn't take his eyes off her, even when the door opened and Manda joined him. 'I've been watching next door. She's pretty amazing, your Belle, isn't she?'

'Not mine.'

Only for a few unforgettable moments yesterday afternoon, when the truth had set them free. When they'd used words that had been locked away.

Until the day he died he'd remember that moment when, poised above him, she'd kissed him, said, 'I love you…' before taking him to a place he'd only dreamed of. *Not his…*

'But yes, she is amazing,' he managed, through a throat aching so much that he could scarcely swallow.

'I was so sure she'd hurt you. I thought…' He put out a hand to stop her, but she shook her head, refusing to be silenced. 'I thought all she wanted was your money, but it wasn't like that, was it?'

'No,' he admitted. 'It wasn't anything like that.'

'Don't let her go, Ivo.'

'Her sister needs her more than I do right now.'

'Maybe she does, but Belle will need you too. We all need someone, a rock to cling to when things are bad.' She leaned against him. 'Or, in your case, a damn great cliff face.' Then, when he didn't respond, 'Her sister will move on, Ivo. Make a life of her own.'

'Eventually.' It didn't matter. Next week, next year, next life, he'd be there, if Belle should need him. Always be there.

Somehow he doubted that she would.

'What's she going to do, do you know?' Then, 'What can she do? The sister.'

'Daisy? I've no idea.' He turned to her, remembering his promise. 'Actually, I did tell Belle that you might give her a job.'

'Thanks for that.' Her standard response when he dumped some tedious job in her lap. He managed a grin, but she shook her head. 'No, I mean it, Ivo. Really. Thank you. For believing in me. Taking care of me. Saving me...' And suddenly his spiky, sharp little sister was the one struggling with words. 'I'll talk to her. Find out what she'd like to do.'

'She's fragile,' he warned.

'I won't break her; in fact she might find it easier to talk to me than Belle.' She glanced back towards the television set, where Belle, holding flowers that someone had thrust into her arms, was smiling into the camera as the credits rolled. 'What about Belle? What's she going to do?'

'I've no idea. She did have an idea for a documentary on adoption and I suggested she form her own production company.'

'That's not really her thing, is it?' Then, 'I can't see her heading up a media company. But maybe there is something she could do.'

'Leave it, Manda,' he warned.

'I hear what you say, Ivo, but are you saying "leave it" because you don't want me involved? Or are you warning me off because you can rely on me to do the exact opposite of what you say?'

'You've grown out of that nonsense.'

'Have I?'

'Don't be clever.'

'I just can't help it.' Then, 'I'll have a little chat with Daisy first, I think. But not just yet. I'll wait a week or two. Give them time to get bored playing happy families.' Then, 'Don't mess things up by sending her flowers or supportive little emails, will you?'

'If you're playing reverse psychology, you've picked the wrong man,' he said.

No flowers. No emails.

Just emptiness.

# CHAPTER ELEVEN

BELLE began, quite irrationally, to hate the doorbell. Not because of who it might be—network people, her agent, who didn't seem to understand the word 'no'—but because of who it wasn't.

Just how stupid could one woman be?

First she'd left Ivo and then, when he'd bared his soul, admitted that he'd been prepared to compromise his own desperate decision, overcome his own fears to give her what she wanted, she'd sent him away. Rejected him, put her sister first. Made it clear that he came second.

No man was going to stand for that, come back for more. Especially not a man like Ivo Grenville.

She picked up the entry phone. 'Yes?'

'It's Miranda, Belle. Can I come up?'

She buzzed her in. His sister was no substitute, but she'd breathed the same air, talked to him, could tell her how he was…

'Great sofa,' Manda said, sweeping into the room in a dramatic swirl of the season's most cutting-edge style, a whisper of some rare scent, picking out the one thing that she hadn't chosen. 'Very eye-catching.'

Oh, right. She was being sarcastic.

'Ivo said your flat had a certain appeal.'

'Really?' What else had he said…?

'I have to confess, I thought his view was coloured by lust but actually he's right. Of course what you really need is to completely restore the house, turn it back into a family home. Maybe convert the lower ground floor into a garden flat for Daisy. So much more suitable for a pram,' she said.

'What can I do for you, Miranda?' Belle enquired sharply, refusing to be drawn into whatever game she thought she was playing.

'Nothing. It's your sister I've come to see. I understand she's in the market for a job.' She didn't wait for an answer but, turning to Daisy, said, 'I saw you on television last month. You've got your sister's smile.' Before Daisy had time to demonstrate it, she continued, 'I have no doubt that the rest of you will catch up in time. Motherhood can do wonders, I understand.' She extended her hand. 'I'm Manda Grenville, Ivo's sister.'

'Ivan the Terrible *and* Cruella de Ville,' Daisy replied, ignoring it. 'A neat match.'

Manda's eyes widened slightly and then, even as Belle held her breath, she threw back her head and laughed. 'The buxom Belle but with an edge. Brilliant. We're going to get along just fine.'

Infuriating though it was, it seemed that they did, perhaps recognising something in one another. And Belle had to admit that the job offer was good news. She hadn't expected Ivo to remember. She should have given him more credit; he might be hurt, but he wouldn't take his feelings out on Daisy.

She had tried to talk to her sister about the future; she was quick, clever, could easily get a place at college. She'd refused to even discuss it with her.

'Is there any hope of a cup of coffee, Belle?' Miranda asked.

About to remind her that if she wanted coffee she knew where the nearest deli was, she held her tongue, glad to have her as an ally on her sister's behalf, even if she'd never been a friend to her.

'Of course. Daisy? Can I get you anything?'

'Is there any of that honey and camomile tea left?'

She boiled the kettle, took the coffee from the fridge and spooned some into the cafetière; wrinkling up her nose at the smell, she decided to join Daisy in a cup of herb tea.

Daisy and Manda were, unlikely as that seemed, deep in conversation when she carried through the tray. She turned down the heating, then opened the French windows.

'Good grief, Bella, do you want us to freeze in here?'

'It's so stuffy in here,' she said. Then, realising that they were both staring at her, 'Maybe I'm coming down with something.'

'It must be something going around,' Manda said pointedly. 'Ivo has matching symptoms.'

'He's not well?'

'Nothing that a decent night's sleep wouldn't fix. Why don't you go and have a lie down?'

'I'm fine, really,' she began. Then, as Manda poured out the coffee and the smell reached her, she realised that was not the case and had to make a run for the bathroom, only just making it before she threw up.

She refused to let Daisy or Manda make a fuss, waving them away. 'It's just some bug. I'll lie down for a minute.'

Manda was still there when she emerged an hour later, slightly fuzzy from a nap and starving hungry.

'Is that pizza…?'

'We sent out for it. Daisy's choice.'

'Bliss. Did she leave any anchovies?'

'What is it with the pair of you and anchovies?' Manda demanded as Belle, spotting one that had been overlooked, picked it off and ate it.

'Belle!' Daisy protested. 'You hate anchovies.'

'I just fancied something salty.' She licked the tip of her thumb. 'What?'

They shook their heads as one and Manda quickly said, 'I'm glad you're back with us. Daisy and I are all sorted. All we need now is you.'

'Me?'

'It's this kids' charity thing I've got involved with. It seems to have been provoked by the huge response to your coverage of the charity bike ride. There's been a bit of a popular outcry and politicians are feeling bruised by the criticism. Things need to be done. The question is what things.'

'You'd like me to give you a list?'

'I was hoping for rather more than that, to be honest. A picture being, as we both know, worth a thousand words, what I need is someone to take a camera crew and show the world just how bad things are. An ambassador for the street kids, if you like. With your credentials, you appear to be the obvious choice.'

Daisy's face was glowing with excitement. 'Manda wants me to go with her on a pre-filming recce. As her assistant.'

'You're pregnant, Daisy.'

'Well, duh! This is the twenty-first century; I don't have to stay at home in purdah. It'll be during the middle three months.' Her voice was pleading. 'We're going to South America, the Far East…'

'I'll take care of her, Belle.'

'Will you?' Then, because she had to ask, 'Was this your idea?'

'You think Ivo is behind it? I promise you, he expressively forbade me from asking for your help.'

'Oh.' Belle felt like a tyre with the air let out. It was like the doorbell, she thought. She understood that it couldn't possibly be him, but she would keep hoping…

'Please, Belle!' Daisy begged. 'Please say you'll do it.'

She weighed up the options. Daisy, sulking and miserable under her feet day and night. Or with an exciting job, a future.

And not just Daisy. This was a new chance for her to do something important. Something that would make a difference.

'I guess you'd better go to the Post Office and pick up a passport application form,' she said.

'You saw her? How is she?'

Ivo might have tried to discourage his sister from whatever scheme she was hatching, but he'd been pacing the library, waiting for her to come home.

'Feeling a little under the weather, if you really want to know.'

Manda settled on the sofa and put her feet up. 'Some tedious little bug, no doubt. It's that time of year.' Then, 'You're right about her flat, by the way. It's charming. Shame about the sofa.' She tilted her head to look at him. 'Did you know that there's one just like it for sale on the next floor?'

'The sofa?'

'Her flat.'

'Not any more.'

She swivelled round. 'You've bought it? When did you organise that?'

'I put in an offer the Monday after Belle left me.'

'Really? Does she know?'

'Not yet.' Then, 'You might as well know that I've bought the other two flats as well. I now own the entire house except the top floor.'

She wrinkled her brow in a thoughtful frown. 'All the flats were for sale at the same time?'

'If you offer enough money, anything is for sale.'

'And your plan is?'

'Shot to pieces, if you really want to know.'

'Oh, I don't know. Once I've whisked Daisy Dreadful off to South America the coast will be clear. You can move in downstairs and lay siege to the fair lady. Ply her with pizza. Just make sure to specify extra anchovies.'

'She hates anchovies.'

'Yes. Interesting.' Then, 'Whatever. Just think about it.'

'What on earth is going on downstairs?' Belle demanded.

The noise was driving her mad. No. Everything was driving her mad. The fact that her perfect minimalist flat had been taken over by the Christmas fairy in the shape of Daisy. That everything capable of carrying a decoration had been lit, baubled and tinselled.

That the freezer was full to the brim with food that made her ill just to think of it.

That all she wanted to do was lie down in a darkened room until the whole thing was over.

'The ground floor tenants are moving out today,' Daisy said. 'They've bought some swanky place in Bankside, apparently.'

'That's the whole place empty except for us? Does everyone else know something I don't?' Then, as Daisy placed a beautifully gift-wrapped package in front of her, 'What's this?'

'An early Christmas present. Something I think you might find a use for.'

She eased herself up into a sitting position, told herself not to be such a Grinch—Daisy deserved this Christmas—and made herself smile. 'That's so sweet. Thank you.' She kissed her sister, undid the blue bow, loosened the silver wrapping paper. Frowned in confusion as she looked at the box in her hand. Then thought for a moment that she was going to be sick again. 'Is this a joke?'

'No, it's a pregnancy test kit. The latest high-tech job. No little blue lines or crosses on this one. It actually says "Pregnant" or "Not Pregnant". How neat is that?' Daisy said, totally pleased with herself.

Belle swallowed. Not neat at all.

'I'm not pregnant,' she said.

'You're sick all the time,' Daisy said, shifting all her weight to one leg, sticking out her hip and ticking off her counter-arguments on her fingers, one by one. 'The kitchen cupboard is stacked with cans of anchovies as if you're afraid they're about to go extinct. You go green if I mention coffee. And yesterday I caught you eating a pickled cucumber out of the jar. Two months ago that was me.' Then, pulling a face, 'Except for the pickle.'

'I like pickled cucumbers.'

'Are your breasts tender?' she persisted. 'I have noticed that you're wearing your softest bras.'

'Well, maybe, but—'

'But nothing. Quit with the excuses. It's time you stopped

hiding from the truth and admitted you're up the duff. In the club. That there is, in the vernacular, a bun in your oven.'

Vernacular? She'd been spending way too much time with Manda.

'No, darling,' she said, pushing her lank fringe back from her forehead with a shaking hand. 'You don't understand. I can't possibly be pregnant.'

'You're doing a very good impression of it.'

'It's just a bug. Something I picked up when I was abroad.'

'They do the delayed action kind now?'

'Please!' she begged. 'I can't... Ivo can't...'

'What?'

'He can't have children.' Daisy did not look convinced. 'He had a vasectomy.'

'Is that a fact? So who's been a naughty girl, then?'

'No!'

'I was kidding, Bella.' Daisy placed the box in her hands, eased her to her feet. 'The bathroom is that way. Do you want me to come and read the instructions for you?'

'This is ridiculous.'

'Really? So prove it.'

Belle sat on the edge of the bath staring at the little wand she was holding. The single word.

*'Pregnant'*

Around her, the world went about its business, unheeding. The bumping and shouting as the removal men shifted furniture.

An impatient motorist hooted.

A child cried.

A brass band in the market was playing a Christmas carol.

'Bella?' Daisy's voice was no longer teasing but anxious. 'Bella, can I come in?' She didn't wait, but opened the door. Took the stick from her hand. 'I really hate to say I told you so...'

'It's wrong.'

'Oh, Bella...' Daisy put her arms around her. 'It's okay.'

'No. No, it's not. It can't be true,' she said. She wanted it to be true. Longed for it to be true. But it couldn't be. 'It would take a miracle.'

Ivo had begged for one. For her sake, she reminded herself. Nothing had changed for him.

'Maybe it's a dud,' Daisy offered gently, as if she were talking to a child. She didn't understand. Couldn't know… 'Why don't I go and get another kit? A different kind.'

'Whatever it takes to convince you.'

An hour later they were surrounded by empty cartons, the little sticks they'd contained, each one telling her, with blue lines, pink lines, blue crosses, the same thing.

Pregnant. Pregnant. Pregnant.

'There's one more,' Daisy said.

'I couldn't squeeze out another drop.'

'So what? You're ready to accept that they're right?' Then, misunderstanding, 'It's not so bad, you know. And our kids will be almost like twins.'

'You don't understand.'

'Maybe I do.' Daisy knelt in front of her. 'It's okay, really.' Then, '*I'm* going to be okay. Selfish. A brat. Afraid that you'd get tired of me. But you sent him away for me, didn't you? Even though you love him.'

'No!'

'Then why hasn't he been to see you?'

'He's busy.'

'He hasn't even called you.'

Belle, unable to speak, just shook her head.

'I'm off to South America after Christmas,' Daisy said, 'but I don't think I can go if you're going to be on your own.'

'Don't be silly. I'll be fine.'

'I don't think you will. No. That's the deal. Call him or Manda will have to find someone else to run her errands.'

'Daisy…' She reached out, caught her hand. 'You know I'd never let you down, don't you? That I'll always been here for you.'

'Yes, Bella, I know.' Then, leaping to her feet, 'Well, what are you waiting for? Call Ivan the Terrible, tell him that, snip or not, he's about to become a daddy.'

Ivo had used work, from his earliest days at school, to block out the emptiness in his life. For the first time in his life it wasn't working.

He'd stopped going into the office, had abandoned ongoing projects to his more than capable deputies, who were doubtless delighted at the chance to show what they could do, using the excuse that he needed to sort out the Camden house.

When he'd seen the flat below hers was for sale it had seemed as if it was meant. Quite what he was going to do with it he hadn't decided. But then Daisy had turned up and it had all seemed so simple. He'd convert the garden flat for Daisy. Move in between them. Be a friend. A father...

Stupid.

Now, the keys in his hand, the empty rooms mocking him, he wasn't able to rouse himself to care about anything very much.

His cellphone bleeped to warn him that he had a text message. His first reaction was to ignore it, but there were people relying on him, for whom he was responsible. He pulled it from his pocket, flipped it open. Stared at it. He hadn't thought his day could get any worse, but it just had.

There was a tap at the front door to the flat. 'It's probably the removal men wanting a cup of tea,' Belle said, drying her hair. 'Can you handle it?'

'No problem.'

She looked at her face in the mirror, pinched her cheeks to put a bit of colour in them. Put on a pair of earrings. Realised that everything had gone very quiet.

'Daisy?'

'Your sister said to tell you that she's meeting Manda for lunch.' Belle spun around on the stool. Ivo was standing in the doorway watching her. 'Your message said you wanted to see me. To talk about the future.'

For a moment she could hardly catch her breath, let alone speak. It had been just over a month and he looked no better than her. Gaunt, hollow-eyed...

'I only sent that text a few minutes ago.'

'I was in the flat downstairs.'

She frowned. 'But it's empty. It's been empty for weeks...'

'Not any more. I've been taking possession of my latest acquisition. What do you want to see me about, Belle? If it's—'

'The flat? You've bought the flat?'

'Actually, I've bought the whole house,' he said impatiently. 'All of it except this floor. Does it matter?'

'That depends on your reason. Are you going to move in?'

'Yes. No...' He shook his head. 'Belle, if you want to talk about a divorce—'

'What? No,' she said. 'No.' She turned and picked up a silk jewellery roll that was lying on the dressing table. Offered it to him. 'It's this.'

Ivo took it. 'What is it?'

'Open it and see.'

He shrugged, undid the tie, then placed it on the bed and rolled it open.

In each pocket there was a small plastic stick. Each one was slightly different. He'd never actually seen one before, but it didn't take a genius to work out what they were. What he didn't understand was what she was doing with them. Telling him. Until the last one. That said it in one simple word.

*Pregnant.*

He thought he knew pain, understood every way in which the heart could be wrenched open, torn apart, bleed. But in that moment, as the possibilities raced through his head, he learned different.

'Oh, my love...' Somehow he was on his knees and she had her arms around him, holding him, crushing him to her. 'What have you done?'

'Me?' She drew back a little.

'Was it a donor? Were you that desperate?'

'No… Don't you understand, Ivo?' She took the pregnancy test strip, knelt before him, holding it out. 'What this is, my love, is a miracle. You asked for one, remember? For me.' She lifted a hand, touched his cheek. 'It's your baby, Ivo. My baby. Our baby.'

He was swamped with confusion. 'Our baby? But…'

She laid a finger on his lips. 'I assumed, from what you said, that the doctor told you that your vasectomy was irreversible. That there was nothing to be done.'

'No. He did his best, but warned me he couldn't guarantee anything.'

'It would have stood a rather better chance if I hadn't been taking the pill for the last three years, don't you think?' she asked, smiling.

'But…' He stopped. 'No. You wanted a baby. Why would you take the pill?'

'I saw your face, Ivo. You didn't have to tell me that you didn't want children. I spent twenty-four hours after you left me alone on our honeymoon island coming to terms with that. At the end of it I chose you for as long as you wanted me. Not for your money. Not for the security. For no other reason than that I loved you.'

'I didn't know…'

She stopped him with a kiss. For a moment he had no thought but to take the blissful moment, forget anything else.

Later he said, 'You stopped taking the pill when you left?'

'Why would I need them? There wasn't anyone else I was planning to have sex with.' She smiled. 'To sleep with.'

'Keep it that way,' he said, then drew back a little, looking at her as if he still couldn't quite believe it. 'Our baby?'

'Ivo, children need parents who want them. Who can love them. I know this wasn't what you wanted. I want you to know that I can do this on my own.'

It was a question. She needed to know. Had a right to know.

'You don't have to do anything on your own ever again,

Belle. You're right. This is a miracle. But the biggest miracle is not that you loved me enough to stay, but found the strength to leave. Forced me to acknowledge the truth. I love you, Belle Davenport, love the baby we made.' Then, 'Or are you telling me that I don't have a choice? That your sister still comes first.'

'It was Daisy who made me call you.'

Belle looked up as the brass band in the marketplace struck up 'Joy to the World'. Then she turned back to him. 'You've seen the decorations? I should warn you that she's planning a traditional old-fashioned family Christmas. How do you feel about that?'

'Here?'

'Could you bear it?'

'I could bear Christmas in a tent if it meant sharing it with you.' He laid his palm over her stomach. 'Both of you.'

'There's Daisy and Manda as well.'

'Maybe not a tent, in that case. I think perhaps I'd better get the flat downstairs furnished, just as a stopgap, or it's going to be a bit cramped.'

'A stopgap?'

'My plan was to restore the house to a family home, bit by bit. Make it so welcoming that you couldn't resist moving in.'

'What about the house in Belgravia?'

'Would you move back?'

'I'd rather take the tent.'

'Then it's history.'

'You're sure?'

'I've never been more certain of anything in my entire life. I just wish I could wipe out the last three years as easily, so that we could start again. Begin anew.'

'You really mean that?'

'With all my heart.'

They were still kneeling, face to face, and she took his hands in hers and said, 'I, Belinda Louise, take thee, Ivan George Michael, to my wedded husband. To have and to hold, from this day forward, for better, for worse, for richer for poorer, in sickness and in health, to love and to cherish, till death us do part…'

Her eyes filled as she said the words, tears flowing unchecked down her cheeks as Ivo followed her lead and reaffirmed the vow he'd made three years before.

'From this day forward,' he said again and tenderly, gently kissed her. 'Until the end of time.'

Once Christmas—starting with a trip to the midnight service to thank whoever was watching over them for giving them all so much—was over, Ivo and Belle had a blissful month alone, while Manda and Daisy took off for foreign parts to explore the possibilities for their film.

They spent it planning their new home together, relaxed in each other's company, discovering the simple pleasures of marriage for the first time. Cooking together, sleeping together, waking in each other's arms. Neither of them in a hurry to be anywhere else.

It was tough being apart while they did the filming, yet exhilarating too. Belle's new-found confidence had given her a harder edge that had the media clamouring for more; by the time she and Manda were helping Daisy through her delivery and she was welcoming her new nephew into the world, it had already garnered half a dozen nominations for an award.

On the night it won the first of them, Belle was panting through her own contractions, Ivo at her side, calm, quietly supportive, even when she completely lost it at one point, told him and anyone else who'd listen that she'd changed her mind about having a baby.

He was totally in control until the moment his baby daughter was delivered into his hands.

Then, tears streaming down his face, he was reduced to incoherent gratitude and joy as he laid their child in her arms.

'So small, so helpless. Like a kitten,' he said, when he was, at last, able to speak.

'Maybe we should call her Minette.'

'You've been working on your French.' He smiled, kissed them both. 'Welcome, Minette.' Then, when the midwife made it clear that there were things she needed to do, 'Manda is waiting for news. And Daisy.'

'Will you call Claire and Simone too? I promised. They said no matter what time of day or night.'

'No problem. I want to tell the whole world that I'm a father.' He kissed her forehead and said, 'Did I tell you today that I love you?'

'With every piece of ice. Every damp cloth. When you massaged my back.' She grinned up at him, 'When you agreed with every word of the abuse I heaped on you.'

'It was all true.'

'Not all of it...' She took his hand, kissed his palm where her nails had dug in, and then looked up, suddenly grave, 'Most of all, my love, when you cried.' Then, 'Did I tell you?'

He looked down at his beloved wife, who was almost asleep.

'I promise you that there isn't a man on earth who feels more loved, more blessed, than I do at this moment,' he said, but softly, so as not to disturb her.

# MARRYING HER
# BILLIONAIRE BOSS
## MYRNA MACKENZIE

**Myrna Mackenzie** spent her childhood being a good student, a reader and an avid daydreamer. She knew more about what she wasn't qualified to be than what she actually wanted to be (no athletic skill, so pole vaulting was out; not a glib speaker, so not likely to become a politician; poor swimmer, so the door to marine biology was closed). Fortunately, daydreaming turned out to be an absolutely perfect qualification for a writer, and today Myrna feels blessed that she gets to make her living writing down her daydreams about ranchers, princesses, billionaires and ordinary people whose lives are changed by love. It is an awesome job!

When she's not writing, Myrna spends her time reading, seeing the latest (or not so latest) movie, hiking, collecting recipes she seldom makes, trying to knit or crochet and writing a blog (which is so much fun)! Born in a small town in Dunklin County, Missouri, she now divides her time between two lakes in Chicago and Wisconsin. Visit her online at www.myrnamackenzie.com or write to her at PO Box 225, La Grange, IL 60525, USA.

# CHAPTER ONE

DESPERATION WAS SUCH an ugly word. Unfortunately it described Beth Krayton's situation. She had roughly forty-eight hours to find a good job and a nice place to live in her brand-new hometown of Lake Geneva, Wisconsin, before her brothers discovered her whereabouts and attempted to bring her back to Chicago.

She knew just what weapon they would use, too. Guilt. And she had never been good at handling guilt. Her brothers and former guardians had always been excellent at ladling it on, but after her "incident" two years ago, things had gotten worse. And lately, since she'd lost her job...

The memory of the totally humiliating scene that had unfolded two days ago sent a sick feeling rushing to her stomach. When she'd overheard her brothers and their wives discussing solutions to "the Beth problem" she had finally realized that, as hard as she had fought for her independence, the older she got the more determined to manage her life her family became.

When her parents died, years ago, her brothers had vowed to raise her and protect her. She'd been convinced that one day they would see her as an equal. But that overheard conversation, which branded her as a woman incapable of making good decisions, had killed her hopes. Now she understood: They would never rest until they felt she was safely in some other man's care. Only by proving that she could go it alone without a husband would she convince them to stop interfering in her life.

"If that's even possible," she whispered to herself as she barely refrained from groaning.

It wouldn't make the right impression in her upcoming job interview if people reported that she had been seen talking to herself and moaning out loud in public places. And she had to make a good impression, because with the clock ticking away, all that stood between her and her goals (and her brothers) was a man named Carson Banick, a wealthy hotelier who had advertised for an assistant well-schooled in the hospitality industry.

Beth didn't have a single ounce of experience in the hospitality industry.

That can't matter, she told herself, heading toward the building where her interview was being held. Perusing the classifieds, she had found few jobs she was qualified for that would pay a living wage. *This* job would ensure basic survival, it hadn't mentioned a college education and, more importantly, it might help her establish a career and an identity of her own. She'd never had either and she needed them with an ache she couldn't explain.

Carson Banick had to hire her. She had to convince him to like her. She had to exude charm in spite of the fact that she had never been called anything close to charming.

"I'll be charming today, darn it," she said, forgetting her vow not to speak to herself as she pushed open the door to the trailer thrown up on the edge of a leveled building site, stepped inside and came face-to-face with the most gorgeous, dark-haired man she had ever seen.

He was frowning at her.

Carson looked up from the stack of papers on his desk, irritated by the distraction of the door opening. He had already interviewed a number of people, but he still hadn't come close to finding what he was looking for. Judging by the appearance of the woman standing just inside the door, it was unlikely that this interview would turn up anything more positive.

It wasn't her dowdy sack of a brown skirt that troubled him. Neither was it the slightly ragged edges on her chin-length, astonishingly red hair. Clothing and hair could be fixed with an infusion of money, and he had plenty of money to spend.

No, it was the wounded, defiant expression in her eyes. The woman clearly had issues, and he was the last person in the world who ought to be allowed near wounded creatures with issues. He'd already proven that several times in recent history. People, important people—his former fiancée, his brother—had been damaged in the process.

Carson tried not to think of how Emily had looked when he'd left her. He fought not to remember his brother's pain-racked face right after the accident or Patrick's complete lack of responsiveness when Carson had visited him last week. He battled like crazy to keep from remembering that he was the one responsible for his brother's fall on that mountain. And he was nearly slayed by the injustice of Patrick losing the use of his lower extremeties while Carson took his brother's rightful place here at this desk.

Rising, Carson fought to keep his hands from curling into fists. Concentrate on this minute and this place and this woman, he told himself. Do the job. Keep things going until Patrick heals. Carson prayed that Patrick would heal, even though the doctors had told him that Patrick wasn't making the kind of progress they had hoped for. The only way Carson could help his younger brother was to hold his position and do the work well.

Carson took a breath. He looked the woman over carefully. No, she wouldn't do at all. He certainly wasn't going to hire someone who would need nurturing or who would remind him of his own failings.

He needed an assistant who was competent and knowledgeable, someone who could help him make a miracle happen at his hotel and help him make it happen fast. The woman before him didn't look as if she'd had any recent experience with miracles. She looked fragile, vulnerable and—

Damn! Why was he even noticing such things, and anyway perhaps she wasn't even here about the job.

She might be a salesperson or someone simply lost. He frowned. No, she had the desperate look of a jobseeker. Carson stepped around the desk.

The woman clenched a fold of that ugly brown skirt.

"May I help you? I assume you're here about the position," he said.

She nodded tightly, but she raised her chin as if he'd just insulted her. "Yes, I'm here to apply for the assistant's job at the Banick Resort."

She looked as if she might be holding her breath, but her chin remained high, her shoulders back, almost as if she was daring him to ask her to leave.

He managed not to sigh. "Then you've come to the right place. I'm Carson Banick."

Those brown eyes blinked. "You...own the place?"

"You don't believe me?"

"It's not that. It's just that I wasn't expecting someone so exalted to be conducting the job interviews."

Carson shrugged. "The person who gets this job will be working directly with me."

She lowered her lashes and nodded curtly. "Do you have an application?"

"Yes, of course, and I'll have you fill one out, but an application is a formality. I'd rather get my information firsthand." There was no point in putting her to the trouble of filling out paperwork when she would be gone in the next two minutes. The people he had already interviewed had not been right but every one of them had seemed more professional than she did.

It was, Carson conceded, proving to be difficult to find the appropriate person. It was high season in Lake Geneva and there were more jobs to fill in the exclusive resort town than there were people to fill them.

That was unacceptable. He had to make a decision within the next few days. He'd known things were falling behind schedule, but he'd waited, hoping Patrick would make a miraculous comeback. He had ignored his parents' demands the way he always had. But, eventually he'd been forced to concede that he would have to take over the building of this hotel, his brother's greatest project. When the doctors had told him that Patrick's lack of progress seemed to be stress-related, Carson had finally stepped in. At least he could help his brother in this one rather inadequate way. He could get the stockholders and Rod and Deirdre Banick off Patrick's back. For once Carson could be the responsible older brother and do what he could to protect Patrick.

The irony didn't escape Carson. His parents had spent years trying to get him to take his rightful place, but he had always rebelled. He'd done as he liked, shunning the family business. Patrick had been the genial one who had sat at the helm of Banick Enterprises for five years since their father's health had forced him into retirement. But now things had changed. When Patrick was healed and ready to reclaim his place as the Banick heir, the hotel had to be up and running smoothly. It had to be a masterpiece. That meant Carson had to do what he'd never done before: leave his rebellious days behind and become a true Banick. It also meant that a top-notch assistant was imperative, but right now the room was empty of candidates except for this lone woman.

The pale curve of her jaw was rigid as she waited for him to take the next step. No wonder. He'd kept her waiting and he was staring at her a bit too hard, he realized.

"Have a seat," he said, motioning her toward the guest chair.

She moved forward quietly, sitting and smoothing the skirt over her knees. There was something innocent and feminine about the gesture, despite that bold chin. Carson wanted to throttle himself. He and innocence didn't belong in the same room, and the woman's femininity or lack of it was none of his concern.

"Tell me something about yourself," he said, moving back to the issue at hand. It was a rotten interview question, but the answer tended to be revealing. Interviewees told him what they thought he wanted to hear. That could be important. An assistant needed to be able to anticipate what was needed in sometimes trying situations.

"My name is Beth Krayton. I'm new to Lake Geneva, but I've visited before. I've always loved it and I hope to build a wonderful life here."

It was a bit of a beauty pageant-style answer, but when Carson looked into Beth Krayton's eyes he saw that she was sincere. He saw something else, too. She had latched on to the folds of her skirt again, twisting it a bit.

When his gaze touched on her fingers, she let go of the cloth. Suddenly she sat up straighter.

"Look, Mr. Banick, I can see that you have no intention of hiring me."

Now he was the one who blinked. He leaned back and folded his arms across his chest. "What makes you say that?"

"Other than the fact that you're frowning, you're clearly capable of hiring anyone you please, and I'm sure you have plenty of qualified candidates camping out on your doorstep."

He waited to see if she had more to say. She had given him the perfect opening to dismiss her, and that was just what he should be doing. But her actions hadn't matched her words. She wasn't rising to leave, and curiosity got the best of him.

He had always been a sucker for the unpredictable.

"So why did you come if you're so sure you wouldn't get this job?" he challenged.

She looked up into his eyes, and something shifted inside him. That wounded look still lurked but there was something else as well, something he couldn't quite name but that he knew was admirable.

Carson almost smiled. His mother had always admonished him to do something admirable. He never had.

"I came because I...really wanted the job. I thought I would be working for one of your employees, someone more like me. Instead...well, it's your hotel."

Not really. He benefited from the family's business

financially, but the hotels were Patrick's. Carson had made his own place in the world, and even when the thrill of that world had palled, he had not come home. Yet here he was, the prodigal son in charge of the company and the family. Only he stood between the company and failure. A disastrous or even a poorly managed project and the Banick's carefully tended reputation and resources could crumble. He held his brother's and the family's future in his hands. Sobering thought, but now was not the time to ponder it.

"So you're bowing out because you don't want to work for the owner?" he asked Beth Krayton.

She stood but instead of turning and leaving, she leaned forward. She actually put one hand on her hip. "Not at all. I may have come here with the wrong impression and I may not be what you expected or what you were looking for, but I really think that you should hire me anyway."

Okay, he couldn't help himself. Carson let a smile slip in. "Why is that?"

"Because I need this job more than any other interviewee will. Because I was raised by four older brothers who all wanted to run the show, so I'm used to dealing with powerful and difficult people."

He tilted his head, and warm pink crept up her throat. "I didn't mean that you would be difficult, but if you're working with contractors and such, I'm sure some of them may be troublesome from time to time. I'm not afraid of tough situations."

"Good. What are you afraid of?"

She didn't hesitate. "Not much." But she dropped her gaze ever so slightly. Bold as she was trying to be, there were definitely things that scared her. Carson wasn't sure if he should applaud her bravado or turn away from her obvious innocence. What he did know was that she suddenly seemed much more interesting than any of the other more conventional and staid candidates he'd interviewed so far. He frowned at that incongruous and ridiculous thought.

Beth Krayton either hadn't noticed that frown or she was choosing to ignore it. She stood straighter. For a tiny thing she was making an excellent attempt at being regal. "I'll be honest with you, Mr. Banick. I might not have all the skills you're looking for, but I learn very fast and I'll devote myself to absorbing everything I need to know as quickly as possible. You'll be able to count on me completely. I'll do whatever is necessary."

"Do you have experience in the hospitality field?"

She shook her head and that unkempt mop of red hair slid against her cheek. "None. And I don't have a college degree, if you're going to ask about that, but I can take direction and I know how to identify and pursue opportunities. I've never shied away from challenges and I don't believe in the word impossible."

"Lots of people say that."

That stopped her for a second. Then she took an almost visibly deep breath. "Yes, they do, but...I tend to live it. The fact that I'm here when I don't have any reason to believe that you would hire me is partial proof of that. I promise you that I will make this job the top priority in my life."

Carson frowned. That was what he needed to hear, but it also sounded a bit too pat. He wanted to ask some follow-up questions, personal questions, but there were boundaries an employer couldn't cross. His next question would have to be phrased carefully.

"If I need you here at night?"

For a second those brown eyes lit. She looked hopeful, almost pretty, which was a ridiculous thought. He liked curvy women, not skinny, nervous ones with bad hair and eyes that were feverish in their intensity. A good thing, since he couldn't get involved with an employee. Frankly, after Emily, he didn't intend to get involved with any woman who wasn't capable of fitting into the Banick world. It just wouldn't be fair to either of them, especially since he had recently decided that he would have to marry. Patrick could no longer father children, and there had to be a Banick heir....

"Mr. Banick?"

Carson gave himself a mental shake and concentrated on Beth Krayton. Despite her obvious misgivings at his so-called "exalted status" she was determined to make her case. She deserved his full attention. "Yes?"

"I said that I could be here whenever necessary. This will not be just a job to me."

"It's a temporary job," he warned. "Once the hotel opens, my involvement and this position end."

She paled slightly. "Okay."

"Okay?"

"I can deal with that. It will still look good on my résumé."

"I haven't hired you yet." More and more he was thinking that while she was definitely the most enthusiastic and driven—and therefore the most promising—candidate, hiring her might prove to be a mistake—on a personal level. There was something intriguing about her, and he couldn't afford to be intrigued by a down-on-her-luck employee.

"I know you haven't hired me."

"Tell me about your last job."

She blanched and then she blushed. "I was a customer service representative in an automotive parts store."

"And you left for what reason?"

For the first time she looked away.

Ah. "Were you…let go?" he asked quietly.

"Yes, in a sense."

He could see she wanted to leave it at that. No chance. "In what sense?"

"In the sense that…" She sighed and turned her attention back to him. "I'll be honest, Mr. Banick. In my younger days I was a bit wild. I did things that got me into trouble and made my already overprotective family even more protective. They knew my last employer and they thought he would make a great husband for me. He seemed to think the same thing. Since I'm not interested in a relationship or in getting married, I was the only one who didn't think Barry and I were well suited.

"No one was forcing me into anything, of course, but the situation still became very awkward. When I declared my lack of interest, Barry asked me to leave. But rest assured that I didn't get fired because of incompetence. And also rest assured that my youthful ways are behind me. If you hire me for this job you won't regret it. I need this position and I do exemplary work. I hope you won't hold the circumstances of my last job against me. For what it's worth, I was very good with the customers. I just wasn't very good at telling my boss that I wasn't interested in him as a man."

Beth finished this long speech, two bright spots of color in her cheeks. It was obvious that the subject of her last employer was more than a little uncomfortable.

She didn't realize it but she had just said exactly the right things. She had been a bit wild in her younger days. So had he, so he knew about trying to move past that. More importantly, she wasn't interested in romance. That simplified things. In a working relationship this close he couldn't afford even the possibility of an inappropriate entanglement, especially given the fact that he'd finally accepted that he needed to marry and produce an heir to keep the Banick line going. Still…

"Ms. Krayton," he began, knowing that his tone was enough to ready her for bad news.

"Don't say no yet. I realize my background isn't ideal, but…why don't you hire me on a trial basis?" she offered suddenly. "If I don't prove useful in two weeks I'll help you find a replacement. I'd even be willing to work those two weeks for free."

Carson raised a brow. She didn't look like someone who could go without a paycheck for two weeks. "That's very accommodating of you, Ms. Krayton."

Carson looked at the clock and then at the calendar. When Patrick began this project, he had planned to complete it by the end of the year. Since his accident three months ago, little had been done and the shareholders were getting restless. Disaster threatened, and the future of the business, Patrick's pride and joy, was at stake. Carson had waited too long to step in. Now he had to move mountains.

The truth was that he didn't know if Beth Krayton was the best candidate, but she appeared to be totally committed to acquiring the position and proving herself. That was more than he could say for any of the other people he'd interviewed, most of whom had been more interested in the salary and benefits than in the job itself. And she had offered him an easy out if things didn't work.

It was tempting to hedge his bets. He was almost as new at this as she was. But there would be no tiptoeing around for him or for anyone who worked for him. Once they began, life would become a whirlwind. The schedule for the hotel was being stepped up.

"No trial period," he said. "I'll hire you until you do something that justifies firing you. Banicks treat their employees fairly." Carson held back a groan. He sounded just like his father. Beth grinned.

"What?" he said.

"You said you would hire me."

Carson allowed himself a hint of a smile. "Yes, I did, didn't I?"

He looked across the desk and saw that his new, petite assistant was practically bouncing. "Thank you, Mr. Banick. And thank you for not making me go through a trial period. I would have gone through with it, but being able to eat for the next two weeks will be nice, too."

He shook his head and smiled again. "I wouldn't want my assistant missing meals. You'll let me know if that's ever a problem, won't you?"

Bright pink suffused her face. "I shouldn't have said that. I was kidding."

She hadn't been. He was sure of that. "Of course. Still, you'll let me know if you need anything."

A curt nod from her was the best he would get. Carson nearly sighed. So the woman was proud and he would have to waltz around that pride. That didn't exactly bode well for their working relationship, but it was too late for regrets. Beth Krayton was officially his new assistant.

He held out his hand and she placed hers in it. Her fingers were unusually long and graceful.

He frowned.

She looked alarmed, and he shook his head.

"Welcome to Banick Enterprises," he told her, trying to smile the way Patrick or his father might have.

She smiled back. "I'm happy to be here."

"You'll start at nine tomorrow morning."

Beth nodded. "I'll let you know where I'm staying as soon as I have an address." She started to withdraw her hand, but Carson was still holding on.

"You don't even have a place to live?"

She shrugged and blushed. "I left home suddenly."

"Suddenly?"

"This morning."

Carson nodded, wondering what exactly he had gotten himself into. He was, of course, going to do a background check on Beth Krayton. He wondered what it would turn up.

Not that it really mattered. He wasn't interested in anything about her except for her ability to help him get this job done.

He was on a mission and nothing, especially not a pint-size woman, was going to stop him.

# CHAPTER TWO

*BREATHE DEEPLY.*

The next morning, standing in the doorway of her creepy little rental room on the far edge of town, Beth coached herself to breathe, trying not to think of how much had changed in one day. This temporary home had been all she could afford, and it wasn't exactly pleasant. It was a far cry from the clean, bustling beauty of most of the lakeside town, but that was all right. For the first time in her twenty-five years she was living on her own, a fact that brought a sense of triumph to her soul. Moreover, she had survived her interview with Carson Banick and she'd landed a decent job. Now all she had to do was keep it, get settled and stop thinking about her new employer's dangerous silver eyes.

Beth took another deep, ragged breath. "Well, that solved one problem," she finally said to herself. She was definitely breathing deeply now.

Too bad it was the thought of her boss's eyes that was causing her to hyperventilate, because that just wouldn't do. This would not be like her last job. No one was matchmaking. Carson Banick wasn't interested in her. It was good that she could think logically about the situation, because she had been stupid about men before.

Beth tried not to think about how idiotic she had been about Harrison, the man she'd fallen so hard for two years ago, thinking he loved her when he'd only wanted a physical relationship. She came from a poor family so they weren't from the same class at all, he had explained, as if she should have known that his words of love had been lies. But what she had realized after she finally stopped hurting was that her foolish mistake had given her brothers even more reason to protect her.

As surrogate parents, they had always worried she would be an easy and naive sexual target. In the past Beth had never told them about the passes men had made. She'd never believed any of the lies until Harrison had lied more convincingly than the rest. Now, her brothers knew for sure that she had been used. At last they had been proven right, and, despite the fact that she was an adult, they had set out to protect her in every way they could.

*Which was well meaning, but...*

Sighing, Beth tried not to think of her brothers as captors. They had raised her after their parents' deaths when she was ten. Her brothers loved her, and she adored them, but as the only girl and the youngest, a somewhat rebellious youngest at that, she had frequently wanted to escape their smothering ways. Now, she had taken the first steps in that direction.

Her brief conversation last night with Roger, her eldest brother—when she'd finally decided to let him know that she was safe and settled—had gone as she'd expected. Poorly. Roger had threatened to come to Lake Geneva, but she'd held her ground.

"I've got a good job and a good place to live," she said, stretching the truth. "If you come up here in your current state, you might jeopardize my situation."

"I wouldn't hurt you, Bethie," he argued.

"You wouldn't mean to," she agreed, "but I told my boss I was capable of acting independently. This job is temporary, but it can be a stepping stone to something better. I'm working directly under Carson Banick of the Banick Enterprises Banicks."

Roger had sworn. "I've read about him in the business pages. He lives a reckless existence."

"I'm not helping him do that. I'm helping him build a hotel. That's all."

"Beth…"

"Roger. I love you and Jim and Albert and Steve, but you're not letting me breathe. Mom and Dad wouldn't want you to stand in the way of my success."

"That's not fair."

It wasn't. She knew they just wanted her to be happy. But they wanted her to be happy by treating her the way they had when she was ten. "When this job is done, then I'll let you know if I'm ready to come home," she promised.

"I'll come now."

"If you do, I'll just have to go somewhere else. You have to let me make it on my own, and I can't do that if you and everyone else are standing around frowning and waiting to see if I fall so you can pick me up. I have to make my own mistakes."

He grumbled at that and told her he would be reading up on Carson Banick. He wasn't leaving his baby sister alone with a man who might try to take advantage of her.

"He doesn't even see me as a woman," she promised.

Finally Roger agreed to keep his distance and let her spread her wings unsupervised.

Not that Beth was fooled by his agreement. Eventually her brothers would show up in Lake Geneva to check up on her. Knowing them, they wouldn't wait long.

"I'd better turn myself into a success quickly," she told herself. When her brothers finally arrived, she needed to be rooted, an independent woman rather than the perpetual little sister. Never again would she sacrifice her pride or dignity for what appeared to be love. She wouldn't live under a man's thumb. Nor would she freely give her heart away, at least not to the wrong kind of man.

Thank goodness Carson Banick was the wrong kind of man.

Carson looked at the calendar and grimaced. Three months behind schedule.

"We need you to get this right," his father had said last night. "The family has fallen down on its commitments to the business, to our communities and to our loyal employees, Carson. One failure affects everyone who associates with Banick. It has always been that way, going back to the European inns where the Banick legend began. People count on us. They trust us. You know that. We can't break that trust."

Now Carson stifled a groan. His parents were stodgy and stuffy. He knew better than anyone how unbending and even unfeeling they could be, but they had principles and they lived by them. They were only being what they'd always been and doing what they'd always done. He was the one who had shrugged off his responsibilities in the past. He was the one responsible for Patrick's current condition, and it was up to him to do something about the existing crisis, not only for the business and the family but for his own peace of mind.

Over the past few months, since Patrick's fall, Carson had watched his loving, joyful brother lose the use of his legs and eventually lose the hope of returning to a normal life. After completing rehab, Patrick had holed himself up in a luxury apartment with only a nurse for company and he didn't welcome Carson's weekly visits. Patrick had rebuffed all Carson's assistance, but he had to help his brother in some way.

He looked up at the clock. It was almost nine. Time to begin, he thought as Beth Krayton came through the door. It was obvious she had been rushing. Her hair was windblown; her ugly navy balloon of a skirt had flipped up slightly in the back. She looked deliciously flushed.

Carson grimaced. Bad choice of words. Delicious shouldn't figure into things.

Carefully Beth smoothed one hand over her skirt as if that would repair the wind damage. She stood up straighter and smiled. "Good morning, Mr. Banick. I'm ready."

Carson blinked at that and tried not to think any prurient thoughts. Ridiculous. She didn't even look like a woman a man would have prurient thoughts about. His brother would never have had such improper thoughts about an employee.

He smiled tightly. "Well, we have a lot to do. We're meeting with the city planning committee in two hours."

"We?" Her voice seemed suddenly a bit weak.

He ignored that. He had hired her. Now they had to make this work.

Frowning, Carson continued, "Yes, I'll need you to take notes and help me focus on any problem areas I might miss. You'll need…" He gazed at her skirt. "You'll need a change of clothing."

Immediately she blushed. "This is what I have right now, other than what I was wearing yesterday. I haven't had a chance to complete my work wardrobe yet."

At the auto parts store she had probably worn jeans. He tried not to think about the fact that her slender body and fresh, pretty face would perfectly complement any pair of jeans known to man.

"Your skirt will be fine for my office, but for this meeting you'll need a suit. We'll take care of that right away." When she held out one hand in protest he waved away her objections.

"Ms. Krayton. This job…well, it's not business as usual. My brother began this project but he's temporarily indisposed. We're well behind schedule and the planning commission was kind enough to grant me an audience on short notice. That doesn't mean they'll roll over and accede to our every wish. They have a job to do and responsibilities to this town. *I* have a job to do and a responsibility to my brother and to my business. In order to win the commission members over on as many points as possible, we'll have to do everything right. Image is important. It's part of your job. I'm buying clothing for you. Right now."

She looked him full in the face and the impact of that nakedly appealing expression was like a blow. Her emotions were written as clearly in her eyes as if a pen had put them there. Pride warred with need.

"All right. I understand," she said. "I'm willing, but—"

He raised a brow. "But?"

She looked away. "I have zero fashion sense."

"I do. Let's go." Rising to his feet, he moved around his desk and held out his hand.

She stared at him as if he'd just suggested something illicit. "You're going to help me pick out clothes?"

Carson smiled. "If you really have zero fashion sense, I'm going to choose the clothing."

"You'll tell me what to wear." Was that a stubborn note in her voice?

"Is that a problem? As I said, appearance is part of the job."

Beth took a visible breath before nodding. "I'm sorry for hesitating. Being raised by four brothers, I've had to argue for the right to do things my way, but you're right. Appearance is part of the job, and you're the expert."

She tilted her chin up and prepared to move toward the door. It was clear that she was a woman with a lot of pride, and he had just asked her to ignore that.

"Beth?" he said gently.

She turned slightly, her hair catching the glint of sunlight, turning it to copper. "Thank you," he said.

Rather than respond to his gratitude, she looked at her watch, a slight hint of pink in her cheeks. "The meeting is in only two hours? Well, we'd certainly better get going if we're to get back and have time for you to fill me in on everything I need to know."

Carson chuckled. "Well, it seems I hired the right person to keep me in check. I tend to be hopelessly late and I have a bad habit of coming and going as I please."

She rolled her eyes.

"What?" he asked as he walked out the door and led her to his car.

"Coming and going as you please might be considered hopelessly arrogant by some."

"Yes. But I'm trusting you to get me there on time."

She laughed, a low, earthy sound that reminded Carson of wine, candlelit bedrooms and sin. He tried not to panic at the images that would only interfere with what he was trying to do for Patrick.

"Here," he said a few minutes later, opening the door to a boutique that specialized in classic clothing.

Beth walked in the door ahead of Carson. He hadn't thought of it before, but the place smelled of class, of opulence. She stood there looking uncomfortable and small and pretty and completely out of place.

"Please…fix me up," she said, her voice husky and thick. "And quickly."

Her words were practical, but they sounded erotic to Carson's ears. He ignored his reaction.

Instead he nodded to a salesperson and forced himself to behave like the businessman he was. "I want something chic, smart and businesslike. Not gray or black," he said, glancing at Beth's pale skin. "Jade, I think. Or gold. We don't have much time." He looked at Beth. "How much?"

She didn't hesitate. "If we need to allow ourselves time to prepare for the meeting, I think…twenty minutes. Thirty, tops."

Carson grimaced. He nodded to the salesperson. "Can you do it? We'll want several changes of clothing, head to toe, inside and out."

Beth yelped. "My underwear?"

He did his best not to imagine the garments she was referring to. He especially tried not to imagine them sliding against her pale flesh. "If you're going to act the part of an accomplished and skilled assistant, you have to feel as if you're used to luxury and privilege, right down to the skin."

She nodded, but he noticed that her cheeks had gone even paler. The saleswoman scurried off, returning with a mountain of clothing. "We'll make her irresistible," she promised.

Carson's last thought before Beth disappeared into the dressing room was, *Oh, no, don't do that.*

He didn't want to desire her. That would interfere with all his plans, and it would ultimately hurt her. Carson had already hurt too many people, and he did not want to see Beth's brown eyes fill with pain.

After numerous changes, Beth finally emerged from the dressing room and heard Carson say, "Perfect. That's the one you'll wear today."

She was dressed in a jade suit with a jacket that nipped in at her waist and a skirt that brushed her knees. A rich cream camisole peeked out from the lapels and beneath that she wore bits of ivory satin and lace. It was the most luscious, luxurious clothing she had ever owned, which bothered her. There was now a sense of obligation attached to this business relationship.

And there was something more. Longing. She hated that feeling. Over the years, she'd trained herself not to envy what other girls had. Her brothers had done their best. Neighbors had often donated bags of ill-fitting clothing their children had outgrown, and she'd always known that people judged her by what she was wearing.

Pretending she didn't care had been a badge of honor. Now…Beth glanced down at the skirt that hung just the way a skirt was meant to hang. She felt as if she were playing dress-up. She would eventually have to put the things back in the box and don her old clothes. But for now…she stroked her hand over the silky cloth.

The movement must have caught Carson's eyes. He glanced at her, and she quickly slipped her hand behind her back, unwilling to let him see her as pathetic or needy or even more untutored than she had admitted to. His gaze never left hers as he told the saleswoman to send the rest of the things he had chosen to the office.

"Ready?" he asked Beth as they left the store.

"Yes." She followed him out into the sunlight. "Thank you," she added. "I doubt anyone would have known if you had spent less money."

He shrugged and smiled. "I would have. This suits you. Think of it as your uniform."

She liked that. It lessened her sense of obligation. "Thank you for the uniform, then," she conceded. "It's much nicer than the red apron I wore over my jeans at the auto parts store. Not as many pockets, but a lot more silk," she said, trying to lighten the mood. "And you were very good at operating within a limited time frame."

Carson chuckled. "Well, those evil glances you were giving your watch helped."

She lifted one shoulder in acquiescence and smiled. "What will help with the planning commission?"

"Not sure. I've never done this before."

Beth yelped. "You haven't? Why not? My landlady said that your family—"

Carson looked grim. She clapped a hand over her mouth.

He shook his head. "Don't apologize for asking questions. The Banicks are well-known around here, and people talk. Gossip is not a sin. Yes, my family has been in the luxury hotel business for years. My father, my mother and my brother, that is. I was never interested, but I'm needed now. My job—*our* job," he amended, "is to hold the fort, to do our best to bring this hotel on line and to maintain the reputation and the solvency of Banick Enterprises."

"Is that all?" Beth tried to joke, but there really wasn't anything amusing about the situation. She clenched her fists, hiding them behind her back.

There was so much riding on her performance, and for a few seconds she considered the fact that she might not have the skills to do this job, after all. In truth, Beth felt as if she were going to hyperventilate. A paper bag would have been nice, but she didn't have that luxury. "All right, I understand. So, what do you think you want me to do?"

He turned those exquisite silver eyes on her. "Take copious notes. Not just about what's being said, but about your impressions of the people on the commission, how they react. What they like, what they don't like, how they conduct themselves. This meeting today is just a formality to ensure that we can begin working again, but in the weeks that follow we may have to go back to them if we make any changes to the structure."

"Will we do that?"

Those silver eyes connected with her in a way that was deeply disturbing, primal, male. "Undoubtedly. There's always competition to be the best. My brother has been out of commission for a while, but the hotel world has kept moving. We'll need to make improvements, to hunt for the next trend, to discover what it is that will bring guests to our hotel rather than to another one." His voice was deep, dark, ragged, earnest.

"I thought you didn't have experience with this," she said softly.

"I don't have much, but I've sat in on plenty of discussions between my brother and my father. I've run my own firms and been a lifelong consumer of luxury products. As fickle as any customer, I've moved from one thing to the next."

For a moment, Beth had the discomfiting feeling that when Carson said "thing" he meant women, his voice was so low and seductive. It was terribly easy to believe that women would parade their wares before him, each trying to outdo the other.

She swallowed hard. "I'll take detailed notes," she promised.

It seemed a simple task when she thought of it that way. Taking notes? What could be so difficult? She would be a great assistant and make Carson glad that he had chosen her. Maybe she could even turn this into a career that would grant her the independence and the future that she needed.

A sense of confidence and well-being filled her soul…until she walked into the office where the meeting was being held.

A row of eyes met her entrance. A wall of men were seated at the table. In other years, Beth was sure, there had been women present, either as members of the commission or as architects or attorneys, but not today. Today she was the lone female, and, she was well aware, the only inexperienced person in sight, no matter what Carson had said.

The minute he entered the room, he seemed to fill it. He was taller, more powerful-looking, more confident than any man present—even though every person in the room looked important. This was no small potatoes meeting.

Everything that happened here mattered. That meant that everything she did mattered.

She could help Carson, or she could prove her brothers right and be a helpless female who needed assistance.

Beth swallowed hard and sat down, pen poised. She cast one look at Carson and found him studying her. He smiled slightly, and she knew instantly that he had loved and left many beautiful ladies.

He might need her help today, but she must never make the mistake of thinking he needed anything else from her. She'd erred that way before. No more.

Dredging up a look of confidence from some

hidden place inside, Beth managed to give Carson a flippant smile. She began to scribble, and she knew that this man could help her free herself from the prison she had inhabited.

Or he could create a new kind of prison for her. If she let him.

# CHAPTER THREE

"WELL, THAT WAS incredibly interesting, Ms. Krayton," Carson said as they returned to the office.

She placed her hands over her face. "I can't believe I did that, said that."

He couldn't help chuckling even though he had been as horrified as she when she had gotten up to speak at the meeting. That certainly hadn't been on the agenda. "You did that," he agreed. "You said that. It most definitely broke the ice."

A look of horror came over her face. "I'm sure that one isn't supposed to tell a commissioner that our pool would be so fun and romantic that he and his wife would feel as if they were giggling newlyweds on their honeymoon. I mean, I didn't even know if he was married."

Carson shrugged. "He is, but I don't think it was the comment about his marriage that intrigued everyone. I believe it might have been your enthusiasm that won them over."

"Well what's not to like about a series of round

stepping stone pools connected by ladders and slides? I especially liked the idea of the slide-away ceiling and the changeable lighting and movable landscaping to take the atmosphere from family swim parties to romantic adult evenings. But, when I stood up I wasn't thinking. I only meant to say that I hadn't seen anything like that in Chicago."

And she had said that…just before launching into a rapt speech about how the commission members themselves might benefit from a stay at the hotel.

The look in her fine brown eyes now couldn't be construed as anything other than guilt. Remorse. A truckload of both. Carson knew those feelings. He lived them every day, and one guilty person in their office was more than enough, especially since she had struck a chord with the commissioners.

"Beth, you were fine."

"I wasn't supposed to talk at all. I just…they were asking so many questions."

Carson couldn't help smiling. "They're supposed to do that. It's their job."

She nodded. "Yes, I know. I mean, now that I've stopped to think, I know that. But the problem was that at the time I didn't stop to think. I just jumped up and butted in where I didn't belong."

She had flung one hand out and Carson caught it, holding her still. Her skin was warm and soft beneath his fingertips, but he tried not to notice that. In that boardroom she had been passionate, electric, her face suffused with a glowing enthusiasm that had spilled over into her speech about the selling points of the hotel and the pool. "Beth, they gave us permission to go on with the plans."

"Because of you. I'll bet mere assistants don't usually hop up during presentations and launch into wild speeches. They were probably too shocked to shut me up."

"Maybe," he said with a grin, "but they knew you were a member of the Banick team. Your speech might have been a bit out of the ordinary, but it was effective and impressive. It's good to see that kind of enthusiasm. It means that you're part of a team that will work toward excellence."

She fidgeted. "I've never been called impressive."

Carson looked down at Beth, remembering the moment when she had put down her pen and gotten to her feet, beginning her speech. Politely at first, but then with more depth of feeling. She had made eye contact with the others sitting at the table. She had spoken to them as if she valued their opinions and expected something from them beyond business as usual.

Beth might not be a lot of things…she clearly couldn't dress herself, he thought, noting that her jacket was riding up, exposing a sliver of creamy skin she didn't even seem to be aware of. Untamed strands of her hair framed her face, the result of her impassioned soliloquy. From what she had said he gathered that she had never met a person with a pedigree outside the working world.

His mother would faint if he brought her home, even for a single dinner. Deirdre Banick wouldn't have liked the speech about honeymoons, either. Her entire life was lived according to a strict set of rules, and she never spoke of anything remotely related to the more sensual aspects of life. Elegance and class were paramount.

She had long been the driving force behind Banick Enterprises, and elegance had always been part of the company's reputation. His foray outside the usual Banick standards in hiring someone as unpredictable, outspoken and untutored as Beth had probably been ill-advised. Nevertheless, that didn't change what had just happened in that meeting. Beth Krayton was one hell of an amazing woman when she got excited about something.

He wondered what else excited her, other than hotels and swimming pools.

Immediately he wanted to slap his own face. She'd been trying to help him and here he was on the road to imagining what the rest of her skin would look like if he lifted her jacket.

"All right, now that we have approval, let's get back to the more boring stuff," he forced himself to say.

She nodded. "Like what?"

Like not imagining you half-naked, he thought. "Contractors," he said. "Details. I want things underway as quickly as possible."

The doctors had said that Patrick should be making better progress given the nature of his injuries. Carson hoped that presenting his brother with something well on the way to completion might help bring back the old Patrick. At the very least, Carson hoped to make up for what had happened, at least in some small way. When Patrick finally felt up to living again—

Carson fought to keep breathing. He hoped that the little brother he knew was still in there somewhere.

"Mr. Banick?" Beth said.

He looked down at her. "Yes?"

"Are you all right?"

He gave a tight nod. "I'm perfectly fine."

What a total lie. He had traveled through life breaking hearts and bringing distress. Because of him, his brother was paralyzed and divorced from all the things in life that had brought him joy. So, it was only fitting that Carson should finally be forced into a business he had long hated. It was retribution. But not enough. Nothing could ever be enough.

He led Beth back to the office in silence. Then, together, they planned a course of action. He schmoozed contractors. She kept records of all that transpired and drew up the paperwork.

The clock's hands twirled around, the hours passed. When Carson heard a slight, quickly stifled yawn, he looked up to see that it was nearly seven o'clock. Beth was still working, but it was clear that she was starting to droop. Her eyes looked tired. She even looked thinner, if that were possible.

"Enough for today."

She glanced up at him and blinked, staring at his

outstretched hand as if she didn't quite comprehend what he meant.

"I'll buy you dinner," he offered.

Instantly she looked alert, wary. "No, that's all right," she said.

A flash of anger ripped through Carson. At himself. Was he looking at her as if he expected something more of her than an after-business dinner between colleagues? It was possible.

"Just food," he clarified. "I'm not proposing anything indecent, Beth."

Automatically she rose, looking flustered. "I didn't think that."

He could swear she was lying, but he didn't intend to engage in a battle of wills. Carson lifted a brow. "Beth, I don't know what you've heard about me… I'm not an exemplary man, but I can assure you that I don't assault my employees and I don't engage in personal relationships with them."

"I know. I know. It's not you. It's just…nothing. I would love to have dinner. I'm absolutely famished." Her voice grew stronger, bolder. The Beth of the meeting had returned and she ended her speech with a smile that transformed her face. For a moment he had the fanciful thought that the light coming in through the window picked up golden glints in her russet hair, turning it a remarkable color that made him itch to touch the soft stuff.

Damn it. Carson was forced to remind himself of what he'd just told her. Was he already going back on his word?

No, he wasn't. He wouldn't. "I know a nice place," he told her as she obliged him by placing those pretty fingers in his grasp. *A very public place,* he told himself.

He refused to keep having improper thoughts about Beth. He had plans. She undoubtedly had plans, too, and plenty of reservations.

He was going to change his life, settle down and provide the long-awaited Banick heir. She would eventually go back to her safe working class family in Chicago.

No one was going to get hurt here, Carson promised himself. That meant no touching, no wanting, no *anything* beyond business.

And that was the end of that.

Well, she had certainly made a fool of herself back there, Beth mused, acting as if he was offering to take her to bed instead of just offering her dinner.

She hadn't really thought that he was doing any such thing. It was just the notion that if word of her socializing with her boss got back to her brothers, they would be rushing up here to defend her honor or something suitably ridiculous. After all, Chicago might be as different from the resort town of Lake Geneva as her red hair was from something tame but it was still only a ninety-minute drive.

Not that she was afraid of her brothers, but their actions made her feel like a little girl. And she found, looking across the table at Carson, tall and dark and sophisticated in his white shirt and navy tie, that for once in her life she wanted to be taken seriously. She wanted to stop feeling like a girl and start taking her place in the world as a woman. And she couldn't do that if Carson ever knew that her brothers were watching her and checking up on his background.

How mortifying would that be!

"Is there something wrong?" Carson asked.

Beth almost jumped. Had she said something out loud again? "I—"

"You're not eating," he said gently.

She looked down at her plate of perfectly prepared food and realized that he was right.

"Sorry, I guess I'm still getting used to the newness of everything…a new job, a new apartment, a new town. Especially my new town. That probably sounds weird."

He gave a slight laugh. "No, actually, I can relate completely. My family is from Milwaukee and I've been to Lake Geneva many times, but usually for vacations. This is a bit different."

"For me, too. The few times I've been here it was because my brother was making a delivery and he allowed me to tag along."

Carson nodded. "What were you delivering?"

"Plumbing supplies. Steve's a driver for a firm that manufactures them. I don't think he was supposed to be carrying human cargo, but it was summer and it was his day to make sure his little sister stayed out of trouble." She didn't want to say more about that so she took a bite.

"You're the youngest, you said?"

She nodded. "By ten years. Steve's thirty-five."

"He the one who tried to match you up with your last boss?"

Beth felt panic welling up inside her. "You don't have to worry. He wouldn't try to match me up with *you*."

Carson almost choked on a piece of steak.

Beth wanted to crawl underneath her plate. "That didn't come out the way I wanted it to. What I meant was that he would know that you're out of my league, that you'd only marry someone rich and sophisticated. If he has any thoughts about you, it's that I shouldn't get involved with you at all."

Which sounded even worse. She closed her eyes and prayed for the flowers on the table to ignite…or anything that would distract Carson and enable her to exit this uncomfortable conversation.

"He's right," Carson said.

Beth opened her eyes. "What?"

"I have a bad reputation with women. Your brother is right to have those kinds of thoughts, although…as I mentioned…"

"I know. You don't get involved with your employees and I shouldn't worry."

A grim smile lifted his lips slightly. "Exactly."

Beth managed to nod. "I'll tell him that. Not that it will matter. Older brothers tend to be overprotective."

She said that last sentence in a casual, offhand, flippant way. She was trying for a light, teasing tone, anything to let him know that *she* wasn't worried, that *she* would never think of him in a romantic or lustful manner.

But Carson wasn't smiling. "Older brothers *should* be protective," he said.

She opened her mouth to speak, but he shook his head. "Forget I said that. I was just thinking of my own younger brother."

He didn't say more. Carson turned the conversation to business, and soon the meal was over. "I'll take you to your car," he said.

"I walked to work. I like to walk." She didn't want to add that the reason she had walked had less to do with her love of walking and more with the fact that her beat-up pickup truck looked like something she had gotten from the junk yard. It didn't fit the image of a success-ful professional.

"Then I'll drive you home."

Panic welled up. "That's all right."

"No, it's not. It's getting late and we have another big day ahead of us. I wouldn't want you to fail to get enough rest and end up being late tomorrow."

"I wouldn't do that."

Carson sighed. "I know that. I just—let me do this. That line you said earlier about older brothers…I haven't always been protective of my brother and there have been consequences. Let me do one good, if small, thing today."

So, what could she say? Reluctantly she gave him her address. To her relief he didn't say anything negative when they turned into the driveway. There weren't exactly any bad neighborhoods in Lake Geneva, but there were some houses that were a bit neglected. The room she was renting was in one of those neglected, dumpy houses. Siding falling off, a crack in the window that hadn't been repaired, weeds turning into a forest.

Carson pulled up in front of the place. Her green truck with the rusty dents sat outside. He looked at the door of the building. Beth realized that there was a hole where the dead bolt should have been.

"Thank you," she said and started to clamber out of his Lexus.

Carson's arm shot out and grasped her by the wrist. Gently but firmly. "Get your things."

Her eyes widened. She turned to face him. "Excuse me?"

"You're not staying here. You can do better."

Instantly she frowned. "This is what I can afford."

"I'll give you an advance. I should have already done it."

"I haven't earned it."

"Yes, you did. Today."

"You're just saying that because you feel responsible. I don't like men telling me what to do."

"Tough. I don't like feeling as if I've acted in an irresponsible manner. Get your things. I'll find you a better place. I'll pay your first month's rent."

"You can't."

"Yes, I can. It's just become a perk of your employment. Room and board. Up-front for the first month. And I can tell you what to do because you work for me."

"Not twenty-four hours a day." But she stopped cold. She remembered him asking her about working around the clock. Rebellion sizzled in her soul, but there wasn't much she could do about it.

"You're as bad as my brothers," she said with a trace of ice in her voice.

To her amazement, Carson smiled. "I'll take that as a compliment. It's the first time in my life anyone has accused me of being overprotective. I think I like it."

"I don't."

He opened his mouth. She placed her fingertips over it, the warmth of his skin burning hers, making her aware that he was a man and she was a woman. "Don't say tough luck," she managed to choke out. "I'll do as you ask, but don't expect me to be happy about it."

"I just expect you to be safe. There isn't even a lock on that door."

"This isn't a high crime area."

"I don't take safety as a given. Unexpected things happen. People get hurt. You're not getting hurt on my watch. So—"

"I know. Go get your things. I'm going." She walked away, her back stiff, her emotions churning. She had come here for independence and now she was working for a man who was just as dictatorial as her brothers. What's more, she was attracted to him. Very attracted, she admitted, resisting the urge to look down at the fingertips that had lain against the fullness of his mouth.

*Don't,* she wanted to scream at herself. *Don't be attracted. He's not for you. Even he has said that much, and you've been there before. This man can hurt you, badly. And you need this job. You can't let it end in disaster, so just...forget the man's mouth and his silver eyes and the fact that there's something wounded about him that makes you want to kiss his pain away.*

The very thought of that made her cringe at her idiocy. *Just do as he says and eventually you'll forget all these very wrong emotions. This is only the result of a long day and the stress of that meeting. It's just because you've never met a man like Carson before. You've got to be strong.*

She did her best. She grabbed the bag she had brought with her, told her landlady she was going and walked back to the car.

"All done," she said to Carson, attempting a smile and to reestablish normalcy. "Everything's fine."

She almost believed it, too, until she looked up and saw Roger's red SUV turning the corner. With him was the collective brawn of the other three Krayton brothers.

"You know those brothers you agree with?" she asked Carson.

He raised one sexy brow. "Yes?"

She sighed. "You're about to meet them. I don't think

it's going to be pleasant. I'll do what I can to head them off, but I think it's only fair to warn you that they're not easy to handle when they're in a group. You might want to prepare yourself."

# CHAPTER FOUR

CARSON TOOK ONE look at Beth's madder-than-hell expression and wanted to laugh. She was incredibly cute when she was angry, and it was obvious that the combination of her brothers' butting into her life along with his own highhanded move a few minutes ago had set off her temper.

He hadn't meant to pull rank on her, but the thought of her sleeping all night in a building where just anyone could get past that broken lock...well, he already had too many bad things he felt responsible for. Stopping to think hadn't even been a possibility. He'd just pulled out the boss card.

Now she was gearing up to do battle with her brothers. Carson had the rather disconcerting feeling that she might even be trying to protect him from them.

He climbed from the car just as Beth's brothers got out of their SUV. They started toward him, tall and sturdy and not looking too pleased about anything.

Interesting.

"Beth, are you getting in that car with that man?" one asked.

"Yes, we're on our way to Vegas to get married," she said, one hand on her hip.

Carson actually chuckled. Beth might be a little thing, but she packed a lot of energy and expression into that small, pretty body.

The Goliath who had asked the question whirled on Carson.

"She's kidding, right?"

Carson was half tempted to tell the man that no, they weren't getting married but he was planning to have his wicked way with her. But he wouldn't. That wouldn't help Beth, and after all, the man was just protecting his baby sister. Carson understood perfectly the need to protect one's siblings. "I believe Beth's simply establishing her right to behave as an adult," he told the man.

Roger's scowl grew. He took another step toward Carson.

"Back away, Roger," Beth said. "Don't hurt him."

"Shut up, Beth. You I'll deal with later."

"Like hell you will. Let me tell you, something, Roger. This kind of thing is why I'm here in the first place. At twenty-five, I reserve the right to live my life by my rules."

"And I reserve the right to check out any guy who might hurt you," another of the brothers said.

"Steve—" Beth's voice was joined by the two other brothers, the conversation getting more heated by the second.

"We don't even know anything about this guy," another brother began. "Well, nothing positive, anyway."

"Jim, as I explained to Roger—" Beth started, and then she turned on Roger. "You told me you would give me time."

"Looks like I was right to ignore my word, then," Roger said. "You were about to get into his car. And you have your suitcase."

Beth let out a shriek of frustration. "I'm an adult."

"You're my sister." Roger moved closer, crowding her.

Carson had had enough. He understood her brothers' concern, but four against one wasn't fair odds. He cleared his throat and moved between Beth and Roger.

Her gasp at his back was almost like a physical sensation sliding down his spinal cord. He could feel her heat behind him. She started to move around him.

He clasped her arm, stopping her when she was halfway around him and nearly at his side. "No," was all he said. "I'm the reason for the trouble. I'll handle things."

She turned toward him, blinking and opening her mouth.

"I know. You like to be independent and do things for yourself, but this has crossed over into my territory. I need you to help me complete the job at the hotel. I'll settle this."

"Settle what?" Roger asked. "Where were you taking her?"

Carson didn't have Roger's bulk, but he topped the man by a good two or three inches. And he'd spent his entire life with wealthy people who liked to one-up others with their power.

Casting Roger a casual glance, Carson pulled himself up to his full six foot four inches and stared down at the other man. "Not that it's any of your business, because as she mentioned, Beth is an adult, but I'm taking her to find a better place to live." He glanced back over his shoulder at the house. "This won't do for a Banick employee."

The fourth brother's glance honed in on the broken lock. "Beth…" he began, his voice low and worried.

"I wasn't going to stay there full-time, Albert," she said. "Just until I got my first check."

Steve whirled to see what Carson would say to that. Carson shrugged. "My mistake, granted. I didn't think about the fact that she might need an advance, but now that I know the situation, it's taken care of."

"That still doesn't explain where you're taking her," Albert said.

Carson didn't even have to think about it. "My family has a lake house where I'm staying. There's a guest house on the premises. It's nicely furnished and secure and it will do."

He turned to face the whole group of men. "I understand your concern for your sister. You want her to be safe and happy, but she's an adult and I'm her employer. I treat my employees with respect and I expect everyone else to do the same. Now, if you and your sister have more family matters to attend to, I'll give you the address where you can reach her as well as my number.

"At the moment, the guest house has no phone service, but I'll get that tended to tomorrow. She's welcome to have whatever guests she likes. But, for now, I need to open up the place and make sure she gets moved in without further delay. We have a lot of work to do tomorrow, and I'm sure she could use some rest."

He glanced at Roger and the man stared back at him unblinkingly.

"I'm not sure I trust you," Roger said.

Beth started to yelp, but Carson held up his hand and she stopped.

"On the other hand, you do seem to have her interests at heart and you definitely seem able to control her better than we ever have been," Roger added.

"Perhaps that's because I'm not her brother," Carson said simply.

Albert growled.

"I'm her boss, and only her boss," Carson said once again. He didn't like having to keep saying that, but he and Beth were never going to get anything done if they had to spend all their time fighting off her bodyguard brothers. "I need her time, but if you're going to interfere… Beth would be very difficult to replace but I'm on a tight schedule. I can't fight battles on two fronts."

"You would fire her?" Jim asked.

"I have a job to do," Carson explained. "Beth told me she was capable of doing the job, but…"

Again he left his words hanging. Roger looked slightly amused as did Steve. Albert was sputtering.

"Are you saying that you think Beth was lying or that she's not capable?"

Carson didn't answer. He could feel the tension rising in Beth beneath his fingertips and he gently squeezed her arm. Instantly she stilled.

"Beth's capable," Jim said. "And she doesn't lie...much. She can do anything she says she can. She's fearless, she's bold. She'll do your job and do it better than anyone else you can hire." His voice rose, becoming more passionate, reminding Carson of Beth's speech earlier today. Roger, on the other hand, was looking more amused.

"Oh," Jim finally said. "You *do* think she's capable. You just want us to back off."

Carson smiled. "Nicely put. I just want you to understand that I have faith in Beth. I need her help and I wouldn't do anything to jeopardize that. I hope you feel the same way."

"So you won't try to sleep with her?" Steve asked, a low challenge in his voice.

Beth broke free and ran up to her brother. "Steven Krayton, I'll sleep with whom I please, but no, Mr. Banick has no designs on my body. My note-taking skills are all he's interested in, and it's very hurtful of you to suggest otherwise."

"I wouldn't hurt you. I trust you. I do." Steven looked down at his youngest sister. "I just don't want anyone else to have a chance to hurt you. Not ever again."

Carson kept his expression impassive, but what had

just been revealed about Beth verified what he'd originally thought about her. Beneath her tough woman image, some damage had already been done.

"This is the first time you've been away from home, Bethie," Steve was saying. "When you left without saying anything, we were scared."

She looked up at him. Carson couldn't see her face, but he saw her brother wipe his thumb across her cheek. "I know and I'm sorry for that. I love you, Steve. I love all of you," she said, turning to face her brothers. "Still…"

"I know. Butt out, big brothers," Roger said, coming over and giving her a hug. "We've heard it often enough. And we're going," he said, even though Albert still looked as if he wanted to object. "But that doesn't mean we're gone forever."

He blew out a breath. "Look, we didn't really come to make accusations. After you left, we just wanted to see for ourselves that you were all right. For now I'm satisfied that you're reasonably safe. But we will be back. We'll want to see where you live."

Beth frowned, but her brother didn't back down.

"I'm putting my trust in you," he told Carson.

Carson hoped he would merit that trust. He tried not to remember how Beth had felt standing beside him. "She'll be safe," he told her brothers. "I'll make it my business to see that she is."

Some less than genial comments of assent from Jim, Albert and Steve followed. They each hugged Beth, then got back in the SUV with Roger. In mere seconds they were headed back to Chicago.

Beth watched them drive away, her back toward Carson. When she finally turned around, her chin was lifted in defiance. "I'm sorry, but they're my brothers. I love them in spite of their bossy ways."

Carson smiled. "They care about you."

Heat flashed in her brown eyes, turning them the color of warm caramel. "Yes, even more so because my parents died when I was ten and left them in charge of me. But I've grown up since then."

She certainly had, Carson thought, trying not to notice the agitated rise and fall of her breasts. "I'm sure they'll learn that in time. You've only just left home."

"You don't have to make sure I'm safe. I am perfectly capable of taking care of myself. It's very important to me that I be able to do that."

He could see how important it was to her, but… "I made a promise to your brothers." He hadn't taken care of *his* younger sibling. Maybe taking care of Beth would make up for some of that.

Beth visibly bristled. "If a man made a mistake, he wouldn't want everyone watching him every minute of every day to make sure he didn't make the same mistake again, would he?"

Loaded question, Carson thought. He'd made tons of mistakes growing up, both at home and at the boarding school where his parents had sent him after they decided that he was too much for them to handle. His parents and teachers had watched his every move. They'd grown to expect him to do the exact opposite of what they wanted. He'd hated that. It had only worsened his behavior.

He gave a sigh. It wouldn't be right to use taking care of Beth as a way to make up for his failure to protect Patrick.

"You didn't answer," she pointed out.

He laughed. "I don't know why your brothers think of you as helpless. You're the most direct, pushy, maddening woman I've ever met."

"I know." She sounded almost forlorn.

"I didn't say it was a bad thing," he reflected. "It is, after all, why I hired you."

Beth looked skeptical. "I don't do it intentionally. Heck, I had to learn to be tough and pushy. Otherwise, my brothers would have run right over me and dictated my every waking moment. Being tough has come in handy at other times, too." But she didn't elaborate.

"Well, we'd better get you settled in," he said, and they got back into the car. The sun was going down over the lake by the time they reached the house. The main building sat thirty feet from the lake, stone and red cedar with a wall of windows that jutted out, facing the water.

"It's gorgeous…and huge," Beth said, her voice almost a whisper.

It was both of those things, far too big for one person. "I don't use a quarter of it," Carson admitted. "The guest house is over here." He flung one arm out to the side where a small two-story cottage also faced the lake.

"I'm going to stay there?" Beth asked. "It's beautiful."

"You haven't even seen it yet," he said, moving toward the building and opening it up. "I haven't been in it on this trip, so I can't vouch for the state of things, although I have a service that takes care of both houses."

He led her through the door, and when he looked back over his shoulder, she was smiling brilliantly, her eyes lit up.

"It's the epitome of a beach cottage," she told him, gesturing toward the large open room with the bamboo flooring, the white and navy upholstery on the summery couches and the lemon-colored accent pieces. "At least, it's what I would guess a beach cottage would be like. I've never actually been in one."

The absolute delight on her face was like the hypnotic glow of a candle in the dark. No wonder her brothers worried about her. Beth spilled out all her feelings for the world to see. She was a sitting duck for a person with ulterior motives.

Not that I have ulterior motives, Carson told himself, leading her through the rest of the house to the small blue and white kitchen, to the sunroom on the back and then simply gesturing to the bedroom. Probably not smart to go in there with her.

"Go ahead and get settled in," he told her. "I'll see you in the morning. I'll drive you to work, of course."

"Of course. I'll need to pick up my car later."

Yes, that rickety, rusty, probably unreliable car. He'd just bet that her brothers hated the thing—of course, not as much as his parents would. He could imagine Deirdre's concerned expression when she saw the car, the meaty brothers and when she met Beth with her nonexistent fashion sense and her tendency to speak her mind without censorship.

His mother had never said one word about any of the women Carson had chosen to date, but her eyes and her tone of voice had spoken volumes. Back then she'd never assumed she would have to rely on him to produce the next line of Banicks. Things were different now.

Carson pushed his annoyance and regret aside. The turn of events wasn't what anyone would have wanted. Not his parents, not Patrick and not him, but they were all stuck with the current situation. He had responsibilities now that he hadn't had a short while ago. He was no longer a young, rebellious boy. He could not afford to indulge his whims and desires with no thought for the future.

But none of that concerned Beth and none of it was her fault. "Sweet dreams," he told her.

She smiled back so sweetly that he wanted to groan. No, he wanted to kiss her. So it was best if he left. Now.

"If you need me, call this number. I won't be home, but I'll pick up my messages."

She blinked. "You're going out? Now?" She glanced toward the setting sun. "Where?"

As if she realized what she'd just asked, she placed her hand over her mouth. "Sorry, not my business."

He wanted to sigh. It wasn't really her business, but she, after all, was the reason he was going out. She and his conscience. If he stayed here, he might touch her, and neither of them wanted that. There was no future in it. "My brother…"

"The one who's ill."

"Yes, Patrick. He was injured in a fall recently, and he's not able to walk. He's living in Milwaukee, about forty-five miles away and I try to get up to see him as often as I can. Patrick…he's the heart and soul of the Banick family."

He felt a hand on his arm and looked down into Beth's upturned face. "Will he get better?"

"I don't know. The doctors think that he should have made more progress, at least in terms of becoming more ambulatory, but he hasn't. The more time that passes only makes a recovery less likely."

Concern filled her eyes. "I'm sure it helps that you visit."

Carson's chest felt tight. An overwhelming desire to pull Beth to him, tuck her against his heart and take the comfort she was offering washed over him. He wasn't about to spoil her dreams by telling her Patrick rarely even spoke when they were together.

"I'll tell him about you," he said, trying to lighten the mood.

Her eyes widened. "What will you tell him?"

"I'll tell him I've hired the woman who's helping me to save his project."

She smiled. "This project meant a lot to him?"

He nodded. "Patrick has made a name for himself in the business, each hotel bigger and better than the last."

"So this one would have been the biggest and the best."

"Exactly."

She studied him for a moment. "Thank you for telling me that. I won't fail you. I'll do all I can to help make this all you need it to be."

Beth stood there, looking like the sweetest woman he had ever seen. She was completely open, completely giving and, therefore, completely vulnerable. A family and a situation like his could rip her to pieces. He could hurt her just by appreciating her…and by wanting her.

"Thank you," he said, "but…"

She tilted her head, waiting.

"This project means a lot to me, to my family, but don't make it your life. You should…get out, enjoy the beauties of the town, the lake. Date a few men."

Beth looked instantly wary. He didn't like that, but he had committed himself. "While you will have long hours, I don't expect you to give up a social life just because you're working for me. Feel free to bring friends to the cottage. I'll still be socializing, for business and otherwise, so you'll have some free time."

"Of course." She nodded slowly. "I hadn't thought of that. I suppose entrepreneurs such as yourself do a lot of entertaining."

"It's part of the business," he agreed. "Every Banick is expected to meet and greet the community and a Banick son is expected to find a bride and have children to continue the Banick legacy." He maintained his grim smile. Did he sound as phony as he thought he did?

"You're expected to produce an heir?"

"As I mentioned, those were Patrick's plans." In truth, Carson knew that Patrick had not relished the responsibility of maintaining the family line but that he had been reasonably sure that Carson wouldn't oblige and so, as in everything else, he had been planning to—eventually—do what was necessary.

She stared at him, her eyes dark. "And now your brother can't father a child."

"Exactly."

"So you will."

It sounded very cold-blooded, but then…it always had. Children were supposed to be the products of a healthy marriage and of a loving family. Unfortunately his family didn't have much experience with the warmer aspects of relationships—with the long-ago exception of him and his brother. They had been close once. That shouldn't be lost.

"Yes, setting out to marry in order to conceive a child seems a bit dry," he said. "But without an heir…" The Banicks' reason for existence would disappear. There would be no one to inherit the empire. All Patrick's efforts over the years would have been in vain. Carson wouldn't let that happen.

"What can I say?" he added. "It's not particularly admirable and it's more than a bit old-fashioned, but it's a family thing."

She gave a small nod. "I know about family things. Not aristocratic families like yours, of course. Still, I understand commitments and responsibilities."

He stared into her eyes and saw sincerity there. She did understand. Why was he the only one still fighting his fate?

"You'd better go," she said, tapping her watch. "Milwaukee isn't far, but you'll want time to get there, visit and get back and still be fresh for tomorrow."

He couldn't help grinning. "You're great at that, you know. I don't even feel as if I'm being reprimanded. You'll be a wonderful mother someday."

Her smile faded. "Unlikely. I don't mind working for a man, but as for marriage…no. I think I've had enough of men who feel they have the right to manipulate or control me."

Carson lifted one shoulder in acquiescence. "Understandable." He turned to go.

The sound of Beth clearing her throat turned him around.

"She won't mind my being here, will she?" she asked.

"Who?"

"Your future wife."

"I haven't started looking yet. The woman has to be…right."

"A woman fit to wear the Banick name?" She chuckled, not a trace of rancor or resentment in her voice.

"It's a bit of an antiquated and stuffy custom, isn't it?"

She shrugged. "I'll keep my eyes open. With all the wealthy women in Lake Geneva, there's bound to be a woman fit to bear the Banick heir."

"You're going to find a wife for me?" He almost choked on the words.

She smiled. "I'm a woman of many talents, and I plan to be the perfect assistant. Anything you need I can supply."

A sudden vision of Beth naked on a bed swam before Carson's eyes. Heat sluiced through him.

"Thank you, but I don't expect you to be my matchmaker." He left before he grabbed her and broke all his promises to her brothers, to himself and to her. When his time with Beth was over, he intended for her to leave him happier than she had been when they'd met, happier than she was now.

And that wouldn't happen if he ruined her life.

# CHAPTER FIVE

BETH STOOD IN the guest house looking out toward the water, holding her palm against the quick thudding of her heart.

This was becoming too personal, and she was getting in too deep. She couldn't blame Carson, either. She'd always had a habit of jumping off the cliff before she checked to see if there was a net to catch her. Sometimes she even felt sorry for her brothers. Much as she complained and chafed, it couldn't have been easy raising her.

Now, due to the fact that she had foolishly let Carson see where she lived she had ended up in this cottage in plain sight of his home. The place where he would be bringing his potential brides.

The brides she had offered to help him find. As if she knew plenty of heiresses.

"Would someone just shut me up?" she asked the empty room. Why had she even suggested such a thing?

She knew the answer. There was something in Carson's eyes that made her want to touch him, to move closer.

Beth placed her hands over her hot face. As if she hadn't learned her lesson with Harrison. Now she was imagining starting something with a man clearly out of her league, one who had told her that he needed to produce an heir.

Offering to help him find the right woman had merely been self-defense, a way of reminding herself that there was danger in thinking of him romantically.

There were parameters to their relationship. Carson was her boss and also a man she could respect. No doubt about that. Remembering how deftly he had handled the meeting and handled her brothers, respect was a given. But she got into problems when she looked into his eyes, or responded to the masculinity of his voice or listened to his laughter. Then he became a very desirable man.

"One who'll be marrying soon," she told herself again. "One who treats you as an equal. Don't spoil that."

*I won't,* she promised herself.

She would not do anything to make him think she saw him as more than a colleague and friend.

Carson studied the flat expanse of land where the hotel would be located. Today was the groundbreaking ceremony. Patrick should be here. But nothing Carson had said had convinced his brother to come out in public.

"Drop it, Carson," his once lighthearted brother had said. "I don't need to be there. Besides, I have pressing social engagements." He nodded toward the nurses waiting to take him to his physical therapy session, even though all the medical personnel had agreed that he didn't really try to complete the exercises.

"Go build the hotel. And do it right. No wild, rebellious stuff. Don't get distracted by a woman or an adventure and mess it up, damn it. It's a Banick building."

It was killing Patrick not to be a part of that, Carson could tell. "You'll finish it," Carson told him, but his brother simply waved him away.

Now Carson stared at the empty piece of earth wondering if the hotel would add to the ambience of this picturesque lake resort town or if it would simply turn out to be just another building. The result was up to Carson. And it meant…too much. The Banicks had money to spare, but the company's pristine reputation had been tried by his parents' retirement and his brother's absence. There had always been a Banick at the helm of the company. Like it or not, this time it would have to be him.

Patrick would have been so much better at this. He was the son who delighted in the Banick mystique. He was the one who wanted the glitter, the glamour and the power. Carson had teased Patrick mercilessly about his ambition, but it was Patrick's ambition that had freed Carson of his parents' expectations.

And it had been Carson's tendency to live for the moment that had talked Patrick out onto a rocky Colorado pass he never would have set foot on if he hadn't needed to prove something to Carson.

So now Carson had to do the proving.

He would start today. He crossed the swath of green grass, headed for the marked-off space that had been set up with shovels and hard hats and a sign hanging from two steel poles that said "Lake Geneva Welcomes Banick Enterprises" in bold green and gold letters.

Green and gold were the Banick colors, and the town representatives had followed the family tradition by wearing the black tuxes with green and gold ties Banick Enterprises had provided. He was wearing the same uniform.

"Gentlemen," he said, coming forward to greet the men who had graciously agreed to take time off from their day jobs to participate in this ceremony. "Thank you for being here." He stepped forward and shook the hand of the first man.

"We're glad you stayed with this project," the man said. "Lake Geneva is historic and scenic but we've stayed vibrant and popular as a resort town by being open to opportunities. The Banick Hotel will be an asset to this area."

Carson nodded. "We intend to do our best to contribute to the community. If you ever think of anything we can do to better integrate ourselves into the region, we're open to suggestions and criticism. The Banick family prides itself on providing quality, comfort and class— to its guests and its town."

"And hospitality, of course," a pretty, feminine voice added. *Beth.* Carson turned to see her strolling across the grass, clad in a bright plum-colored dress belted with a gold and green scarf. Her arms were laden with bags and a small boy followed behind her pulling a green wagon.

She frowned, glancing at all the men in black and then down at her dress. "I'm too bright," she said. "Black would have been more sophisticated."

"But not as pretty," one of the men said, stepping closer to her. And the man wasn't lying. The dress lay softly against Beth's creamy skin. The contrast of green and gold and plum perfectly enhanced her copper hair. "Here," the man continued, "let me help you with those things."

His voice was merely friendly, but Carson felt a twinge of annoyance. Friendliness could easily segue into more, and hadn't he promised her brothers that he would watch over Beth?

"I'll help, too," another man volunteered, giving Beth a brilliant smile. Carson wasn't sure who the guy was. He wasn't on the planning commission, and he wasn't dressed in a tux. But he was looking at the neckline of Beth's dress as if he was planning where to nibble. Other men were murmuring assent and moving in Beth's direction.

"Oh, we can't put our guests to work," Carson said to the men, smoothly wedging himself between them and Beth as he held out one hand. "Banick Enterprises is very appreciative of your presence. So…just relax and enjoy this brilliant weather. I'll assist Ms. Krayton and her young friend." He reached out for the bags she held, leaning forward enough to whisper near her ear. "What's all this?" He glanced toward the boy.

She leaned close enough to hand him the bags and turned her head so that she could speak low enough not to be overheard. "The caterer called this morning. It seems there was some sort of a mix-up. She didn't think she could get everything made on time. So, I...well, I went to the store and then back to the house and made up a few things. Nothing fancy. I hope that's okay. Jimmie's mom was out on the pier next door, and since she knew who you were, she volunteered him to help me out.

"He's a very good helper, too," she said loudly, for the boy's benefit. She flashed him a brilliant smile.

The boy smiled back, his eyes big and dark, a dimple in his cheek. He reminded Carson a bit of Patrick when he had been that age. Always cheerful and willing to do what was needed.

"Is this all right?" Beth asked. She was biting her lip. "I'm not much of a cook."

"I don't know about that, not having tasted your cooking, but you're a great assistant," Carson said with a smile.

"I had folding tables delivered," she said, "because the caterer was bringing her own, but I see they just dropped them off without setting them up." Beth motioned to an area where the folded tables rested. "I suppose it will look tacky to set them up as we go." Her eyes looked dark and troubled.

No doubt she was right, but nothing would convince Carson to agree with her and cause her to be even more uncomfortable. He'd had a lifetime of being told how to salvage a less than perfect situation. Useless information, he had always thought. Until now.

"Nonsense, Ms. Krayton," he said, his voice firm and strong and low enough to carry to the commissioners. "Setting up the tables gives a man a chance to show that he's more than just a paper pusher. Come on, Jimmie, let's go attack those tables."

Immediately a chorus rose from the other guests. "We're not just pretty faces, either," a woman who had just arrived said.

"And this gives us a chance to show we have a few muscles," a man added.

The guests moved forward to set up the tables and chairs. Beth directed them and then began opening bags and boxes.

A small cry from her had Carson spinning around. "It's hideous," she said, staring down at a cake that had collapsed in the center. It looked a bit like an inverted volcano.

"It's original," Carson said, refuting her statement.

"And, honey," a woman said, "chocolate coupled with a big, strong man is enough for me. Absolutely perfect, in fact."

Carson looked down to see the woman staring at him, even though she had been speaking to Beth. The woman had long blond hair, blue eyes and a short, black very expensive dress that fit everywhere a dress was supposed to fit. The diamonds in her ears could have bought enough food to feed an entire metropolitan area.

"Sheena Devoe," she said, holding her hand out to Beth and then immediately placing that same hand in Carson's grasp.

"Of the crystal merchant Devoes," he said.

"None other. I have a place in the area. I saw all the fuss—and you—and thought I'd stop by and say hello. I believe our parents know each other."

He nodded and told her it was nice meeting her.

"It was nice meeting you, too. Very nice," Sheena said. "We definitely have to get together another time when you're not so busy. We'll talk."

"Yes," he agreed politely as the woman moved off.

Beth groaned. "I can't believe I was planning to serve deflated cake to a woman who could buy all the cake she wants," she said. "What was I thinking? I should have just tried to hire another caterer."

Carson couldn't help grinning.

"What?" she asked.

"They're happy, Beth. Relax. Have some cake." He motioned to where the guests had finished setting up the food and were eating, talking and laughing. Jimmie circulated among them, helping himself to cookies.

"What choice did they have?"

"Great cookies," someone said, turning and calling out to Beth.

Carson laughed. "See, your cookies are a success. No one cares that there wasn't a caterer. Great cake, too," he said, scooping up a piece of the fallen mess with his fingers.

"It's not—" she began, but Carson found another small piece and popped it into her mouth.

"Now chew and swallow," he directed.

She did.

"Better?" he asked.

"I only allow you to order me around like that because you're my boss and I have to do what you say," she said, a trace of stubbornness in her voice.

"Of course," he agreed, then laughed again when her eyes turned storm dark. "Thank you," he said, more softly.

She raised a brow.

"You saved the show," he said. "At least the first part."

"I'm not sure about the rest."

He shook his head. "This is my part," he said. "Wish me luck. I've never done this before, never even attended one of Banick's groundbreakings, and I don't have a clue about what I'm doing."

Then he stepped into the fray and began talking.


Beth had never attended a groundbreaking ceremony, either. She'd seen one once, when she had walked past a news crew filming a groundbreaking for a shopping center. A few men dressed in hard hats, suits and work boots had smiled for the cameras, then shoved their shovels into the earth while bulbs flashed. Except for the applause and a few speeches, that had been it.

Carson, however, obviously had other ideas. Besides the catered refreshments, which had been his idea, he'd instructed an employee to mark out the perimeter of the hotel and the major parts of the building. Now he proceeded to lead the dignitaries on a tour of the hotel.

"I want this to be a home-away-from-home for our guests and a point of pride for the townspeople," he said. "There should be interaction between those staying in Lake Geneva temporarily and those living here on a more permanent basis, a sense of connection. In that spirit, the hotel's amenities will be available to the townspeople, not just to hotel guests, which will give our resort a heart. That's my goal, to create a sense of home right from the start. Thank you for welcoming us. I hope you'll feel that you're a part of this. It's possible only because of you."

He made eye contact with every individual present. He had memorized their names, allowing each person to feel as if he knew them. He had them leaning closer to make sure they didn't miss a word, Beth saw. And when he called for more shovels so that each person could be a part of the first attempt to break ground, even those who had simply shown up to watch, applause broke out.

"Beth, come here," he said.

Her eyes blinked wide. "I'm not part of the town."

"You live here," he reasoned. "And you made food. You provided the chocolate."

"And she'll look real pretty in the picture, too," someone said.

For just a second, Beth saw a frown form between Carson's brows. He was right. Her looks or lack of them had nothing to do with the hotel. He waited patiently, and she realized that by holding up the proceedings she was spoiling the mood.

"You're important, Beth. Without you, the movie doesn't roll," he said. "That's why I hired you, to help me make things flow."

He held out a small shovel, and she reached for it, her fingers brushing his as they made the exchange. His hand was hard and strong, and her breath whooshed out of her.

"Come on, Carson, darling. I'm ready," Sheena Devoe said. "I want to be in the picture with you."

Another man chuckled. "I'd do as she says, Carson. Sheena doesn't make those kinds of requests every day." Beth looked again at the woman Carson was walking toward. Tall, elegant, with old money, class and beauty, she made an impressive statement. She was worthy of bearing the Banick heir. Carson's family would approve. The two of them fit.

Beth needed to remember that and she needed to promote the relationship. She was, after all, Carson's assistant, and that meant she was here to assist in any way she could. She had offered to find him a wife.

Beth felt something hard and painful in her chest, and she knew it wasn't a true physical ailment. It wasn't anything she could pay attention to, either. Instead she grabbed her shovel and, using as much force as she could, scooped up a big shovelful of dirt, her too quick movement nearly causing the cameras to miss the shot.

She hoped she wasn't in the picture, next to Carson and Sheena. Her absence would remind her that she was here for the job, not for the man. And if she kept reminding herself of that, then she couldn't very well start caring for him, could she?

# CHAPTER SIX

HOURS LATER, Carson gazed through the wall of windows separating his house from the outdoors and stared at the woman walking along the lakeshore. The fading sunlight turned Beth's thick, silky hair a brilliant and golden red.

*What if I never get to touch it?* The thought came out of nowhere, totally inappropriate. He had to keep his distance from Beth. She was…too much. Too passionate, too alive. That made her dangerous. People in his world concentrated on goals, on business…on protecting the family name. He needed to stay focused, and Beth, wonderful as she was turning out to be, was a distraction.

Born into circumstances that his mother would have labeled as serving class, Beth would never be a Banick. She would never feel comfortable in that world. The Banick life would wear her down and eat her up and destroy all that life and stubbornness and glorious spontaneity that she exuded.

If he kept her around too long, eventually she would

meet his mother. Deirdre liked to drop in while a hotel was being built. She would, at the very least, show up once the building was completed. When that happened, she would most likely end up hurting Beth. And so would he.

Carson remembered the look on Beth's face when she realized that her soggy little cake had collapsed. She had been embarrassed and afraid that she had spoiled things. That kind of doubt didn't come from spoiled cakes. It came from somewhere much deeper. She had been hurt in her life, maybe many times. To expose Beth to his mother would be like feeding a baby chick to a wolf.

So, he wouldn't do it. Beth was his employee, nothing more. Even if today she had been…adorable was the word that came to mind. Until he thought of her eyes.

Heat flowed through him. Then other words came to mind. He ignored them. The safest thing to do right now would be to stay in the house and pretend he hadn't seen Beth.

But he had, and she deserved to know how instrumental she had been in making this day a success. She should have more than the tepid thank-you he had given her at the groundbreaking.

It was his duty to walk down to the lake and speak with her, wasn't it? A good employer saw to his employees' needs, and Beth needed to know she was valued.

Without allowing himself time to consider, Carson left the window, exiting the French doors to the deck.

Beth's head came up at the sound of the door clicking

closed. "I'm sorry. This is your part of the lake. I shouldn't be hogging it."

He smiled. "Your part of the lake, too." He motioned toward the guest house. "Hog away."

Her laughter wasn't the soft, tinkling sound of the girls he had grown up with. It wasn't small or ladylike. It was a full-bodied bark, the kind of laugh a girl growing up with four males would adopt. It was genuine. He moved closer.

"You made the day today," he said.

Beth whirled, her hands coming out of her pockets as she crossed her arms and howled. "You must have had some weird days in your time. Let's see. The caterer canceled. I wore vivid purple into a crowd dressed completely in tasteful black. I cooked when I seldom cook, so I know it wasn't good stuff—"

"You look nice in purple," he said, cutting her off. "And the food was home-cooked. People like that. They appreciated your efforts. They liked pitching in to help with the tables and they liked knowing that in a pinch we still came through."

"I stuck my shovel in the ground too soon."

"Is that a euphemism?"

"Are you making fun of me?"

He smiled. She kept making him do that. "Maybe a little. But today was simply ceremony, a chance to let the townspeople meet us. It worked, and you helped make it work. The timing of shovels was immaterial."

She turned away and when she turned back she was

smiling, her eyes rolling. "You're very good. You know that?"

He raised a brow. "Good at what?"

"Good at schmoozing people. I saw the way you handled those people today, the officials. You had them completely captivated and willing to do your bidding. You're a natural."

"A natural what?"

She laughed again. "I don't know. A natural…aristocrat. People want to get close to you and do your bidding. Even important people."

"Hmm, that sounds stuffy and boring." Was that what he was turning out to be?

She shrugged. "I suppose that kind of thing could be stuffy, but it wasn't. Everything worked today, didn't it?" She looked up at him, and those warm brown eyes seemed even warmer than he remembered. For the first time he actually felt good about his role in this project.

"Everything worked," he agreed. "I think things are going…all right."

She laughed. "I'm sorry, but are you always this subdued?" she asked. "The town officials are practically kneeling before you in obeisance and you think that things are merely going all right?"

Carson frowned. "Okay, better than all right."

"You could tell them you wanted to build a moat with alligators and they would consider it," she argued, chuckling again.

The sound went through her body and made Carson's

fingertips tingle. "I'm not infallible, Beth. Not even close. Don't make the mistake of thinking that I am."

She shifted slightly at his dark tone, her breath hitching visibly. "I won't," she promised as Carson told himself to leave her there. Yet he didn't.

"But you have given me some ideas," he said, trying to ignore the idea that was insisting on being heard. The one that told him to pull her close, to taste her.

The sound of footsteps coming down the shore path snagged his attention. Carson immediately turned Beth toward her house.

"What kind of ideas?" she asked.

He looked down and saw that she was staring at him intently. Her lips were parted slightly. Somehow he kept from groaning, from touching.

"When Patrick and I were young, we used to play at the sites when the workers weren't there. Probably not the safest thing in the world, but my father would get busy with contractors, and Pat and I would sneak away. Sons of hoteliers, we would play dueling hotels, each grabbing whatever drawing materials we could find and squaring off in our corners. The point was to plan the biggest, best hotel and then to compare and see who was the winner."

"You poor babies," Beth said. "Didn't you have base-balls or Frisbees?"

He laughed. "Yes, we had all the requisite toys and then some, but my parents—" He frowned. "They lived and breathed Banick Enterprises. If you wanted their attention—"

"You had to prove you were worthy?" she asked.

"Not really. I never took Banick seriously even though as the eldest I was the chosen son for a long time. My parents took even the most outrageous designs seriously. I tended to goad them by suggesting just the kinds of things you mentioned. No alligators, but I believe I suggested mermaids in the pool and piranhas in the pond. A horse for every guest."

Beth's mouth curved upward. "Did your parents ever consider any of your fine ideas?"

"No, they admitted the obvious. Finally. Because of that and…other things I said and did. Patrick was the true Banick and I was going to be trouble all around."

"I don't believe it."

"Believe it. I'm not complaining, mind you. Everything worked out for the best, and we all got what we wanted."

"But you're here, doing this." She held her arms out to the side as if the hotel was right on this spot. Her eyes were wide and confused.

"I'm here, and yes, I'm finally taking my place in the Banick empire, but after having been away for years, I need to catch up, do it right. Better than right. I need to make this hotel a masterpiece. Different. Unique. And maybe if, as you suggested, I have some leeway to be creative…"

A slow smile turned Beth's berry-colored lips upward. The last sinking rays of the sun painted her skin golden. "I definitely think you do. So, let's go brainstorm, let's plan, let's dream and let's be creative," she said. It sounded like an invitation to climb into her bed...or maybe that was simply what Carson wanted to do.

"Let's do it," he agreed.

Two hours later they sat on the thick rug in his living room surrounded by paper and two empty champagne flutes.

"White noise machines, classical tapes and sleep masks for the occasional insomnia caused by sleeping away from home," he read. "Hmm, maybe."

"A set of *Harry Potter* books in every room?" he read, ending on a whoop.

Beth wrinkled her adorable nose and leaned in to him, trying to look intimidating even though her small size prevented it. "Hey, I love *Harry Potter.*"

"Me, too. We'll see." He picked up another piece of paper.

"How about this? A series of separate and cozy sitting areas off the lobby with circular couches and fire pits," he read.

"Cozy. I love that idea. I can't think of anyone who wouldn't want to stay in a hotel with such warmth and appeal. Here's another," she said, blindly picking up a bit of paper. "Window seats and library shelves in the guest rooms." She smoothed the edges of the slightly crumpled sheet as she fed it into the pile, then looked back over her shoulder, smiling at him.

Carson's heart lurched. His whole body lurched. To distract himself, he poured her a glass of champagne and then one for himself. When he finally handed her the glass and looked at her, she was shrugging.

"Yeah, maybe not. Too provincial," she said. "Little girlish."

He shook his head. "No. Not provincial. Don't criticize it just because it was your idea," he said. "I like that idea. I like it…a lot." His voice deepened as he watched her drink, watched a tiny trickle of liquid slip down the stem of the glass and splash onto the hollow of her throat. He swallowed hard. Then, without thought, he leaned over and licked the pale liquid from her skin.

Beth dropped the glass. She closed her eyes. "I'm sorry."

"Don't be. It's only champagne. It's only a rug. I'll buy another."

"No." She looked up and placed both hands on his chest, so lightly that he should barely be able to feel it.

Carson felt it. He groaned at her touch, but he could feel the tension within her. It wasn't a good kind of tension, either. "No," he repeated. "You're right."

She shook her head slowly, then leaned forward and pressed her lips to his, breaking away so quickly that he almost didn't have a chance to savor the touch. And yet, he thought, as heat and light and longing seared him, she had marked him, indelibly.

"I'm an idiot," she said softly. "I should know better than to drink champagne when I don't handle it well."

Knowing he shouldn't, he reached out and tucked her hair behind one ear. "I won't take advantage of you."

"You didn't, Carson. *I* kissed you, but I shouldn't have. You're my boss. We're not the same. Besides, Sheena Devoe wants you."

He struggled to clear his head as Beth got to her feet and he stood up to meet her. For a minute he didn't remember who Sheena Devoe was. And then he did. "Sheena?" He frowned.

"You don't like her?" she asked.

"I don't know her," he admitted. But he knew that she was interested in him and that she was Banick material. Somehow that seemed unimportant. He fought to remember his brother. Carson had always dumped all the pressure on Patrick when by rights it had been his to bear. "Sheena Devoe?" he muttered beneath his breath.

Beth frowned. "Don't make a quick decision. She might not be the one. Nice, but too pushy. You can do better. Remember, I said I would help you find more."

Something hard and heavy shifted inside Carson's body. He had come on to Beth. She had kissed him and in the next minute she was offering to find a bride for him.

He was deeply afraid that he had somehow hurt Beth, And yet he wanted nothing more than to touch her again.

Beth lay in bed, staring at the stars through the skylight and trying not to think about what she had just done.

She had kissed Carson.

Well, he had touched her first, she thought, her whole body shivering at the erotic memory of his lips against her skin. But he was probably the kind of man who kissed lots of women all the time without even thinking.

She had known exactly what she was doing when she had pressed her lips to his. The thought of being so close to him and not touching had seemed unbearable in that moment. Of course, she had immediately realized her mistake. The minute her mouth had met his and she'd felt his warmth, his breath, everything had turned to mindless sizzle. She'd been lost and she would have asked for more if she hadn't run.

Carson was much more potent, more exciting, more intelligent and giving than any man she'd ever known. He was more forbidden as well.

Sheena Devoe wanted him, and Sheena was of his world. Despite Beth's earlier critique, she knew Sheena was the type of woman Carson was seeking. She could be a Banick.

Beth let out a groan. "Stop it," she told herself. "Don't think about Carson as a man. He's not a man you can have. He is your employer. He was born into a world where you would never fit."

*And where he hadn't always fit, either.*

She sat up in bed, frowning. Why hadn't he fit? His parents had been disappointed in him and had favored his brother. But now that his brother was incapacitated Carson had to save the day. Who were the Banicks, anyway? Why was Carson so insistent that this one project be perfect?

"None of your business, Krayton," she said out loud,

but Beth had never been one to listen to orders. A mere twenty minutes later, she was at the computer Carson had provided, pecking away on the Internet.

"This is nonsense," she told herself. "It's nosy."

She considered that for a minute. Then she typed in a few more search terms. What harm could a little snooping do?

# CHAPTER SEVEN

BETH ARRIVED AT the office early the next morning. She'd had a restless night. The things she'd discovered on the Internet had been sketchy, bits and pieces from old tabloid articles. The information could have been put online by anyone. Competitors. People harboring grudges. All she knew was that she'd been left with more questions than answers.

When Carson had been eight, his parents had sent him to boarding school while his younger brother had never gone. Carson had been disciplined for breaking the rules numerous times and had been arrested for underage drinking. Broken hearts left behind had appeared to be the norm. In fact, during his younger years, Carson had been the type of boy her brothers had warned her about. He'd been a hell-raiser and a rule breaker. His brother, in contrast, had been the good one, the hope of the Banicks.

But things had obviously changed. Carson wasn't a boy anymore. More recent accounts on the society pages still had him breaking hearts. Only his businesses had succeeded.

"And now he's taking his rightful place at the head of the family." She said the words to herself just as the phone rang.

"Banick Enterprises," she said into the receiver.

"I'd like to speak to my son," a woman's rather deep, commanding voice said.

Beth almost jumped. For one terrifying second she had the awful thought that Deirdre Banick knew that Beth had been snooping into her affairs.

Or that she'd been kissing her son. The son who was supposed to be marrying a socialite.

Closing her eyes and her mind to…everything, Beth struggled for the cheery tone she had used when dealing with customers at the auto parts store. "I'm sorry, but he's not in right now. May I have him call you, Mrs. Banick?"

"No, you may not." The woman's tone turned to ice. "You may find him right now. I'll wait."

Beth blinked. Her immediate instinct was to politely and firmly reiterate that the woman would have to wait, but…what was she thinking? This wasn't a person coming in to the auto parts store to complain to the manager that their tire pressure valve had failed after six months. This was Carson's mother, a woman who commanded audiences with political and business giants. "I'll try to find him," Beth said.

"Don't try. Do it." The terse answer was even more frigid than her previous comment had been. Beth quickly placed Mrs. Banick on hold and looked up Carson's cell phone number. She was punching it in when he came through the door. He smiled at her and immediately froze. She knew why. After last night she'd decided to dress more conservatively…for her own good. And she wasn't good at fashion, as she had explained.

But right now she couldn't talk about her dress. She looked up at him, big-eyed and taking a deep breath.

"What?" he asked, his voice instantly concerned. "Beth, I—are you all right?"

"Your mother." She gestured to the phone.

He didn't answer, just gave a terse nod and moved over to his own desk. "Hello, Mother," he said, picking up the receiver. "I'm here."

There was a period of silence while the woman spoke. "Her name is Beth," he said quietly, "and stop complaining. She did as you asked and found me. You can't expect me to be here around the clock." More silence. "Yes, I changed my cell phone number, but it had nothing to do with you. My other one conked out and I only just got this one. I've been busy and haven't had time to give you the new number."

He leaned his hips back on the desk and glanced over toward Beth. She wished the black dress looked a bit more stylish, but she hadn't chosen it for its beauty. It was baggy and unattractive and it helped remind her that she and Carson were from completely different worlds. Wearing this, she couldn't possibly think of doing something stupid like kissing him again.

"You've spoken to the planning commission and you don't like everything we've agreed on," he said, his voice devoid of emotion.

More silence as he listened to the woman on the other end of the line.

"No," he said firmly. "I'm not changing the plans and don't go bringing this to Patrick. The doctors feel that he's already too stressed. It's affecting his recovery. If you're going to visit him, it can't be to complain."

He listened a bit more.

"I promise you that I have Banick's best interests at heart, Mother. I intend to do all I can to help Patrick recover completely. I don't want him to have any interferences with his progress, so if you insist on visiting the site and reviewing the plans, bring your concerns to me. I don't want Patrick worrying about anything other than getting better."

He had barely stopped speaking when Beth saw him blanch. "Of course, I believe he'll get better. His health is all that matters right now. The doctors have spoken to Patrick. He knows their prognosis concerning everything, including his ability to walk again and his inability to father children. There's nothing he can do about the latter except rail against his fate. None of us can reverse history, so there's no point in discussing it with him." He listened. "Mother, yes, I know you're worried about him, too. Just…call me if you need to discuss your concerns."

Carson released a long sigh. "I assure you that I'll

take the responsibility from Patrick and fill the gap. There will be an heir…in time. You'll just have to be satisfied with that for now."

In the silence that followed, Carson's whole body grew suddenly tense. "Yes, I know that I'm being highhanded for someone who has never given a damn before. And no, he hasn't brought up the subject of who was at fault for his accident. For what it's worth, I *have* apologized, but an apology is, of course, inadequate and too little too late. To pursue it further would only distress him more." His voice had turned weary and sad. Beth could see the tension in the long lines of his body. She tried to concentrate on her work, but it was impossible. As Carson listened to what was being said to him, a frown marred his forehead.

"I'm sure you disagree with my methods. But sometimes Banicks *do* need to apologize."

Beth could hear the sound of the woman's voice coming through the receiver. Even though she couldn't understand the words, it was obvious that Deirdre Banick was angry.

"No, I wasn't talking about you needing to apologize, Mother." He ran his thumb and forefinger across the bridge of his nose. "It was good speaking to you, Mother. And yes, I understand you'll want to see the drawings and that you may drop by. Just don't yell at Beth if I'm not here. She'll find me, but the results may not be instantaneous. You know what a lot of legwork a project of this magnitude involves."

More noise from the other end of the line.

"She's excellent. The best. Don't go there. I mean it. You're out of line. Goodbye, Mother." He hung up the phone. Just before the receiver hit the cradle, Beth heard the woman's voice. She was still talking. That couldn't be good.

Beth looked up at Carson in disbelief. "Did you just hang up on your mother?"

He crossed his arms.

Beth frowned. "Forget I asked that. What goes on between the Banicks…" she began.

"Stays with the Banicks? Don't believe it. The Banicks' squabbles tend to leak out. People talk."

"Were you defending me?"

He grimaced before giving a harsh laugh. "Don't take it personally. My mother likes to complain. Usually about me, but when she runs out of arguments…you were simply convenient. Don't worry. I won't let her get near you."

Unsure how to respond, Beth nodded, but what she was thinking was that Carson was protecting her and obviously protecting Patrick. Why had he inferred that he had been the one to hurt his brother? She'd read the newspaper accounts. Carson and Patrick hadn't been near each other on that trail. She didn't believe he was to blame. She did believe, however, that she was adding stress to Carson's already stressful life. He had to help Patrick, to save the family and the business. Now he had to protect her?

*No.* She almost said the word out loud. She was not going to cause Carson any stress. That meant she needed to remember that she was, as his mother would have told her, merely the hired help.

She glanced down at her dress. This black monstrosity was supposed to help her remember her place. But when she looked up at Carson and he gave her a reassuring, melting smile she forgot everything but him.

Carson tried to go about his business without thinking about the conversation he had just concluded. He was used to his mother's ways and had learned to let her judgmental comments slide when they pertained to him. Even her stilted way of voicing her concern about her youngest son wasn't a surprise. Deirdre Banick had never been particularly maternal.

But her venomous remarks about Beth had nearly made him lose it. He knew where that venom was coming from. His mother was frustrated, and Beth had seemed to be an impediment, a lesser being standing in her way. His parents felt strongly that their employees should be paid well and given generous benefits, and they also felt that in return for those benefits, a Banick employee should be a model of servitude: efficient, dependable, submissive and invisible. Beth was neither submissive nor invisible, and Carson was sure that Deirdre had already written Beth's name down on her black list of people she would see to later.

It wasn't going to happen. He wouldn't let it. But his mother's attitude wasn't the reason for his black mood. Deirdre was predictable. He was used to dealing with her, and her reaction to Beth wasn't exactly a surprise. He would simply make more of an effort to protect Beth. He was prepared for that. He had promised her brothers he would watch over her, and even if he hadn't…no one was going to hurt her. Not even himself.

The hotel wasn't the source of his concern, either. Construction was proceeding smoothly even though it was only in the early stages, and his call to a designer who would be involved in the latter stages of the process had been concluded quickly and satisfactorily. It was one of those days when all aspects of the job were flowing smoothly. Things were going so well, in fact, that he should have been ecstatic.

He wasn't. And after fighting his conscience for a while, Carson admitted that he knew why. Because his mother's call had upset Beth and turned her unusually quiet, he had been loathe to add to her distress. But, ignoring the situation wasn't changing things. The silence between them lay deep and heavy.

So, Carson turned toward Beth now and gave her a long, slow look, finally focusing on what was bothering him. She had come in this morning wearing something black. That was the best description he could give. It wasn't one of the dresses he'd bought for her and it didn't touch her body anywhere. But it *was* tasteful. And expensive. He had been born knowing such things. She must have spent every last penny he had paid her thus far for the loose, flowing cloth.

Carson muttered an oath beneath his breath.

Beth looked up from her paperwork and gave him a quizzical look. "Something wrong?"

"Not a thing." Except for the fact that he could still feel her hands on his chest. That the brief meeting of lips last night had only made him hungry for something longer, deeper, with more touching and less clothing.

He frowned at the dress and admitted what he'd been avoiding admitting all morning. He knew why she was wearing that sack. Because he had shown her that he desired her. He had stepped outside the bounds of acceptability for an employer. He had driven her to hide herself. She did not deserve to be treated like an object. Like a man's plaything. Not someone with her brightness and spirit.

"Carson?"

From somewhere he found a smile and the ability to lie. "I'm just thinking about…things. The plans," he amended when she looked alarmed.

She still didn't look happy. "Your mother didn't like the plans. If it's all right…may I ask why? What did she say?"

Finally something he could do to ease Beth's distress. He crossed the room to her desk. "Don't worry. It's not as bad as you think. I talked to my father via videophone this morning. His response was 'Looks acceptable,' 'It's about time you got more involved,' 'Could you make sure the sign is just a bit bigger but still tasteful?' and

'How about putting bright red flashing lights and rotating beds in the guest rooms?'"

Beth blinked. Then her eyes got wide. "Well, I—" Her mouth fell open just a touch.

Unable to stop himself, Carson reached out and gently placed a finger underneath her chin, causing those pretty pink lips to close. "I was kidding, Beth," he said with a smile.

"Oh." She fiddled with a bit of her hair. "About all of it?"

"Just the part about the beds and the lights. They do want the sign bigger."

"But still tasteful."

"Always. That was my mother's complaint."

"Well. We could do that. Couldn't we?"

"We could. If we wanted to."

"Do we want to?"

"I haven't decided yet." He didn't add that he wanted to bring it up to Patrick. Carson didn't care one iota about what size the sign was, but Patrick had always been as particular about the details as his parents. He didn't want to distress Patrick, but perhaps there was a way to snag Patrick's interest in a no-stress way. Maybe if he presented his brother with a plan that didn't meet his sibling's idea of perfection he could get a rise out of him. Anything that got Patrick involved in life would be welcome.

Beth was about to say something when a man came up behind her. "Ms. Krayton?"

She whirled and looked at him. Carson recognized

the man as part of the construction crew who had been working on the south wall.

"I just wanted to thank you for the lemonade you left for us this morning, ma'am. It's some of the best I've ever had." The man paused, raising his head briefly to glance at Carson. His look was clear. *Butt out, buddy,* was what it said. *I'm the one talking to this woman now.*

"Oh, well, you're entirely welcome. It was the least I could do," Beth was saying. "I have brothers in construction, and I appreciate how hard your work is." The warmth in her husky female voice and the smile he knew she was giving the man even though he couldn't see it made Carson want to snarl. Instead he offered the man a quick nod, then moved off.

But not far. Not nearly far enough, since his desk was only a few feet from Beth's. For what seemed like hours but was really only a few minutes after lunch had concluded for the crew, a steady stream of muscled, sweaty and smitten men entered the trailer and tried to hit on Beth.

When the line finally thinned, Carson came over. "You need to eat. You've missed your lunch hour."

"I will. I'm fine." She hummed as she reached into her desk for a brown paper bag and a thermos.

He should definitely go back to his desk and leave things alone. "Beth, those men—"

She looked up at him, her eyes wide and warm and far too innocent. "It's okay that the workers come in here, isn't it?"

"Of course, but—"

"I just gave them something to drink. I knew you would want them to have something since it's so hot today."

That woman. He hadn't even considered the men working in the heat, even though he should have. "Thank you for doing that. But they were here for you, not just to thank you for your lemonade."

She frowned. "I wasn't trying to encourage men to come on to me during business hours."

"I didn't mean to imply that. I'm not accusing you of anything."

He knew he was handling this badly, and finally the elephant in the closet came tumbling out, what he and Beth had avoided discussing all morning: the thing that it was obvious that both of them had been thinking about. "I just wanted you to know that if someone comes on too strong, if anyone in any capacity pushes you too hard…that's unacceptable. Tell me. I will do something. You should never have to put up with someone making you uncomfortable or taking advantage of you no matter who that someone is."

He stared into her eyes, which were dark and worried. "No one has pushed me," she whispered. "It wasn't like that."

"I know you need this job. You told me so."

Beth looked to the side. "You sound a lot like my brothers. And yes, I *do* need and want this job, but I know how to take care of myself. I know how to stand up for my rights when I need to, and I won't let myself be pushed around or prodded into doing something I don't want to do." Her voice began to rise a bit. "Carson…are you accusing yourself of sexual harassment?"

Ah, there it was. Finally. "I fed you champagne. I touched you."

"You didn't force me to drink the champagne and you didn't force me to accept your touch. I never felt threatened or exploited. I realize that it was just the situation, and the champagne."

Carson crossed his arms. Then he shook his head and reached out one hand. "Come on."

She stared at his outstretched hand. "Where?"

"Lunch." His words were like a bullet. "We both need some, and we need a break."

"And you need to make a point," she accused as she slid her palm across his.

"Exactly." He ran his other hand through his hair, mussing it, and she laughed.

"What?"

She shrugged as they exited the trailer and started down the short staircase. "I know what you're going to say."

As she reached the last step, he stopped, looking down into her eyes. She was so close he could swoop in and kiss her. And because that was what he wanted to do, he started walking again. "What am I going to say?" he grumbled.

"You're going to tell me that I'm naive, that I only see what I want to see, that I don't understand how men operate. Which is patently ridiculous."

"You thought those men were really coming in to talk about lemonade."

"They were…partly. And okay, yes, I knew they were flirting a bit. It's not the kind of thing a woman wants to discuss with…her boss."

*Or the man who had licked champagne from her neck the night before,* Carson thought.

"You're right. I shouldn't have interfered." It was just that there was something fresh and spontaneous about her and…damn it, it made a man want to think about things he shouldn't be thinking about. He didn't like knowing that other men might be thinking the same kinds of things.

"I know you can take care of yourself. You talked me into hiring you when I never intended to."

She gasped.

"And I'm glad you did. You were a gift. You were, hands down, the best person for the job."

"But you still think I can't handle a man leering at me while he discusses lemonade?"

Carson didn't answer at first. "I don't think that."

She gave him an evil look. "When I was growing up, my brothers worried that boys would think I didn't know how to take care of myself because I didn't have a mother to watch over me and give me advice. They figured guys would assume I was more open to…earthier things, that I would be wild. And they were right."

Carson turned to look at her.

She grimaced. "I was wild to break free from four overprotective brothers who threatened to beat up any boy who asked if he could borrow a piece of notebook paper. But my brothers were right, too. Boys *did* try things with me that they didn't try with other girls. They cajoled and tricked and charmed to get under my skirts any way they could."

Carson's breath stopped. Anger flowed through his veins. He fought to control his reactions. "What did you do?"

"I learned to be polite and smile and wait, and as long as no one tried anything other than talking, things were fine. If they tried more, I learned to hit and humiliate and defend myself."

The thought that she would have to do any of those things sent a blackness through Carson that he could barely contain. "Good. I hope you broke a few noses."

Beth's laugh rang out, and Carson relaxed a little. "I did," she said. "You'd think that would have reassured my brothers, but it didn't."

"I can understand that." He could also understand why she wasn't all that interested in relationships if guys had treated her so callously.

She stopped and turned to him, pulling her hand free to place it on her hips. "What do you mean, you can understand that?"

"Your brothers wouldn't have liked the fact that you had to break noses. They would have wanted to prevent that in the first place."

"Carson, this is the twenty-first century. Women fight their own battles."

"I know that, and I admire you for it."

"So why are you warning me to watch out for men on the prowl when I've already proven that I can take care of myself?"

He didn't know, or maybe he didn't want to know. He certainly didn't want to think about how much he hated the thought of men coming on to her. They were foreign feelings, this anger and jealousy and protectiveness, and they weren't emotions he wanted to cultivate when there was no chance of anything developing between him and Beth.

"Why am I warning you? Probably because I'm an idiot."

She twirled around and clutched his hands. They stood next to the Driehaus fountain with the blue sky and that gorgeous lake filled with colorful bobbing boats as a backdrop. It was a magical setting. She was a magical woman with hair like fire, a smile that bewitched and laughter that begged a man to do something stupid.

"How can you say that? You're not an idiot. You're a good man, Carson," she added.

And that was her fatal mistake. Because he knew her last words were a lie. He couldn't bear for her to think he was good.

"No. I'm not," he said. "I've done things I'm not proud of, Beth. My former fiancée...Emily was everything my mother detested. I'm not sure...but Emily was probably part of my rebellion. It ended badly. I hurt her because I didn't love her."

Beth took a deep, visible breath. "I read about that. I'm sorry."

Carson swore. "Don't be sorry, but don't make me out to be better than I am. Because all the time I was warning you about those other men, I was wanting more. I was wanting this." He cupped her elbows, pulling her against him and kissing her in full view of the throngs of people on the lakefront. He opened his mouth over hers and drank from her lips, tasting, teasing, savoring.

"I want even more of you when I know I can't have it and I definitely can't give anything in return," he whispered fiercely against her lips. "So hit me, Beth. Punch me, tell me no, break my nose." His words were urgent, fueled by the fact that she had kissed him back, that she was still pressed against him, and the lemony scent of her hair, the soap-clean scent of her skin was driving him wild.

He felt her tremble against him, and he hated himself. He started to let her go, but she grasped the front of his shirt with both hands. She kissed him once, very hard and very fast.

"You think only men want things that they can't have? I want you, too, even though I agree that this can't be. It's wrong."

"So promise you'll hit me if I ever do this again."

"I'll do better than that," she said, rising up on her tiptoes and brushing his lips with her own. "I'll stop wasting time and I'll help you reach your goals so that neither of us will have any regrets when we're done. As a top-notch assistant who can do it all, I'll make it my business to help you find the woman who will grace the Banick cocktail parties and corporate dinners and give the Banick family an heir with a pedigree."

"No."

She leveled a look at him that dared him to argue with her. "Don't tell me I'm too weak to handle this, Banick," she said.

Desire such as he'd never known licked through him. Admiration for her grew in leaps and bounds. "That wasn't my point, and weak wasn't the word I was thinking of," he said.

"What was the word?" she demanded.

*Gorgeous, desirable, amazing, wonderful* all came to mind. But he knew those words would only fuel the fire they were both trying to extinguish. "Spunky," he said, trying desperately to tease her and lighten the mood. "Or maybe perky."

"Spunky?" She socked him on the arm. "Just for that you owe me a lunch," she said, giving him a shaky smile.

That smile hit him hard. For a moment, he envisioned her with his child in her arms. He couldn't think about Banick heirs, dinner parties, family responsibilities or even healing Patrick. She was all. She was his. He wanted her, and he didn't give a damn about Banick Enterprises.

But his family—his mother in particular—would make Beth's life miserable. All the power he had wouldn't protect her. She was too smart, too intuitive. She might be capable of keeping men at bay, but she had never dealt with Deirdre Banick. Emily had. He'd exposed her to that and he didn't want Beth to experience that kind of pain. "Forget about the Banick pedigree. That's my concern." He would give up Beth. He would focus on the business as he'd planned. He would set Patrick free, something he should have done years ago instead of throwing all the work and duty and responsibility into his younger brother's lap while he did as he pleased.

"Forget about all of it," he reiterated. "For now I owe you lunch." *And freedom from the heartache a long-term association with the Banick clan could provide.* He would protect her and free her…just as soon as they were done with this job.

# CHAPTER EIGHT

CARSON WAS TRYING to protect her, Beth thought later that night as she sat on a bench outside the most expensive restaurant in Lake Geneva. Yet, for some ridiculous reason she didn't resent his attempts the way she did her brothers'. Why?

"Don't go there," she muttered to herself, but it was too late. She'd already thought of two reasons. The first was okay: he really did believe in her abilities. The other one, however, wasn't okay at all. She was attracted to him. Massively. That wasn't right or smart. And if she didn't follow her instincts and find some way to take a large step back, her attraction was going to lead her into the worst heartache she had ever experienced.

"So, I'll build some barriers," she said. The clothes were a start, she thought, looking down at her unattractive dress and trying not to think about the lovely things in her closet. But the clothes weren't enough. Kissing—great, hot, wonderful kissing—had still taken place while she was wearing this dress.

Carson needed a bride, but it was pretty clear he wasn't rushing to get to that part of his life. And he had told her to stay out of it, she reminded herself with a frown.

Make no mistake, the man could find his own women. There were probably plenty besides Sheena who were salivating over him.

And he just wasn't a man who would ask anyone to help him do what he thought he should be doing himself. Since he had asked—no, ordered—her to steer clear, she should obey him, but...she couldn't do that, and it was far more than her usual rebellious streak that was at fault.

*If Carson were engaged, she wouldn't dare think of him in the wrong way, and he wouldn't touch her. He was too honorable for that.*

A long, low ache slithered through her. She ignored it and her conscience as she walked into the restaurant with a pad of paper and a pen. *Hey, what's a good assistant for, anyway?* she reasoned.

All through the meal, as she sipped her tea and nibbled at the least expensive appetizer on the menu, she scribbled loudly on her notepad in order to attract the attention of the nearby female patrons.

Intentionally she sighed and ripped a piece of paper off the pad, then started over. Several times. When she got up to leave, she picked up the discarded scraps, allowing one to flutter to the table, seemingly unnoticed. Then she left the restaurant.

Beth hoped that the piece of paper she had left behind

would be noticed and talked about. It was a scrap from a Banick Enterprises memo pad, the logo prominently displayed. On it, Beth had written her name with a list of "Things To Do For Ms. Krayton." Along with several mundane tasks such as "file receipts," "make copies of contracts" and "make sure all workers are provided with stocked water stations" she'd embedded and underlined "compile list of eligible, successful women of good families to attend hotel opening ball."

For half a second, Beth's throat nearly closed up. Her breathing became labored. Usually an honest person, she had made up that whole scenario. There was no hotel opening ball, or if there was going to be it would be far in the future. Of course, Carson was capable of pursuing his own women, but after more research on the Internet, she knew a few things about the man she hadn't known before.

Carson's parents had been ecstatic at the birth of their first son but they obviously hadn't been capable of dealing with a young man's rebellion. That kind of behavior would have warred with all the Banicks' aristocratic sensibilities. So, the boarding school exile had followed. Eventually an almost complete rift had occurred, because Carson, the eldest son, the natural choice as heir to the hotel empire, had disappeared from the family photos and Patrick had taken over the hotels. Things had continued in that vein until Patrick had been injured in a fall on a perilous mountain hike.

Now Carson was in charge of everything, but he

clearly hadn't wanted to be. There were lots of empty spaces in her knowledge, but she did know this: Carson was feeling guilty about a number of things and he had the world on his shoulders.

But if he could rid himself of his guilt and find the right person to care for and make everything right with his family, then he might finally be happy.

Beth knew that no matter how things seemed between the Banicks, they were still a family just as much as the Kraytons were. If she were estranged from her brothers…Beth tried to think of what that would be like—the loneliness, the regrets. In such a situation, she would do all that she could to set things right. Marrying and producing an heir would bring Carson back into the family fold. It would make everyone, including him, happy.

"The woman has to be perfect," Beth whispered. "She has to be right for Carson, for his family and for his position. She must be found, examined and preapproved, and I'm just the person to do those things. No woman will get to him unless she gets through me first. And I am, as all Kraytons are, one stubborn individual."

"Are things still all right, Bethie?" Roger asked later that night as they talked on the phone.

Beth considered her answer. She thought back to how many times Roger had fixed up her skinned knees and let her cry on his shoulder. He'd even given her the stilted, edited version of the birds and the bees. He had done it all. He had always been there for her, and even though she still needed and wanted to claim her freedom, she now knew from what she'd discovered about the Banicks that she and her brothers had something pretty special.

Roger deserved the truth. But if Roger even began to suspect that she had kissed Carson or that she was matchmaking in order to stop wanting him to kiss her… Roger deserved not to worry, but her concerns and her plans regarding Carson were private. She couldn't bear to reveal her weakness for the man yet.

The dilemma warred within her. "Bethie?" Concern made his voice harsh. She knew her silence was upsetting him.

Her decision made in that instant, she feigned a yawn. "Don't worry, Roger. Things couldn't be better."

Which was such a lie. She was seriously besotted with Carson and no matter what her plans were to rid herself of her obsession, she still had to get through tonight. She had to remain in her house, in her bed and not do something stupid like run across the lawn and bang on Carson's door.

Carson was rushing the next morning. The faster he did things, the less time he would have to notice what Beth was doing.

Not that he thought she needed supervision. The woman was a powerhouse. She thought of things that needed to be done ten minutes before he did. She took care of all the paperwork and charmed everyone who came into the office, leaving him free to deal with design issues and the political and practical aspects of actually overseeing the building of the resort. Today she'd been especially busy and there had been a large number of people trooping in and stopping at her desk. *It's too much,* he thought. Her eyes, normally so bright, looked tired, as if she hadn't gotten enough sleep last night.

*He* hadn't gotten enough sleep. He'd been far too aware that she was only across the lawn, that if he went over and knocked on her door, he could see her. He could...do more.

Carson suppressed a growl.

Beth looked tired for a different reason, anyway, he reminded himself. There were too many demands on her time. She couldn't handle all her paperwork and still shepherd people around. Another employee might be a good idea. He was getting ready to attend a meeting with the architects to discuss some minor design changes and already Beth had produced a copy of the original blueprints, the proposed blueprints, copies of letters from the planning commission regarding the procedure for handling minor changes *and* she was handing him a cup of coffee.

"For the road," she said. "And there's a thermos in the car and some sandwiches from the deli in case you get stuck for any length of time."

"Food for the architects, too?" he teased.

"Of course," she said with a sudden smile that turned the room ten times brighter and significantly warmer. Had he ever really considered not hiring her?

"Care to come along? You tend to think of little things the rest of us miss," he said. "And it looks as if you could use a bit of a break from all this." He gestured to the papers piled on her desk.

For a minute her eyes lit up, but then she shook her head. "I have too many things to do right now."

Carson was about to try to persuade her when the door opened and a woman walked in. She was tall and willowy with long brown hair and she gave him a very intense look. Was it his imagination or had there been an unusual number of sleek women dropping by today?

He stared back at the woman. She greeted him and gave him a smile that could only be called inviting. She held her hand out in a graceful gesture that had clearly been bred in her.

"Nice to meet you," he said, and then he moved away, suspicious. Beth had twice joked that she would help him find a bride. He had warned her not to, but…this was Beth. Had she failed to do anything she had said she would do in the brief time he had known her?

Foolish question. Of course, she hadn't.

Suppressing a groan, he took out his cell phone and made a few calls. Then he waited for the woman to leave before he strolled over to Beth.

"Change of plans," he said. "I've postponed the meeting until tomorrow."

"Excuse me? I thought you needed to talk to the architect as soon as possible."

"Something else came up that was more important." Carson tried to be casual but he knew he was failing, especially when Beth started to fidget with the pen she was holding.

"What came up?" she asked.

He reached out and took the pen from her. "You. Them," he said, leaning over her desk, looking at her memo pad. There was a list of names with notes such as "too pushy," "too flashy," "he could do better" and "a possibility." Beth started to try to move the paper away.

Carson gave her a long, intense look. "I could do better?" he tried to tease.

"Yes, you should ask for a lot. For everything." But she wasn't teasing. She was solemn.

He swore. "Let's get away from here. We'll go for a ride...and then we'll go home."

She opened her mouth. To object, he was sure.

"One-half day of missed work won't hurt. You need a break. I need a break. Don't worry. We'll just talk. I won't bite...or kiss...or touch you in any way," he promised. "I won't hurt you, Beth. I would never willingly hurt you."

"I know that."

But she still looked nervous, like she didn't believe him. Somewhere along the line someone had hurt her. If it happened again, it wasn't going to be him.

But they had to get the rules straight. Both of them

needed some boundaries, it seemed. This was a talk they should have had from the first.

He couldn't let things slide anymore.

The small white boathouse where Carson led her perched above the shore on the edge of his property. She had, of course, seen it but she had never been inside. Now, as he opened the door for her and she brushed past him to step over the threshold, she realized just how cozy it was. Screened in and with a hardwood floor, it boasted a raised fire pit centered between a navy and white striped couch and matching chairs. A small dining table ideal for two was placed near the wall.

"What a perfect place to sit and watch the lake," she said.

He nodded. "I used to hide here when I was a boy."

Glancing around the single square room, Beth raised a brow. "Where?"

"Ah well, the furnishings were different then. There was a table with a cloth that swung to the floor. I'm sure everyone knew just where I was, but I lived with the illusion that no one could find me."

Beth raised her eyes to his. She wondered how many times Carson had needed to hide from the world as a child. "Don't get that look," he said.

"What look?"

"The devious one, where you start plotting to save someone. I've seen you do it before. When the caterer didn't arrive, with the men at the work site, with me. I'm not letting you do that today. It's you we're hiding away. You need a rest. You look…lovely, but tired."

What could a woman say to a man who looked at her with both concern and desire in his eyes, especially one who had told her he wasn't going to touch her?

"Have a seat," he said. He gestured toward the couch, but once she was seated he moved to one of the chairs. Obviously he intended to abide by his word.

*I should be grateful,* Beth thought. So why was she thinking that he was too far away? As if he hadn't always been too far away—in social standing, goals and desires. No, not desires. He wanted her just as she wanted him. He just wouldn't give in.

*Nor will I.* Knowing she had to force her determination, she asked, "Do you still come here often?"

Carson tilted his head. "When I'm in town, yes, I like to sit out here. It feels like neutral territory, less Banick somehow."

"And yet…" She held out her hands.

He turned to the side, the breeze drifting in from the lake and ruffling his dark hair. "Yes, I'm a Banick, through and through. That, I've realized, is inescapable. My lineage is part of why I brought you here. I don't want you to get hurt."

There was sadness in his voice, and finality, and Beth felt dread lurch through her body. She remembered that day when Harrison explained why he couldn't marry her. She had survived dread before. Beth took a deep breath. "I won't."

"You might. People who get entangled with my family do get hurt at times."

"I'm not *people*."

He smiled and leveled a hot look at her that drove past all the defenses she was so hastily erecting. "No, you're not just people," he admitted. "It was obvious from the beginning that you were different."

"Pushier," she provided.

His smile grew. "A bit, yes, but what I was going to say was 'more involved,' 'more caring,' possibly 'more intense.'"

"Possibly?" she asked, daring to smile herself.

"Okay, definitely."

"It's a bad habit."

"It's one I like." That direct look was back and it was focused completely on her. The pace of Beth's breathing notched up. Something warm and melting and frightening in its urgency slipped through her.

"You care, you help," he added. "But there are limits, Beth."

She took another deep breath. That was what Harrison had told her: she needed limits. But that had been different. She'd been involved with Harrison, he had lied to her. Carson had never promised more than employment. He had never pretended that the chemistry between them was lasting or welcome.

"I know about limits," she said. "I'm not trying to cross any lines that shouldn't be crossed."

"I don't mean *your* limits, Beth. I mean… I'm the

one who has breached the barriers. I have to put a stop to that, in whatever way I can."

Oh, no. Beth's heart felt as if something was squeezing it. Was he going to fire her or send her away?

The sound of a boat on the lake drifted to them and she used that as an excuse to look away from Carson's silver gaze.

"Beth." Carson's voice was low and soft and coaxing. Almost against her will, she looked at him. "Come with me to the house. I want you to see something, to understand." He took her hand. For a minute he just gazed down at their linked fingers, his palm warm against her skin.

She followed him across the lawn and into the house she had never entered, into a two-story foyer where sunlight streamed in and lit the gleaming cherry wood of the floor. "This way," Carson directed as they ascended one side of a curving double staircase. When they reached the top, he pulled her close and walked with her down a long hallway carpeted in royal-blue.

"Did you…grow up here?" she whispered as if the ghosts of generations of Banicks would show up and accuse her of being an interloper.

"No, but we spent a fair amount of time here." He pushed open a door. It slid back smoothly, revealing a long room with low shelves around its perimeter. Photos and paintings covered every available inch of wall space. "The Banick shrine," he said with a harsh laugh.

Beth blinked and stepped forward. She gazed at a

picture of a man who, except for his clothing and too stiff and stern demeanor, looked very much like Carson.

"My grandfather," he offered. "And here is my father." He pointed to a man a bit more portly than himself but with the same nose and chin and height. "And my great-grandfather." The portrait hung over the fireplace. "He was knighted for his service to the hospitality industry. I think perhaps it was that bit of history that turned the business from merely business to duty for my parents."

"Your parents talked about him a lot when you were growing up?"

Carson's laugh was harsh. "In place of bedtime stories."

"Oh, Carson."

"Beth, I'm not telling you any of this because I'm looking for sympathy but because I want you to understand my family and why you don't want to get too close."

"I'm not fantasizing about you," she lied.

He frowned. "I'm not accusing you of that. It's just…you're trying to help me. Don't. At least not beyond this job."

Beth took a breath, trying to sort through her thoughts.

"When I was relatively young, my parents brought me in here," Carson said, "and they showed me my ancestors. They told me that I would be next in line after my father. It was an honor to be a Banick and it was my duty to uphold the family name in every way.

"Don't," he said when she started to respond. "Don't be nice. Don't say something soothing. It's not necessary. Just understand this. I was allowed to play and be relatively normal, but within limits. I was to associate with children of my rank, to spend a fair amount of my summers with my father at work, to learn the business from the ground up and to, eventually, marry well and produce the next Banick heir. Any grade below an A was cause for punishment; getting dirty was cause for censure. Developing crushes on girls or friendships with boys who were not worthy of the Banick name was not allowed. On the one hand, I knew I was lucky. I never wanted for anything. But the better part of me hated the restrictions. I rebelled in every way I could."

His voice was cold when he discussed his parents, colder still when he discussed his own reactions. He blamed himself for his rebellion.

"Any boy of spirit would fight back," she said.

"But I had a younger brother, so when my parents finally grew frustrated with me, Patrick was left to take my place. He wasn't strong or rebellious. He had no one to speak up for him." Carson's cold voice had turned even icier.

"He hated it, too," she said softly.

"No, I think he was born for it. Eventually, at least, he became good at it. The problem was that he was never allowed to enjoy it. Patrick took my place but he was always made aware that it was conditional. He was stepping into my shoes because I wouldn't behave. So, he worked harder, tried harder, learned the business inside out, sideways and upside down. He sacrificed everything he was to the business, and I let him do it."

"You were a boy."

"A boy who grew up and still stayed away. I came home for summers and holidays and as soon as I was old enough I left for good. All the burden fell on him. He didn't have a choice."

"Everyone has a choice."

"Patrick was different. He was easygoing, fun, good-hearted, but he grew up without having time for fun while I got to play and run free. I worried about him, but I didn't step in and help him. Instead I teased him about being too serious. I was the one who skied and hiked mountain trails. I accused him of allowing our parents to dictate his life. So he took the bait and came with me that day."

Carson didn't have to say more. Beth knew the outcome. She took a deep, shuddering breath. "I'm so sorry, Carson."

"I'm not after your sympathy, Beth. That's not why I brought you here and not why I'm telling you this."

She stepped closer and looked into his tortured eyes. "Why *are* you telling me this?"

He placed his hands on her shoulders. "So that you'll know what we're like. Everything gets sacrificed to the business. Nothing is more important."

"You blame yourself for your brother's accident. So you stepped in to take his place, in the office and in providing an heir."

"Yes. It's my turn to let him have the time he needs. Do you understand, Beth?" He held her there, so close she could feel his chest rising and falling against her, so close his breath was warm on her face.

"I understood some of this already."

"Is that why you're trying to help me find a bride? It just won't fly. Like Patrick, you're stepping in to help me do what I should have been doing myself. I don't want to see you get caught in the Banick mess. I don't want you to be Emily."

"I won't," she promised on a whisper and she wasn't sure if she was talking to herself or to him.

"Finding me a bride wasn't part of your job description. Why are you doing this?"

*To protect myself from wanting what I can't have.* That was the right answer, but it couldn't be spoken. "Because you're the first man who ever thought I could do more and be more than what I am," she said, and that was the right answer, too. "I *want* to help you."

Carson slid his hand up to her jaw. He rubbed his thumb over her cheek and, even though she knew she shouldn't, she turned into his touch.

"Don't look for a bride for me."

"You don't want a bride?"

He rested his forehead against hers. "It's not a matter of wanting. I don't want a bride, but I'll have one. I just…I don't want you to find her. She'll be found and married in time."

"With no thought to her feelings?"

"She'll be the right one, but I can't promise she'll have feelings for me. Promise *me* you won't look anymore. If my mother came back and found you involved…"

He didn't have to say anymore. "She doesn't like non-Banicks getting involved in Banick personal matters?"

"She can be ruthless. She's shredded the feelings of people before. I don't want that for you."

Beth nodded against him. "All right. I promise." But a part of her felt shredded already. Up until now, Carson marrying for convenience hadn't seemed like a reality. Now, the situation was undeniable. And no matter what he wanted she was going to get hurt. She had developed feelings for him, and they were growing stronger still.

"I'll walk you home," he said. "It's already getting dark."

She went with him, silently, moving across the soft grass.

"Don't shortchange yourself," he said as they walked. "You said that I made you feel like more than you were. But I'm not buying that. You didn't see yourself that first day in my office. You're an amazing, strong, capable and beautiful woman. If people don't see all of that, they're missing the obvious."

"Maybe it's not their fault."

He stopped and faced her on the lawn. "What does that mean?"

She shook her head. "When you lose your parents early, sometimes you have a chip on your shoulder.

After my parents' deaths, I was angry. Every Mother's Day I had no one, not even an aunt or a sister. The teachers hemmed and hawed when it came time to inform me of the 'miracle of my body,' knowing that I lived in an all-male household. I've already told you about the clothes. I was an anomaly. It made relationships with girls difficult and relationships with boys impossible."

He frowned. "I don't see how any of that was your fault."

She reached up and touched the lines on his forehead. "I knew I was different so I didn't let anyone get close. I didn't let boys too near and when I grew up they saw me as a challenge, not a person."

"You are a beautiful person."

Beth smiled. "You feel that way because you didn't know me growing up. You treated me like a normal person from day one. That's why I want to help you."

A low growl emitted from Carson's throat and he pulled her against him. "You are so much more than normal, Beth. Much more."

Beth's heart soared even as it plummeted. She was getting in too deep. That meant she would have to leave this job, and him, soon. Very soon.

She pulled away and opened the door of her house.

"What's wrong?" Carson asked. "What have I said that hurt you?"

Whirling, she looked up at him angrily. "You haven't done a thing. Not a thing. None of this is your fault. It certainly isn't your fault that I like having you touch me when I know I shouldn't."

Carson groaned. He stepped inside and closed the door behind him. "I probably shouldn't have heard that, but Beth, I'm a red-blooded man and knowing that you want me—"

He pulled her to him, his lips coming down on hers. "I just have to taste you," he whispered against her mouth.

"Because I'm a challenge?" she asked.

"Because you're you."

Beth rose up on her toes. "Good. I want you because you're you, too, and if we're only going to get to do this once…"

Carson swung her into his arms and started up the stairs. "Let's do it in a bed," he said.

# CHAPTER NINE

CARSON LAY BETH on the gold and jade comforter and just stared at her for a moment. "You're incredible," he told her.

"I have red hair." She said it as if it were a crime.

"Yes. Beautiful red hair." He picked up a strand and slid the silky stuff between his fingers.

"No one has ever said that about my hair before."

For a minute, Carson felt a lurch…because she had not had the kind of experiences he wished she'd had. And because he wanted to make this special for her. He wanted it too much.

"I have to warn you that I'm not very experienced," Beth said.

Carson's breath hitched in his throat. He stroked a finger down her cheek to her throat. "Then I'll want to make this right for you."

Slowly Beth shook her head. "I'm not very experienced, but I want you enough that right doesn't matter. I'm going to like touching you and having you touch me no matter what."

It wasn't what he'd expected, but when had she ever been what he'd expected? It wasn't what he was used to, but who wanted the same thing over and over? Beth had surprised him a hundred times in a hundred ways. He smiled at her.

"What?" she asked, seeming worried.

He shook his head. "I'm going to like touching you, too. More than you can ever know." He kissed her, slowly, deeply. He tasted her mouth, then her earlobe, then nipped at her throat and her shoulder, the curve of her breast.

She shivered beneath his touch and placed her hands against his chest, struggling to unfasten the buttons.

He did it for her.

"Am I...a challenge?" she asked as he moved from his own clothing to hers. Wanting to rush but sure that she needed more from him, he carefully undressed her, revealing her like a precious jewel emerging from velvet.

"Are you a challenge?" he asked, gazing down at her. He brought his hand up her side, slowly, so slowly, her soft skin making him want too much.

He gazed down into those luminous eyes so filled with uncertainty. "Beth," he whispered. "You're not a challenge. You're a treasure."

His lips descended to hers, she curled around him and for once in his life he knew paradise—even as he knew that paradise never lasted forever.

By the time Beth woke the next morning it was already nine-thirty. She shrieked, rolling toward the edge of the bed. Then she stopped short. She was naked, she had whisker marks on her side and she was alone. Briefly she remembered what had seemed to be a dream: Carson kissing her and telling her to go back to sleep just before the warmth of his body had left her side.

Dragging herself from the bed she realized that it was raining, matching her mood completely.

Last night had been wonderful and amazing and…wonderful. And it was over. For real. For good. For all time. Carson might not be engaged but he would be soon. He was taken and she was just here to do a job.

Beth repeated that to herself about a million times as she got ready for work and dragged herself into the office.

Carson was nowhere in sight, but there was a pot of coffee and a note. Her hands shaking, she opened the note. *I'll be back soon,* it read. *There's a glitch at the site.*

Beth sat down to work, to do anything to keep from remembering last night. She tried not to think that Carson was avoiding her in the way of men who had gotten what they wanted from a woman.

Ten minutes later, the door opened and Carson came in, dripping. He peeled himself out of his slicker, took off his work boots and stepped farther into the room.

"Good morning," he said. Was his voice a little tense?

She looked up into his eyes, willing herself not to seem needy and desperate or too happy and confident, either. This was a new situation for her, sleeping with a man when both of them wanted it but knew it was a one-night stand. What was proper after-lovemaking behavior, anyway?

"Coffee?" she offered, then realized that sounded like an invitation to something else.

"Yes," he said, his voice hard and hot and filled with naked desire.

Beth took a deep breath.

Carson scrubbed a hand through his hair.

"This isn't going to work," she said as brightly as possible.

He stepped up to her desk, leaned right into her space. "Beth, I'm sorry. I shouldn't have grabbed."

"I shouldn't have asked you to, but…we both knew what we were doing. It was just that one time."

He frowned.

"We have plans. You have to marry and I have to…not marry," she added.

He opened his mouth. She could see he was angry, so she held up one hand. "It has nothing to do with you. I had already decided that," she reminded him. But her conviction had just gotten deeper. How could she marry when this man was the only man she wanted to be tied to? He was not free and he belonged to a different world.

Carson nodded. "I still shouldn't have touched you."

"Then I would have had to tie you down. I wanted you last night."

He leaned closer. Her heart started to tick away terribly hard and fast. She was close to reaching out for him, so she leaned back. "But I'm over that now," she said. "I'm ready for work. What's new at the site?"

She rose and got the coffee. Subject dropped. At least she wanted him to think she had forgotten it.

For a long moment there was silence behind her. When she turned he was staring at her, his eyes unreadable. Fearful of her own response, she took a step forward this time…to show that she was no longer thinking of him in that way. She handed him the cup, carefully angling it so that the coffee stayed in the cup but her fingers didn't touch his.

He took it, his brows drawn together in a furrow.

"Trouble at the site?" she asked.

He turned around, let out a breath, then turned back around again. "Yes. We have to stop until the weather clears. And they're predicting rain for the next five days."

"Oh, Carson." She knew how badly he wanted to bring this project in as close to schedule as possible. It was late, but now it would be later still.

"I'll just have to ride it out…and work on other things."

Both of them would be closed up in this little trailer with each other. Beth wondered how she was going to keep from touching him.

*Work* she told herself. As the only girl in her family she had gotten good at playing alone. It was a good skill to have. She moved toward one of the many file cabinets in the back and started pulling out drawers. "You don't mind, do you?" she asked Carson. "They look neglected. Maybe I can get some of this cleaned out."

"You don't have to do that."

She looked up and their glances connected. "I need to be busy," she told him.

He gave her a terse nod. "All right. I trust you to know what needs saving and what we can safely get rid of."

He understood…and he trusted her. It would have to be enough.

But hours later, Beth wanted to scream that it wasn't enough. She was completely aware of him, all the time, every minute and she could barely concentrate on the files.

When the day finally ended, it was a relief. She threw a bundle of files in her bag, told Carson good-night and rushed out the door.

*Four more days of this?* she asked, turning her face up to let the raindrops fall full on her face. *I'll just have to get over my infatuation with the man. By the time the rain stops, I'll be done with him.*

But the rain kept falling. Four days turned into six and then seven. And she didn't get over Carson. On day seven she wanted him more than ever. She was all but ready to throw herself across the trailer and into his arms and beg him to kiss her again.

But she didn't. And he spent as much time as possible out at the site checking the puddles. Thank goodness.

The file cabinet was getting emptier. It was the only thing good that was happening, she thought one night as she flipped through another dusty file filled with old receipts.

The phone rang. "Beth?" she heard as she picked it up.

Immediately Beth's brother alert turned on. "Hi, Albert."

"You haven't called lately."

She hadn't. She'd been too afraid that one of them might hear her misery.

Beth sat up and smiled, just as if Albert could see her. "I'm just a bit tired, Albert. It's been raining for days and I've been cleaning out file cabinets to keep busy. But I'm great. It's supposed to stop raining tomorrow."

"You're sure it's just the weather making you sound so low?"

"Albert," she said, striving for brightness. "You know that nothing gets me down."

"Is there something going on that would get another, less perky person down?" he demanded.

Uh-oh. She had phrased that last comment badly. "Of course not. I'm great. Just sleepy. I stayed up last night reading a good book. I probably should get to bed early tonight. But I'm glad you called." And, she realized, she really was. "I miss you. Tell Roger and Steve and Jim that I love them and miss them, too."

In a few minutes she was off the phone. Lonely. Hurting. She could see the light on in Carson's house. She'd been looking at it for days. He was so close…

"He'll never be close," she reminded herself. "You knew from day one that he wasn't for you. He gave you a job. He gave you more. And what have you done for him lately other than look sad and wail to yourself? Files don't count," she said to the offensive things. "Stop acting so moody and get things back to normal. Do not look toward Carson's house again. It's his home, not yours and that's the way things are."

*That's the way things are.* It was a mantra she'd quoted to herself many times while growing up. It had gotten her through a lot. Now it was time to stop moping and go back to what worked.

Beth took a deep breath. She squared her shoulders, opened up another file and gave it her full attention. On the first page were some childish scrawls.

*A basketball court on the lower level* was scrawled in blue marker.

*A really cool library with pirate books and science fiction and mysteries and pillow-filled nooks to hide in or read in and a soda fountain* was written in the same scrawl.

*A 3D theater, a lap pool, an indoor running/walking track, an underground shopping center with comic book stores and popcorn stands and toy stores and a playroom with tunnels and bridges and mirrors and slides.*

The list went on, all in marker, all written by…Carson? By Patrick?

Beth remembered what Carson had told her about their games. Her first instinct was to rush to his house and show this to him.

"So he can decide if it's important," she told herself.

*So you can be alone with him in a house with a bed,* she admitted. If she showed him something he liked, he might kiss her and then she might kiss him back and then…

"He'll still end up married to Sheena or someone like her," she reminded herself. "All you would do is make him feel guiltier for touching you again."

The truth couldn't be denied. She could see the guilt in his eyes every time he looked at her. He already lived with enough guilt. How could she even consider dumping more on him?

She couldn't. Beth put the papers back in the folder. It would wait until tomorrow.

Carson was already in the office the next morning when Beth rushed in. Instantly he saw that something was different about her. For the past two weeks he'd been doing his best not to focus on her, not to want her.

It had been completely impossible, of course. He'd been miserable and she had been a shadow of herself. He should never have touched her. How could he have risked hurting her?

But how could he not have touched her? As it was, an ache had settled into him that he did his best to ignore. If the darn rain would stop, they could finish and be done with each other. Everything would be fine. He was already looking into other jobs, better jobs where she would be appreciated and be able to rise through the ranks. Then she could be happy.

And he could do the things he needed to do. Maybe Patrick would talk to him, start thinking about walking, living.

But for now, Beth was…fidgeting was the only word

for it. For the past few days she'd seemed tired, dull and withdrawn. Today there was an energy trapped within her. She kept looking at him and then looking away again. A trace of the old Beth, his Beth shone through. He couldn't keep from smiling. He rose to his feet and strode toward her desk. "Something's different about you."

She opened her mouth, then closed it again, her hands fluttering. She latched onto her dress in that way she had. He noticed that she was wearing something more fitted than the sacks she had been sporting for the past couple of weeks.

"What?" he demanded, placing his palms on her desk and leaning toward her.

"It's probably nothing," she said, biting her lip.

"Say it anyway."

"I found something." She reached into a desk drawer and pulled out an old blue folder. He'd seen her looking at it earlier. "I'm not sure you'd be interested…or if it matters…or if you want to keep it, but—"

He took it from her. His fingers brushed hers. Sensation flooded him, and it was only with great effort that he kept his hands from shaking.

Concentrating on what she had given him, he flipped the folder open. A piece of paper fluttered to the floor and he picked it up. Almost instantly a lump formed in his throat.

"Yours?" Beth whispered.

He looked into her eyes and saw that she was worried. No wonder. He was clutching the paper so hard that it was wrinkling. Carefully he loosened his grip and cleared his throat, shaking his head.

"Patrick's. One of his best, I must say." He managed to smile.

Beth reached out as if to touch him, her hand hovering just inches from his before she hid it in her skirts again. "You're joking, but…I thought some of it *was* very good. Not conventional but intriguing. Not that I know anything about building hotels, but I know what I would like if I were a guest. I'd want something more than just a room. Something fun. Some of those ideas could work, don't you think?"

She was talking fast, but her voice wasn't completely certain. There was a nervousness to her as well as an excitement. Like the day he had first met her.

Carson moved around her desk, standing beside her.

"What are you doing?" Her voice was low, anxious.

"Nothing." He bent and kissed her cheek. It would have been brotherly, except there was heat even in this. "Thank you. You're right, or at least I want you to be right. Let's discuss these ideas." He shook the folder for emphasis just as the phone rang.

She frowned as she picked up the phone and said "Banick Enterprises" into the receiver.

Then her frown deepened. "Yes, Jim, he's right here. Why do you want to talk to him?"

Carson could hear what was undoubtedly Beth's brother Jim through the phone as his voice got louder.

"It's my job to screen his calls. You can talk to me.

I'll decide if what you have to say to him is something he needs to hear," she said in a perfect, prissy receptionist voice.

Carson couldn't hold back his grin. He reached over and gently pried the receiver from her fingers.

She tried to slap his hand away. "I don't want you to talk to him."

"Sorry, Beth, I outrank you and this is a call I want to take." He put the phone to his ear.

"Jim, what's wrong?" he said.

"You tell me," Jim said, not a trace of a smile in his voice. "Albert spoke to Bethie last night. He said she sounded tired, even worn-out…and not cheerful. Beth is almost always cheerful. If she's not, then something's wrong. I want to know what's wrong. She'll tell me that nothing is wrong, so I'm asking you. What do you say?"

Carson looked at Beth. Jim was right. Something was wrong. Beth's smiles had dimmed of late and he was undoubtedly the cause, but she wouldn't thank him for offering his opinion on the state of her smile to her brother.

"I'm glad that you love Beth enough to call and ask about her, but she's an adult. How she's feeling is something she can choose to share or not to share and neither you nor I should try to control that."

Jim swore. "I'm her brother."

"But she's her own woman. I won't treat her like less."

"You know what this means, don't you?"

Carson wanted to groan. "You're planning to come here. That would be a mistake."

Beth squawked and he held up his hand to silence her so that he could hear Jim.

"Why?" Jim was saying. "I'm family."

"Exactly. You should have more faith in her. Beth isn't shy. If she needs something or wants something, she'll speak up." He hoped that was true.

Turning to look at her, he saw that her eyes were luminous. "Are you all right?" he asked her.

"That does it," Jim said. "Why are you asking her that?"

"Because I want to know," he said and his answer was more for Beth than for Jim.

She nodded, taking a deep, visible breath. "I'm good," she said loudly enough that her brother could hear her. She took the phone from Carson. "I'm fine," she said. "Tell everyone not to worry. Having you worry…worries me."

When she finally hung up the phone, he waited a whole two seconds before he stared her in the eye. "Now tell me what's wrong."

She put her head down. She placed her palms on the desk, then she looked up and into his eyes. "Nothing. You trusted me. You thought something was wrong and yet you didn't tell my brother that. You let me be me. These are happy tears."

Carson studied her carefully. "You're sure?"

She narrowed her gaze. "Don't make me change my mind by turning into an overprotective male."

A harsh chuckle erupted from him. "You make it very difficult sometimes, Beth. Believe me, I want to be

overprotective even if I know it's not what you want."
He looked at her to see she was smiling brightly.

"I...like you," she said, her words slicing through
him, nearly stealing his breath. Like was a far cry from
what he felt for her.

"Now what about your brother's ideas?" she asked
as if she hadn't just stuck a dagger in his heart. "What
are you going to do about them?"

He thought for only a minute. "I think...I'm not sure
how to play this, but—"

Carson flipped through the folder again. "Beth, I
think you may be right, but...I can't do anything about
these without asking Patrick. These are his, from his
childhood. I don't want him to feel as if life is leaving
him behind, as if it doesn't matter whether he's here or
not. Some of these ideas have merits, but I won't touch
them without his okay."

She smiled softly, touching his hand. "Then you
should go see him. Right away."

"Yes." He turned to go. "Don't be disappointed if this
amounts to nothing. Patrick doesn't speak to me much
these days, and he doesn't have much interest in the
business."

"But you will have tried," she said. She picked up her
purse. "Let's go."

Carson blinked. He eyed her purse. He started to speak.

She shook her head. "Don't say no. I realize that this
is a delicate situation, and Patrick *is* your brother, but
I'm your assistant and this is business. You might need

someone to take notes and you might need someone to just…be there."

"Beth," he said. "Patrick isn't…he doesn't…"

"I know he might not be a pleasant person right now. I told you on day one that I was used to dealing with difficult people, and you might be too close to him to present things properly. Just the way I am with my brothers. Carson, you helped me. Let me help you. I promise not to say anything that would upset Patrick, but I would like to meet him. Who wouldn't want to meet the person who envisioned a butterfly garden on the grounds of a hotel?" she asked brightly.

Carson closed his eyes to keep them from tearing up. "He's not that boy anymore," he explained.

"I know," she said softly, taking his arm. "But I'd still like to meet the person he is right now. He is, after all, the reason you're managing this project. That makes him the reason I got this job. I can at least tell him that I'm enjoying working for his company."

Nodding, Carson tried not to think of how right she felt standing next to him. He wondered how Patrick was going to react to Beth.

*I wonder what I'll do when she's gone,* he thought.

# CHAPTER TEN

BETH LOOKED FROM Carson to his brother and then back again. "You look so much alike," she said.

"You don't know what you're talking about. We're nothing alike," Patrick said. "We never have been."

Carson grasped her arm gently as if he was trying to protect her. His body tensed beside her, and she could almost feel him forcing himself to relax, muscle by muscle.

"Patrick—" he began, but Beth rushed on.

"Well, you may be nothing alike. The two of you would know that better than I, but you must have had something in common." She looked at the folder Carson was holding.

Patrick looked aside. "What a ploy! I suppose you want me to ask what that is."

"It's a page from our Hotel Days game," Carson offered. "It's one of yours, and…it's brilliant. I'm surprised you never used any of this stuff."

"It's not the type of thing we do at Banick Enterprises," Patrick said.

"But they're such good ideas," Beth said.

"They're rubbish," he said with a sneer.

She put her hands on her hips. "Who says?"

For a second she thought she saw Patrick blink. She definitely felt Carson breathe in more deeply. Had she just questioned the credentials of a man who had been in the hotel business all his life? Darn it, she was always doing this kind of thing, speaking her mind when she should just shut up.

"That is, *I* like them," she said a bit lamely.

"That's because they're good," Carson said. "They *are*, Patrick."

"Then use them."

"Not without your blessing. I won't force you into anything." But when Beth turned, she could see that the look the two brothers were exchanging was filled with deep meaning. Both of them felt that Carson had forced Patrick onto that trail and neither of them could forget it. Patrick had to live with the results every day.

Her heart sank. She hoped that by coming here she could somehow help Carson, to give him something other than filing or note-taking or meaningless clerical tasks. He had seen into her heart and had broken through a barrier with her brothers…twice now. How foolish to think she could tap into Patrick's heart in some magical way and make things right for Carson. This wasn't the same at all. This man was truly suffering…and so was Carson.

"We should go," Carson said.

She nodded. "It was nice meeting you, Patrick." She

held out her hand and he looked at it as if it was made of something he didn't want to touch.

"I suppose you know that Carson never stays in one place for long," he told her. "He's here one day and gone the next. You can't rely on him. Just because he's sleeping with you, don't think it means a thing. He's not the marrying kind."

Beth sucked in a breath.

Carson stepped in front of her. "I didn't bring Beth here so you could insult her."

"Why did you bring her here?"

"Good question." Carson's voice was low and tense.

Beth pushed around Carson. "He brought me here because I asked him to. I wanted to meet you. Now I have. And for the record, you're not very good at hurling insults. I've definitely heard worse. I've given worse. But you know what? None of that changes a thing. You can be as hateful as you like but you still came up with some brilliant ideas once upon a time. You could still have them. I don't see why you need working append-ages to plan beautiful buildings. It *was* nice meeting you, Mr. Banick."

She held out her hand again.

To her surprise, Patrick looked flustered. He took her hand. It was barely a touch, but he made the effort.

She turned to Carson and found he was as stiff as a wall. "I'll see you, Patrick," he said.

His brother waved him away. Carson and Beth left the building, walked out into the sunshine and moved toward the car without speaking. When they got there, Carson stood for a long time, not moving, staring into the distance.

She wanted to touch him but she was afraid he might shatter. "I'm sorry," she whispered.

That was all it took. He grabbed her; he held her; he kissed her, his lips coming down hard and taking hers with a ferocity she had not imagined him capable of. She tasted desperation and despair in his touch.

Beth crowded in close and placed her arms around Carson. She kissed him back just as hard.

"I shouldn't have made you bring me," she said against his lips. "It hurt him…and you."

"I didn't know he'd speak that way to you," he said, running his hands up her arms. "I'm so sorry. I shouldn't have let you come."

"You couldn't have stopped me. You know that."

"I know, but I should have tried."

"You can't blame him," she said, plunging her fingers into his hair as he kissed her until they were both panting and in need of air. "I said things to him that I shouldn't have said."

"You said what needed to be said. That's all. Come on."

She wrapped her arms around his waist and rose on her toes to kiss him again. "Where?"

"Anywhere private. I need to be alone with you." They climbed into the car and headed back to Lake Geneva.

Beth barely remembered the drive, but when they got to town and he headed toward the house she stopped him. "The office. No one will be there." It was closer, and she didn't want to wait any longer.

Carson led her from the car to the stairs. He opened the door, whisked her through and kicked it closed behind him.

Instantly he had her in his arms, his lips wild on hers, his hands rough. "I don't want to scare you," he said.

"You couldn't. Touch me."

With that, he shoved the papers off her desk, lifted her onto the slick surface and followed her down. "You make me crazy."

"You make me weak."

Carson's hands slowed a bit. "You could never be weak." He flipped them and she ended up on top. "You lead."

Beth smiled down at him. She plunged her fingers into his hair, kissing his jaw and then returning to his mouth. Trailing a finger down his chest, she flicked a button open and then another. She could feel Carson's heartbeat go wild beneath her fingertips.

Her hands began to shake. She wanted to touch him. She wanted…so much more.

Patrick's words drifted back to her. She hated what he had said, but she knew that he was right. Carson wouldn't stay.

She hesitated.

Immediately Carson sat up, pulling her onto his lap. "Beth," was all he said, as if he knew what she was thinking.

"It's…nothing."

He shook his head. "No, it's something. It's everything. I shouldn't be touching you this way. I shouldn't even be thinking of touching you like this."

"I can't stay," she said as if it was her decision. Darn it, she wanted it to be her decision.

"I know," he told her, his voice breaking. "You told me. I knew that. I wasn't trying to force you."

She hit him then. "Do you think I thought that?"

"No, not really."

Immediately she felt contrite. She rubbed the spot where she had pounded him. "Did I...hurt you?"

A growl emanated from him. He cupped her face in his hands. "It's not you who's wrong here, Beth. It's me. I—"

The phone rang. She reached for it automatically, the result of years of ingrained training.

"Leave it."

She started to, but she didn't want to go back to their conversation. She was in too much pain. She didn't want Carson to spend more time blaming himself when it was she who was at fault. She had known she was falling in love with him, and that she couldn't have him.

"Beth, give me Carson." Patrick's words were terse. She didn't even hesitate, just handed the phone to her boss.

Seated on his lap, she wasn't far enough away to ignore the voice coming through the line even though the receiver was snugged up against Carson's ear. "Don't bring her here again. You owe me that much." And then the phone clicked off.

Carson sat silent for a long moment. Then he hung up the phone. "I'm sorry you had to hear that. He wasn't always like that. Before the accident he was…joyous, loving, everyone's friend. He would never have said something hurtful like that." Carson's jaw was tense. His whole body was tense.

Beth took his forearms in hers. "That's not your fault."

"It is. You weren't there. I was. I talked him up there and he fell and both of our lives, his and mine, were changed forever. I owe him."

He looked directly into her eyes. "I never want to hurt you, Beth. Kick me, punch me, scream at me, fight me, but don't ever let me do anything that might harm you. Promise me."

She didn't speak.

"Beth." The word was a command.

"You can't hurt me. I won't let you," she promised and she knew her words were the truth, because she was the one who had fallen in love. She was the one who had hurt herself.

And now *her* life would change, too. It would never be the same again.

A few hours later, Carson stared out into the night. What had he been thinking? How could he have forgotten himself so much that he could have come onto Beth like that after what Patrick had said to her?

*You were thinking that you had to have her, that she was more necessary to you than anything else in that moment*. He had not been thinking that he was falling in love with her. But he was.

That only made the situation worse, because Patrick had been right. He hadn't stayed in the past and he couldn't stay now. Carson owed Patrick his dedication to the business, he owed his family an heir and, above all, he had to protect Beth from his family. After the way Patrick had spoken to her and knowing the way his mother would speak to her, he could never ask her to join his family. And…she didn't want to get married.

Carson groaned. She *did* like kissing him, but Beth was no fragile flower. She was a modern, independent woman who went after what she wanted. The fact that she desired him didn't mean she wanted a future with him. She'd had enough of controlling men. Marriage would be a cage to a woman like her.

He clenched his hands into fists. Touching Beth again could be fatal, to his sanity and to her happiness. If she ever realized how he felt about her, that would hurt her. No matter how strong and independent Beth was, she liked to make things good and right for people. Guilt…he knew too much about guilt, and he wasn't going to let a drop of the stuff touch her.

So he'd stay away or at least stop touching her or thinking of her as a woman he wanted.

A great plan, but one he didn't seem to be carrying out very well. He needed a barrier, a deterrent, a constant reminder to keep his hands off of Beth.

That was what he was thinking when he went to

sleep. When he woke up after a restless night, he had the solution.

But Beth wasn't going to like it one bit.

The next morning, Beth sat forward on the white Adirondack chair on her patio, her hands clenched on the wide armrests. The pink and white roses that framed the brick scented the cool morning air. A pretty yellow and white sailboat drifted by on the lake, and the willow at the edge of the water swayed in the slight breeze. It was a serene setting…but Beth felt anything but serene as she faced Carson, who was, she noted, standing tall and gorgeous in a gray suit that made his silver eyes more intense.

"You want to invite my brothers up for a vacation and you want them to stay at your house?" Beth's voice rose. Her heart started to thud. She looked at Carson warily. "Why?"

He stepped closer. The breeze lifted a lock of his hair, and Beth forced herself to stay seated, to not walk over to him, stand on her toes and brush that hair back the way she ached to do.

He dropped to one knee beside her. "Beth, I'm not doing this to harm you. I don't trust myself with you and…well, I know you miss them. Lately you've been spending most of your time with me. That can't be good."

Beth bit her lip. He was right. Look what happened every time they were close. Her hands shook, her throat hurt, she wanted to touch him, and her heart—

"No, you're right about that," she managed to say, hoping her voice came out sounding normal. "We shouldn't spend so much time together."

Carson touched her hand with just one finger, then drew away. He stood and moved back, putting distance between them. "I'm not asking them here so they can police you but so that they can love you." He held a hand out. "This isn't a bad place for a vacation. You don't think they'll like it?" he asked with a smile. She could tell it was a forced smile, but he was trying. How could she do any less?

"They might think it's a bit puny," she teased. "Only four whirlpools when they're used to six. And the view?" She gestured toward the gorgeous clear water and the pretty skyline. "Not up to their usual standards, but I'm sure they'll make do."

"Ah, that's good then."

She sighed. "You're right, you know. I do miss them and they miss me. They don't get many exciting vacations and this would be heaven. Can they bring their families?"

"Of course. The more the merrier."

Which was…so true. The more people between them, the less likely she and Carson would do something ill-advised. She smiled.

He slid a lock of her hair between his fingers. Her breath stopped. She forced herself not to lean closer. "I won't let anyone bully you, Beth. Your life and your choices should always be your own. If you had objected to this plan…"

She touched his sleeve. "I know. You would have withdrawn it, but you're right. It's a good plan and a smart one. Thank you for accommodating me and my family."

His eyes grew suddenly darker. He leaned in and kissed her lips. "Don't thank me. I'm being selfish, as usual. Mostly I'm doing this to keep myself from stepping out of line."

She nodded. What he was saying was that he would be marrying soon, and getting involved with her would be a mistake.

*Well, he's right,* she told herself later. Besides, she didn't believe he was only being selfish. Carson did care about what happened to her. He was doing this for her more than he was doing it for himself.

So that was that. Now all she had to do was wait for her brothers to arrive and for this project and her time with Carson to end.

But, she thought with a sigh, she had never been good at waiting. And, frankly, she wasn't any better than Carson at keeping herself in line. Her brothers had never been much of a deterrent to her making unfortunate decisions, so no matter what Carson thought, she didn't think their presence would keep her from touching him. Having her brothers come to Lake Geneva wasn't really going to solve his problems or make him happy.

What would? Carson had done so much for her. He had given her a chance when she had no true credentials; he had listened to her opinions, believed in her ability and stood up to her family. Now he was taking her family into his home. She wanted to do something for him, something more than being his assistant. He didn't want her help in finding a bride, so what would work?

Closing her eyes and holding her breath, she picked up the phone and dialed. "Mrs. Banick?" she said when the woman answered. As soon as the woman responded in that imperious and querulous tone, Beth knew that she had chosen a path that might have questionable consequences.

But she also knew that there was no going back. Risk nothing, gain nothing.

"Mrs. Banick," she said softly. "This is Beth Krayton, your son's assistant, and I have something I need to speak to you about."

Then she waited for the sky to fall.

# CHAPTER ELEVEN

CARSON GLANCED TOWARD Beth's desk for the forty-second time this morning. It was only a few hours since he had told her of his plans with her brothers and she was looking pale.

He swore beneath his breath. Softly, he had thought, but she looked up, anyway. "Problems?" she asked, a worried look in her pretty eyes.

Yes. He wanted her, cared for her and couldn't have her. "Nothing much," he told her.

She nodded, playing with a pen she was holding. A nervous habit. Beth could keep her feelings from her face but they always shone through in some other way. "Carson," she said suddenly. "About that conversation with your brother yesterday…"

He tilted his head. "I told you that wasn't the real Patrick talking."

"I know, and I know you're worried about him. But…that accident…it wasn't your fault. I've read all the papers, Carson. It's perfectly understandable that he's miserable, but for you to blame yourself…"

"Leave it, Beth. Things are as they are, and much as I appreciate what you're saying, there are some things that just can't be changed. I'm dealing with it. Okay?"

She gave him a worried look. "Yes," she finally whispered. "Has he called again?"

Carson felt the familiar dull ache in his chest. He cleared his throat. "No. He won't, but that's understandable. I'll visit him tomorrow. In the meantime, let's just—"

He stopped. Her eyes were sad. She was leaning toward him. She had stopped fidgeting with the pen and was giving him a look that made him want to lock the door and finish what they had started yesterday.

"Work," she said suddenly. "Let's just work."

"Yes," he agreed. "Let's stick to that." He would. If he could just trust himself, he would do that.

But damn it, he didn't trust himself. He hoped her brothers would arrive soon.

Beth tried not to think too much as she climbed into her car and headed toward Milwaukee. Acting without thinking had often worked for her. It had also often backfired, but in this case…well, she had to do this.

Soon she would be gone from Carson's life. And she couldn't leave knowing that he would still be berating himself for something he hadn't done.

That didn't mean her heart wasn't thumping erratically when she finally got to the huge red brick colonial. Her hands were shaking and damp. The part of her that was supposed to prevent her from doing stupid acts was screaming in her subconscious.

*Too bad,* she thought and turned it off. She rang the doorbell and entered the house when the housekeeper let her in.

In only seconds, it seemed, she was back in the room where she had stood with Carson just yesterday. Patrick was in his wheelchair, facing a window, looking away from her.

"What are you doing here?" he finally said.

Beth hesitated. So much was riding on this. So little was possible, she conceded, staring at the hard line of his jaw. What had she been thinking? This was the man who had railed at her and who had told his brother not to come back with her? Was there really anything she could say to him that would make a bit of difference to anyone? That is, in a positive way? She could do a lot of harm.

"I'm probably doing something incredibly idiotic," she conceded. "It's a bad habit of mine. I thought I'd outgrown it, but it seems I haven't."

He turned his head slightly then turned his chair so that he faced her. He studied her for a minute and she noted that although she'd read that he was only twenty-five he looked much older. Slightly battered.

"What is it that you want?" he asked her. "I assume it's something important if you drove all the way from Lake Geneva."

"It's important," she agreed. *Almost too important. She couldn't handle this wrong...*

"Does Carson know you're here? Did he send you?"

Oh, no. She shook her head vehemently. "No, to both, but he's the reason I'm here."

Patrick's frown deepened. "I told you about him. If you're here to see if I can plead your case and get him to marry you, then you're mistaken."

Now shock had Beth's mouth dropping open slightly. "If I wanted anyone to plead my case, I would do it myself. I'm not here about me. I'm here about him. And you."

"Leave me out of this."

She shook her head. "I can't. You're in the middle of it."

He crossed his arms. Beth didn't know if it was a protective gesture or an angry one, but she knew she would have to tread carefully.

"Look," she said softly. "I know very well that I'm interfering where I have no business interfering, but in a few weeks I'll be gone. I can't begin to understand how you feel or how your life has changed. I know what the doctors have said about your recovery, but I would never presume to tell you what you should or should not do about that. I'm not here about your injury. That's your affair."

Patrick raised a brow. "And yet you've come to see me. You've said I'm in the middle of whatever situation you're referring to. I can't imagine—"

"He blames himself for what happened to you."

That shut him up, or so she thought. At least he didn't speak for a while. "I know that," he finally said.

A moan of frustration welled up in Beth. "And you let him feel that way."

The eyes that met hers were no longer disinterested or even angry. They were haunted. "Yes."

"Why?"

"I *was* there because of him. I wouldn't have gone otherwise."

Beth felt the whole situation slipping away from her, spiraling into destruction…as if success had never been a possibility. What price would Carson pay for her foolishness?

"Did Carson force you onto the trail with him?"

Patrick wheeled his chair closer to her. "Look at me. Look at what has happened to me. I was always second to Carson. My parents wanted him to be the one who took over the business. And do you know what? He *was* the more talented son. That was the thing I couldn't deal with. He had everything I wanted and he threw it away.

"I worshipped him," he continued, his voice growing softer. "I wanted to be like him. I always wanted to be like him. And that day…I'd had a drink or two. Not much but enough so that when he teased me about staying at my desk while he played and had a real life, I went along. Oh, we didn't go out on the trails tipsy, but once I had told him I'd go…"

"You didn't feel you could back down," Beth said. "I know what you mean."

He studied her for a second. "The trail wasn't all that dangerous, but I was angry at having agreed to do what I didn't really want to do. I didn't like feeling that I had allowed myself to be teased, and my pride was acting up. I wasn't as careful as I should have been. I don't remember much. Just waking up in the hospital with my parents wringing their hands and my brother looking as if he'd just shot a puppy."

"And you blame him…not just for the fall. Well, I guess that means you finally win. You have something he doesn't have."

He didn't answer at first. Then he sighed. "All right, I'll take the bait. What do I have?"

"Revenge."

Patrick blinked. "I guess you're right."

"And I guess I'm wasting my time thinking you might give him absolution." She turned to go, her shoulders slumping. "He told me you were once laughing and joyful. He admired your spirit, your work ethic and your talent and he's never going to get over this," she told him. "Even if you walk again, I don't think he'll forgive himself."

And when Carson heard that she had come to plead on his behalf, he wouldn't be happy that she had badgered his brother.

As if Patrick had read her mind, she heard him call out, "Aren't you going to ask me not to tell him that you were here?"

Beth glanced back over her shoulder. "I assume

you'll do as you please. You're a more powerful man than you think, Patrick."

Carson was barely dressed the next morning, his shirt half-unbuttoned, his hair a bit unkempt, when he found Beth standing on his doorstep.

She was a beautiful mess, her hair a flyaway mass around her face. She was wearing a turquoise v-necked shirt and white shorts that showed off her pretty legs.

His first thought was to reach out, pull her inside and kiss her until he had his fill of her...as if that would ever happen. That is, until he looked at her face more closely. She was pale and there were dark shadows beneath her eyes.

He pulled her inside anyway. She needed a safe place. He intended to provide it. "Are you okay?" he asked.

"Yes. No. I have to tell you that I went to see Patrick yesterday."

He had been meaning to let her go once she was inside, but his fingers froze on her skin. "I see." But, of course, he didn't.

"I won't go into details. I don't have time. Suffice it to say that I was meddling and I was hoping to get him speaking to you. It didn't work and I'm sorry, and there's more."

He pulled back and crossed his arms. Clearly it was confession time, and clearly she was miserable. He didn't know how he felt about her going to see Patrick.

He didn't feel good, but he couldn't think about that now. She was distressed. "Tell me about the more," he coaxed.

"Yes, well…" She looked to the side as if there might be an escape route there. Interesting, since she had been brave enough to come over to confess. "I called your parents yesterday. They'll probably be here later today."

Carson did a double-take. A part of him was confused. Another part was amused. Mostly he was concerned. What was going on?

She frowned up at him. "Did you hear what I said?"

"Absolutely. I'm just trying to figure out why you would call my parents."

"Well, you could have just asked. I'm planning on telling you." He did his best not to smile at her.

"I'm asking," he told her.

"You told me that you invited my brothers here because we needed barriers and because I needed my family nearby. I'm thinking that that's all well and good, but what about you? You should have someone, too. And furthermore—"

The sound of a car pulling in cut her off midsentence. As if they were joined by a string, Carson and Beth moved to the window. There wasn't just one car pulling in. There were two vans…and down the road Carson could see his parents Rolls-Royce gliding toward him.

"Uh-oh, that's them, isn't it?" Beth whispered.

He held out his hands in acquiescence. "You seem concerned, but I thought you invited them."

"I did, but the timing isn't exactly what I expected.

I thought I'd talk to my brothers and settle them in at my place and then when your parents arrived we'd all be separated."

"No mingling?"

"None."

"Bad news, Beth. There's bound to be mingling."

"I know." She sounded unhappy.

"I have an idea," he told her.

"What?" She turned to him eagerly, as if he could save the world.

He wished he could do that. For her. "Let's go meet them," he said.

She followed him out onto the front steps. "Roger," she said, hugging her brother. "And Edie." She hugged a tiny, dark-haired woman she introduced as her sister-in-law.

"Very nice to meet you," Carson said as he took the woman's hand.

"Nice body," Edie said to Beth with a wink, just as Carson's mother stepped from the Rolls-Royce and glared at Edie.

For a second he thought he heard Beth whimper, but then she continued with the introductions. The vans, it seemed, could hold a lot of people. Adults and children kept tumbling from the vehicles' depths. His parents hung back at the end of the long line of Kraytons.

Beth looked at him. "Maybe we should skip the introductions to my family," she whispered in his ear.

He shook his head. "That would be rude."

"We Kraytons are used to rudeness."

"I'm not." He continued to say hello to each man, woman and child as he reconnected with her brothers and was introduced to the newcomers.

By the time his parents reached him, all of Beth's relatives had formed a noisy group to one side.

"Beth, this is my mother and my father. Mother, Dad, this is Beth Krayton, my assistant and the woman responsible for inviting you here today."

Beth held out her hand and Deirdre, impressive as always in a cream Valentino suit and matching Sergio Rossi shoes, shook it limply. Not her usual style. "I must say that I'm not used to being summoned," she said, her voice acidic.

"Well, heck, then you're not used to Bethie. She's pretty forceful," Steven said with a laugh.

"Yeah, just don't get her mad," Steven's wife, Angela, added. "Beth is a firecracker, but we love her to pieces. And we don't like people looking at her as if she's unworthy."

Carson winced. His mother, never one to change her ways, looked down at Beth's shorts and the blue and white flip flops. "Be that as it may," she said, staring at Angela, "I have a few questions I'll want answered. Beginning with why all these people are at my house." She said the word people as if it were a synonym for "hideous worms."

Out of the corner of his eye, Carson saw Jim and Roger approaching, determination and condemnation in their expressions. He gave them a warning look then turned back to his mother. "They're here because I invited them, and this house belongs to the Banicks. All the Banicks," he reiterated.

His father cleared his throat. "Welcome," he said to the Kraytons. "We're happy to have you."

Carson wanted to laugh. His father didn't look happy, but he had never escaped the role of hotelier. He would exude congeniality no matter what his true feelings were. "Perhaps I should take my family over to the guest house and you can take your parents inside," Beth was saying. "I'll come over once everyone is settled."

One of the toddlers started to wail and stumbled over to hug Beth's leg.

Deirdre glared at the child as if the sound was a personal affront. Beth picked up the baby and cuddled her, and Carson couldn't help noting that she looked as if she was made to cuddle children.

"Shall we do that?" she asked Carson, just as Albert took the child from her. Albert was wearing a shirt with a beer logo on it. He smiled at the baby and winked suggestively at Deirdre. Intentionally provocative, Carson thought, trying not to laugh as his mother gasped. When Albert pulled the child away, there was a wet stain on Beth's shirt where the baby had drooled.

"We're not sending your family away," Carson said calmly. "We'll all stay here."

"I'll make the decision about where I go or stay," Deirdre said. "Carson, this is completely uncalled for. This 'Beth' insisted that it was important that I come here. It sounded like a life-or-death issue. I assumed there was a major problem and now your father and I find that this is merely a…an excuse for some sort of picnic. A ruse. Are you involved with my son, young woman?" she demanded. "Sleeping with him, perhaps? Because I have to tell you—"

"You don't have to tell her a thing," Carson said, stepping in front of Beth, shielding her from his mother.

He felt a nudge from behind. "Don't do that," Beth said, moving around him to face Deirdre. "I can do this. I started it and I'll see it through. And yes, Mrs. Banick, you're right in your reasoning. I did call you because I thought there was a major problem. I had this naive idea that if you came here, if you and your husband and Patrick could take a trip out to the new hotel and see what wonderful things are being done, if you could get together on that one issue, then something good might happen. As a family, you know. I meant it to be a chance to be together for the first time in a long time. I guess…I'm not sure what I really expected to happen. But it certainly turned out to be a mess, and I apologize for dragging you here."

Turning to Carson, she looked up into his eyes. "That day you hired me I forced myself into your life, and it looks as if I've continued to force a lot of things. Thank you for letting my family stay here. I'm sorry for today."

He took her hands. "Beth…don't. You've done nothing wrong."

She shook her head. "I spent so much time telling

you how I hated people to interfere in my life, and look at how I've barged into *your* life."

"I'm glad you see how things are, my dear," his mother said, maintaining her traditional role of queen mother.

"Oh, I do," she said, looking from her family to his mother and father. "I definitely see much more clearly. And…it's okay, Carson. I really do need to spend some time with my family. Thank you for inviting them here. We're just going to go home now and get reacquainted."

"Beth."

She shook her head. "No, I want to go now. It was nice meeting you, Mr. and Mrs. Banick," she said. "And, in response to your earlier question, I never expected a thing from Carson. He's going to do his duty as a Banick, and that's how it should be."

She turned and linked her arms with Roger and Steven and headed toward the guest house. Her flip flops flapped, her shorts rode up and showed a bit too much of her delicious legs. She looked like a wanton. She looked like everything he had ever wanted.

Behind him he heard the sound of one person applauding. He turned slowly and saw Patrick wheeling up to the doorway.

A rush of feeling swept through him at the sight of his brother. "How long have you been there?" he asked.

Patrick motioned toward a van sitting at the edge of the driveway, the driver leaning against the vehicle. "Long enough to hear a few things," Patrick said. "So…am I late for the party?"

"You're right on time," Carson said past the lump in his throat.

"Good. Hate to miss an occasion. Mom, Dad," he said, acknowledging his parents. "By the way, Carson, I have to tell you, your assistant is a master of the exit line. That's the second time in two days she's left everyone with their mouths hanging open. I applaud your taste in women."

And to Carson's astonishment and relief, he saw that his brother was smiling.

# CHAPTER TWELVE

BETH BARELY MADE it through the next few hours. Her face hurt from fake smiles. Her sisters-in-law were being so nice to her that she completely forgave them for that incident with her boss at the auto parts store. After all, they and her brothers had meant well. At least their actions had been motivated by love.

It was good to be loved.

"Stop feeling sorry for yourself," she muttered beneath her breath.

"Talking to yourself, little sister?" Roger's voice came from behind her, and Beth spun around, nearly knocking over the vase of flowers she had been pretending to arrange.

"Bad habit," she said with no embarrassment. Roger was used to her ways.

"You don't look happy. Should I punch him?"

She didn't ask who. "He wasn't the one who did anything wrong. I was the one who invited his family here without telling him."

"Trying to fix things for him? Yeah, I know about those urges. Been there."

"I'm so sorry I've been mean about all your efforts."

He shrugged and ran his knuckles down her cheek. "You had to grow up sometime. It's just hard for us to let go. We like to think of you as ours."

"I *am* yours," she said. "Nothing will ever change that."

"In some ways, but you've grown up now. And you're in love."

Beth looked up at him and to her distress, tears ran down her cheeks. "Yes, I am."

"And you're in pain."

She nodded.

"He doesn't love you?"

"He's going to marry a woman of privilege and produce an heir for the family."

Roger's jaw hardened. "Then he's a dead man." He turned to go.

Beth shrieked. "Roger, no! Wait! It's not like that."

He turned back. "Then tell me how it is."

"It's…I knew his plans from the first. I knew he had family obligations. It's all tied up in the past and things that happened between him and his brother. I think he's doing it mostly for his brother."

"The man in the wheelchair."

She blinked. "How did you know about him?"

Roger shook his head. "He was there. A van drove up while we were talking. I saw him out the window. With the door open he must have heard everything."

Beth closed her eyes. "He came. It may not mean much, but at least he came to see Carson. Before the accident, Patrick was supposed to marry well and produce the heir."

"I see. Are they pretty tight?"

"Used to be. I hope they can be again. And if Patrick is here and Carson's parents are here…well, no matter what happens, Roger, I have to leave. It's time."

"Then you should tell him." He nodded toward the door. "He's been here three times. Steven and Albert wouldn't let him past."

Beth's eyes widened. "Did they hurt him?"

A harsh laugh fell from Roger's lips. "He almost hurt them, but they convinced him that they were only following your orders. That got him to leave."

Beth stood on her toes and kissed her brother's cheek. She patted him on the arm. "You guys are so sweet. That's why it's going to hurt so much when I kill you for misrepresenting me." She turned on her heel and headed toward the other house, but she had barely stepped outside the door when Carson met her.

She tried to force her heart to behave but it was useless. Instead she decided to ignore it. "I want to talk to you," she said, trying to sound confident and authoritative, not emotional.

"I thought you didn't want to see me."

Beth shrugged. "You know how my brothers are."

He smiled and touched her hand. She did her best not to let him see what even that simple contact did to her. "I'm glad they care about you so much."

"I'm sorry for what happened earlier."

"Beth, don't be sorry. I'm the one who should apologize. My family—"

She shook her head. "Is your family just as mine is mine."

"All right," he agreed. "I won't go down that path except to tell you that Patrick showed up. I have you to thank for that."

She took a deep breath. "Is everything all right with him?"

"I don't know. Probably not. But just the fact that he showed up…it's a bit of a miracle, Beth, and you made that happen."

When he said the words, she knew the opportunity had come. She had to make the leap. Do something desperate. Even lie a little. "Well, good then. It looks as if my work is done." She pasted on a brilliant smile.

Carson froze. He studied her carefully. "What do you mean?"

She held out her hands. "Well, you know, having my brothers and their families here, I discovered how much I missed them and missed home. The project is moving along so nicely you won't have any trouble at all replacing me."

"The hell I won't."

His voice was fierce, his look fiercer. She wished…it didn't matter what she wished. Nothing had changed. She was who she was and he was who he was. "I have a list of acceptable candidates," she told him, even though it wasn't exactly true. While doing her job, she had met some likely individuals. She just hadn't known she would need their names. As soon as she left him she intended to write their information down. "I'll give it to you before I leave."

"When will that be?" His voice was cold, hard, demanding.

She didn't hesitate. "Tomorrow."

He moved closer. He reached out. "Beth."

Quickly she stepped back, not trusting herself. "I want to go, Carson. I need to go. Don't ask me to stay. Please don't ask me to stay."

Silence followed. He studied her, and she prayed he would stop soon. The tears were close. It was costing her so much to hold onto what little composure she had. "Please," she whispered again.

He swore beneath his breath. "All right, then," he said. "You're your own woman. You know what you need and want. I'll expect those names on my desk in the morning."

"Of course," she said. But in the end she took the coward's way out. Slipping the list of names beneath his door, she ran back to her car and headed toward Chicago. Her great adventure, her great love, was over.

It had been eight days since she had gone, Carson thought, ignoring the ringing of the phone. Eight miserable days.

Sure, he and Patrick were talking, at least about

superficial things. Sure, the hotel was moving ahead full force. Driven by a near insane need to forget Beth, he'd thrown himself into work, hassling the contractors, driving everyone to finish.

None of it mattered. Beth was gone.

*She wanted to go,* he told himself.

But a part of him didn't really believe that.

He wanted her to be here. Forever. He loved her, and that was so incredible, wonderful and terrible. This wasn't like the other relationships he'd had. He wasn't just killing time or having fun or trying to prove to his parents that he was as bad as they believed him to be.

He wanted to protect Beth: from his parents, from everything bad, from himself.

A small, choked laugh erupted from him. She would have punched him for that one. Beth hated to be protected.

But he didn't care. He wished she were here, mad at him or not. He just wanted to see her again.

But he couldn't. He remembered how his mother had spoken to her. It was laughable in a way. His family was privileged, the ones who should have been setting the example for others and yet…Beth was so much kinder and more compassionate than the Banicks. She could give lessons to families like his. And she might. If she were here.

But she wasn't.

He had to accept that.

The best way to get his mind off of Beth was to go to work. So Carson drove to the work site, reluctant to enter the trailer where he and Beth had worked together. Instead he stood to the side, watching the morning rays of the sun hit the raw building where the crew would go to work in less than an hour.

The stone and cedar exterior was rugged-looking but warm, like a lodge rather than the typical Banick brick and granite luxury buildings.

It was beautiful. A bit rough, yet golden and good, like Beth and her family, he realized. Had he thought of her when he'd asked for the changes? He didn't know.

Probably. She *had* changed him, after all. He breathed in the cool morning air, the scent of grass and pine. He watched the sun climb, on its way to brighten the earth, and all he could think of was Beth. She brightened everything. She was in this building, in this air, in every thought he had. She was special, more special than anyone he had ever known, and a coveted family name or distinguished pedigree wouldn't make her more so. Just knowing her had made *him* feel special in a way he never had before.

*She should see this.* The thought ran through his head and it stuck. He needed her to share this with him. In many ways, she *was* this project. She had given him what he needed to complete it. He wanted to give back to her.

But she'd asked him to set her free, and he didn't want to do anything to hurt her.

What could he do? How could he pay her back for all she'd given him?

Carson paced the site. He studied the building from

all angles as if the structure itself could supply him with the answers. And in the end, it did. He left in a hurry, on a mission.

He hoped, he prayed, he was doing the right thing for Beth.

Beth's heart was in her throat as she walked up the hill to the site of the Banick Resort, her brothers at her side. She didn't want to be here.

In the time since she'd been gone, she had done her best to get over Carson. Nothing had worked. Coming back here would just start the pain all over again.

But the gold and cream invitation she now clutched had come in the mail last week. *You're invited to a preview of the newest Banick Resort.* Her heart had clenched at the scrolled writing. She had thought of a thousand excuses she could give for not showing up. *I love you and I can't see you again* had been chief among them.

She really didn't have to be here. She was incidental to the world of the Banicks, a blip in their history. "What if she's there?" Beth had whispered to herself. "His new fiancée?" It would be foolish to show up and subject herself to that. She would just call and pleasantly make her excuses.

And she would have if not for the writing at the bottom. "Please come, Beth," had been written in Carson's bold scrawl. "I really need you to be there."

She took a deep breath, disgusted with herself even now, five days later. Because just like that she had agreed to come. All Carson had to do was use the word "need" and she folded, melted, burned.

"And here we are," she whispered, her throat scratchy from the tears she had shed the past few days.

"Don't worry, Beth, we're here to support you," Albert said. Her brothers had insisted on coming and she hadn't even argued. For once, she needed their protection, even though she knew they couldn't really protect her heart.

"I know. Thank you," she said and continued walking. At the top of the hill was the building, tall and beautiful. Beside it was a tent where the Banick family waited, and outside the tent, looking down, was Carson, his dark hair lifting slightly in the breeze.

Beth looked at him and her knees nearly buckled. Roger caught her arm as she stumbled. Carson came barreling down the hill. He looked at her brothers then held out his hand.

"Beth." That was all he said, but as if she had no mind or will of her own, she placed her hand in his. They walked up the hill together, her brothers following.

When they got to the top, Carson let go of her before turning to his family and to her brothers. "I'm sure you're all wondering why I've called you here."

"It's highly irregular," Deirdre said. "It's much too early for a preview. This isn't the way we do things, and this building…it's nothing like a Banick hotel. I don't know what you were thinking. When Patrick was in charge—"

"Mother," Patrick said. "Let Carson finish."

"Yes, let the boy talk," Carson's father said. Carson

raised a brow and Beth could understand why. His father was reputed to be a quiet man, deferring to his wife.

Carson looked at Patrick and the two of them exchanged a smile. Beth's heart soared. If nothing else had come of her time with Carson, at least something good was happening there.

"You're right about the building, Mother," Carson said. "It *isn't* a typical Banick hotel. This will still be a luxury resort with the guests' comfort and entertainment of foremost importance. But there are differences, good differences, wonderful differences. This is a combination of Patrick's plans, mine and Beth's. I think the results are going to be wonderful, mostly as a result of her input. That's why I'm naming it The Bethany, as a tribute to Beth and how I feel about her."

Beth's heart tripped wildly. She looked at her brothers, who were shifting uneasily; she looked at Patrick who gave her a thumbs-up and a smile; and she turned to Deirdre and Rod Banick. Rod's expression was unreadable, but Deirdre's was shocked. Then Beth turned to Carson who was staring directly at her, his silver eyes fierce.

She didn't know what to think. What exactly was he saying beyond the fact that he valued her work?

"It's preposterous," Deirdre Banick said, "naming a hotel after a woman. That's a bit like tattooing a woman's initials on your arm. When you change your mind and break up, you just look ridiculous."

"Stop it, Mother," Carson said. "Don't say anything else that both of us will regret later."

Beth realized that her brothers had left her side. They were advancing on Carson.

"Don't subject Beth to this, Banick," Steve warned. "If you do anything today to hurt her, you've got us to deal with."

Carson raised a brow. "That's good to know. I'm glad Beth has you as champions, but in case you haven't realized it, your sister is perfectly capable of defending herself. She can hold her own with anyone. It's one of the things I most admire about her."

Beth felt her eyes misting up. Stupid man. He was going to tick off everyone and to what purpose? Why *was* he saying these things?

As if he heard her heart's question, he turned to his family. "I brought all of you here because I don't want there to be any confusion later. I love Beth, and I'm sorry if that makes you uncomfortable or messes with your plans, but frankly, I can't let that matter. She has more integrity and compassion and kindness and character than any woman I've ever known, and I adore her."

Beth looked at her brothers, who were shifting awkwardly as if they didn't know how to deal with this unexpected change of subject. Carson's mother looked confused and concerned and stunned. Patrick alone looked amused.

Beth's hands began to shake. Her heart began to pump wildly. Fear gripped her with an intensity she couldn't control.

Without thinking, she stepped forward. "Carson,"

she said, her voice breaking and wobbly. "I don't know what's happened here since I've been gone, or what you and your family have gone through. But…I can't let you sacrifice what you've worked so hard for. I don't want to be your means of making a point. And I can't be your next rebellion, your next Emily." Her voice rose on the last line. She was staring up at Carson, her eyes round with anger and a terrible, aching fear.

In the buzz that followed, she became aware that everyone's attention was focused on her. But she didn't care. She wouldn't look.

There was only one person Beth cared about, one person whose response mattered. She faced Carson, waiting for his answer, waiting for her heart to be broken again.

Carson felt as if he was standing on a ledge with a one hundred foot drop-off on either side. There were no rules and only one thing was certain: if he made one wrong move, he would fall.

But there was really only one move he could make, good or bad. The fact that it was his heart's choice, too, didn't guarantee a thing. If she didn't want him… he had to let her go.

Carson swallowed hard. "It's not like that. You're not Emily," he said. "You were never Emily. I never loved her and she knew that from the start."

Beth opened her mouth to speak, but Carson stepped forward. He had to finish and he had to do it now, because he could see that he was hurting her, and that was unacceptable.

"I'm not throwing you in anyone's face, Beth. I would never do that to you. Besides, I don't give a damn what anyone thinks, other than you. You're all I see, all I want. You're everything."

"Carson?" Beth broke in, her voice fainter than he could ever remember it. She didn't believe him. He could tell.

Fear bit at him. If he didn't convince her…

"Damn it, Beth," he said. "You were the one who always told me that I should demand more from a woman than a family name, that I should ask for more in a *wife*. Well, here and now, I'm asking, Beth. I'm asking for you."

Carson stared directly into her eyes as he said the words, but he could see that she still didn't quite believe. Maybe she didn't want to believe. Maybe she didn't care.

"I can see that you might not feel the same way I do, Beth," he managed to say around the lump forming in his throat. "But I'm telling you and everyone here that you're the only woman I love or ever have loved. You're the only wife I'll have, and if you won't have me, if you can't love me, then I'll have no one. Are we clear on that?"

She stood there, staring at him. For what seemed like forever.

His heart fell. He looked at Roger and thought he saw sympathy in the man's eyes.

Then, Beth came hurtling toward him. She launched herself into his arms, twining herself around him.

"I think you might be making a massive mistake, Carson. I really do. I seriously doubt that you have control of all your senses if you still want me after the way I butted into your life and made a mess of things with your family. But I'll have you. I love you madly, and you're the only man I'll marry. Are we clear on that?" she whispered.

Carson answered by bringing his lips down to hers. "Oh, yes, we're clear," he whispered to her. Then he kissed her again. "Crystal clear."

Beth rose on her toes and pressed her full length to his, winding her arms around his neck and raining kisses on his face.

Somewhere in the distance, Carson heard his father harrumph. He heard Roger clearing his throat.

With a grin, Carson raised his head and looked at the crowd. "Beth and I are getting married. So, if anyone has any objections, make them now. Not that it will make any difference. The deal is done as far as I'm concerned."

"You'd better treat her right," Albert called.

Beth looked over her shoulder. "Does it look as if he's treating me wrong, Albert?" she asked.

Albert shrugged. "Just making a point."

"Point taken," Carson told him, not letting go of Beth. "She's safe, and she's mine," he said.

Deirdre cleared her throat. "Beth, you should know that Carson has always been rather headstrong and difficult," she said. "He's impulsive and I'm not surprised that he has chosen a less than conventional path to matrimony. As for me, I just want to make sure that you will be a credit to our family."

Carson thought he heard Patrick groan. "Mother, you had better be a credit to Beth," Carson said on a growl. "She at least knows how to treat people."

"Carson," Beth said, from the safety of his arms. "Watch your tongue. Your mother is just trying to protect you the same way my brothers protect me. I'm sure you'll feel the same if we have children. I would certainly expect you to watch out for their welfare."

"Thank you, Beth," Deirdre said. "I see that you do understand."

Carson granted his mother a small smile. For her, to concede even that much, was a lot. He didn't have high hopes for a close relationship between his mother and Beth, but at least this was a civil start.

Patrick rolled up beside them. "So, does the brother of the groom get a kiss?" he asked as he pulled Beth down and kissed her on the cheek. "She's a special lady, Carson," he said. "Believe me, I know. She's the reason I'm here."

Carson took his brother's hand. "This means a lot to me. You mean a lot to me."

Then Patrick dragged him down for a hug. "Hey, Carson, you and Beth did a fine job on this hotel. When my health improves, I just might take a vacation. Maybe I'll even take a turn at being the wild brother."

Deirdre gasped, but then she and their father looked at each other and Carson saw hope written on their faces. Carson supposed that having Patrick show any interest in life, even in a wild life, made them happy now. Perhaps his parents were mellowing just the slightest bit.

"Go for it," he told Patrick, "or stay and help us build the next Banick masterpiece. We're with you, no matter what."

Beth gave Patrick a smile and a thumbs-up. "I'll expect a play-by-play on your exploits," she said.

"I'll send pictures," he told her with a grin.

Beth's brothers came up to shake the hand of their future brother-in-law and to give Beth a hug. "Knew you'd be good for her," Steve said, and everyone laughed.

And then the hugging was over. Carson took Beth's hand. "Come on," he said.

"Where are we going?" she asked.

"Doesn't matter," he said. "Anywhere you'd like. As long as it's you and me together."

"Always," she answered. "Now, about that honeymoon suite in The Bethany…"

He grinned. "Do you have anything you want to say about the plans?"

She rose on her toes and kissed him. "Yes. I want us to be the first occupants. I want us to get married here."

Carson picked her up and swung her around. "I knew that I liked the way you thought. From the minute I met you I loved you. You're a woman who goes after what she wants."

"Well," she said with a grin, as they walked toward the hotel. "It's good then that I want you."

"It's more than good. I'm one lucky man. At last."

From behind them, they heard the sound of applause. They turned and saw that Patrick and Roger were leading the way. Then the rest of Beth's brothers joined in, and then…Carson's father nudged Deirdre and the two of them, a bit awkwardly, applauded as well.

"I knew you were a miracle worker," Carson whispered to Beth with a smile.

"I knew you were the man for me," she countered. "Now let's go see our first project. Later, we'll start on our next one."

"The heir?" he asked.

"Absolutely, my love," she told him. And who could argue with that?

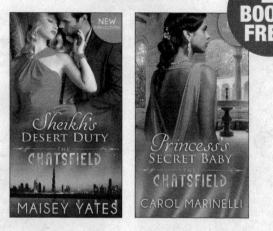

# MILLS & BOON®

## Seven Sexy Sins!

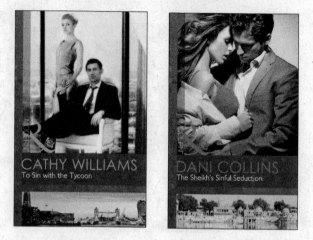

### *The true taste of temptation!*

From greed to gluttony, lust to envy, these fabulous stories explore what seven sexy sins mean in the twenty-first century!

Whether pride goes before a fall, or wrath leads to a passion that consumes entirely, one thing is certain: the road to true love has never been more enticing.

### Collect all seven at
**www.millsandboon.co.uk/SexySins**

0315_ST_9